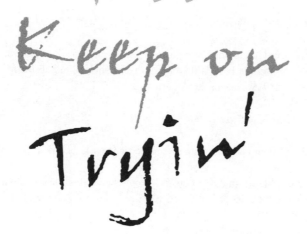

Gotta Keep on Tryin'

VIRGINIA
DeBERRY
&
DONNA
GRANT

A Touchstone Book
Published by Simon & Schuster
New York   London   Tokyo   Sydney

TOUCHSTONE
A Division of Simon & Schuster, Inc.
1230 Avenue of the Americas
New York, NY 10020

Copyright © 2008 by Virginia DeBerry and Donna Grant

First Touchstone hardcover edition January 2008

TOUCHSTONE and colophon are registered trademarks of Simon & Schuster, Inc.

For information about special discounts for bulk purchases, please contact Simon & Schuster Special Sales at 1-800-456-6798 or business@simonandschuster.com.

Designed by Mary Austin Speaker

Manufactured in the United States of America

10 9 8 7 6 5 4 3

Library of Congress Cataloging-in-Publication Data

DeBerry, Virginia.
    Gotta keep on tryin': a novel / by Virginia DeBerry and Donna Grant.
        p. cm.
"A Touchstone book."
1. African American women—Fiction. 2. Friendship—Fiction. 3. Women-owned business enterprises—Fiction. 4. Life change events—Fiction. I. Grant, Donna. II. Title.
PS3554.E17615G68 2008
813'.54—dc22   2007011584

ISBN-13: 978-1-4165-3167-8
ISBN-10:   1-4165-3167-X

*To the gift, power, laughter, comfort, strength,
and blessing of friendship.*

WE GRATEFULLY ACKNOWLEDGE

Hiram L. Bell III. Thank you. Always. DG

Gloria Hammond Frye, Juanita Cameron DeBerry, and the late John L. DeBerry II, for the right stuff.

Alexis, Lauren, and Jordan, Brian, Christine, and Arielle, the future—which becomes more present with every book.

Kenneth Dell, Cheryl Jenkins, Jeanette Frankenberg, Carol Valentin, Bob Gore, Leigh Haber, Valerie DeBerry, D. Michael Bennett, John L. DeBerry III, Victoria DeBerry, for their support and faith when I needed it most—VDB

Arlene Hamilton, for your unfailing encouragement and support.

Our ART—Advance Reading Team: Gloria Frye, Juanita DeBerry, Keryl McCord, Valerie DeBerry, and Liz Opacity, for taking time out of your busy lives to plow through pages, give us feedback, and remind us why we do this.

Tyrha Lindsey and Tracey Kemble, for keeping 4 Colored Girls Productions going during our extended absence.

Peter Meme, Stuart Smith, and the rest of our Makeda family for love, hugs, and gomen.

Mark Pascal and Francis Schott, the Restaurant Guys and owners of Stage Left Restaurant for their generous hospitality during our photo shoot.

Ron Henry for being a bad gambler and a good loser.

Bill Wylie, whose photos have been making us look good for more years than we care to count.

Tony Nakamura for cards, posters, and other graphic wizardry.

The good Dr. V, for the inside scoop on mergers, acquisitions, buyouts, and other things corporate and for all the rest.

Victoria Sanders, our agent, for her guidance, advice, encouragement, and for being either "Mother Hen" or "Mama Tiger"—depending on the need.

Our editors in transition, Cherise Davis and Sulay Hernandez, our cheerleaders at the start and finish lines, respectively.

And all of our friends and family members—you are too numerous to name individually—whose continued love and support is surely the grace of the Creator at work.

Friends are the family you get to choose.

PROLOGUE

. . . crossed hearts and promises . . .

Maybe we are through. It droned in Pat's head like a chant, propelled her blindly along Broadway in the April twilight. She didn't smell the bus exhaust, the dirty dogs languishing in their daylong steam bath, the greening scent of new spring that hung tentatively in the evening air. Indifferent to the chill, Pat's trench coat flapped open like sails in the breeze. *Maybe it's time.* It was her occasional refrain, but how could that be the answer?

Oblivious to blinking crosswalk signs, Patricia Reid followed the crowd—stopping or going with the packs of pedestrians who challenged cars for the right of way. At the corner of Fortieth Street she pounded the hood of a Jeep that came too close when the light turned green. "What the hell's wrong with you!" Pat glared at the driver, but she never really saw him or heard what he yelled as he sped off. There was too much wrong and it whirled in her head. Truth was, she'd felt it coming, tried to blow past the rough spots, sure they'd take care of themselves. And they had, more or less—until now.

A *lawyer—first thing in the morning I'll call—who?* Pat knew *their* lawyer wouldn't touch it—too much invested in *them*—too personal. But hadn't they been together too long to be talking about separate attorneys, who was entitled to what? When did the "stuff" outweigh decades of trust?

For several strides Pat walked next to a slim matron, wielding a cane in one hand, a cigarette in the other, and for the first time in years Pat wanted one—smoke sticks Marcus used to call them when he would bug her to quit. She wanted to suck the heat and the burn into her lungs, blow out the smoke like a dragon. She settled for a deep drag of second-hand smoke, remembered when crossed hearts and promises used to be enough, and kept walking.

As kids all any of them had was scraped knees, and dreams that took them on separate journeys for a while. But ten years ago Gayle and Marcus had come back into her life. It was as if Pat got back her right hand and her left, the two halves of her heart, the friend who was her sister and her partner in a business they had grown from nothing, together. And the husband who was her friend, her lover, her safe place.

How could she be on the verge of losing one of them again?

Pat felt the phone vibrate in her pocket and kept walking. She'd had enough talk for one day. And she hadn't changed her mind. This wasn't their first fight. Since they were kids, they had disagreed too many times, about too many things to count. It certainly didn't stop because they loved each other. But there was no yelling this time, just mean, hateful words. This may not have been their nastiest quarrel, but was it really their last?

Less than a block later the phone quivered again, and again before she walked another two. There was so much going on now, so much at stake she couldn't afford to brush off.

She yanked the phone out—saw the number and almost hit "ignore," but something—the need to go another round? the need to have the last word, again? the hope for an apology?—she didn't know what it was, but she answered.

"Yes." Pat's tone was flat, challenging, cold. And she had no warning the temperature would drop so suddenly, flash-freeze her anger. "Where? . . . I'm on my way."

Pat waved frantically for a taxi, wanted to stand in front of one, make it stop. Finally a cab pulled over. "Madison and One Hundred and First." She willed the lights to stay green, the traffic to clear, but it seemed to be taking forever, like they were driving over shifting sand. Perched on the edge of the seat, she prayed for this to be alright and tried to remember that even a bad day has good parts.

CHAPTER 1 •

. . . from what-ifs to reality.

"I can't look." *Elbows planted on her* drawing board, Gayle clamped both hands over her eyes. Ever since she'd sent the final sketches, specs, and fabric samples, she had worried she'd left out something important, or that it wouldn't look the way she imagined. Or that it was a great big mistake.

"What are you worried about?" Pat dug through the squeaky mass of packing peanuts as if she were searching for buried treasure. Yesterday the doll maker they had contracted said the original doll was on the way, and all morning Pat had worn a rut between her desk and the big windows at the front of the third-floor walk-up office, scanning the horizons of West Twenty-third Street and Eighth Avenue, willing the FedEx truck to round the corner before its usual mid-morning run. Pat grabbed hold of an arm and pulled. "She's beautiful!"

Gayle peeked through her fingers, then she was out of her seat. "Oooh. Let me hold her." Gayle had started drawing Ell Crawford, with her two fat braids crisscrossing the top of her head, blue jeans, a pink velour shirt, and big brogans like the clunky ones her daughter had to wear to support her feet, after four-year-old Vanessa tossed her shoes down the laundry chute, fully expecting they'd be lost forever. Gayle created a s/hero whose formidable footwear fit her as well as Cinderella's slipper and magically transported her to far-off times and places. Ell helped Vanessa feel better about having to wear "boy shoes," and even after the industrial-strength lace-ups were gone, Vanessa still looked forward to Ell's next adventure. It was hard to believe, but five years had passed since Pat convinced Gayle that other little girls would enjoy Ell's exploits. Twelve books later they still did—and clamored for more. Now the first Ell doll was cradled in Pat's arms, looking so much like Vanessa it gave Gayle chills.

"Thought you couldn't look." Pat tucked the doll behind her back, enjoying a playful moment now that she could see the two years she'd spent on the project—the first convincing Gayle it was the right move, then working with a doll artist—were going to be worth it.

"Changed my mind." Gayle couldn't believe Ell Crawford

looked like she had just leapt off the page, from the mischievous gleam in her big brown eyes, to the grosgrain laces in her sturdy oxfords, tied with big bows the color of bubble gum. Gayle had come up with the ploy to make the shoes special. She would change the ribbons to go with Vanessa's outfits. The doll's shoes were patent leather, but Vanessa's father had kept hers polished so they gleamed, a memory Gayle chased out of her head. *I will not let Ramsey spoil this.*

"OK. I'll share." *Like when we were eight.* Pat handed over the doll.

Gayle and Pat had gone from sharing a room with twin beds when they were kids, to an office with twin desks, arranged face-to-face, today. In the semi-early days—after they'd made the leap from dining-room table to a real office—they would clear both desks to create mailing central, where they packaged and labeled their orders, excited about each and every one and where it was going. And they celebrated across the desks with champagne and a sausage-and-mushroom pie from the greasy pizzeria on the corner when they shut down the assembly line and hired a fulfillment house to handle getting the books from printer to customer—definitely slumming it after Pat's days of luxe expense-account dinners and her plush office in a sleek glass tower, but this felt even better. She and Gayle had built it from what-ifs to reality.

The dueling desks also made it easy to talk. Some days they did a lot of that, about ad buys, color separations, and production schedules. But also about Vanessa's grades, Pat's anniversary surprises, shoes on sale, and where to get the best manicure. Articles written about the slow and steady growth of The Ell & Me Company and its catalog of fanciful picture books always played up the lifelong friendship shared by founders Patricia Reid and Gayle Saunders. It still made them smirk and shake their heads because they remembered how it started—in kindergarten when Pat was too country, Gayle was too prissy, and nobody else wanted to be their friend. As kids they pretended to be lots of things—mommies, gypsies, private eyes, and the Vandellas—but copresidents of their own company had never been on the list.

Pat, the Ivy League ex–advertising exec who regrouped after a musical chairs merger left her with no desk when the music stopped, and Gayle, the former stay-at-home mom who turned a reversal in life into a creative springboard, made for a study in opposites, one hard-driving and business-savvy, the other whimsical and creative. Like they planned it, or even thought about it that way. Each just did what she did best and somehow it worked out.

"Sure she's not too big?" Gayle placed the doll in the stand that was included and leaned back to examine her.

"Don't start." Pat knew that look and tone. Gayle's exuberance was about to dissolve into a sinkhole of doubt. "We've been over every finger, toe, eyelash . . ."

"I know. You're right." Gayle lifted Ell's pant leg, smoothed a polka-dot sock.

"She's perfect." When it came to how Ell looked, Gayle had specific notions, and getting to "just right" had plucked Pat's bottom nerve. They had weighed and debated the possibilities from pocket-size to life-size and decided on eighteen inches as a manageable height for all ages. It took months to get the right complexion, a special blend of chocolaty golden hues their artist called sun-kissed cinnamon. And the hair—

curly, kinky, wavy, and cornrowed—they had been through it all. Pat was not about to revisit their decisions.

"I just want to be sure." Gayle perched on her stool. Pat had anted up the money to start the business since she said Gayle had created their product. Besides, at the time Gayle only had enough to get back on her feet and buy a little breathing room. But it was Gayle who suffered the sleepless nights while they set the wheels of their fledgling company in motion, terrified Pat was wasting her time, talent, and a heap of her termination-agreement money. And anxious herself about what she would do for a living if this crazy scheme didn't work out. But they were equal partners, fifty-fifty. They split the proceeds and made decisions jointly.

All the paperwork they had to sign when they incorporated made Gayle's stomach hurt, but Pat explained every move. Gayle had been amazed at the way Pat called in favors from former associates to get them going and didn't break a sweat negotiating toe-to-toe with contractors. After their first print run was sold-out and they went back to press, Gayle was thrilled, but underneath it all she had worried when the devil would jump up and take it all away. She still did. Her marriage was the last thing she had counted on, and that turned out to be so much smoke and mirrors. When the air cleared, Ramsey was gone, her mother was dead, and she and Vanessa were homeless. The big house, expensive clothes, luxury cars—all lost. Gayle accepted that some of what happened was her fault. Ramsey didn't hide his gambling that well. She just spent too much time squinting through rose-colored designer glasses instead of seeing what was in plain sight. With Pat's help she'd been able to put the shelter far behind her, but post-Ramsey stress disorder still lingered.

"You're never sure." Pat sat at her desk.

"You don't exactly have a crystal ball. There are lots of dolls . . ."

"And none of them speak to the little girls who adore your stories."

My stories. Gayle had a hard time taking credit. She was only a high school graduate with no formal training. Drawing came naturally to her, since she was little. And the stories—just something she had made up to entertain her child. Except that when she read them to Ell's fans at libraries and schools, and they called her Ell's mom, it did give her a charge. And when she examined her bank and brokerage accounts, which she did regularly, and balanced them down to the penny, she was proud to be paying her way in life—finally.

"So rude." Rosalind, their receptionist, office manager, cheerleader, and sounding board, came around the half wall. "People just bang the phone in your ear when they dial a wrong . . . Will you look at her." Lindy stopped, put both hands on her hips. "Standing up there like she's about to talk. The very first one, and goo gobs more to come. Ah, sookie sookie now." She did her victory shimmy. Not much bigger than a doll herself, Rosalind flitted like a hummingbird and watched over Pat and Gayle like a hawk. And made sure they marked special occasions properly. "Where we having lunch?"

"Rain check, Lindy." Pat picked up the phone. "Our new star has an appointment. Gotta plan her first photo shoot. You can order me a Greek salad. I'll eat when I get back."

"Chicken Parmesan, side of spaghetti," Gayle added.

Pat looked at the remnants of Gayle's breakfast bagel and cream cheese. That was the same as when they were kids too. Gayle never gained an ounce and Pat still battled the pounds that threatened with every forkful. "It's just not fair."

Lindy shuffled back to her desk, and Gayle tried not to vibrate off her chair. Planning the doll had been an exercise for Gayle. Seeing her there, discussing pictures for the cata-log, that made it too real. Pat had asked Gayle if she wanted to go. She begged off, wanted to finish the drawing on her board. It was for the book that would go with the doll launch, so she felt pressure to make it extraspecial. All morning Gayle worked on the illustration—of Ell in a covered wagon, ging-ham ribbons in her shoes, heading for the Oklahoma Land Rush of 1889—but it seemed as though the doll were look-ing over her shoulder, questioning every stroke. By the time Pat packed her up for the trip across town, Gayle felt like she'd done more erasing, pencil sharpening, and staring at the kaleidoscope of photos, swatches, knickknacks and what-nots she collected for inspiration on her Brain Strain bulletin board than actual drawing.

Just as Pat was putting on her coat to go, she heard Lindy buzz someone in. "Sure you won't come?"

"Are you sure this is a good idea?" The question had haunted Gayle all morning. "We could eat the loss on development—"

"Wasn't I right the first time—when we started all this?" Pat slipped on a glove.

"Yeah, but—"

"If I listened to you, the stories would be in a trunk collecting mold." Pat thought she'd nipped this bud, but the roots were deep. She understood Gayle's reluctance, but she also knew that forward was the only way to go—her own life had taught her that.

"But we don't know anything about the toy business."

"Will you cut it out. This is going to be huge. Enormous. Colossal." Pat picked up the bundle. "Gigantic. Stupendous. Mammoth—"

"*No. You'll have to leave.*" It was Lindy's I'm-not-playing voice.

They looked at each other, then Pat went to investigate.

She rounded the corner and saw the fresh-faced cutie. Cornrows released a cascade of curly hair that brushed the shoulders of her jacket, a snowball of white fake fur.

Haven't had one of these in a while. Every now and then one of Ell's fans would show up in person to tell them what the stories meant to her. This one looked to be in her late teens. *A little old. Must have read them to her baby sister.*

Lindy shot Pat a "Get lost" look, which she thought was odd. The girls were always sweet, although sometimes they had a big weepy breakdown when they met Gayle.

"Mrs. Carter?" The voice was small, like a fairy or a six-year-old. A beauty mark punctuated the upturn of her smile.

Pat went from warmhearted to wary in four syllables. "Can I help you?" Nobody called her Mrs. Carter, unless she was with Marcus at some sports shindig. That's how she could tell it was somebody who knew him by name and reputation only. Everyone else was aware she'd kept her own name. It was just easier doing business that way. *And what business do you have with me?*

"My name is Tiffani Alexander. *Tiffani* with an *i*, not a *y*."

"And Miss Tiffan-I would like to get in touch with her supposed father." Hands on hips, Lindy cut to the real nitty-gritty. "Marcus Carter."

All morning Pat had been hanging ten on the crest of a can-do wave. Now she felt sucked into the undertow, unable to breathe and unsure which way was up. Early in their marriage, she and Marcus weathered a spate of accusations by women with cuddly babies and lawyers who offered to keep matters confidential for a mutually agreed-upon settlement. And while he admitted that before they were married, he hadn't exactly been a saint, Marcus assured her he hadn't been stupid either. Well, she hadn't exactly been Sister Patricia of the Order of the Crossed Legs, but her playmates had the good sense to stay gone. And while none of the claims received the DNA seal of paternity, Pat still found it unsettling being confronted with Marcus's ex-"thangs," who were definitely more cinnamon buns and fruit tarts than a well-balanced meal. "But who did I marry?" What was she supposed to say? You *have* to eat your vegetables, but would you really rather have a Twinkie? Still, nobody had shown up damn near grown, on her own, and on Pat's doorstep until now.

Gayle came out, not liking the sound of this.

"Where is your mother?" It was the most logical thing Pat could come up with.

Tiffani's smile froze into a grimace, then the corner of her lip began to tremble. She hid it behind her hand. "She died . . . last November . . . I'm sorry." She swiped at fat tears that dripped down her hand. Unzipping her pink miniback-pack, she handed Pat a glossy white folder.

Behind her Lindy mouthed, "I can get rid of her."

Pat shook her head and rifled the folder, not letting herself focus on any of the articles and photos taped to black construction paper. "And what makes you think my husband is your father?" Pat, who rarely referred to Marcus so possessively, was suddenly feeling proprietary. She couldn't say she saw him in Tiffani—her caramel complexion, the shape of her face, her nose. *What would his child look like?* They didn't have any to go by.

"I never asked her till she got really, really sick. It was always just the two of us. I was so scared of losing her . . ." Tiffani sniffed back more tears. "She said they met one summer, when he played for the Orioles—in Erie . . . Pennsylvania . . . that's where I'm from."

Gayle's ears perked up. That would have been back in the days when she and Marcus were young and engaged to be engaged. Before she let Ramsey sweep her into his fantasy.

"And what made you decide to show up here?" Pat folded her arms across her chest.

"I read this article, about you and Mr. Carter and your, like, companies. I put it in the scrapbook." Tiffani motioned for the book so she could find it, but Pat didn't budge. "I went to his building this morning, but the guards wouldn't let me upstairs. So I came here." Tiffani managed a shy smile.

Pat knew getting past security in the G&C Pro Sports building required photo ID and a phone call to reception. No appointment, no ride to the fortieth floor. "So you just got up this morning and took the bus from Erie—"

"I took the train, Mrs. Carter. I live with my aunt in New Jersey now."

"Whatever. And if you read the article, you'd know my name is Ms. Reid."

Gayle could tell Pat was rattled. "What is it you want, Tiffani?"

"Just to talk to him. About my mother and stuff." Tiffani looked down at her feet, then back at Pat.

"I'm sorry for your loss, but I can't help you." Pat held out the folder. "If you insist on pursuing this, you should have your lawyer handle it." The girl hardly looked like a threat, but her appearance out of nowhere was creepy.

"I don't have a lawyer." Tiffani looked wilted. "My phone number and stuff are in the scrapbook . . . I made it for him."

The injured ache in Tiffani's voice threatened to crumble Pat's hastily constructed control of the situation, but she wasn't about to open the door to some stranger, no matter how sad her story. Pat tucked the folder under her arm again, but didn't say another word.

It was clearly the end of the audience. Tiffani picked up her purse. "Thank you, Ms. Reid."

"Do you have a ticket home?" The mother in Gayle couldn't help but make sure Tiffani would be alright. *She's about Vanessa's age. Maybe a little older.*

Tiffani nodded, gave a little wave. "Bye." And she was gone.

"Could be one of BeBe's Kids as soon as Marcus's." Lindy was unmoved.

Pat stormed into the office.

Gayle got the emergency bag of macadamia-nut, chocolate-chunk cookies out of Lindy's bottom drawer and followed.

"I don't want to talk about it." Pat tossed the folder in the trash and slung her coat on the chenille sofa in their sitting area. Playing I've Got a Secret was absolutely not on her agenda for the day.

"You're going to have to tell him." Gayle offered Pat a cookie, but she was too busy fuming to take it.

"Why? She had no business—"

"At least you have warning . . . some control." *The magic word.* Pat always hated being out of control, even when they were kids. Gayle retrieved the folder. The first page had a death notice with a postage-stamp-size picture of a woman who had a warm smile and Tiffani's eyes. Simone Rae Alexander had worked at the Jewelry Chalet for twenty-one years. Seven years older than she and Pat, on November 18 she passed from ovarian cancer. "So young."

"What?" Pat turned, saw Gayle flipping the scrapbook pages. "Oh, come on." She marched across the room to confiscate it, but saw a photo of Tiffani and her mom over Gayle's shoulder. Simone had sunken shadows beneath weary eyes, but the sparkle of her spirit still showed in them. A red-and-black turban covered her obviously bald head. "It's a sad, sad story, but what am I supposed to do about it?"

"Give it to Marcus. It's his hot potato. Let him handle it." Gayle turned the page, to a wobbly snapshot of Simone and Marcus, cheek to cheek. Gayle remembered the summer Marcus came back from Erie wearing the thick gold chain he had on in the picture—one he was not wearing when he left St. Albans. "The good news—it was before you two were together, so it's not like he was cheating on you." *He was cheating on me. Not that it matters.*

Pat's breath made a foggy circle on the window as she peered outside. "It's weird. Like she's out there somewhere."

"She's just a sad little girl."

"Exactly what I don't need." Pat pulled on her coat, picked up the doll, and barreled out of the office for her appointment.

The midwinter sun was unseasonably warm, and since she had angry energy to burn, Pat decided to hoof it, striding like she had the answer before anybody else had the question and you better not get in her way. She had half a mind to head for Marcus's place, but one office surprise was enough for the day. She was not interested in acting like some crazy shrew for the delight of his staff—so unprofessional. Besides, he wasn't having the greatest week.

As a championship baseball player turned sports agent after an injury ended his career on the diamond, Marcus had the marquee name in their household, but his clients were a lot harder to handle. The last week or so he'd been bellowing like a bear with his paw caught in a trap, severely PO'd that one of his hot prospects, a hard-throwing lefty with a promising curveball, was acting shaky. After all the time, attention, and money they had spent grooming him, now he was making noises about jumping ship, leaving Gallagher & Carter Pro Sports in favor of one of the mega sports-management companies, just as he was on the verge of the majors and a real payday. Ouch.

After a few hours of brainstorming with the photographer, Pat recouped some of the morning's excitement. She couldn't wait to get back to the office to share the ideas they had come up with. Ell would get her own portfolio, consisting of studio shots against a rainbow of backdrops. Pat even had Polaroids in her purse of some samples they had taken. They would have a miniature of the latest book created so Ell could hold her own copy. They would also cast for little girls to be pictured hugging Ell, which was really the whole point—putting the me in Ell & Me. When all the proofs were in, she and Gayle would decide which picture would herald their entrée to the next level of the game.

For a while Pat had missed the high-octane action of her former career. But before they had cut her loose, she'd been kicked upstairs, away from the daily dose of adrenaline she got from producing commercials, and the endorphin rush of seeing them air. She had a prestigious title and a better office, but riding herd on the other producers to keep their bottom lines from getting flabby had sent her down a lonesome road with no trailmates and no glory in the end.

Now she got to cut her own path, with no office politics to navigate, and no boss who needed anything kissed. Each day brought new challenges and rewards. Whether it was the afternoon she and Gayle got wired on a twelve-cup pot of coffee and a batch of snickerdoodles and came up with a name for the company—they were so giddy, neither remembered who suggested The Ell & Me Company, but they knew that was the one. Or the day they sent out their first catalog—a trifold brochure really. She couldn't get Gayle to stop crying because she was sure no one would place an order. But Pat was certain they had a winner. And the spring in her step as she zigzagged along the crowded sidewalks was because she felt the same way now. Gayle was Ell's mom, the public face of the company, and Pat was happy to stay behind the scenes and plot their course.

It was dark by the time Pat got back to the office. She would have gone straight home except she wanted to drop off the doll, show Gayle the pictures.

Lindy passed Pat on the stairs. "V-attack."

"Great." It was their code for Vanessa having some kind of meltdown.

"Just needs one good butt-whipping. Night." And Lindy made her exit.

Pat hoped it was just one of Vanessa's near weekly emotional outbursts. Honestly, she didn't know how Gayle could take it. Pat loved her best friend's only child, but Vanessa had been challenging even as a tween. That was nothing compared to these teen years. But they had had more than one go-round about Gayle's discipline style, which usually ended with Gayle saying, "You talk to me when you're a mother." If this was motherhood, Pat didn't know how anybody could take it.

"Nessa . . . I know how hard you practiced. . . . Oh, honey. You thought it went so well . . ."

Whatever it was wasn't tragic, so Pat dropped some of the photos on Gayle's desk. She'd hear the Vanessa saga tomorrow. She stuffed Tiffani's folder in her bag. Pat still wasn't sure what she would do with it, but it was making the trip home.

*   *   *

"Simone." Marcus sank to the brown suede sofa when he opened the scrapbook. *Sweet, sexy Simone.* "I can't believe it."

Not the response Pat had bargained for. She didn't even like the way he said her name, like a warm, soothing secret. On the bus ride up to West Seventy-ninth Street she'd had time to find some logic in the situation. All Marcus really had to do was give up a little DNA—a swab of the cheek would tell the whole story. There was no reason to think Tiffani was his daughter any more than the others had been, so Pat decided to start the evening with her, get it out of the way so she could get to her good news.

"Did she say how long her mother was sick?"

"I didn't ask," Pat snapped, and cinched the belt of her leopard-print robe. If she'd known Marcus was staying late to work out contract minutiae with a manager on the West Coast, she'd have booked an hour of tennis at the club near her office so she could smack something. Instead she took a long hot shower and drank some green tea in search of serenity. She was still searching. And if she'd known Simone would bring back such fond memories . . . "Is there something you need to tell me?"

"No. It's just a shock." He closed the book, pressed it between his palms. "Simone was a long time ago."

Pat could see the one dimple in Marcus's cheek that appeared whenever he clenched his jaw. She'd known that expression since they were kids, since his brother Freddy's funeral. It meant he was holding back, holding on. And what was he holding now? His thoughts? His sadness? *Let him handle it*. Deciding to hold her tongue, Pat came up behind him, rested her hands on his shoulders. He let out a deep sigh.

Marcus had retired from professional sports, but not from the gym. His body was as sleek and sculpted as any of the athletes he represented—said he had to give the young punks something to aspire to. But Pat could feel the tension knotted beneath the surface, so she kneaded his muscles, pressed circles across the swells of his chest with the heels of her hands, pulsed down his biceps, his forearms. Marcus closed his eyes, let his head loll against her belly. Looking down into his face made Pat calmer too. Some mornings she still woke up and got the flutters when she saw him across the pillows.

Not to say being married was easy. Everything, from finding an apartment that suited them both, to figuring out what to put in it, had required negotiation and compromise, and neither was a natural at diplomacy. For a while Marcus had tried to convince her a houseboat on the Hudson would be cozy, but Pat was not about to live with him in less space than they already had and with floors that swayed with the tides. Eventually they found a place on Riverside Drive, with a wide-open view of the river. Combining his macho utilitarian decor with her metropolitan chic proved challenging too, but eventually they found a balance between comfort and style.

Except it wasn't just the big things that required work. Which brand of mayo, where to go for vacation, whose bank—the day-to-day decisions took energy and effort as well. Then add all the career pressure that came with being a two-entrepreneur household—pressure to stay ahead, be on top, see and be seen at the right places, with the right people, say the right thing. It was certainly never dull. And she never, ever wanted to be dull—the kind of woman who got lost in the shadows, left behind.

Pat pressed fingertip spirals along his temples, across the buttery skin of his forehead. And the daytime pressure didn't subside at night. Their mismatched schedules meant their bed was mostly for sleeping. She couldn't pinpoint when that had happened—little by little, over time. Some racy lingerie and a long weekend used to be enough to get them in sync, but somewhere along the line those interludes stopped making it into their calendars.

Pat was about to lean over, press an upside-down kiss to his lips . . .

. . . when Marcus opened his eyes. "I'll give Tiffani a call tomorrow."

"What for?" That snagged Pat's groove like a needle scratching vinyl.

"To see how she's doin'. To express my condolences."

"Marcus, the girl shows up out of nowhere, says you're her father, and you're talking about a sympathy call. It doesn't make sense. Unless you already know—"

"I don't know squat. Aw-ite." Except Simone was his first, his burning sands to cross, his guide. He was a lame teenager in man clothes, with milk breath, and she was patient, taught him a little about life, about himself. Simone threw him a line before he knew that's what he needed, then tossed him back because she knew he wasn't grown enough to reel in—all in one summer. He never forgot her for it. And now her daughter had shown up to tell him she was gone. *My daughter?*

"So are you planning to take her word you're her daddy? Maybe she could move in the guest room."

"It's what her mother told her, so it's all she knows. I can't blame her for that." Marcus stood up. "You, of all people, should have a little sympathy."

"That's different." Marcus had snatched Pat, headfirst, back to the pursuit of her own father, a fact she'd conveniently overlooked when Tiffani appeared.

"How? All you had is what *your* mother told *you*. You

never believed anything else the woman had to say, but you took that for gospel."

What could she say? Pat had worked so hard for so long to make herself successful, worthy of her father's acceptance. But he had dismissed her with a brittle cackle. *I have all the children I plan to acknowledge.*"

Marcus saw the hurt in Pat's face, came over, and surrounded her in his arms. "I'm just saying I'll check it out." He tilted Pat's face up to his, met her mouth with a slow kiss. "You got nothing to worry about."

"Me worry?" Pat slid her arms under his cashmere sweater. Turned on was about the last thing she expected to feel after her encounter with Marcus's potential progeny. Especially since it had been so long since they were both tuned to this channel at the same time.

"That's what I like to hear." Marcus continued the lip-to-lip conversation, then steered them toward the bedroom.

And the urge to share their deep connection allowed Pat to be swept along. She'd had enough talk for one day. The doll could wait until tomorrow. So she lounged on the bed, waited for him to slide in beside her.

Marcus pulled her on top, looked into her eyes. "You know, you and me make a little somebody, wouldn't be no questions about who's the mommy and who's the daddy."

Nothing was a faster fire extinguisher. *Why would you bring that up now?* "Come on. You leave for Florida in two days. I've got a doll launch to plan . . ."

"Think of it as on-the-job training." He eased his hands under her gown, let them explore familiar hills and hollows. "Might inspire new stories. Another doll . . ." He nibbled kisses along the curve of her neck, down her collarbone.

Pat considered not answering, just going with the flow, but she couldn't let her silence be mistaken for yes. "Now is not the time."

"It's never now." The tender moment quickly congealed. Marcus slid Pat to the side and sat up.

"That's not fair." Pat sat up too, wrapped the sheet around her, feeling the need for cover.

They retreated to separate isolation booths, each staring straight ahead.

"There's part of me that hopes that girl is mine." Marcus got up, stepped into the pants he'd dropped in a heap.

For the second time in the day Pat felt herself drowning, swallowed this time in waters that had always seemed safe.

"At least I'll have one child." Marcus left the room.

Leaving Pat adrift.

• CHAPTER 2 •

Whoa, whoa, whoa . . .

W hat a day. *Gayle stepped out* of the cab. Normally she took the bus, but between the doll and Pat's surprise visitor, Gayle felt so drained she was running on fumes. And she wasn't too sure what was waiting upstairs.

"Evening, Mrs. Hilliard." The doorman nodded as Gayle walked inside.

Every time she heard herself called that name, his name, it was like pouring salt in a big hole in her side that had never healed. But it upset Vanessa for her to have one name and Gayle to have another, so for business and her own sanity, she was Saunders. At home and as Vanessa's mom she was Hilliard. It didn't make either of them completely happy, but it was the best she could do. She owed Vanessa at least that.

"Feels almost like spring, don't it?"

"Guess so, Mario." Frankly, she'd been too preoccupied to be conscious of the weather, traffic, or how long it actually took to get home. Long enough to chew through a twelve-pack of Juicy Fruit, the wads of foil-wrapped gum a mass in her pocket.

"But I think you'll find it's gonna be stormy later." Mario glanced upward—not at the sky, but in the general direction of 6B, Gayle's apartment.

Swell. She knew he meant no harm, but some days she found the doorman's bulletins irritating, and this was one of them. Besides, it was hardly breaking news. From Vanessa's phone call, Gayle knew the thunderclouds had rolled in.

Gayle mustered a semismile and headed for the mailbox, fishing in her bag for keys. With the eye of an eagle and the nose of a gossip columnist, Mario monitored not only the ins and outs of the building residents, but also their moods, feuds, and dudes—and he didn't miss much. The updates had started when this was Pat's apartment and Gayle first moved in—his way of alerting Gayle to the current climate in Vanessa's world. Occasionally the days were sunny, but cloudy, stormy, and showers had been the most common forecasts.

Who could blame her? Vanessa had been through major upheavals in her young life. And while she was never an easygoing child, the loss of her father, grandmother, her home, friends, school, and for a time her own mobility had made her that much harder to handle.

Gayle got in the elevator, heard the "yip yip" and the tap tap of doggy nails on the marble and pushed her floor, willing the doors to close before she had company. No such luck. A beefy arm—the one not clutching the Pomeranian—thrust through the opening. Her neighbor, a mountain of a man with a mass of wiry, black hair with white roots, got on and pretty much filled the small elevator car. Gayle muttered hello and flipped through her mail, hoping to avoid idle chit-chat. And until he got off on three, Grizzly Adams as Vanessa called him, obligingly whispered baby-talk gibberish to his puffy orange furball, the pair living proof that people and their pets do not necessarily look alike.

The apartment was dark and quiet—not a good sign. Usually Vanessa had music blasting and lights blazing in every room. Gayle dropped her coat on the chair in the foyer, stopped in the kitchen and wolfed down a snack box of raisins to hold her, then headed down the hall and knocked on Vanessa's door.

"Yeah."

Taking that for an invitation, Gayle entered. "What in the . . . ?!" Reflective stars on the ceiling twinkled faintly in the dim light from the desk lamp. Vanessa, in yellow sweats cut off just above the ankle, which she wore over pink tights and red socks, sat on the floor, scissors in hand, surrounded by what looked like the remnants of New Year's Eve in Times Square. "Nessa, what did you do?" Her room had been a shrine to the dance, the walls plastered with posters and photographs, some of them signed—Katherine Dunham,

Josephine Premice, Alvin Ailey, Garth Fagan . . . She had collected, rearranged, and obsessed over them for years. Now, only dust shadows, torn corners, bits of tape, and picture hooks remained. Gayle felt as if someone had grabbed a fistful of her guts. *Stay calm.*

"It's obvious, isn't it?" Vanessa shrugged, continued to snip. "What do I need them for?"

"Honey, you loved those. Just because you didn't get into Performing Arts doesn't mean—"

"What? That I suck as a dancer? Why did I bother auditioning for that stupid school? Only like sixty kids out of a thousand get in. Oh, yeah. I know. It was your idea. I knew I'd never make it." Vanessa sliced through the dynamic arc of Bill T. Jones. "I told you, you have to know somebody. That's what everybody says."

"It's a New York City public school. Anyone with the talent can go there." Applying to LaGuardia had been Gayle's idea. After three private schools in the last five years—all-girls, Quaker, and progressive—Vanessa still hadn't found one that fit. She hadn't found new friends either, and she adamantly refused to contact her old ones—the circumstances that caused her embarrassment were now history, but it wasn't ancient enough. So when it came time for high school, Gayle urged Vanessa to consider the school *Fame* made infamous.

At first she was reluctant, not wanting to be the new girl again. "Everybody in your class will be new," Gayle had told her. After the school tour, the history, and talking with students, Vanessa changed her mind. "Arthur Mitchell went there. And Lola Falana and Edward Villella." It was the first time in ages Gayle had seen her genuinely excited about anything.

"Guess that means I don't have talent, huh?" Vanessa went to work on a Philadanco poster, shredding it into ribbons.

"That's not what I meant." Vanessa was expert at turning Gayle's words against her. They didn't so much have conversations as confrontations, balancing on a tightrope. Gayle was usually first to lose her balance. "I'm proud of the way you prepared for that audition."

Vanessa had come a long way from Miss Judy's in Scarsdale. When Ramsey heard that enrolling your daughter was de rigueur for the "right people" in their tony community, Gayle was assigned the task. She had no idea if Vanessa would like dance class or not, but the moment she put on her first cap-sleeved leotard and joined the cadre of little brown girls in pink tights on Tuesday afternoons and Saturday mornings, she was captivated. Gayle was prepared for her to outgrow this phase, like horseback riding and violin, but Vanessa's interest didn't fade, even as she advanced and the classes became more demanding. She practiced diligently and really shone in the spotlight of recitals. Some of Gayle's fondest memories were of the performances they saw together—from ballet to Broadway—Vanessa's wide eyes gleaming in the darkened theaters. Afterward she'd chatter endlessly, about the costumes and the staging, and reenact her favorite parts, choreographing jetés and pirouettes across the great room since it didn't have carpeting.

"Yeah, well, you're not a judge, so what difference does it make?"

"Doing your best always makes a difference."

Vanessa rolled her eyes. "You're trippin'."

Choosing to sidestep the trap, Gayle picked up a handful of confetti. "You're going to be sorry. You can't just replace these." She let the shards of paper slip between her fingers, float to the floor. Gayle's parents had seen her artwork as a childish diversion—like jumping rope or watching TV. She didn't fault them. They looked out for her the best they knew how. Her father stressed school so she could get a decent job, her mother encouraged her to find a good husband. Drawing pictures wouldn't help in either category. Ramsey was no better—called the books she made for Vanessa "mammy-made junk." She wondered what they would say now. Her parents, at least, would be proud. Vanessa only acted as though Ell Crawford was a big deal if somebody else brought it up. But Gayle was mindful not to crush Vanessa's dreams.

"I don't care. This stuff is all stupid. I'm never going to be a dancer anyway." With nothing left to cut, Vanessa laid her scissors down.

Her teachers had always been supportive, told Gayle Vanessa was good, strong, dedicated, and had a dancer's body—lean, lithe with a long neck and legs. No one ever said she was extraordinary, a star in the making, but as long as Vanessa believed and tried, Gayle vowed to do her part. Especially after the fall that had shattered her body. So once her doctors and physical therapist had cleared her to dance again, Gayle did what she could to get Vanessa back to the barre, even finding an instructor who worked specifically with injured dancers.

"Maybe I should have died in the fire too."

"Enough." It didn't take much to shove Gayle back to

that day, the smell of smoke, the utter panic and desperation. "You know you don't mean that."

"Right. Like you know anything," Vanessa mumbled, but loud enough so she knew she'd be heard. "You thought I'd get in."

Gayle cringed, and somewhere not too far from the surface she knew she could never have spoken to her parents that way and still had lips. Vanessa mostly kept her comments in check when others were around, but when the two of them were alone, she let them fly. Yes, Gayle thought Vanessa would make it. She wished and hoped and prayed it too. "Of course I did. Because you're a beautiful dancer and you worked really hard." But Vanessa was so disappointed. Gayle could see it, and that left jagged little holes in her soul.

"Which means exactly nothing!"

"Maybe you're right. What do they know?" Gayle dropped down on the floor beside Vanessa. "When you're a star and you're getting the—what's the dance award?"

"The Capezio."

"Then you can *not* thank them!" She took Vanessa's hand. "So you'll stay at Breton—they have a strong arts program."

Vanessa shrugged, but she was listening.

"You'll still have your lessons with Miss Ducelle." Gayle took a deep breath. "And maybe we'll look into one of those camps you're always talking about for the summer."

"Really?" Vanessa brightened, actually looked at her mother.

She had begged to attend performing arts camp, but Gayle always found excuses—not the right time, the right place, the right money. But really, six weeks was so long. And what could Gayle do to fill them, besides work and worry? She knew it was just a camp where kids took music and mounted plays in addition to volleyball and swimming. But she hadn't been able to protect Vanessa when they lived in the same house. What could she do hundreds of miles away in a world where people snatched children into panel vans and flew planes into buildings? But the offer was out there now. And it made Vanessa look so happy.

"Yes. Really. You call for the brochures."

"Interlochen and Stagedoor are the only two that matter. You know how many famous people went there? And sometimes they come back to teach and stuff. A couple of summers and I'll be set, way better than stupid LaGuardia. I'll make some real connections. That's what I need." The weather had changed and Vanessa was off and running toward a sun-drenched summer adventure. "I mean you have to be good and have training, but if you don't have connections, you're dog meat."

"What about all those ballerinas who were discovered by George Balanchine. It was their dancing that got them noticed."

"And you think that was all?" Vanessa gave her mother one of those you're-too-hopeless-to-breathe looks. "What do you think would have happened with your little stories if Aunt Pat didn't have a hookup? Nada."

"My stomach is full of nada." Deciding it was time for an exit, Gayle got to her knees and stood up. "You can come help with dinner, or stay and clean this up."

"Why would I do that? Rosie comes tomorrow." Vanessa sprang up from her cross-legged seat in one fluid motion.

"This is beyond vacuuming. You made this mess. You'll have to clean it up."

Vanessa huffed and followed Gayle to the kitchen. Hair knotted loosely at the nape of her neck, she posed in the doorway, feet in the usual turnout, like a penguin, and no evidence of the typical teenage slouch. She had only recently abandoned her ragamuffin *Les Mis* period and was now exploring her inner Bohemian, which looked pretty much the same to Gayle except the colors were brighter. A supersize forest-green sweater draped her delicate frame and she combed her fingers through the fringe on the six-foot scarf she had wound around her neck.

Gayle was glad for the company. The evening was actually going better than she'd anticipated. She peered in the fridge, grabbed a handful of cashews. "We finally saw the doll today."

Vanessa looked bored and baffled.

"Our Ell Crawford doll. I should have brought one of the Polaroids. She's beautiful." Gayle shook the jar of nuts toward Vanessa, who shook her head no. "Looks so much like you!" *And you look so much like your father.* Although she had three inches on Gayle, Vanessa wasn't yet as tall as her dad, but her bronze skin, strong nose, and lean, muscular body, those were Ramsey's gifts. Gayle found it hard to see any of herself in Vanessa. At least on the outside. Granted, no one who knew them now had ever met Ramsey, and people always remarked how much daughter favored mother, especially since Gayle had let her hair grow long again—the almond-shaped face, the flashing brown eyes. But Gayle could hear her mother say, "She's just like you." That was not about their physical resemblance. It was the impulsive, vain, superficial young woman with tunnel vision and a stubborn streak her mother referred to. And Gayle was terrified it was true.

"Great. Like the books weren't bad enough." Vanessa pulled out a stool and sat at the breakfast bar.

"Oh, you love it. There'll be little Nessas everywhere!"

Vanessa screwed up her face, like she'd just downed castor oil with a prune-juice chaser.

"Besides what do you think pays for all your clothes, and private school, and dance classes, and this Interwhatever camp—"

"Whatever."

Gayle dug in the pantry, pulled out a box of fusilli. "Pasta?"

"I don't care."

"We had another surprise at work today."

"Uh-huh."

Gayle put a big pot of water on to boil, dumped a two-pound bag of frozen shrimp in a bowl of tepid water to thaw, gathered onion, peppers, olive oil . . . waiting for Vanessa's curiosity to kick in.

"Why do you make so much food? I don't eat that much. You say we'll have leftovers, then you toss them 'cause you hate leftovers. It's stupid."

"Everything is stupid to you these days." Gayle turned away, chopped vegetables, heated the pan.

Vanessa shrugged. "So what happened?"

"I knew you wanted to know!" Gayle brightened. "This girl came by the office—"

"One of your no-life Ell-heads?" That was Vanessa's name

for the legions of girls who wrote heartfelt letters about what the Ell stories meant to them.

"I wish you wouldn't call them that. And she wasn't."

"So?"

"So . . . she's from Erie, Pennsylvania. A little older than you." The onions sizzled as Gayle dumped them in the hot oil. "And she says she's uncle Marcus's daughter." Gayle had hoped adding the *uncle* would blunt the impact of actually saying those words, but it still stung. *Stupid.*

"Oh, man, wish I'd been there. I bet Aunt Pat was deranged."

"She actually handled it very calmly." *Calmer than me.* "Would you make the salad please."

Vanessa jumped off her stool, got a bag of ready-made salad from the crisper drawer, and dumped it in a bowl.

Gayle sautéed garlic and shrimp as she filled in the blanks.

"Well, he was a jock. You know how they are."

"How are they?" Gayle put the two plates of pasta *del giorno* on the counter and sat down.

"Come on, Mom. You've seen the press conferences. In this corner you have the crying skank." Vanessa licked her finger and dabbed wet spots below her eyes. "He was sooo big. He overpowered me. There was nothing I could do." She batted her eyelashes. "And in the other corner you have the guy looking all humble." Vanessa straightened her imaginary tie, deepened her voice. "'I never meant to dishonor myself, my team, and my loving wife in any way.' Yeah. Right. Meanwhile, wifey is standing behind him looking like 'Sucker, I own you.'"

"It wasn't like that when Marcus and I—"

"Whoa, whoa, whoa. Marcus and who?"

Damn. All that talk about the old days. It was kind of an unspoken rule that the three of them hardly ever revisited that time, certainly not with Vanessa. Not that there was anything wrong. But today it was in the spotlight. This was a cat Gayle had meant to keep in the bag and drown in the river, but it was out now and Vanessa would never let it go. Gayle popped a forkful of food in her mouth to give herself a moment to figure out what to say.

"Back when we were kids, high school really, Marcus and I, we used to . . . date."

"So he was your boyfriend?"

"Well . . ." Gayle felt this conversation slipping out of her control. Another forkful. "Yes. Pat was in boarding school, then she was away in college. We were all friends. She and Marcus used to fuss all the time."

"Like they do now?"

"Kind of. But, yes, Marcus and I went together. It was childish really."

Vanessa couldn't hold the excitement anymore. She ran into the living room, around the coffee table, and back again. "So that means you did it, right? Holy—"

"No. No. No. There was no *it*. I told him there would be no *it* until we got married."

"You're kidding me, right? 'Cause that's the stupidest thing I ever heard. Tiffani probably is his, 'cause he had to be getting it somewhere."

"That's enough."

"Be real, Mom. No guy is gonna keep it in his pants waiting for you. A pro baller too. And what, you left him for my father? Great move." Vanessa slid back in her seat. "You didn't make him wait."

Gayle looked at her daughter, stunned.

"I'm not stupid. I can add." Vanessa stabbed at a shrimp, looking triumphant. "Guess you gave it up to a loser."

"What did you say?" Like she hadn't heard it loud and clear. Gayle didn't mean for her voice to come out so shrill. The muscles in her face, her neck, tightening.

"I mean I guess I should be glad since otherwise I wouldn't be here. But Uncle Marcus is kinda hot for an old dude. And he didn't jack up anybody's life, then jump in the ocean. Yep, a prime-time loser."

"Stop it."

"Whatever."

"He was your father." *Is your father. Wherever he is.*

"So? You chose him. I didn't." Vanessa grabbed a shrimp by the tail, popped it in her mouth. "For what he did, he deserves to be dead."

"Vanessa!"

"I'm done. Going to clean my room. If that's alright with you?"

Gayle wanted to yell, make her apologize. But for what, telling the truth? All she could do was glare, swallow Vanessa's contempt. She had earned it, hadn't she? Without thinking, Gayle picked up her plate, shoveled pasta and shrimp into her mouth, down her gullet, not tasting, just swallowing until it was gone.

Then Gayle rolled up her sleeves, scrubbed the pots, cleared the table, telling herself she had no right to feel hurt about what Marcus *might* have done. So she choked down her disappointment that he was what, human? Didn't play her little power game way back when? She was about to scrape Vanessa's uneaten pasta into the trash, but she found herself picking at it, one shrimp, another, then the pasta until the plate was empty and she was disgusted with herself. So she rinsed it clean, shoved it in the dishwasher, put away the leftovers, and left the room.

But she couldn't sit still, couldn't relax. Gayle looked at Vanessa's door, wanted to go in, but didn't know what she would say. She wanted to call Pat, just to hear somebody else's voice, because sometimes in the evening she felt so alone. But Pat had her own problems to unravel tonight. So she paced back to the kitchen, got a peanut butter cookie from the jar. And another. *That's enough.* She left the room, but the tension kept rising and she needed to stuff it down with something, and she kept ending up in the kitchen, for another pinch of pasta, some cheese, another cookie until there were no more.

Except food didn't fill the space, could barely stifle the scream that threatened to escape every day she walked into her office, unsure she would ever have another worthwhile idea. Yes, the doll was great, but that only made her feel worse since there was more to lose. Pat was always confident, and Gayle was grateful her friend had pulled her along, helped her back on her feet. But Pat wasn't the one filling the blank pages, needing to satisfy the little girls, who wanted another story as soon as they finished the last one. Of course she was happy about the doll, happy about their success and all the plans they had for the future. But she was terrified of failing, of letting Vanessa down, of screwing up again.

She changed into her nightgown, brushed her teeth. Sometimes the minty burn of mouthwash would keep her from putting one more thing in her mouth. But tonight she was back in the kitchen, staring into the refrigerator, the freezer. Then she had a spoon in the carton of cherry vanilla ice cream. She didn't even like it. Vanessa did. The cherry scraps felt like trash in her mouth, but it didn't matter. She needed to feel full. So full her stomach cramped and she felt clammy and dizzy. She shuffled to the bathroom, locked the door, turned on the shower, bent over the toilet. It didn't take much to make it all come exploding out of her in spasms, eyes tearing, head aching. But when the retching was over, and she panted for breath, a cloud of calm passed over her and it was peaceful for a moment. And when she left the bathroom, she was back in control of everything but her shame.

CHAPTER 3

What will be, already is.

"Wow, you look different in person. But the same." Tiffani lit up like the star on top of a Christmas tree as she swept into the office and saw Marcus. He grinned, momentarily disarmed by her bubbly greeting, and by actually seeing this girl, who could be his daughter. Before he could move, she had crossed the room, and what Pat thought should have been a handshake became a hug.

"Tiffani." Pat's clipped tone wasn't so much a welcome as

an acknowledgment that said, "I know who you are, but we're not pals." Then she greeted Tiffani's aunt Stephanie, whose plain-faced, wait-and-see reserve Pat found reassuring. *Not everybody has gone crazy.*

It had taken a month for Pat and Marcus to work out arrangements they could both live with for this confab. Pat tried to convince him there was no need to meet at all before there was a lab match, but when he said, "You don't have to go. I can take care of this by my damn self," it hit her like a brick and she backed off. First Marcus wanted to invite the girl to their apartment, but Pat wasn't having it. Then he suggested driving to her aunt's house in New Jersey, but Pat nixed that too. "You don't know those people." Finally she convinced him that her office was at least neutral ground. "She's been there already." So they would all converge at ten thirty—postbreakfast, prelunch, all-business. Pat and Gayle already had an appointment scheduled that afternoon to brainstorm the Ell Crawford publicity with their PR firm, so the meet and greet couldn't drag on forever.

Pat also convinced him to have someone from Millennium Security present. "You'd insist if it was one of your players." And that was true. He and Rich retained the company to handle a variety of delicate romantic matters, some death threats, lunatic fans, the usual fallout of life in the public arena. Gayle had vouched for the company owner, Teresa Stuckey, the retired detective who had been so helpful and attentive when Ramsey disappeared, even after Gayle had moved out of her jurisdiction. Stuckey took this assignment herself since it was Marcus's situation and because, as she said, "I'm less obtrusive than a big, burly guy." So she sat toward the back of the office, out of the way, but with full view. Pat wanted a lawyer too, but Marcus wouldn't go that far. Not yet.

Pat and Gayle gave Lindy the morning off, although she begged to come in to show support. "Ride shotgun," as she put it. Gayle would wait at the coffee shop around the corner. Pat would call when the dust settled. It wasn't exactly Gunfight at the OK Corral, but Pat was feeling ambushed.

"You look like your mother." Marcus had seen the pictures, but the resemblance was more startling in person. He had tried to go into the day with a blank slate and no expectations. But over the last few weeks, when he was in the shower or buckled in his airplane seat staring at the clouds, he wondered what it would have been like, all those years ago, if Simone had said she was pregnant. Would he have been chest-pounding proud or upset he had gotten her knocked up on his first dip in the pool? Could it have been a beginning, or the end of his big league dreams? Now he didn't know if he was mad at Simone for leaving him in the dark, or mad at Pat for making him wait, making him beg, like it was some kind of conceit or inconvenience for a man to want a baby with his wife.

"Thanks. Mom was pretty cool." The past tense made Tiffani's eyes well, but she blinked back tears. "She was like my best friend."

They settled in the lounge area, Tiffani and her aunt on the sofa, Marcus in the club chair. Pat pulled her executive desk chair around, staying slightly outside the circle, and above it. She wasn't interested in turning this into a cozy lovefest. She was already annoyed at how much care Marcus had taken getting dressed, picking out the right tie. He'd even had a fresh haircut, like this was a date with his special girl.

"I have to say, my sister never mentioned anything about you." Stephanie's lips pursed like she'd been sipping lemon juice straight from the bottle. "Didn't know she was expecting till after Tiffani was born."

Pat crossed her legs. *Guess Tiffani likes surprises too.* Seems Aunt Stephanie didn't know about her niece's expedition in search of her roots until she'd already sniffed out a tree.

"And I didn't know till now." Marcus looked Stephanie square in the eyes. "I would have been involved before if I had." He wanted to make sure she didn't think he was the kind who liked to hit it and quit.

"Well, we weren't close—in age or otherwise." Her hair was curled and fluffed like a poodle's, too young for the hardness of her face. "Simone danced to her own tune."

The independent streak certainly fit the woman who had picked Marcus out as somebody worth knowing. He ignored the bite in big sister's voice, like she wasn't too keen he'd been Simone's dance partner. He leaned in toward Tiffani. "Tell me about yourself."

"I don't know. Not much to tell. Really." For the first time she looked hesitant, as though she wasn't sure what she'd gotten herself into. "I'm in tenth grade. I was a cheerleader."

"I used to think cheerleaders were pretty special, getting the crowd all fired up. They'd at least pretend to believe you could get on base, even when you weren't too sure." Marcus settled back in the chair. "I used to go with a cheerleader, back in the day."

Pat cut him a look that would slice stone, but it didn't appear to make a scratch.

"Really?" Tiffani smiled. "I sorta hung with this guy who

was on the basketball team, till he got all funny. Like he owned me or something."

"Jocks can be jerks," Marcus said.

No kidding. It was hard not to jump in, but Pat figured the less she said, the better.

"That's what my mom said. Oh, I mean, not about you."

That made them laugh a little, lighten up.

"My new school doesn't even have cheerleaders. They hardly have computers."

There was a blue note in Tiffani's voice, and Pat found herself nodding, wondering how Tiffani fit in her make-do household. Pat had been just five when the woman who loved her like a mother died, and she had to move in with the mother who couldn't love her. But that wasn't on the table for discussion. Nor did it make Marcus responsible for righting what had gone wrong in Tiffani's life.

Tiffani shrugged. "That's about it. Nothing special."

Marcus continued to prod, and Tiffani revealed a regular teen, who earned B's and a few C's. "Mostly in science. I hate memorizing formulas and stuff." Pat could barely keep still while Marcus conducted the Tiffani crash course: What music do you listen to? What do you watch on TV? What do you like to do?

"Go to the mall," Tiffani answered that one immediately.

"That's not an activity." It slipped out before Pat could catch it, but after the cheerleader crack she figured she and Marcus were even.

"It sort of is. There's all different stores and different people. What they wear. What they buy." Tiffani warmed to the topic. "I was a stocker at this juniors' shop. In the mall where Mom worked . . . we used to come home together. Anyway, the stuff was kinda cheesy, but you could make it look alright. Like these pants." She held out a leg to show her tweed trousers. "With the thirty-percent-off sale and my discount they were seven sixty-nine. Not too shabby." Tiffani crossed her ankles demurely, obviously proud of her bargain-hunting skills. "You'd see the same girls in the store every week, 'cause they like being first with the style. So we got merch every week to give them something new to buy. Then, some of 'em only come for the sale. They usually want the hangers too. It's interesting. To me anyway."

Marcus was impressed. "You're an expert people-watcher."

Even Pat had to admit Tiffani sounded like she had a head on her shoulders, making pretty astute observations while doing grunt work. Pat couldn't imagine Vanessa going to school and holding a job. They had offered to have her work the summers, pay her a little something, let her get familiar with the business. She made it sound as if they wanted to sell her to the highest bidder.

"Mom managed a jewelry store forever, that's what made her name me Tiffani, but you don't get nothing but a check . . . anything but a check. Little one at that, compared to all the gold and diamonds. I'd rather have some kind of store of my own. Like one of those chains or franchises or whatever." Then she turned to Pat. "That's why I think it's so cool Ms. Reid, you and your friend starting a company together."

Pat was surprised to hear her name come up in conversation. "Thank you. I've really enjoyed it . . . even more than I expected." It was usually the mothers who considered the business, and Pat and Gayle's role in it. *Awfully mature. But then, so was I.*

After a few more rounds of Getting to Know You, Tiffani lobbed a question of her own. "What was my mother like, when you two were together?"

Marcus inhaled deeply, searched for the right words.

And Pat decided it was time for a station break. "It might be best you leave those question until . . . until we know what we're dealing with."

Before Marcus could object, Aunt Stephanie seconded the motion. "I agree."

Pat figured it was because Stephanie didn't want to hear the gory details. Frankly, neither did she. Right now Pat was just happy for an ally.

"Uh, yeah. Aw-ite. Why don't *we* do that." Marcus's expression tensed just enough to let Pat know he was annoyed.

Tough. They were in this boat together, and somebody had to pilot while he was lost in a sea of old memories.

"Let me just say, Tiffani is still a minor. All my sister's money went for doctor bills . . ."

"It's not about money." Tiffani looked distressed.

"I'm being realistic. That's my job, as your guardian. And I have my daughter's three kids, just until she gets herself straight, you know."

"Without question." Marcus came to attention. "And I will be monetarily responsible for all the necessary tests. And whatever else is required."

Pat was glad to hear his negotiator voice click on. It meant he hadn't completely melted into a puddle of slush, although she wondered what would be required. And not just out of their checkbook.

"That's not why I came." Tiffani got up. "See. That's messed up. I'm sorry." She headed for the door.

For an uneasy millisecond Pat understood why her father might have thought she saw dollar signs when all she wanted was for him to know her. And why it hurt so much because that wasn't her intention. She intercepted Tiffani. "It's not messed up." She wrapped an arm around her. "There are just some details to straighten out." Then she had an armful of Tiffani, crying on her shoulder. Marcus swooped in, offered his handkerchief. This instant family tableau, with Pat in the mother position, made her woozy. Unsure what to say or do, she patted Tiffani's back, waited for the sniffling to subside.

After that, the meeting drew to a close. Marcus introduced Stuckey, said she would be in touch to arrange the necessary tests. Then he gave both Tiffani and her aunt his card, home number scribbled on the back. When he put it in Tiffani's hand, he added, "Call me anytime."

Not our home number. But it was a done deal. Forward, back, and side to side, every part of this process left Pat dancing the confusion cha-cha. And when the music stopped, she was exactly where she started—not knowing where any of this would lead.

"Hope I see you soon." Tiffani gave Pat a peck on the cheek, and a honeyed smile, capping off the morning.

Pat heard herself say, "Me too," but it sounded strange, like it came from somebody else's mouth.

Marcus accompanied Tiffani and her aunt downstairs to put them in a cab while Pat wondered if Tiffani was going to become a permanent part of her universe. That made her what? Pat's stepdaughter? Way too much to process.

"That went well." Stuckey shoved the folder with Tiffani's information and her aunt's into her folio and zipped it shut.

"Is that what you call it?" Pat felt drained, like she'd been battling the flu.

"No yelling. No finger-pointing. No blood on the floor." Stuckey nodded, bouncing an ash blond curl onto her forehead. "Good outcome."

"I thought *my* job was stressful."

"But I'm never bored." Stuckey's cell phone vibrated in the pocket of her well-tailored black suit, her stylish postcop uniform. "Kid seems kinda advanced for a sixteen-year-old."

"I was like that."

"All my nieces wanna know is 'Where's the party?' Takes all kinds." Stuckey took a quick glance at the phone, then put it away. "Listen, there are a few things I'd like to run past you and Gayle. About your office security. Or the lack thereof."

"That doesn't sound good. Give me a few. I'm meeting Gayle around the corner." Pat decided to switch the plan. She needed air and a change of venue. "We can grab a bite and talk."

Marcus breezed back in. He and Stuckey spoke briefly by Lindy's desk. Then Stuckey poked her head in, said she'd wait for Pat downstairs. Leaving Pat and Marcus to confer.

"Well?" Pat stiffened, girding for a fight.

"She's a good kid. Hope I can help her out." Marcus seemed loose, almost giddy.

"But you don't know . . ."

"She's the daughter of a friend. Nothing wrong with a little help." Marcus gathered his overcoat and dodged her pointy attitude.

"You make it sound so simple."

"Maybe it is." He gave Pat a kiss . . .

. . . which she suspected was to keep her lips from moving.

"Besides, seems like you made more of an impression on her than I did." He buttoned his coat, headed for the door. "Terry asked if I wanted a background check. I said no." Then, seeing the "Why?" on Pat's face, he added, "The DNA test is all the background I need. What will be, already is."

"What do you want it to be?" It was already too late for what Pat wanted, which was for Tiffani's aunt to live in Detroit or Phoenix or Fiji—someplace not so convenient. Or for Simone to have taken her damn secret with her. Anything that meant this was not in the middle of Pat's life. Not right now.

"Whatever it is. I gotta go." And Marcus made a clean getaway.

Leaving Pat carrying her emotional baggage alone, yet again.

•   •   •

Gayle had snagged a booth facing the door and waved as soon as she saw them. She'd gotten to the coffee shop early—well before the hard lunch crush, because she couldn't stand waiting at home anymore, wondering what was going on. So she had nibbled on some fruit salad, a corn muffin, a Reuben . . . The waitstaff knew her so they didn't hassle her for holding the booth, but she had to order something.

"I won't take up much of your time." Stuckey crunched a half sour pickle from the bowl on the table. "But I gotta tell you, you're a sitting duck for psychos in that office. Your intercom sounds like snap, crackle, and pop, and you've got no monitor, so basically you buzz people in blind."

"I hate that," Gayle agreed. "If I'm by myself, I look out the window and try to see who it is."

"You worry nonstop." Pat was not looking for another problem to solve. "We do children's books—it's hardly controversial." The rest of the afternoon was supposed to get her mind off the unpredictable and onto circumstances she could handle—a doll who didn't walk, talk, or ask questions.

"Thieves don't look for controversy. They look for cash, computers, anything with street value. And who knows, maybe there's some nutcase whose question you didn't answer when you visited her daughter's second-grade class and she's been mad ever since. Pat, Tiffani found you because of an article she read. There are lots of people you don't know who know you. So basically you only have a glass door between you and chaos."

Gayle hadn't thought about it in such stark terms. "What should we do?"

"Move." Stuckey laid the metal napkin dispenser on its side, positioned the salt and pepper shakers behind it. "You need barriers—security guards, metal detectors, surveillance cameras—a full-service building, like Marcus and Rich."

"Not in the budget. Not right now." Pat saw it as case closed. Stuckey was obviously not privy to Marcus's moaning about the monthly nut to support his bastion of polished chrome and athletic prowess. Amenities would have to wait.

"Do you think it's really that dangerous?" The worry wrinkle appeared between Gayle's brows.

"You're absolutely taking a risk." Stuckey rested her hands

on the fortress of napkins. "And if there's anything at all dicey in your personal life, that can follow you to the office. I mean, I doubt little Tiffani Sunshine is packing a Glock, but under other circumstances . . ."

"Come on. So far our biggest threat is being overrun by take-out menus." Pat was determined not to give in to unnecessary panic.

"I don't know . . . sometimes we get these hang-up calls . . ."

"Come on, Gayle. Everybody gets hang-ups." Pat waved at their waiter.

Stuckey perked up. "What happens?"

Gayle looked sheepish. "Nothing exactly *happens*. Lindy answers the phone and after a few seconds the line goes dead."

Stuckey took out pad and pen, jotted a note. "How often?"

"Not a lot. A couple of times a week maybe. It just makes me feel a little squirmy."

The waiter, a meatball-shaped man with a cascade of small silver hoops from the top of his ear to the lobe, appeared at the table. Pat ordered the split-pea soup, Stuckey took a pass, and Gayle had an order of fries, just to keep Pat company.

"I hate to bring this up, but have you had any contact with you former husband?"

"No. Nothing. It's like Ramsey disappeared from the planet."

"If we're lucky." If he wasn't dead, Pat couldn't imagine Ramsey would have the nerve to show his face. Not after what he put Gayle through. Whenever she remembered the day he showed up and tried to trick Gayle into giving him the money he had hidden, she still got furious and wished

Stuckey had caught him. Pat would have relished seeing him in handcuffs, thinking about him rotting in jail, because what he did—that was simply unforgivable.

"You know, I always meant to write a letter to your chief of police, about how helpful you were that night Ramsey showed up."

"You didn't, did you?" Stuckey's eyes darted up from her notes.

"No. I was such a wreck back then."

"No need to explain. I mean, if you had, I should have seen it, you know. They usually show you that stuff before it goes in your file. And I never did. See it." Stuckey closed her pad. "Anyway, don't hesitate to let me know if you get that squirmy feeling. It could be there for a reason." Stuckey stood up. "I'll put together some recommendations to button down your office better."

She walked away, and Gayle leaned in, almost whispered, "How are you holding up?"

"Fine." Pat was too busy catching the crap coming her way to think about how she was holding it. She had thought talking to Gayle afterward would be a relief, but right now it just reminded Pat of all the years when Gayle and Marcus had been the couple, which made this whole trip back in time even weirder.

Gayle knew the clipped answer meant her friend was absolutely not fine, but it would take some prodding to get Pat to admit it. So Gayle asked questions, about the meeting, about what would happen next.

"Check please." Pat wanted to close out the discussion along with the bill. "We gotta head downtown."

• • •

"Two hundred bucks deposit. You get it back when you move out, if you don't trash my place." The landlord's voice was hoarse, as though he'd been sick, but you could still hear the Brooklyn in it. "Ninety a week, cash or money order, paid in advance every Saturday by eight p.m.—and my watch runs on time."

Ramsey followed the man up two flights of rickety stairs. Stood aside as he unlocked the dead bolt with one of two keys on a dirty string and flipped on the light—two naked bulbs in a four-socket fixture. The room reeked of cheap pine disinfectant. Ramsey had stayed in enough hellholes to question if the place was really clean, or if the pungent cleanser had been splashed, like cologne on a whore, to mask odors there wasn't time or inclination to wash. Bottom line—what difference did it make? It's what he could afford.

He walked across the scarred parquet floor to the window, wondered what it looked like in the house's glory days—like that had anything to do with him now. From the pockmarked mantel, and what was left of the plaster moldings, he could see the old girl used to have some class. Ramsey tilted the aluminum blinds. The window was streaked, like somebody had attempted to wash it recently, but this was not a room with a view—a concrete slab impersonating a yard, ramshackle wood and stockade fences, and the rear of a row of houses identical to the one he was in. The view could have been a reflection.

"No kitchen privileges. No cooking in the room. Bathroom at the end of the hall." A snowy halo of hair sat on the man's head—like he was wearing a cloud. "You share it

with three other mens. I don't supply no sheets or towels."
He swallowed hard, coughed, then tugged on his bottom lip.
"I don't mind a little liquor, long as you can hold it. But I
won't have no dope. This a quiet house. No loud music. No
fussin' or fightin', or you find your ass on the street. No questions. No excuses." The man folded his bony arms across his
sunken chest. He didn't look like he could remove the trash,
much less an unruly tenant. But Ramsey had no intention of
testing him.

There was a lumpy twin bed on an iron frame, dresser,
desk, chair, table, lamp—none of it from the same decade.
Four wire coat hangers dangled from a metal rod that
bridged a recess in the wall—the closet. A small braided rug
lay by the bed, a cloudy mirror above the dresser. Ramsey
caught a glimpse of himself, something he didn't care to do
much. Thanks to Bessie, Detective Stuckey—the cop in
his pocket—and their associates he looked different these
days.

"Oh, yeah. If you have a woman up in here, she have to
be out by midnight. Like Cinderella. No questions—"

"—no excuses." Ramsey pulled a roll of bills from the
pocket of his green work pants. "I'll take it." He slid off the
rubber band, counted a stack of crumpled fives and tens and
exchanged it for the keys The old man never looked twice at
Ramsey's hand.

• • •

Gayle continued the barrage of questions in the cab, and by
the time they got down to Hudson Street, Pat was sick of the
whole mess.

The capper—right as Pat entered the revolving doors,

Gayle said, "You and Marcus should have a baby. That's why he's so excited about this girl."

Pat spun around backward and spoke through the glass. "Did he tell you that?" She saw Gayle shake her head no. At that moment she wanted to do a 360 and head for . . . where? Instead she waited on the other side and hissed, "What would a baby solve? Exactly nothing."

"What are you so afraid of?" Gayle walked beside her. "You and Marcus would make great—"

"I'm done talking about it." But Pat wasn't done steaming.

They rode the elevator in silence, but once they opened the purple-and-red-striped door to Now What?—their PR firm—it was hard to stay in a sour mood. When Pat left advertising, they had been a hot new shop with a commitment to business un-usual. They had taken on The Ell & Me Company because they had an affinity for clients with an adventurous spirit and room to grow.

Pat and Gayle followed the neon sign that read THIS WAY, across the AstroTurf carpet to the Lucite reception desk, filled this month with giant gumballs. Just as Shirley Bassey came through the speakers and warned of the kiss of death from Mr. Goldfinger, their rep, Drew Voight, swept out to greet them.

"Hail, hail, the gang's all here!" The excited tousle of dusty brown hair hinted at the energy that was Drew's not-so-secret weapon. He was one of the few people on the planet who could wear a kiwi green shirt, like he had on today, and look handsome, not like a Muppet. From the beginning Pat had liked the way he took every assignment as a game to be played and won, and he brought the fun with him. "Ell and me have something to show you."

Drew ushered them into his office, a floor-to-ceiling gallery of vintage amusement-park posters.

"First, some housekeeping." Drew handed them the current schedule for their upcoming Atlanta-area events. "I've sent this as an e-mail attachment as well. There's still a radio interview I'm trying to tie down, and I'm sure there will be more changes before the trip."

"There's already two radio spots and a cable taping." Gayle started obsessing immediately. Both Pat and Drew told her she was good at interviews, but that didn't stop her from worrying until the moment the ON AIR sign lit up. Afterward, she'd fret about what she should have said.

"Just trying to keep everybody happy. You'll still have plenty of time for Toy and Doll Sourcing Expo events, but a little press on the side never hurts." Drew reached for two large manila envelopes on the credenza behind him.

Pat examined the itinerary. "Did you schedule in sleep?"

"You only need that every other day, right?" Drew smiled and passed them the envelopes. "On to the good stuff. I think these will be fantastic in the media kits."

"Wow." Gayle opened the color foldout mock-up of Ell.

"It's life-size. I wanted a piece with some impact. Media contact info will go on back. We can also do plain ones as a takeaway for the fans. Something to put up on their bedroom walls—show Mom, Dad, and Cousin Keisha what they really want for their birthday, Christmas, Kwanzaa, good report cards . . ." Drew scrolled down the list he had open on his laptop. "Oh, and, Gayle, it would be a good idea to get some photos of you with the doll . . . Ell-and-her-mom type of thing."

Pat gave it a quick once-over and put it back in the envelope. They discussed the e-mail blast to go out right after the official announcement. The foldout would also be the centerfold of the catalog. Normally she loved this kind of kicking around ideas, but she couldn't get her head tilted in that direction today.

Gayle went for a ladies' room pit stop before they headed out. Pat started to wonder what the next round with Marcus would be like. *If he's acting like a kid on Christmas Eve when I get home, I'll . . .*

"You know, none of this is final. I can work up some other—"

"No. It looks fantastic."

"That was pretty unconvincing."

"No, really. I'm just . . . distracted." Pat took a deep breath.

"I can always make it better. Just tell me what you want." Drew stretched back in his chair, clasped his hands behind his head.

What she meant to tell him was he'd done a yeoman's job of putting together events for the weekend, and she loved the way he'd designed the Ell foldout so it would be multifunctional. But she looked over at him and all the stuff she'd been holding came spilling out. "You're a man. Would you be happy if some girl, a teenager really, showed up out of nowhere and said she was your daughter?"

Drew cocked his head to the side.

"I just don't get it. Marcus is practically gleeful. Gayle's brilliant suggestion is for me to have a baby. Tiffani, that's the girl's name, is Miss Congeniality, all perky and breathless. And I'm . . ." Pat was about to inhale for the next part of her rant when she looked over at Drew. "And I am really sorry. That was completely out of line." Pat stood up.

So did Drew. "No. Look. Not a problem."

"Tell Gayle I'll meet her in the lobby." Hot with embarrassment, Pat gathered her things. "I need some air."

Drew came around his desk, took her coat, and held it while she put it on. He rested his hands on her shoulders. "No harm, no foul. My door is open if you need to vent."

Drew's touch shot through Pat as if she'd been Tasered. "Thanks." She tried not to trip over her feet as she walked out the door.

• CHAPTER 4 •

. . . living somewhere in the space between.

"Open your mouth please, Mr. Carter."

As far as Marcus was concerned, she may as well have said, *bend over and spread 'em.* This wasn't his first time, and the procedure was a lot simpler now than a few years ago. Still, even seated in the privacy of his own kitchen, taking a paternity test felt as if he were being accused of some deed that called his character into question. Maybe it was the forms to be filled out, his ID checked, his mug shot taken, just like an arraignment, all to verify the accompanying skin cells belonged to the correct party. Or maybe because Pat kept popping in and out, for more coffee, vitamins, a banana. He had had Stuckey schedule the test for nine thirty because Pat was always gone by then. But not today.

Marcus complied and opened wide. The buccal swab took only seconds, and the evidence was popped in its handy carrying case to be sealed with the rest of his documents. It reminded him of the occasional drug test he'd taken during his playing years, when they made you feel guilty until proven innocent, even though he knew he hadn't smoked, ingested, or anointed himself with anything questionable. Just as he hadn't abandoned Simone. And he hadn't shot Freddy on purpose. . . .

"How long does it take . . . for results?" Pat put her mug in the dishwasher as she spoke to the technician over Marcus's head.

"Four to five days after all specimens are in."

Pat sauntered out, tight-lipped, without giving Marcus a glance.

He followed her into the bedroom. "What was that about?"

"What?" The room was dark. Pat opened the blinds and the sun came in like a spotlight.

"You." The other times he'd been accused, they were a team, united in their outrage. "Acting like I'm some kind of criminal."

"That's in your head. I didn't say—"

"You don't have to. Look, forget it." Marcus threw up his hands, turned to walk out.

"This is hard on me too, you know."

He turned back to her. Sometimes he caught a glimpse and Pat reminded him of when they were kids, and she would put up a tough front so no one could see she was afraid. Then there were moments, like in Gayle's basement during that thunderstorm, when she let him see through the act. Marcus wanted to wrap her in his arms, just like then.

"Uh, Mr. Carter . . ."

"Yeah." He headed back toward the apartment door, let the technician out.

By then Pat was bundled and ready to leave.

"I'll give you a lift." Marcus reached and caught her shoulder. "I'm driving."

"That's OK. I'm fine. The train will be faster." Pat's vulnerable underbelly had been wrapped and tucked away. She dotted a kiss on his lips and left. "Busy afternoon."

And so did he, heading for the office. He needed to be busy too.

· · ·

"Son of a bitch!" Marcus balled up the faxes and hurled them against his office wall like a fastball with a lot of juice, just missing the three-foot model of his boat, *Brother's Keeper*, which Pat gave him for their fourth anniversary.

"Already called the rat bastard." Rich was a pocket-size wheeler-dealer, given to custom blue shirts with high white collars, worn with a gold collar bar that made his precise half-Windsor knot sit up like an extension of his Adam's apple. "Had his mommy answer the phone and swear he wasn't home." He squeezed his ever-present wad of exercise putty with extra rancor.

"Why can't we sue the slimeballs at UMG?" It's not that

Marcus didn't feel it coming. Randall Piccone appeared to be a quiet giant—a twenty-year-old, six-foot-five, Wheaties-eating, churchgoing baseball savant, who pitched with both power and finesse. It wasn't a question of whether he would make it to the show, but how soon he'd have his first twenty-game season. He had a sixth sense about baseball, maybe even a seventh. Rich always said it was fortunate Randall had found the outlet for his talent because "The boy is dumb as a turkey and twice as ugly." But from day one he was a major league whiner—called the office at least once a week, carping about what some other player got that he didn't—mentions in the *Sporting News,* his picture and stats on one of the Web sites devoted to minor league ball, tickets to Skate America. Hell, United Management Group owned Skate America. They gave tickets away by the handful, but Randall acted like they were gold.

Marcus had turned inside out to keep that kid happy—practically held his hand on his first-ever plane ride, went with him to open a bank account, got a dentist to fix his snaggly teeth. Marcus tried to make him understand it was all coming his way, via the express route, if he'd just keep his nose clean and his head in the game. All of which was an investment in his future earnings potential since it wasn't really until they hit the majors that players made enough to pay their agent a percentage. A lot of guys went it alone until they made it to the show, but Marcus knew Randall would have drowned without support, which made this slap in the face especially hard to take.

"You know a lawsuit won't do jack, except cost us time, money, and heartburn. The ungrateful little punk has already cost us enough." Rich slid a hand over his gelled dome of hair. "This sucks. It's like we're in the mines and they get to wear the diamonds."

UMG wasn't the only pirate. Several giant sports conglomerates handled every field of athletics from auto racing to water polo and produced massive events as diverse as the Super Bowl and the pope's arena masses. Marcus and Rich's take was that it was fine for the folks at the top of the food chain, but the little fish could get lost or swallowed before they had a chance to grow. Their strategy was to concentrate on baseball and develop relationships early that would last a whole career. They sold the prospects and their families on the individual attention and grooming a boutique agency like G&C Pro Sports provided for their precious future all-stars.

Marcus knew the inner workings of baseball, and his easygoing manner allowed him to maintain valuable ties to both players and management. He took a personal interest in his guys, guiding them through the gauntlet of distractions, giving them the benefit of his experience. And Rich was a fox at the negotiating table—agile, always looking for the opening, the advantage. He just about worshipped baseball players, but since he'd never made it much past ball boy, he loved being around them, protecting their interests, talking the game. But clearly somebody at UMG had been whispering sweet *Sports Illustrated* covers in Randall's ear. Making him feel that his representation was negligent because he wasn't on par with Roger Clemens yet. So the "Dear Agent" kiss-off had been waiting when the office opened. The kicker—Santos Taveras, an acrobatic shortstop with solid hitting skills, was going with him.

"I know Piccone talked him into it. He's too big a chickenshit to go on his own, and Taveras isn't dominant enough for UMG yet except as Randall's sidekick." The big guys always skimmed the cream, leaving the curds and whey—serviceable players, but not the marquee talent.

"Randy and Santos should at least be man enough to tell me to my face." But Marcus knew they weren't men. He hadn't been back in his early playing days. What mattered more than anything then was his career with a capital C. But he had been loyal, a word that didn't exist in the vocabulary of most of the young guys. They were half as dedicated and twice as impatient. They all wanted to be like Mike, with burger commercials and endorsements for their own "eau de sweat" cologne, without putting in the Mike time and effort. But he knew the mega-agents displayed their superstars like jock porn, driving tricked-out cars, sporting babes, bucks, and bling. Then made it sound as if they could deliver it on a platter.

Rich headed for the door. "You gonna call him?"

"Hell no." Marcus had tried that tack before. All he got was humiliated by pimply-faced egos in jockstraps and cleats. Once they sent that letter, on plain white paper, like you weren't supposed to know the fax came from their new agent's office, it was a done deal.

"What do you think we should do?"

Marcus thought a second. "Right now, I'm going for a drive."

Since he got his first wheels—the Black Firebird he bought with his signing bonus—Marcus often took to the road to think. It was only 10:24 in the morning and he already had a mindful.

The morning's events looped in his head as he made his way to the garage. He managed to wave or nod at the people who acknowledged him on the street. Even after years of retirement, he still got regular high fives and photo requests from passersby. Marcus had never played for a New York team, but he was still a hometown hero.

The thunk of his Range Rover door closing meant Marcus was in his own world. Pat rode in but rarely drove the big green truck she called The Hulk. More than their apartment or his office, it was his sanctuary, his tan leather cocoon. With sax playing softly in surround sound Marcus edged the car across town, heading for the Lincoln Tunnel.

The Randall debacle burned like a brand. When he first became Rich's partner, Marcus was pumped, bringing substantial energy and capital to the enterprise. And they'd had their successes, moved to tony offices in the heart of midtown, power-steak-house territory. G&C Pro Sports had a good reputation, but they were basically breaking even. This was supposed to be a business, moving forward, like the one his wife was building. Instead, it was beginning to feel like an expensive hobby, and he already played golf. His agency had a higher gross, but by the time you added it up and carried the expenses, Ell was in the lead—which wasn't supposed to matter.

Marcus squinted as he exited the tunnel. The sun hadn't seemed quite so bright when he'd entered on the New York side. He reached across to the glove box, grabbed the shades he kept there. *Move out the way.* He flashed the Honda doddering in the left lane and the driver applied his brakes. *Ya dumb* . . . Marcus do-si-doed around him, then left him in the dust.

He was all hyped to call DeJohn Henderson's father when he got to the office this morning. Marcus had been following the heavy-hitting high school senior for more than a year, spoken to his coach and parents, sent scouts to check him out, watched the videotape. Now DeJohn was the star of his suburban Augusta varsity team, and one of the High School Top 100 Prospects. Marcus liked DeJohn's swing, his stance. At his young age he had quick hands and a quiet bat, and Marcus sensed a familiar intensity, the drive to take it to the next level. He'd been in touch with the family for some time, answered their questions, gave them advice when they asked. And they sent Marcus regular updates on DeJohn's activities—summer leagues, showcases, his schedule for the season. Now, since it was DeJohn's last high school season, Marcus wanted to set up a face-to-face in Georgia—well before the draft. *What the hell for? To get him in shape for UMG?*

As he approached exit 15W, Marcus found himself making his way to the right. When he got in the car, he didn't exactly know where he was heading—just away. But as he drove, he realized he had something else to check out.

Marcus followed signs to the Garden State, exited onto the wide avenue. There was no pain or pressure from the test swab this morning, but he'd been worrying the spot with his tongue, wondering if . . . He hadn't had Millennium run a check on Tiffani, but he knew the basics—where she lived, went to school.

There was a picture in his head of what the house would look like—a neat single with a pitched roof, a tidy yard, a lot like the house he grew up in, since he figured Aunt Stephanie ran a tight ship. But as he searched for Tiffani's street, he realized that a lot like his old neighborhood, the reality was grittier than his imaginings. The avenue was lined with two-story storefronts—brick and the remains of old signs and awnings—built back when they would have housed ice cream parlors, five-and-dimes, and barbershops with a red-and-white pole out front. Now, the ones that weren't boarded up or for rent were occupied by dingy tattoo parlors, pint-bottle liquor stores, fried-chicken joints with greasy tables and Plexiglas security barriers. Even in the foggy-breath cold, men in do-rags and shearlings loitered on corners. After a tight-jawed mile or so, Marcus saw her street, made a right at the no-name gas station with the rusty Buick behemoth in the repair bay, drove another two sorry blocks.

It was a rambling wreck of extensions, three stories of free-form, aluminum-sided enclosure, ringed by fire escapes and sharing the lot with a dilapidated shed. Marcus counted six doorbells with crossed-out name stickers beside the peeling front door. Next house was a scorched shell with a garbage-filled claw-foot tub abandoned in the driveway. He had seen enough.

By the time he got to Tiffani's blond-brick school building, hordes of students spilled outside for lunch. Marcus pulled across the street, watched the sea of teens swarm the sidewalk, in clusters, and two by two, laughing, fussing, and cussing like in a locker room. Then he thought he saw her—the bubble of curls, and the furry white jacket. But the tweed trousers had been replaced by camouflage cargo pants and a new accessory—a chunky ruffneck with a black-and-silver down jacket and baggy pants held her in a headlock embrace. And Marcus wanted to make him let her go, had his hand on the door handle. That's when the squad car rolled alongside and blocked him in.

Damn.

The officer took his time getting out, strolling over. Marcus rolled the window down, noticed the hand the cop kept near his gun.

"You got business here?"

Marcus could see his eyes darting around, checking out the inside of the car. "Just checking on a friend's daughter." This was supposed to be a simple trip, not an event, but nothing was simple these days.

"Let's see your license and registration."

Marcus dug for his wallet, handed over the two cards. He clutched the wheel with both hands, keeping them in sight. This wasn't the first time he'd been stopped.

"Move along." The cop shooed the students who had gathered along the sidewalk to watch. Then he chewed a corner of his mustache as he examined the license, looked over at Marcus.

Marcus took off his shades to give the officer an unobstructed view. He tried to chill, but he wanted to rip the wheel off the steering column as he waited.

"You're him . . . ballplayer."

"Uh, yeah." Although Marcus wasn't feeling much like himself at the moment.

The officer grinned, handed back the ID. "Usually we see a vehicle like this, it's here for some other reason, stolen, or drugs, that type of thing, you know?"

Marcus hadn't thought about what he was driving, but right now he wanted to drive it out of town.

"Mr. Carter?" Tiffani had come down from the steps. "Hi." She grinned.

"I was, uh, just in the neighborhood." It sounded more like an excuse than he intended.

"Oh. It's nice to see you." Tiffani looked at Marcus, then the cop. "Guess I should go back inside. See ya." She practically skipped across the street.

"If that's all . . . ?"

"Yeah. A pleasure. Wait till I tell the guys at the station. Drive safely."

It was after two when he got back to the city. Rich asked if he was alright, Marcus said, "Yeah," and that was the end of it. The only Tiffany Rich knew about was the one with the blue box, which was how Marcus planned to keep it until he found out otherwise.

Alone in his office Marcus reared back in his seat, feet on the desk. He looked around, examined the poster-size print of the photo taken as a home run ball screamed off his bat in the fifth game of the World Series—the one he actually played in and helped win, as opposed to the one he spent in the hospital after he wiped out his motorcycle. That moment at the plate was as good as it gets. Then he took out his wallet, opened the cracked photo he kept folded behind his driver's license, the one of his brother at fourteen, bat balanced on his shoulders. The colors had faded, but the image was still sharp in his mind's eye, an emblem of Marcus's worst day. And for all these years he'd been living somewhere in the space between.

Marcus laid the picture on his desk. He flipped through his Rolodex and dialed. "DeWitt Henderson? This is Marcus Carter. I hear DeJohn's been tearing it up this season." Whatever UMG and all the others were throwing, he would find a way to hit it. Just like in his playing days, if he was going down, he was going down swinging.

• CHAPTER 5 •

. . . the happy family kit—deluxe edition.

T here *was no room for conjecture* or doubt. Marcus sank to the sofa like a stone, didn't look up as he handed the report to Pat, who was hovering.

This is it. She braced for her life to turn upside. *Probability of Paternity—0.000%?* "Yes!" Pat knew where to look. It took only seconds for her to find the zeros, and she wanted to open her windows and shout it into the velvety night. It took a moment longer for her to realize she was the only one celebrating. "You're in the clear." She perched on the sofa arm, feet on the cushion, brushed a bit of sparkle off his pant leg. Their concierge had signed for the two overnight packages—one from Genes R Us, the other from Millennium. Pat was glad to see he'd come to his senses and had Stuckey do a background check. All evening she had walked past the envelopes, picked them up, shaken them. She was close to zipping off the pull tab, but there was no way to reseal them. That would have been a big blowout.

"Glad you're so happy."

"And you're not?" Pat had waited up for him, way past her bedtime. Marcus was out again, entertaining the boys from some team's front office. The smell of Opus X cigars clung to his suit, which meant they'd probably been to Lush, the happening Harlem nightspot. Millennium handled security there so Marcus and Rich felt reasonably sure they and their guests wouldn't be hassled and that confidential conversations would stay that way. Pat had been a few times, but mostly it felt like she was invading his territory so it wasn't her favorite hangout.

"I don't know, Pat. But it doesn't feel right." Marcus got up, shoved his hands in his pockets, went across the room, leaned on the entertainment unit.

"And what would feel right, Marcus?" *So we can please put this behind us.*

"Hell, I don't know. I just know this doesn't." In some ways he had already made Tiffani part of his plans. He was just waiting to make it official. "I still want to help her."

"Help her what?" All Pat wanted was to get out from under this cloud. Now Marcus seemed determined to keep his umbrella up until he found some rain. "What do you want to do? Adopt her? Support her? Send her to Hawaii? This girl has nothing to do with you."

"What if she did?" Marcus looked at Pat, held her gaze until she answered.

"But she doesn't! Why can't that be it?"

"You didn't see where she lives."

"Tell me you didn't go to her house?!" Pat was about to stand straight up on the couch, but remembered to put her feet on the floor first. "Are you insane? Or are you trying to get sued as a stalker? Or maybe a pedophile? That would do a lot for your public profile."

"I checked out her house . . . and her school."

"So you rode through a strange neighborhood, in a car that probably cost as much as some of those houses, and figured nobody would notice? What were you thinking?"

"You think too damn much." And there was no point mentioning Officer Bob since nothing happened, but his wife would turn it into a catastrophe. Marcus hadn't thought out what he wanted—just to *do* something that made a difference. It didn't seem that complicated. "Somebody helped you out when you needed it."

"You're right, OK. Gayle's parents took me in, but I wasn't a stranger." Pat was in no mood to rehash the details of her pitiful past. "They knew me since I was five years old. We're not responsible for every lost lamb who comes to our door."

"Look, I'm done talking about it." Marcus headed off toward the guest room. "I'll just do what I'm gonna do." Whatever that was.

Pat watched. They hadn't had a fight that required separate rooms in a while. Usually one of them would go away on business and upon their return they would resume normal cohabitation, like everything was peachy.

Marcus stopped and turned. "The other envelope is for you."

Pat had plenty more to say, about how dare he disregard her wishes, and how helping this girl seemed more important than his own wife's feelings, but she knew from experience that talking when he had stopped listening infuriated her more. She plopped on the couch, in a hard, mad knot, landed on top of the other envelope. She pulled it out, tore it open. Pat's eyes narrowed in disbelief.

Millennium had dug up some background alright—on Pat's mother, Verna, who it seemed had left St. Albans and moved back to Swan City. She couldn't read any more than that. "How dare you?" Pat practically levitated toward the guest room, flung open the door.

Marcus's suit was a crumpled mound on the floor and he'd already gotten in bed, turned off the lamp. An arrow of light pointed at him from the hall.

"It's bad enough you're trying to make up some kind of family with this girl. Now you decide to go look for mine?! Are you out of your mind? Why would I care if she's in North Carolina or even on the planet? I have all the family I need."

Marcus looked at her a long moment. "I don't." Then rolled so his back faced the door.

Which hurt more than any big, flashy argument they could have had. Pat could handle volume, but seeing him look so sad, that hurt her heart. She shut the door, poured a glass of wine, and curled up on the couch.

The whole family thing just wasn't that simple—like you pick up the happy-family kit, deluxe edition, with the Christmas-card photos and the swing set, follow the directions, and voilà, another satisfied customer. *And if he thinks bringing Verna into the picture will help* . . . The thought of her mother raised the hackles on Pat's neck. Verna was proof that love isn't some kind of by-product of giving birth. And what could she do now? Say I'm sorry, kiss the boo-boo, and make it all better? *I don't think so.* And as for daddy dearest? Tidbits about Turner Hughes's behind-the-scenes political ploys, business coups, and social machinations were regular fodder for reporters with column inches or airtime to fill. But as far as Pat was concerned, his self-deprecating apology moment years ago, using her doorstep as a confessional, was too little, too late.

Pat had tried to make the idea of being pregnant feel like cause for celebration, but right now all it conjured up was helplessness, uncertainty, and guilt—for that time in her twenties, the time with PJ, when she had let herself believe for a moment that love was like a fairy tale with a happy ending. Even Gayle had abandoned her then, and lying up on that table, all alone, Pat swore she would never let herself get pregnant again, not until she knew it was right, until she was ready. She had kept her promise, although she'd never found a way to let Marcus in on the secret. *He'll just have to wait.*

• • •

"You need to leave that man alone." Aunt Stephanie leaned against the bathroom doorframe, watching Tiffani bathe two-year-old Tory. "You already worried him enough—embarrassed your mother. . . . Y'all stop all that noise and go to sleep." The twins, Troy and Trey, were already in the bed they shared in the living room. Judging from the grunts and thuds, tonight it was a steel cage for their own bedtime smackdown.

"How did I embarrass her?" Tiffani knelt by the side of the tub, trying to aim a washcloth for the wiggling baby's ear. "I just thought—"

"Makes it look like Simone didn't even know who your father was. That's a dis-grace." Aunt Stephanie tucked the edges of her hair under a satiny sleep cap. "Even though it woulda been nice to have somebody in the family with some money."

"I just want to call and say I'm sorry, that's all. Don't you think that's polite?" Tiffani's hair was already wrapped for the night—one scarf up front for the braids, and one in back for the curls. "He gave me his home number."

"It's not *polite* to accuse somebody of being your daddy who's not. Folks get shot behind that mess. Just leave it at that." Stephanie walked down the hall.

"I wasn't *accusing*." Tiffani threw the balled-up towel in the water and Tory was happy to join in the splashing game. "Quit it!" She shook the baby's shoulders. Tory's lip started the pre-cry quiver. "OK. OK." Tiffani reached back for one of the mismatched bath towels, wrapped Tory, and lifted her out of the tub, bounced her enough to make her smile. Then Tiffani swiped on some lotion, dressed her baby cousin in one of Stephanie's dead husband's old T-shirts they used as pajamas, and deposited her in the crib in a corner of her aunt's crowded bedroom. Tory fussed until Tiffani gave her the Binky and the stuffed duck.

"You wanna watch TV?" Stephanie consulted her *TV Guide*. "Let's see, tonight—"

"Nope. Got schoolwork." The last thing Tiffani wanted was to watch reruns with her aunt on a crappy twelve-inch portable. Tiffani went to the kitchen, got her folding bed from the back hall, and opened it up in the narrow space between the counter and the table. The room was dark except for the light above the sink. That made it feel more private.

When she first arrived, Tiffani shared the queen-size bed with her aunt, but she couldn't take the farting and snoring all night. The apartment where she and her mom had lived was no great shakes, but next to this, it was a penthouse. Stephanie bragged her house was paid for, which appeared to be her husband's major accomplishment before he died. And between the insurance he left her and rent from the tenants, she managed to get by. Every now and then Monique, the children's mother, sent a money order, which Stephanie would go on about like it was the lottery. But Tiffani had arrived without a stipend. Stephanie sold whatever of Simone's anybody would buy. And Tiffani was not so subtly reminded—usually when she balked at playing nanny—that her aunt had taken her in out of Christian kindness.

The twin's muffled talk and laughing drifted in, but Tiffani paid it no mind. It was part of the constant hum of traffic, sirens, boom cars, and gunfire she had learned to ignore since moving to her new neighborhood.

She got out a pen and her spiral notebook, turned to the back where she had taped the picture of the Range Rover she'd torn out of a newsmagazine in the library. The halls of Tiffani's school lit up the afternoon Marcus had shown up. She didn't exactly tell them who he was, or why he had come, but they had seen the ride, seen her talk to him. Word went out he was Tiffani's squeeze, that he must be a gangbanger or a rapper. Nobody came up with father, maybe because there weren't many of those around. She rolled with the buzz. It was better than being the new bitch from Shitville, Pa. Even the guy who was trying to talk to her at lunch that day showed more respect.

Tiffani had pages and pages of pictures in her notebook. It had started with jewelry catalogs her mother would bring home. They'd pick out their favorites—diamond watches, ropes of pearls, ruby cocktail rings, things they would have when they bought their own jewelry store. Really it was Tiffani's dream. Simone hadn't dreamt past salesclerk, which is really what she was. Tiffani said *manager* because it was too pitiful her mother didn't have more to show for all her time. Through the years Tiffani diversified her dream catalog, added posh mansions, crocodile boots, sable coats—beautiful things that other people had, that she would too someday, instead of a cot in a crummy kitchen.

Carefully, she tore out a sheet of paper, folded back the jagged edge. She let her pen hover above the page, thinking. Then she began—*Dear Mr. Carter, I don't know what to say. It's what Mom told me . . .*

. . . room for the slow build and simmer.

"I'm *down this way. I'll drop* my stuff and meet you two at doll central, by registration." Drew glanced at his watch. "Fifteen minutes? Can't wait to get a look at the competition with my own baby greens."

"Vinaigrette or blue cheese?" Pat waved.

"Zesty Italian." Drew headed off down the hall.

Gayle unlocked the door, already feeling as if she'd been caught in a tornado. The car had picked her up at four thirty

in the morning, and they hit the ground at Hartsfield running—two radio spots before they checked into the hotel.
"It's not hideous." A three-and-a-half-star, generic convention hotel—perfectly acceptable, and utterly unremarkable.
Gayle tried to keep it light, since Pat was still in a snit about
Marcus and his "obsession" with Tiffani. Two days before this
trip, she'd had Lindy change her flight so she came straight
home instead of meeting Marcus in Wilmington at his father's
house, like they planned. Gayle tried to convince her not to
switch, said maybe time away from the daily pressure cooker
would give them a chance to talk. "You can't talk to somebody
who doesn't listen." First thing out of Gayle's mouth—"Takes
one to know one." Pat had no trouble expressing herself about
that. And after the Verna discovery, Pat was ready for the
whole state of North Carolina to splinter off and join Atlan-
tis at the bottom of the ocean. "Doesn't smell moldy."

Pat hung her garment bag in the closet, feeling bad that
she'd been such a pill lately. She knew Gayle was due a mea
culpa. So she did the best she could, offered up one of their
favorite war stories—"You mean like the room that was so
funky we slept in our clothes on top of the covers—"

"—and wouldn't set foot in the shower." Gayle finished
the story, apology accepted. If they could laugh through that
night, they could laugh through anything. In the beginning,
when they were catalog-only, Pat, Gayle, and cases of books
went anywhere they were invited, and some places they
invited themselves. Some of those early events were real
doozies—a huge downtown auditorium where twelve people
showed up, the tent that collapsed in a windstorm worthy of
Dorothy and Toto.

Pat headed into the bathroom with her toiletries, poked her head back around the corner. "No mildew. No mouse turds on the soap. We have officially arrived." At least it felt like they were about to. She and Gayle had worked their collective butts off to get this far. Now it was all about to come together. They were in Atlanta for two days to surf the Toy and Doll Sourcing Expo and get some face time with manufacturers. In the hierarchy of dolldom trade shows, the TDSE was a minor spectacle. Nothing like IDEX, the Shan-gri-la of the doll universe, where perpetual youth—from life-like infant replicas, to coiffed and haute-coutured collector models—was displayed, bought, and sold. Then there was Toy Fair, the mammoth utopia that was the granddaddy of them all. Pat and Gayle weren't ready for the big time. This regional event seemed just the right size, and they hoped to find an American factory that could do their limited run of ten thousand dolls for a reasonable price.

At the last minute, Drew decided to tag along. The doll world was new to him too, and he wanted to get a feel for what they'd be up against, so the twosome became a threesome.

"Ready?" Pat knotted her cardigan loosely over her shoulders.

"Need to call Vanessa." Gayle sat at the desk. "Let her know I'm here, like it matters." Gayle opened the box of snack crackers from her carry-on, grabbed a handful. "You want?"

Pat shook her head. "Did she ever decide which camp?"

"She's leaning toward the one in upstate New York, which I want. But you know how she is. If I say that, she'll decide to go to Michigan. So I'm crossing my fingers and keeping my mouth shut."

"Smart move."

"I make one now and then. Mostly by accident. I'll be down in a minute."

Maybe it was the "let's pretend" spirit that encouraged perfectly respectable adults to dress like dolls, teddys, clowns, whatever they fancied, but strolling the convention floor was like entering a toy box come to life, to the tune of chipper, chirping music. Gayle always got a kick out of the spectacle. For Pat, who was admittedly play-challenged, her favorite game was imagining an Ell empire with her and Gayle at the helm.

Pat spotted Drew across the lobby, deep in conversation with a woman, swathed chapeau to toe in frothy aqua ruffles and bows—full Azalea Trail Maid regalia. *What could they be talking about?* Pat stared in their direction, willing Drew to look her way, leave Missy Mint Julep and come over. When the mental telepathy failed, she smoothed her slacks, popped a breath mint, squared her shoulders, and tried to look casual instead of vaguely annoyed. *Why do I give a shit?*

Pat had to hold in her laugh when it turned out an over-rouged seventy-year-old face and a Bronx accent went with the bonnet and ringlets. Sylvia Stein and her twin sister, Sheila, now of Riverdale, had been designing nineteenth-century dolls for forty years.

"You a first-timer too?" Despite the lace glove Sylvia's handshake was firm.

"No, Drew here's the only virgin, but we'll try to be gentle."

"You got any questions, you look for me. Or my sister. Looks just like me, but dressed in yellow. Not quite as bright as cutie-pie here's shirt."

The look on Drew's face as he watched Sylvia swirl away made Pat laugh. "I told you it was gonna be different."

Drew had their badges, and as soon as Gayle showed up, they hit the show floor. The sights in the hall barely hinted at the fifty-ring circus that awaited them. Deciding that divide and conquer was the best strategy to get the lay of the land, Pat went scouting manufacturers, and Gayle's mission was to check out the fabric, notions, and accessories suppliers with the ideas for Ell's first three outfits in mind. And Drew was all about promotionals, display styles, packaging, inserts, hand-outs. After hours of talking about molds, joint assembly, hair rooting, head-attachment methods, plastic, polymers, vinyl, laminate, flat-fold, paper and plastic packaging materials, and examining teeny umbrellas, hats, socks, and shoes, the shell-shocked trio reconvened to compare notes and map out the next day.

"Can't we do this somewhere else? Like over dinner?" Drew suggested.

"There's the welcome cocktail reception and a seminar about how the use of computers has improved mass production." Pat examined the TDSE schedule, certain that an extra dose of work would keep her mind off how mad she was at Marcus.

Drew turned to Gayle. "She's kidding, right?"

"Sorry to say she's probably not." Gayle plucked the schedule from Pat's hand. "Enough. We can start again tomorrow, bright and early—maybe with the session on eyelash implantation?" Gayle smiled and batted her own.

"We still need a plan. I want to leave here with as many production pieces in place as we can."

"Yes, my ambitious partner, but right now, my head is pounding. You two go ahead. I'm going up to the room. We're at the studio tomorrow at what time?"

"Seven thirty." Drew knew their schedule by heart.

"You're killing me." Gayle put her hand to her head. "I'll order something light from room service."

"If you're not feeling well, I'll come up with you." Pat looped her arm through Gayle's.

"Then it definitely won't be quiet." Gayle playfully pushed her away.

"I know when I'm not wanted. I'll come up and drop this."

"Gimme." Gayle took Pat's TDSE tote bag, chock-full of flyers, brochures, and samples. "Later."

"And all this time I thought you two were living it up on the road," Drew teased Pat on the cab ride to the restaurant. "Now the truth is out. You're working your tails off." He paid the driver.

"You'll never tell, will you?" Pat followed Drew out of the taxi. Dinner with associates was usually a tedious extension of the workday, but she always enjoyed Drew's company. "Look at all these people—walking!" Pedestrians ambled in pairs or packs, peering in kitschy shops displaying everything from doggie pastries to surfboards, and deciphering menu boards in front of a cosmic array of eateries. The fragrant spring evening felt like early summer. The avenue was not the multilane thoroughfare she had come to expect, and the neighborhood's historical architecture and graceful, tree-lined streets made it seem like the town center in a cozy village, decades and miles from the bustling Southern metropolis. "I've been to Atlanta a zillion times and never been here."

"Virginia Highlands. Couple of years ago I had dinner with a friend who relocated here. She brought me." Drew touched the back of Pat's arm to direct her. "Right over there. It used to be a gas station."

"You're kidding."

He held the door. Nothing remained from the fill'er-up-and-oil-change days. The space was open and inviting, with glazed concrete walls, a huge polished-wood bar, and dangling light fixtures that looked like molten-glass ice cream cones. They were shown to a table by a window, near a painted orange sunset.

"Food's good too."

Before Pat could open her napkin, her phone started vibrating in her purse. She dug it out, glanced at the screen, considered a second. "Excuse me. I need to take this."

Drew nodded and opened his menu.

"Yes, Marcus." Pat's voice went flat. She turned her head and looked down. "It's going fine. . . . Yep. All day tomorrow. . . . Yep. You'll be gone before we get in. . . . She's fine— uh, just about to grab dinner. . . . OK. . . . Hi to your Dad. . . . Have a good flight." Pat dropped the phone in her purse. "Sorry about that."

"No problem."

Well it is, but it's not yours. Pat looked around for their server. "I need a martini."

"I was going to have a Coke. Now you've upped the ante."

"Don't let me lead you astray." Pat laughed.

"Margarita. Up. No salt," Drew told the waitress. "I go willingly, senorita."

Pat considered mentioning she was really a senora, but let it slide.

They were halfway through their entrées, and twenty minutes into the final phase of Drew's bilevel marketing plan for the Ell Christmas launch, when Pat put her fork down. "Did you ever believe something, find out it wasn't true, but keep supporting it anyway?"

Drew laughed, took a swig. "It's been known to happen. Frequently there's a check involved."

"And if there's not?"

"Sometimes just to be ornery. Sometimes to prove it really isn't false. Galileo took a lot of heat, no pun intended, for believing the earth revolved around the sun, but he was right." Drew cut into his pan-roasted skate wing. "But I'd hazard a guess you're not talking about scientific theory."

"You'd be right. Sorry. I'm tired. I'm pissed at my husband." Pat took a sip of water. "Now what were you saying about the September mailer?"

"Beats me. But I think we can go officially off the clock. Floor's open for discussion. What's on your mind?"

Pat pushed a scallop around her plate, searching for a glib answer, but at the moment her head only had two gears—dolls and Marcus. "What does a guy like you make of an arena full of rabid doll lovers?" First gear. "I mean, it's gotta seem a little weird."

"No weirder than, say, spelunking."

"Spe-whating?"

"Exploring caves."

"Why would anybody want to do that?"

"Damned if I know, but whatever turns you on."

The busboy cleared their plates and they both ordered coffee to linger over.

"And what turns you on, Drew? I mean, in your nonbillable hours."

"Early-twentieth-century amusement parks, like Luna Park and Dreamland, black-and-white photography, and classical guitar, although I do like a song with a good beat you can dance to."

"I'd have taken you for a techno-color guy."

"No soul or shadows. Everything I do has to snatch your attention in four seconds, hold you hostage, and make you want more. Doesn't leave room for the slow build and simmer." He sprinkled sugar in his coffee.

Drew was a lefty. Pat had never really noticed. Although she had noticed there was no wedding band. "That must be great for your girlfriend." *Why the hell did I say that?*

He didn't miss a beat. "Maybe. If I had one."

"Oh, come on. A dashing man-about-town like you?"

"I'm not a monk—and I'm not saying there haven't been applicants—but since—" Drew added cream to his coffee, took a sip. "I'm just choosy." Drew smiled. "And you?" He held her gaze over the rim of his cup.

"What? Oh." She'd been drawn in by the slow build and simmer, emboldened enough to venture into truly personal territory, and found herself more intrigued than she expected by his response. *But since what?*

"What turns you on?"

"I'm very dull these days. It's all about the business—planning, problem solving, execution . . ."

"You looked a little too gleeful when you said *execution*."

"Don't worry. You're not in the line of fire."

"Sounds like somebody is."

Pat let out a deep sigh, sank back in her seat, shifted into her second gear. "I just don't get it, Drew." She knew this was a breach of something—PC, loyalty, or good sense—but if she didn't say something to somebody, she was going to explode. Besides, they had already crossed a conversational boundary. Hadn't they? "If the jury finds you not guilty, would you insist on serving the sentence?"

"OK, I'm a little thick. Help me out."

Pat sighed again, reminded Drew of Marcus and the Tiffani situation. "He is off the hook, free and clear, but he won't let it go. Now he thinks we should help her. I mean, he's always a decent guy, but this is crazy."

Drew sat back. "So tell me about this girl. Is she nice?"

"I don't know. And neither does he." Pat rolled the edge of her napkin with her index finger. "I mean, I guess she seems like an OK kid. A little naive, but in a way it's refreshing."

"Unless you're leaving out some relevant details, like green scales, claws, and fangs, she doesn't sound like a monster." Drew sipped his coffee.

"Maybe she had a facial and a manicure before our meeting."

"Maybe she's not all bad. And maybe she's not bad at all—just an ordinary kid who caught an unlucky break." Drew leaned back, put his fingertips together. "What if—now just hang with me a sec—but what if you did help her?"

"Now you sound like Marcus. What is it with you guys and the need to rescue the damsel in distress? I thought it was just women who were brainwashed by fairy tales."

"I don't mean move the girl into your house, or buy her a yacht, but we all need a little help from time to time. At least I did." A smiled curled the corners of Drew's mouth, his right eyebrow arched. "Hmmm."

"I've seen that look before." Pat recognized it as the early-warning signal that he was about to unleash some crazy idea.

"I don't mean this to sound crass or mercenary, but the whole thing has great story potential, Pat. Not that I would encourage you to offer her a helping hand because you could get some press out of it. That would make me a spokesweasel. But your company is all about empowering girls."

"Terrific." Pat watched the waitress clear their cups, wondered how old she was, what she wanted to do with her life, had anyone given her a break?

Side by side in the taxi, neither said much on the ride back to the hotel. The evening's conversation had come full circle. Business, personal, and back to business, all in the course of a meal. Pat decided not to wonder about what Drew had started to say but backed away from. Instead she thought about Gayle and her parents, about Miss Cooke, her teacher at Jackson, her teachers at Southridge and Princeton, Minnie Littlefield. Even Althea Satterfield, a mentor and colleague, had opened a door Pat would never have known existed, although she later slammed it on Pat's fingers. What would she have done if they hadn't taken an interest, urged, encouraged, guided her. *Would I really have made it this far on my own?* But Pat felt strangely calm, relaxed in a way she hadn't in weeks. And why didn't Drew's suggestion to help Tiffani piss her off? *Must have been the martini.*

"Busy night for dining in." Drew remarked on the dozen or so trays and carts lining the hallway on their floor. "Maybe doll people don't go out after dark."

"Shhh." Pat held her finger to her lips. "We don't want them to know we know, or we'll wake up tomorrow with rooted saran hair and rotational neck joints." She took in the folding service tables on both sides of their door and across the hall, piled with empty plates and upturned metal lids. "Looks like our neighbors had a party."

"Gayle's seems so lonely." Drew glanced at the soup bowl and bread basket by their door. "We'll make it up to her tomorrow. I have a great spot for lunch, before we head to the airport. They do the best shrimp and grits you've ever had."

"*Merci.*" Pat grasped his hand, like they would shake.

Instead they held hands. He brought the other one up to cup hers. "*Pas de quoi.*"

Pat watched him head down the hall, disappear into his room, still feeling the heat from his hand as she opened her door, secretly glad Gayle had pooped out and it was "their" evening. The TV was on with the volume turned way low—the way Gayle usually fell asleep. Pat heard water running. She really needed to use the bathroom, but while she waited, she undressed, turned back her bed, and Gayle finally emerged from the bathroom in her nightgown, hair pulled up in an elastic on top of her head, wiping her face with the towel around her neck. Her eyes looked red and watery.

"Are you OK?"

Gayle was startled. "When did you get here?" She dabbed her forehead, pushed back the damp tendrils that curled around her face. "Sorry I was in there so long. Something I ate disagreed with me." She perched on the edge of her bed.

"Should I call for a doctor?"

"No. It's better."

"Didn't look like you ate enough to get sick."

"Just soup and salad." Gayle stretched out. "I'll be fine in the morning. Marcus left a voice mail."

"It's OK, I talked to him."

Gayle pulled the covers up to her chin. "You and Drew have a good dinner?"

"It was OK. He got some really good packaging ideas today. We have our game plan set for tomorrow." And Pat found her mind wandering down the hall to his room, wondering whose messages he was returning.

Gayle was, in fact, good to go the next morning, and they completed their rounds an hour before the show floor opened to the general public. More than satisfied with the textile offerings, she looked forward to a new selection of sample books, swatches, and trims that would keep Ell in style for a few more adventures. Drew was convinced they had a winner with no real competition except the American Girl dolls—which was good company to be in. And Pat found a plant in Tennessee that could handle their initial minimum run, but was also equipped to step up production without outsourcing when they were ready to up their numbers. Their rep, a walrus of a man with hands the size of bear claws, looked as if he should be talking hunting not dollies, but he knew the business inside and out, understood the particular needs of freshman companies, and promised to have paperwork on her desk by Tuesday.

· · ·

"This is a mistake you know . . . the car." Gayle ducked from under the driver's umbrella and into the limo, needles of uneasiness pricking her skin. "I mean it's nice, but we never order a stretch. You can look up our records." Throughout the trip she struggled to keep down her distress about how much they were spending, and what they were about to commit to. Drew sounded upbeat when he left them and headed to the monorail to begin his trek home to Hoboken. But Gayle was well past overload when she and Pat walked from Terminal A and spied the limousine instead of their usual black sedan.

"I guarantee you won't be charged extra." The driver closed the door and went to stow their luggage.

"That's his problem." Pat pulled down the armrest and copped a lean. "Lindy can straighten it out tomorrow. I don't care if he's driving a sleigh with eight tiny reindeer, he's taking us home." A line of violent storms had planes stacked up all along the Eastern seaboard, meaning their 7:48 p.m. arrival took place at 12:10 a.m. "I'm beat."

"Me too." Gayle suppressed a shiver, brought on by both exhaustion and the damp spring night. She drew her cashmere shawl around her. "But you just woke up."

"That's not real sleep. It's avoidance." The trunk thumped closed behind them.

Gayle always marveled at the way Pat could buckle in

and will herself into slumber before takeoff, her escape from noisy, nosy people and cramped seats at thirty thousand feet, since they still didn't splurge on first class. Gayle would no more nod off on an airplane than jump out of one. She fished for the seat belt, snapped it closed.

In one move the driver tossed the tent-size umbrella to the passenger side and got behind the wheel. "Busy night. You had a reservation and you're a client, a buddy client at that." He spoke to them over his shoulder. "G and C is one of our best customers."

"Good to know." Pat wondered exactly how many thousands made a good customer, but Marcus and Rich certainly put on a good show, even if their bottom line looked anemic.

"Can you tell me your name?" Gayle dug in her purse for something to write on. "In case we have problems with the bill."

"The name is Miles. They all know me." He inched the long, black Lincoln away from the curb and into the phalanx of cars snaking out of Newark Airport. "This was the next car available. Well, there was the white Excalibur, but it seemed a little flashy for you ladies—maybe another time though."

"Miles, from Miles Ahead Car Service." Pat put her feet up on the long sofa section beside her. "Could it be more perfect?"

"I don't think so." The disembodied voice floated back to them. "Care for music?"

"Rain on the windows is music enough for me." Gayle could still hear the hum of the convention center.

"Sure thing."

So for the first time in days there was quiet—no pitches, no bells, no drums. Each stared out her own window, preparing for reentry.

Since her conversation with Drew, Pat had decided that helping Tiffani wasn't such a hideous idea after all. "I was thinking about flying to Wilmington." Pat looked over at Gayle. "And offering to help Tiffani, since it means so much to Marcus. Maybe see if I can get her into Southridge." She'd written plenty of checks to her alma mater. "Tiffani said she had pretty good grades and she seems to have some kind of ambition."

"I think it's fantastic, but what made you change—"

"I don't know." Pat shrugged. "Time I guess. Lindy's gonna kill me."

"She'll be happy you're going to see Marcus." So was Gayle. Their fights made her nervous. She knew them both so well, knew they loved each other, but it was impossible when they both wanted to be right. "I won't stop for Vanessa tonight. It's too late."

"Did you call Danitha?" Pat, who always had the latest gadget, knew Gayle sometimes forgot she had a phone in her purse.

"While you were in the ladies' room, my little Gizmo Guru."

Vanessa stayed with Danitha Hemphill when Gayle traveled. They'd met at Gayle's first post-Ramsey job as the receptionist for a fledgling law firm. Danitha was a paralegal and law school night student, holding it together for her two children in the aftermath of a husband who had traded home and family for a new love—crack. Gayle admired her resilience and learned from it. Without Danitha's wisdom and support, espe-

GOTTA KEEP ON TRYIN'

cially after the fire, Gayle didn't know how she would have survived. Gayle had worried that Pat and Danitha wouldn't hit it off, but she shouldn't have. And when Danitha finished law school, The Ell & Me Company was one of her first clients.

Another was a couple of Brooklyn Polytechnic students with a text-messaging innovation and little capital. More than once Danitha accepted stock options in lieu of current payments because she understood it was hard to turn sweat and an idea into hard cash.

When the start-up blossomed under the greenhouse effect of the dot-com bubble, it was plucked by one of the industry giants, and Danitha's equity, together with her work on the buyout, netted her a mint. Instead of going mad with her moola, she took her kids on their first ever vacation, to the Magic Kingdom, then invested, set up college funds, and bought and renovated a brownstone in Manhattan Valley. With no family of her own, she imported her ex's mother from Cleveland. She was as disappointed with her son as Danitha had been and was grateful for the chance to be grandma in residence. And because Danitha remembered her own desperate struggle, she started a practice dedicated to helping women who were tryin'—to get an education, get child support, get a house, get a job, get away. But Danitha was a natural born negotiator, who loved making a deal as much as Monty Hall, so she held on to a few corporate clients—among them The Ell & Me Company.

"We're not moving." Gayle had watched the soldier in the bus next to them start and finish a jelly doughnut. They were heading north toward the George Washington Bridge, but traffic had come to a standstill.

"Excuse me—" Pat leaned forward and spoke to the driver. "Is there a reason we've stopped?"

"Don't know yet. I called the dispatcher but she doesn't have word. Weather's been causing problems all day."

"We won't be charged for this time, will we?" Gayle switched her worry focus back to money.

"Absolutely not."

Gayle caught Miles's eye in the rearview mirror, then looked away.

After another ten minutes in park, Miles grabbed his umbrella. "I'm going to see if anybody can give me a heads-up. Be right back."

"Is he supposed to go off and leave us like that?"

"What's the difference? We're all stuck."

"Suppose something happens."

"Right. On an interstate right outside the busiest city in the country, with about a hundred thousand of our closest friends? I'd go check it out if it wasn't raining. At least I could stretch my legs."

A tap on her window nearly sent Gayle through the sunroof. She lowered the glass and Miles's face filled the opening. In the airport she hadn't paid much attention to him aside from the sign he held with their names on it. He had on a black suit, like all the other livery drivers. She did notice he wasn't particularly tall—maybe five-nine. Now she could see his skin was as smooth and clear as polished amber—no mustache, no goatee or soul patch. Sparks of silver flecked his close-cropped hair—just enough to make him look like he'd been somewhere, seen something.

"Talked to a guy from another service. There's a jackknifed tractor trailer at the toll plaza. Could be stuck for a while." Miles patted the door. "Better close up—stay dry." He got back inside.

Pat slumped back in her seat. "I could feel another nap coming on."

"I need a sandwich." Gayle had finished her roll of chewy mints.

"If you open that console, you'll find snacks." Miles gestured through the open privacy window. "And the compartments below the glasses are stocked with sodas."

"No liquids, thanks. Unless you've got a compartment I don't know about."

"Patricia." Gayle elbowed her friend and went for a bag of pretzels.

"What? It's true."

"Those are in our luxury buses and location vehicles." Miles rested his elbow in the opening. "Now, instead of soft drinks, the big spenders, like your husband's athletes, they special-order ahead of time—usually Dom or Cristal—to impress a 'lady.'" He made quotes with his fingers. "But they wouldn't get one of these—they mostly prefer superstretch SUVs."

"You're like a walking company brochure Miles, from Miles Ahead." Pat figured she'd make conversation to keep herself awake. She hated to check out on Gayle.

"These are good." Gayle crunched another of the spicy pretzel squares.

"Glad you like 'em. They're new for us. Always looking for something different."

"How long have you been with the company?" Pat asked.

"From day one." He smiled and nodded. "Twenty-one years."

Gayle tried to remember what she was doing twenty-one years ago—living at home, going to school, making her bed. "You don't look like you had a driver's license twenty-one years ago."

"I'm flattered. But the company's been good to me." Miles turned front to check for movement. "I have a confession to make. I'm not a regular driver . . ."

"Now he tells us." Pat perked up. "He's been trying to pass the permit exam for twenty-one years."

"Nothing like that. My chauffeur's license is up-to-date, but I'm only out tonight because we were shorthanded."

"Well, if you're not a driver, you must be in sales," Pat said.

"You might say that."

Gayle wanted to join in, but felt somehow tongue-tied, so she finished the pretzels and went for a six-pack of cheese crackers.

And after eighteen of the twenty questions, Pat established that Miles was, in fact, the president of Miles Ahead, a business he had started as a freshman at Fordham, while driving part-time for his uncle who was an undertaker. He would borrow a car on Saturday nights to make some extra bucks ferrying his buddies to and from the Bronx campus to nightspots in Manhattan. He even picked up some Sunday weddings. When his uncle got new cars, he let Miles buy an old one, "on time." Four years after graduation he had half a dozen corporate clients and thirty cars. "We can even get you an armored car if that's what you need."

They had been in the car over an hour when the traffic started to move. "Maybe I can get you ladies home to your husbands before sunup."

"Only *one* of us has a husband," Pat said sweetly, and grinned at Gayle.

"That's good news for some lucky man." Miles put on his blinker and merged left, following the cars in front of him.

It was Pat's turn to nudge Gayle and mouth, *"He's kind of cute,"* like that would mean anything to Gayle—whether he drove for a car service or NASCAR. Pat had tried to get her back in the mix. "I have Vanessa to think of," she would say—which struck Pat as an airtight excuse for never living again.

Pat was on the West Side, so she was the first drop-off. "Call me when you get in." Miles opened the door.

"But I'll be delivered to my door, Mario will still be standing guard."

"So?"

The call was a ritual. Wherever they had been, if it was after dark one called the other, just to make sure they were both home OK—like something bad couldn't happen in the daylight. Gayle knew it was really for her. After the dead-or-alive, now-you-see-me, now-you-don't game Ramsey had played, Pat wanted to be sure Gayle and Vanessa were safe.

"So, I'll call you when I get in."

"I like that—watching out for each other." Miles pulled away from the curb.

"Always have. Since we were kids." No point talking about the ten years they didn't speak. That could never happen again.

The rain had stopped by the time Miles parked in front of Gayle's building and came to open her door. "It was a pleasure being stranded on the turnpike with you—at least for me." Miles helped her out of the car. "Makes me want to get out of the office more often." He retrieved her suitcase and passed it off to the doorman.

"Good night." Gayle was about to head into her building.

"Here's my card—in case you have trouble with that bill." Miles didn't step aside.

Gayle smiled, looked at the card. "Thank you, Miles Thomas."

"And I'd probably can one of my drivers for this, but I'd like to take you out sometime."

"No. Um, I'm sorry, but, no." Gayle couldn't look at him. "It's not you. I just don't."

After Ramsey, Gayle went cold turkey on men and happily ever after. Pat gave her a couple of years in peace, but after that she started to nudge, poke, and badger her about shutting herself off to the rest of her life. "Even in baseball you get three strikes. Then they let you get up and try again the next inning." So to get Pat off her back, Gayle had gone out a few times, nothing serious—nobody she brought home to Vanessa. She didn't trust them, didn't trust her own judgment, and it all felt like too much pressure.

Gayle stepped around Miles and hurried inside. Meeting Ramsey involved a car too. Once was absolutely enough.

The phone was ringing when Gayle opened the door. "Give me a break, I just got in." She knew it was Pat.

"Someone has an admirer."

"You're crazy. I'm tired and I'm going to bed."

"I'm telling you, he's—"

"Good night, Patricia Ellen."

By Monday afternoon a big box from Miles Ahead landed on Gayle's desk.

"What do you have to say now?" Pat came around to investigate.

"We're clients. It's a thank-you." Gayle fiddled with the tape, found a loose end, and pulled.

"It's not addressed to the company. It's addressed to you." Pat pointed out the label.

It was a case of the pretzel squares Gayle liked, and a note: *Here's to rainy nights. And a real lady. Call me, if you decide you "do."* He signed it, *Hopefully, Miles.*

The silliest look came over Gayle's face. "Don't say anything."

Pat smirked. "I just want to know, do you?"

●　●　●

Everything he owned had fit in an army-surplus duffel bag, so it didn't take much time to settle in. Ramsey's to-do list wasn't long, and every day since he'd put money down on his apartment, he accomplished a little more. A trip to Fulton Street netted the rest, including a radio and his one luxury—a prepaid cell phone. Contrary to house rules, he even smuggled in a small microwave. He scrubbed the room—hands and knees—put a mattress cover and new sheets on the bed. It was a room—not much else to say about his four walls at the end of the hall on the third floor of the Bed-Stuy brownstone. But it was a palace compared to some of the places he'd been in Louisville—it was home, for now.

Ramsey whistled a hollow, haunted tune as he stripped down to his boxers and undershirt, sat on the edge of the bed. The springs creaked under the weight of his stocky frame and the strain from countless others who had sat in that spot with nothing to do on a Saturday night. And the strain of some who did.

He fished a worn photo from his wallet, studied it like it was new to him. Gayle had on red shorts and a striped tank top she bought when they were on vacation in Aruba. Two-year-old Vanessa, in a yellow sundress, sat on her hip. Both were barefoot, out by the pool. Their pool. It was just about sunset—that had been a Saturday too. Gayle never even knew he had snapped that picture, much less that he always kept it in his wallet behind his driver's license, and the wad of credit cards he no longer had. He propped it against the lamp on the table next to him.

After a while Ramsey got under the covers, turned out the light. Tomorrow he would get the papers, look for a job. If it rained, he'd go to the library. He wasn't a big bibliophile, but enjoyed reading magazines and newspapers—he could watch movies and he'd gotten surprisingly good at using the computer. He had no idea so much of the world could be at his fingertips. And if the day was sunny, he might go into the city—do some people watching.

• CHAPTER 7 •

Pas de who?

"Ah, man, *those are da bomb.*" DeJohn noticed Marcus's World Series rings exactly when he was supposed to—as soon as Marcus walked in the Hendersons' house and shook hands.

They would live at the bottom of his sock drawer if it were up to him, but Marcus figured out early in his agenting career that those glorified school rings—gaudy chunks of gold and diamonds awarded to commemorate a championship season—were the baseball Holy Grail, the trophy recognized by everyone, from peewee league on up, who ever stood in the on-deck circle with a moment to dream.

"Here." Marcus handed them over, feeling, like always, that the second one was unearned, but that wasn't the story he was selling tonight. This was about fresh talent and wide-open possibilities.

DeJohn's father, DeWitt, hadn't had time to change out of the green tie he wore as part of his car-rental manager's uniform. The rim of hair and the belly pooch made him look older than he probably was, but he looked content, in his home, with his family. He clapped Marcus on the back, shook his hand. "It's an honor," and it sounded as if he meant that sincerely. Marcus had been putting on the last-lap press, even had other players he represented give the Hendersons a call. Randy Piccone had at least been good for that. He had advised them about DeJohn's college-versus-pro options. Now it was time to get the commitment.

"How many Derek Jeter got?" The rings were big for DeJohn's fingers, but he made a fist, made them fit, stared at them with small but piercing eyes, as if they gave him a boost, a charge, an important piece of the puzzle.

"What kind of question is that, DJ?" His mother, Marvella, was a tall woman, with long dark hair, probably worn the same as when she went to Bennett and met DeWitt at an A&T homecoming. DeWitt had told Marcus that story when they spoke on the phone, sounding like it was just yesterday. Marvella guided them from the foyer to the living room, where Marcus could smell there was sho 'nuff cooking going on in the kitchen, something savory, buttery, and homemade. He never knew what he was going to walk into on these excursions. He'd been to trailers, apartments, and gated communities—homes where a career in professional sports was seen as demeaning or salvation.

"Baseball is a game of numbers, Mrs. Henderson." Marcus stood next to DeJohn. "Derek's got four. But Yogi Berra's got ten."

"Who?" DeJohn was a good-looking kid, a shade under six feet, so Marcus figured he had a few more inches to grow. Even under the baggy rugby striped polo you could detect his frame—lean, schoolboy muscle with not an ounce of fat—a good base to build on. "A ring for every finger. That's crazy. Who he play for?"

"The Yankees—a long time ago. After that he was a manager." Marcus was about to deliver a baseball history lesson, but decided to save it for another time.

"Then I don't have to sweat him. Old dude, musta been bad though. . . . Hold up, Calvin."

DeJohn's little brother took a flying leap and hung off the forearm of his big brother's ring hand like it was a chin-up bar. It reminded Marcus of roughhousing with Freddy, when there was no crying uncle.

"Let go, champ. I can't replace those if you lose one." Dad wrangled Calvin and they settled on the sectional. Mom brought them a pitcher of lemonade, matching plaid glasses, and coasters, then went to get dinner on the table, the way dinners in the Carter house used to be before . . .

Marcus had shown up for DeJohn's afternoon game without announcing he was coming, so as not to affect the young man's performance. Marcus sat at the back of the stands, kept a low profile. These days, he got more of a charge watching budding ability than seasoned professionals—they were supposed to play well. When DeJohn was up to bat, he was firmly in control of the microgame, between hitter and pitcher. He seemed to read the ball as soon as it left the pitcher's hand and zero in on the one with his name on it. There wasn't much challenge in the field. DeJohn handled the few balls that made it out to right with ease, although he did showboat one grab, sliding for the catch when it wasn't really necessary. It brought a cheer from the crowd.

Dad wanted to know about the players Marcus had met on the way up, the odds of making it all the way.

"Odds mean you're gambling. It ain't a gamble when you know you're gonna win." DeJohn had other concerns—what car Marcus drove, what stars had he met, did he have a boat, what did he make for his old Tastea ads? "Used to make my moms buy that stuff when I was little."

"My wife produced those ads—before we were married."

"You got a wife? With babes all over the place?"

"DeJohn . . ."

"I'm just sayin' . . ."

"There's no shortage of babes. But it's hard to know who to trust." And he trusted Pat more than anyone else, since they were ten.

"What I gotta trust 'em for? Just gotta be smart, which I am."

Marvella called them to the dining room, set with a table-cloth and napkins, roast chicken, gravy, biscuits, and string beans, like Sunday dinner. They bowed their heads, DeWitt said grace, Calvin kicked DeJohn under the table, the way Marcus used to kick Freddy.

Dad's big concern was turning down bird-in-the-hand college scholarships for the wild-goose chase of a spot on a major league roster. "There's some talented players never make it further than our Green Jackets." DeWitt hadn't touched much of his dinner.

"That's Class A ball, Pops. They don't make it past that, they ain't that talented." DeJohn went for another biscuit.

"They're *not* that talented," Marvella corrected.

"But you could come out in four years with an education and still be drafted."

"Suppose nobody's looking for me in four years? Suppose I break my back and can't do jack—end up renting cars or something."

"DeJohn!" Marvella gave her son a slant-eyed warning.

It sounded to Marcus like she had refereed this fight before.

"You could do that in the minors, Son."

"Least I'd be trying to get where I wanna go."

It was as if they were following a script in Marcus's head from twenty years ago. He watched Calvin, watching his big brother, almost ready to bust with excitement and pride. Mom looked concerned, and a little amazed that her son was almost a man. And father and son locked horns, each sure of what was right. Marcus knew which side he was rooting for, and it wasn't about seeing dollar signs.

Marcus wiped his mouth, laid his napkin aside. "I won't try to make up your mind, one way or the other. There are excellent college programs, and many players, probably most players, are drafted from them. What I do know is DeJohn has tremendous talent. Not middling or maybe talent." Marcus looked at DeJohn. "You've gotta bring the will and the work."

"Got it covered. You'll be seeing me at Turner Field."

"Can't guarantee which teams will be interested, and you'll be on the bus, playing at cracker-box stadiums for not much more than you probably get in allowance before you're in anybody's lineup. Derek spent four years in the minors."

"Yeah. Aw-ite." DeJohn slouched in his seat, draped an arm over the back.

Marcus stifled a grin. "I know you've been talking to other agents—bigger ones than me. But nobody will take more of an active interest in guiding your son's career." Marcus stopped short of begging, but he wanted to be there, wanted a hand in DeJohn's success.

Peach cobbler and coffee and Marcus was on his way, but not before Calvin got to try on the rings. He was more still than he'd been all evening, as though he was afraid to break the spell. DeWitt promised to call within the week to let Marcus know their decision.

DeJohn walked Marcus up the gravel driveway to the car. "You know I'ma do this, right?"

"You know it's gonna be hard, right?" Even the ones who had the goods had to have the stomach for the nonstop, in-your-face competition. "And what was that slide in the sixth? You could have caught that ball on the run."

"Looked pretty, though, didn't it?" DeJohn lit up, reliving the moment. "Got to give the people what they want."

"Not if you get hurt. Rule one, use your head. Protect your body." Marcus ran a hand over DeJohn's whisper of hair.

"We gon' do this, for real?" DeJohn cocked his head to the side.

"For real." Marcus held out his fist.

DeJohn gave him a pound. "Solid."

And Marcus made his way to I-20 East, heading for Wilmington, North Carolina, to look in on his parents. By rerouting regular trips and building in layovers, he found ways to visit them regularly—sometimes just long enough for dinner with his dad and a swing by the nursing home. Or he'd manage a weekend, and the two of them would go fishing or play eighteen holes—Marcus paid for annual membership at a local golf club for his father. At first he said the place was too stuffy and kept playing the public courses, but eventually Booker got the hang of it.

Originally, Pat was going to swing in from Atlanta, but she and Marcus were still not on the good foot. And arguing in that tiny guest room where his father could hear—that was out. In all the time he'd lived under their roof, Marcus couldn't remember his mother and father arguing. His dad would keep the peace—just walk away. That's what Marcus did.

It was a four-hour-plus drive, which would get him in after midnight. Soon as he got to cruising speed, he checked in with Rich, dictated to his assistant, including a thank-you to the Hendersons. DeJohn's potential was sky-high with the right guidance, and Marcus was going to get him there. He could just imagine DeWitt and Marvella in the stands beaming, and Calvin, in a near frenzy, wearing his brother's jersey. They were clearly a family who stuck together, just like his parents, and in the crunch they would stick by him. He thought about calling Pat, but what was the point of another "Hello. How are you?" phone call?

By the time he got to I-95 he was preparing to enter his parents' orbit. He called his dad, said he'd be in late. "You know how to let yourself in." Marcus had been on top of the world when he surprised them with that first house—brand-new and fully decorated, with more bathrooms than their place in St. Albans had bedrooms. But when he got them moved in, they looked so small in it, and he had worried it was too much for them to handle. Booker pooh-poohed his son's concerns, managed the house, and Ethel too for the first nine years. It wasn't until later Marcus found out she sometimes rubbed toothpaste in her hair instead of Vitapointe if Booker wasn't watching, or that she still wandered off, asking the neighbors if they'd seen Freddy. But the night Ethel swallowed her wedding band and a topaz birthstone ring as though they were candy, right off her fingers, and had to be rushed for emergency surgery, shook Booker up, bad. He finally admitted it was time to find a place where his wife couldn't hurt herself. After that, he had Marcus sell the dream house and downsized to a small town house in a condominium community, not far from Ethel's nursing home.

And just like always, Booker didn't complain, he did what had to be done—like a man.

By the time he parked behind his dad's new ride—a sporty coupe because he didn't want another "old fogy" car—Marcus was whupped. He walked around back toward the patio. No matter how often Marcus got after him, his father's sliders were always unlocked. "This is the country. Ain't nothing coming in here after me."

Although the Atlantic was only a few miles away, the condo complex had been built around a man-made lake. Booker's ground-floor unit looked out on the shoreline—boat slips, dunes, sea grass. Winding paths lined with benches led to a white sand beach. Marcus stretched a moment, took in the incandescent moonlight shimmering on the water. He was a stone city boy, but it felt as if there was more air to breathe out where the buildings didn't touch the sky. It was a long day, but a good one. He'd get a kick out of telling his dad about his new recruit.

Four strides across the patio and he could see the door was not only unlocked, it was open. They'd have to talk about this at breakfast. Hand on the screen, just about to open it, he stopped. Some cop show repeat played on the TV. A half-eaten plate of cookies sat on the coffee table. Fistfuls of blood pumped through his heart. His father sprawled on the couch—mouth open. And his arms were wrapped around some woman, who was not Marcus's mother. She snuggled beside Booker, head on his chest. Both breathed deep, in sync, like falling asleep entwined was completely normal, not the seismic shock that rocked Marcus.

He banged the screen door open so hard it came off the track. They both started awake.

"What time is it?" Booker scratched his head and sat up.

"Time for me to get home." The woman finger-fluffed her steely gray hair. "Messin' with you and dessert. Marcus, I'm Roberta. You're father's told me much about you, and I can't wait to hear more—in the daylight."

"Roberta brought over some fresh-caught amberjack. Tomorrow I'll show her how to cook it—on a charcoal grill."

"No wonder I can't stay awake. Been up since 'fore dawn, fishing." She patted his leg. "Come on, Book, walk me home."

In the midst of the pleasantries, nobody seemed to notice Marcus hadn't put his bag down or said a word.

Roberta put the uneaten cookies in the canister. Booker put his shoes on. They both put on windbreakers from the Goose Creek Golf Club.

"Get yourself settled. She lives right cross the way. Let's go, Bert." And they were out the door.

Marcus didn't watch, didn't want to see if his father kissed her good-night. He sat at the round, glass kitchen table. Waiting—until his father returned. "What was that?"

"What it look like?" Booker hung his jacket on a lighthouse peg by the door. Still tall and proud, the uneven slope of his shoulders was a souvenir from the mailbag he carried for decades.

"My father laid up with some woman."

"Don't come in here with no foolishness. And don't insult my friend. Roberta is an awful nice lady."

"Mom's not dead."

Booker got one more cookie. "Your mother and I are still married. And I still love her—will until the good Lord takes me home, but she ain't been a wife to me in more years than I'm gonna count. Most days she don't know me from the president, who she still thinks is Jimmy Carter."

"What's that supposed to mean?"

"I know you ain't no dummy." Oatmeal-cookie crumbs sprinkled the front of Booker's shirt.

"So now it's Book and Bert, like Bonnie and Clyde." Marcus's insides churned. "That's not how you raised me."

"I raised you to face your responsibilities, and not you or anybody else can tell me I didn't do that. But I got some needs too. And I need to be happy, have a little companionship. While I still can. I'm goin' to bed."

Marcus did too, but it wasn't restful—couldn't get that image out of his head, his father and Roberta. He'd never seen his parents argue, but he hadn't seen them snuggle either or walk hand in hand. He got mad that Roberta had made the golf club more attractive to his father, that she brought him fish and he was going to cook it for her, that they had special names for each other. His parents had always been Booker and Ethel, even to each other. And he was mad that his father needed companionship his mother couldn't give him. Marcus knew why, and that got him out of bed early, showered, dressed, and packed. His flight wasn't until the next evening, but he'd change it at the airport because he couldn't stay for grilled fish or go and look at his mother's blank eyes.

"Where you going so early, Son?" Booker shuffled out of the bedroom in a new-looking navy-and-white-striped robe.

It made Marcus mad to hear his father call him son, because there used to be two and now there was just him. "I gotta go, Dad."

"You ain't still upset 'cause—"

"I gotta go."

* * *

"What are you doing here?" Pat was startled to see Marcus. She was in the bathroom, hair done, one cheek blushed, when she heard the key in the door. She had pulled on a robe, all set to read the super for coming in without warning.

"Wasn't expecting you either." Marcus had gotten an early flight out. He figured he'd have a few hours alone, to get his head straight, maybe go in to the office.

"Actually, I just finished packing."

"Going where?" He didn't remember she had another trip planned, but that had happened before.

"Wilmington."

"Oh." He put down his bag, but stayed by the door, not yet ready to bridge the safety zone between them. "For what?"

"To see you." Pat had been holding her robe closed with her arm. She let it go, revealing a sliver of black lace bra and pantie. "It's called a surprise. I was going to call your dad as soon as I got dressed. My flight leaves at three, so I'd be there for dinner." And by then she'd have practiced what she was going to say about Tiffani, without the Drew part of course. "Guess I can cancel the car."

Marcus smiled. "I'm still surprised." He wasn't expecting a peace summit.

"Something happen?"

"Naw. Just wanted to come home." He was not interested in repeating the Roberta story. He hadn't digested it yet.

No point in waiting. "I've been thinking... about Tiffani."

"And?" So much for the summit. He braced for the debate.

"There's no reason to punish her any more than life already has, whatever her mother told her. And you were so upset... about her neighborhood and her school. I was thinking I could make some calls . . . to Southridge. As long as it's OK with her aunt . . . and you."

"Thank you." Marcus crossed the room, surrounded Pat with a hug, suddenly aware he had missed her arms around him, wondered why it couldn't always be this simple.

Case closed. And if assisting Tiffani satisfied Marcus's parental urge for a while, what was the harm? *"Pas de quoi."* She wanted to reel that back as soon as she'd said it.

"Pas de who?" He whispered it close to her ear, nibbled the top with his lips.

"De you." She raised her head to look at him, fill herself with him, tried to stop the wheels of her mind from spinning.

"You know how long it's been since we played hooky together, just you and me?" Her hair smelled like lemon and honey, and he was tired of thinking, about his business, his parents, his duties and disappointments. He just wanted to be—with his wife.

"Hmmm." It had been months since they'd played at all. Not that she was counting. But the time dripped by—drops became bucketfuls, became enough to swim in. Now it was time to just dive in. "Are we gonna get in trouble?"

"I'm counting on it."

Marcus had no problem picking up where they'd left off. He backed them to a dining chair, pulled her astride his lap so he could see her, feel her. Cheeks in the palms of his hands, he tasted her neck, just above the doubloon he'd given her to symbolize a timeless love. His lips moved up her throat, her chin, until they found hers, tasting them one at a time, like sweet fruit.

Pat closed her eyes, tried to let go, let it flow, to be with him, be outside herself. She knew the sounds, the moves, the rhythms, like a dance she had learned, could repeat by rote. But she couldn't feel the music, so she immersed herself in him, what he needed, at least what she could give him. She rode the waves with him, till he came ashore, wet and panting, hot breath on her shoulder. She had kept her head above water, but tears surprised her, sliding down her face, onto his shoulder.

"You alright?" Marcus brushed them away with his thumbs, held her tighter.

"I'm fine," she said, knowing there was no way to explain all that was wrong, not even to herself.

CHAPTER 8

. . . plenty plenty to spread around.

By the time Marcus left the Hendersons' house that day, he was sure DeJohn would be his client—he felt the connection, felt their trust. So when DeWitt called to make it official, it was more like another item Marcus crossed off his checklist than a cause for celebration—one step closer to the goal, getting DeJohn drafted.

And the actual day of the draft always felt odd—kind of an anti-event. Marcus and Rich met for their traditional draft-day breakfast at 6 a.m. on that June morning—their usual Eleventh Avenue diner, the 24-7 choice of cabbies, hookers, and theater stars. Fortified with steak, eggs, and enough coffee to float the Staten Island ferry, they headed for the office—to wait for the chaos to start.

There was no televised coverage of the major league draft. No anxious but hopeful draftees seated in the spotlight, trying not to sweat bullets and look ill as somebody else's name was called. No fans with banners eating hot dogs, cheering and booing their team's next choice, maybe the key to a winning season. There is no actual event, just a conference call—thirty teams on the line, fifty rounds, a speed drill with two minutes a pop for teams to stake their claims and move on.

There were no personal calls in the office that day. All lines stayed available for anxious players and parents, but mostly for "the call." The one that made it official, that meant your player had been selected—let the dealing begin. G&C Pro Sports had a number of prospects in the hopper, but DeJohn Henderson was the first name they expected to hear. Rich cracked jokes, rapid-fire, like a bad comic on open-mike night, pumping the office morale and adrenaline.

Marcus got real quiet, answered necessary questions in as few syllables as possible. He remembered Pat telling him good luck before he left, but he wasn't sure what he said back, if he said anything at all. He wasn't as edgy on his own draft day—youth and ignorance had made him cocky enough to be sure it was going to happen. Marcus couldn't sit still, had to keep moving. And for the first time in years he had to have a baseball in his hands. Not to autograph or throw out the ceremonial first pitch. He needed to feel the cowhide in his hand, hear it slap in his mitt. He had a hundred scenarios for how the day would play, which teams were the right fit and needed a player with DeJohn's skills. But he just needed one to pan out.

Everybody hopes for the first round, but Marcus was realistic enough to know it would be at least the second. As he got word the second round was over, he felt his tie was too tight, his jaw tensed. He slapped the ball in his mitt, snapped at his assistant for asking if he wanted anything. There was only one thing he wanted, the right phone call.

And it came toward the end of the third round, from the Brooklyn Cyclones, the new Mets A team. The staff exploded in hoots and dog barks loud enough to raise the roof. Rich mounted the conference table, pumping his fist. Marcus exchanged high fives, celebrated with the rest, but really it was more like somebody had unlaced his straitjacket and he could breathe again.

Marcus closed himself in his office, dialed the phone. "He's in." He cleared his throat, choking back a swell that caught him off guard.

Marvella had answered in one ring. All four of them were home, sitting their own phone vigil. She couldn't talk, handed the phone to her husband. Calvin roared like a lion. Marcus imagined him tackling his brother. That's what he would have done to Freddy.

DeJohn was Mr. Cool Breeze, no sweat, knew it all along. "Got me a new outfit for school tomorrow. Gotta look like a pro."

Two weeks later DeJohn was considerably more unhinged about the signing bonus Marcus negotiated. It was all crazy money now. Back when he signed, Marcus remembered staring at his check, late into the night because he couldn't imagine that much money was his at one time. Soon as it cleared, he spent it all on the Firebird, because it fit his image, whatever he thought that was. But DeJohn could buy a whole lot more than some wheels with $690,000.

"Yo, that's almost a million! That's more than my pops made, probably in his whole life."

"Remember, it's just because you're good at a game."

"That makes me a playa."

"And if you're smart, you won't get played." Marcus had to talk him down, throw some foam on the fire before it burned through DeJohn's pockets and out of control. "This is just a down payment on what you can make in the future. It'll keep you tight till you get past the dress rehearsal and up to the show." All those zeros made it hard to keep DeJohn's attention for stuff like accountants and taxes. So Marcus decided it was time to bring DeJohn to the city, show him the lights, school him about what's in store.

* * *

"That's what I'm talkin' about!" DeJohn tugged his shirt cuff and eyed the crowd watching him exit the Hummer limo. A night out was Marcus's reward for the day DeJohn spent taking care of business. Sporting pinstripes that cost more than his parents' monthly mortgage, DeJohn stood aside, waiting for Marcus to join him. "Looks like Hollywood." The limestone exterior, sandblasted back in time to its original chalky white, was bathed in cool blue light. Ornate Moorish arches made it clear you were about to trade in today for the sleek art deco of the 1920s. It was Lush.

"Bessie has offers to open branches in other cities, but he says there'll only be one Lush."

"He? Some dude with a chick name owns this place?"

"There's a dozen stories about how he got the name, but when you meet him, you decide not to ask." Marcus told the driver what time to return, then led the way past the horde hoping to be admitted, and through the towering, etched-glass flamingo doors.

The three-story building reigned over the block on a grand Harlem avenue that had regained some of its faded luster since Bessie Austin closed his Westchester restaurant and reclaimed his roots. Lush harkened back to a uniquely uptown glamour, brought back the Renaissance to a part of town in danger of losing its flavor, gentrified into below–Ninety-sixth Street sameness. It was the place to be after dark.

"Good to see you." The doorman and Marcus exchanged a soul shake, bumped shoulders. The doorman unhooked the rope from the stanchion. Marcus pressed a fifty into the big guy's hand and let DeJohn enter ahead of him, because Marcus remembered what it felt like the first time.

"Da-yum!" DeJohn stopped. The cascading crystal chandelier reflected a starburst on the vaulted foyer ceiling and bedazzled the black-and-white tile floor. The sweeping ebony staircase tempted you upstairs for more.

"This is just a taste of what's out here for you—if you keep your game up and your head on. You see Jaleel back there—on the door? Could've had a monster football career. Blew it on women and blow—got cut after his rookie season. Now he's a gatekeeper instead of a newsmaker."

"That's messed up. . . . Whoa . . ." The hostess, clad

in body-skimming silver lamé, cooked DeJohn's cool.

"Good evening, sir." Deep bangs accentuated kohl-rimmed eyes. A curtain of raven hair kissed her shoulders. "Welcome to Lush." She smiled at DeJohn from behind her desk—a frosted-glass oval wedged between ten-foot bronze nudes. "Reservation for Blue, Pink, or Black?"

"What?" DeJohn was lost watching her hands, the nails lacquered cobalt blue, silver half-moons at the base. They were poised above the three books, each patent-leather-bound in one of the signature colors.

Lush had three levels, each catering to a specific clientele with distinctive offerings—fine dining, swell cocktails, posh entertainment or other distractions. Lush Blue, on the entrance level, welcomed the general public, who for only a semi-outrageous price could sip and sup, the stars of their own special night fantasy in the azure, alabaster, and sterling restaurant that heated up into a club vibe after midnight.

"Mr. Carter! I didn't see you." Her voice had a slow smolder. "Are you together?"

"We are indeed. How are you tonight, Rain?"

"Luscious. Thank you for asking." She looked down, then back up at Marcus through thick lashes.

Marcus had been one of The Five Hundred, the individuals invited, for reasons fully known only to Bessie, to become members when Lush first opened. What they had in common was clout and cachet and they received exclusive privileges—preferred seating in Lush Blue, Pink, or Black, no reservation required, a personal humidor, VIP-room access on all three floors. Membership was lifetime and nontransferrable. The chosen would remain at five hundred, with no additions unless a member passed away or had membership revoked. Marcus had heard of a Lush Privé, but if it was true, he had not ventured through those doors.

"Tables at Black and Pink as usual?"

"Yeah. Rich is probably coming later and I don't know who he might bring. Rain, this is baseball's newest hitman, DeJohn Henderson. DJ, Rain holds the keys to the kingdom. Get her on your side and you've got smooth sailing around here."

DeJohn grinned sheepishly, shoved his hands in his pants pockets, muttered something akin to "Hey." As he and Marcus walked away, DeJohn regained some of his bravado, turned, and looked back at Rain. "She's sure in your shit."

"I'm a married man. You can't have everything you see."

DeJohn shook his head. "How you pass that up?"

"I'm not blind, and they're still looking. Makes for a pleasant evening." Marcus winked and kept walking, led the way into Blue, where he greeted the maître d' by name, paused at a table near the door long enough to pat a back and shake a hand, before moving to the bar, where he found his favorite imported beer waiting in a chilled pilsner glass. DeJohn hesitated when asked for his order, then requested a ginger ale. He smiled when it appeared in the same tall, frosty glass.

Marcus took a swig, surveyed the room. "Whether you're here, at the barbershop, or the Piggly Wiggly, you can run into any and everybody—teammates, classmates, the woman who helped you at the bank, or the sportscaster who ragged on your game. And pretty soon folks are going to know your name or your face. Mostly that's fine, but someday some fool is going to try to earn points by kicking your ass."

"I can defend myself."

"I'm telling you now, if it smells like trouble, walk."

"I ain't no chump."

"You will be if you take on a sucker fight. Even if you win, you lose."

Marcus finished his draft, led the way out.

"Hey, we didn't pay." DeJohn, feeling like the Almost Million Dollar Man, pulled out his new eelskin wallet. "I got it."

"They bill me."

"You don't sign or nothin'?"

"They know all the members."

"That's phat."

They rode the elevator two floors up to Black. Piano, bass, and drums cushioned hushed conversation punctuated by a robust laugh or lyrical giggle, a sharp contrast to the chatter and clatter they'd left down in Blue. An opulent ebony, ivory, and gold sanctuary where sharp angles met sweeping curves in jazz-age moderne style, the space was dominated by the bar, a half-moon of brass and leather. Deep club chairs in black-and-white calfskin orbited the bar, and the room was ringed by gleaming lacquered dining tables, some partitioned into private sanctuaries by etched-glass surrounds. The patrons were quietly elegant—jackets a must for men, sophisticated couture de jour for the ladies. Dining was leisurely, service unobtrusively impeccable.

"Your table is ready, Mr. Carter. How are you tonight, sir?"

"Just fine, William. Keep that for me, will you? I'll wait for Rich downstairs."

DeJohn was dumbstruck. "Ain't that—?" He pointed to a table across the room.

"Yes." Marcus put his hand on DeJohn's arm, exerting just enough pressure. "But don't point." The world light-heavyweight champion was deep in conversation with an equally imposing man in a white dinner jacket. "And the guy he's with—that's Bessie."

"Oh. Uh. Sorry. I just—"

"I know. You wanna meet them?"

"Uh—naw, man," DeJohn whispered to Marcus. "Don't want to interrupt." Meeting the champ and this Bessie was more than he was ready for. But this place, this life, it's what he wanted—all of it. The store Marcus took him to for his suit, it was unlike any place he'd ever been, and the people fawned all over him, called him sir. The limo, people knowing your name and what you want before you ask, feeling as if you belong in a place like this—now he'd seen it, up close and personal, knew it was real, and within his reach. That was enough for now.

Or so he thought until they made their way down a floor. Nineteen-year-old DeJohn couldn't even imagine Lush Pink, a rosy red Valentine box, wrapped in satin, velvet, silk, and leather from the palest blush to the deepest claret. Sandwiched between Blue and Black, Pink catered to a clientele in search of a more specialized kind of entertainment experience, where gentlemen and sometimes their ladies could partake in a visual feast of flesh and fantasy.

They arrived midperformance and were shown to a tufted banquette that offered an intimate view of the stage. The dancer winked, swerved a hip in their direction, and blew Marcus a kiss over red-fishnet-gloved fingers. DJ elbowed Marcus his approval and tried to slouch casually in his seat—

like this was as regular an occurrence as it appeared to be for Marcus. "Yo, man, this is stompin'!" This was not the bump, grind, and shake your behind he had seen in movies and on bad videos in the basement with his friends while their parents were out. "I could get used to this." The music, deliberately planned to fuel anticipation and imagination, had a sultry texture that caressed your skin with every note.

"I bet, but a little entertainment goes a long way, man. It's fun, but it ain't where you hang your hat."

"You only sayin' that 'cause you got it like that."

"No. Your job is to play ball. Theirs is to separate you from as much of your cash as you're willing to part with, but—"

"Hey, Marcus." He was interrupted by the young woman who had been onstage moments before. She came up behind them and draped her shimmering, well-toned mahogany arms over his shoulder. "Like the show?" Her voice was as soft and dusky as the night air.

"Don't I always?"

The dancer oozed around, slowed enough for Marcus to slip another fifty under the waist of her thong, and came to a stop in front of DeJohn. "No Rich tonight? Who's your new friend?"

"Xenia, this is G and C Pro Sports' hottest new bat."

DJ stumbled up so quickly he almost tipped the table over. "DeJohn Henderson, ma'am."

"Ma'am? Damn, you know how to hurt a girl." She sank down on the velvet bench where DeJohn had been sitting.

The song changed, a new girl took the stage while DeJohn looked down at Xenia, or more specifically at the glittering, red pasties that did their own hip-hop as she talked. He stared at the place she patted next to her, then looked over at Marcus. "Um. Sorry, ma'am, I mean Xenia."

"DJ is a Georgia boy, Xenia. He's just being polite."

"We could use a little more polite around here. Come sit next to me, DJ. And show me some of that Southern charm." Her laugh was bright, a light DeJohn actually thought he could see. "I know!" She wiggled in her seat. "You show me yours and I'll show you mine."

DeJohn cleared his throat. Palms and pits sweating to beat the band, he sank to the bench. Xenia draped a strategically posed leg over his knee and rested her hand high on his thigh.

"Hey, Xe, give the man a minute." Marcus laughed. "The ink isn't even dry on his contract. But he's close by—you'll see him again."

"You know how much I like your friends, Marcus." She moved her hand a little higher, pressed a little harder. "They always know how to make a girl feel appreciated. But I'll run along now. Leave you boys to your mischief." Xenia pushed out her bottom lip in a mock pout, then jumped up. "Ya'll come back soon now, ya hear?" She bent forward, tassels dangling, and cupped DeJohn's face. "How's my Southern DJ?"

"Fine." The word practically squeaked out. He swallowed the *ma'am*, took a breath, and tried again. "I'll definitely be back."

Xenia waggled her farewell, blew them kisses, and they both watched her rump bump as she sashayed away. She stopped by another table where a short, portly gentleman with a balding pate got up and followed her out of sight.

"Private client. Probably a regular." Marcus noted DJ's confusion. "Lap dance."

"For real? That's stompin', man. Right up in here?"

"But it's *only* a dance and you don't get to lead. You lay one hand, or any other part, on her, and you'll find your ass on the sidewalk and a permanent not-welcome mat at the front door."

Rich showed up, and before heading back to Black, they watched a torrid redhead whose acrobatics demonstrated that her collar and cuffs definitely matched. Once they settled at their table upstairs, Rich and Marcus took DeJohn to school. "You goin' out—to a party or a club? Never drive. You hear me? Never, ever drive yourself. Use a limo service—the one we use or not as long as it's somebody's."

"But what if you got a stompin' ride? Why you wanna—"

Rich held up a hand. "This is not multiple choice. Do *not* drive no matter *how* much you *dropped* for a *car!*" Rich spoke in exclamation points. "And don't go by yourself. Go with your buddies. There's safety in numbers. And you need witnesses—and I don't mean the honeys." Rich got up in DeJohn's face. "I know what you're thinking. Why should I listen to this little crazy bastard? I don't care if you think I'm nuts. *You* are a *potential target* for crazies, and for plain old-fashioned thugs who won't give a shit whether you got LoJack."

"Don't forget the gold-diggin' baby's mamas," Marcus added. "If you can't keep it in your pants—and I know that ain't possible—don't even think about hittin' it without a glove. And if you're smart, you'll take it with you."

"Damn, that's nasty."

"So is a paternity suit. I don't care what *she* says, or how sweet she says it. Until time proves otherwise, you gotta expect they're after what you can do for them, and that's about the Benjamins."

For the last lesson of the night Rich pulled out his cell phone. "See this? I got six pictures of you on here."

One was of DeJohn draped with Xenia's leg, her hand up his thigh.

"How you do that?" DeJohn was horrified.

"Doesn't matter, but I bet if I threatened to send them to your mother, you'd trade me some bills for 'em."

"Man, you can't do that." DeJohn pleaded.

"I won't." Rich pressed a button. "Gone. But don't do anything in public you don't want to see on the news."

DeJohn looked deflated.

"We're not picking on you. Every rookie gets this speech. And some of the old ones get a refresher course." Rich punched DeJohn's arm. "Not necessarily in this setting. You're on the fast track. And you come to a place like this—you gotta remember it's entertainment. Period. These women are spectacular—they can make you forget your mother's name. Damn, they can make you forget you got a mother, but girl-friend material they are not. This is a job. They like you as long as you have a big contract and plenty plenty to spread around—hell, they'll even love you. Just don't get your needs and theirs confused."

DeJohn ordered a porterhouse the size of the Manhattan phone book, because he could, drank iced tea, because he should, and tried to commit every detail of the night to a memory he would use to impress his friends back in Augusta. Before they left, there was a stop in the men's room where the valet made sure they were suitably brushed and lint-rolled, removing telltale flecks of glitter and sparkle from a close encounter with a Pink lady. What a gentleman said or did after he left Lush was up to him, but it was the attendant's job to erase traces of the evening that might anger a wife or girlfriend, ultimately costing Lush a customer.

The night ended with a Hummer ride back to DeJohn's hotel.

"Be by tomorrow at eight to pick you up," Marcus announced as DeJohn climbed out.

"In the morning?"

"Play hard. Work harder."

Marcus was still perking, but he needed to squash the excitement before he got home. He'd been there before, made a big deal to Pat about some rookie and the stratospheric potential, and had it fizzle in his face. This time he'd just keep it under wraps. "Take me back uptown."

Jaleel smiled, nodded when Marcus got out of the limo. He wasn't the first man who came back for a nightcap. Xenia wasn't surprised either.

CHAPTER 9

*Time to put your mouth where
your money is.*

"If it's green and it grows, I can take care of it." Ramsey watched the pudgy woman, dirty glasses perched on the end of her nose, go over his application. He wasn't worried. He had seven prospects and one of them would pan out. Driving around New York, tending plants in high-rise office buildings, pricey co-ops, and hotels was a long way from having his own landscape company with his own employees, but what he needed right now was a foot in the door. There was a lot to do before he was ready. The rest would come in time.

"It certainly seems as though you've had experience. Let me do a hypothetical." She took her glasses off. "If I have a large container—with a ficus that is failing to thrive and it's surrounded by—let's say amoema . . ." She leaned forward, clasped her hands on the desk—her cuticles were ragged, the raw, hot pink of a longtime biter.

Ramsey leaned back. "Dieffenbachia—what kind of cultivars are we talking about? Camille? Tropic Snow? And are they failing to thrive too, or is it just the ficus?" He knew she was testing him and he wanted to cut to the chase. "Ficus is pretty hearty despite its reputation. You just have to let it settle in, get used to a home, but you know that. And it's obviously not aphids or mealybugs because you could *see* what the problem is. So I'd check for root rot, maybe a fungus or bacteria in whatever you've been using to fertilize—which maybe you've been doing too much of. Now if the trouble is with both plants, I'd check the soil—most likely a drainage problem."

"Well, you do know your plants." She smoothed a lock of limp blond hair behind her ear, smiled.

"Yes. That I do." Ramsey smiled back. It had taken him over a year to be able to smile again. He barely had a face left when that trucker found him at the rest stop.

"And you can start right away?"

"This very moment if you like."

She laughed. "A week from today is more what I had in mind. The person you're replacing is with us until Friday. Now, you do understand that your shift would begin at six a.m.?"

"Not a problem. I like early morning—before the day knows exactly what it's going to be when it grows up."

"Well, yes." Cynthia Abbott didn't have a clue what he meant, so she told him where to go to fill out the rest of his paperwork, get his ID card and uniform. "Welcome to Inner-Scape." She reached, offering her hand, but was startled when Ramsey extended his. It was OK. He'd learned to expect that reaction when people first noticed the shiny puckered skin covering the stubs where his last two fingers used to be.

*   *   *

"Think they'll get along?" When Pat arranged for Tiffani to meet her after school for a chat, Gayle decided it would be a good day for Vanessa to stop by too—to shop for dance-camp gear. Not that Gayle was trying to engineer a friendship, but Tiffani seemed so grounded, and if they happened to hit it off . . .

"Who knows. I'm not exactly ready for this tutorial." Pat paced like a sentry. She was fearless in most situations, but counseling a teenager had her wigged.

"Trade you that for my root canal." Gayle had just regained feeling in her lips and tongue, but her embarrassment still burned. Her usually chatty dentist had been quiet as she examined Gayle's mouth. Then she wheeled her chair up so she faced Gayle, removed the drain from her mouth. "You have a fair amount of enamel erosion." Gayle knew why. Same reason she had bottles of antacid stashed wherever she might need them—the acid gushing from her stomach, back up her throat, into her mouth. Sometimes it felt like she was breathing fire, but that was too repulsive to talk about. Before the dentist could continue Gayle had babbled something about intestinal problems, said she was seeing a specialist. At the end of the visit, the dentist prescribed a fluoridated mouth rinse, said she could recommend someone if Gayle wanted to talk about any problems she might be having. Gayle told Pat she'd cracked her tooth on a candy-coated almond. And Gayle swore to herself she'd get control, stop stuffing herself, over the summer while Vanessa was away. "Sit down. You make me dizzy."

"Fine." Pat plunked down at her desk, logged on to check e-mail for the ninety-ninth time. She hadn't laid eyes on Tiffani since she arranged her Southridge scholarship. Pat's inquiry was past the application deadline for the fall semester, but the admissions committee agreed to consider it. After Tiffani's interview and Pat's diligent follow-up, they not only accepted her, they waived tuition. After all, Pat had been one of their first urban scholarship recipients—or hardship handouts as Gayle used to call it. Pat was now a distinguished alumna who had been asked back as a commencement speaker. Marcus and Pat would cover room, board, uniforms, computer, books, and her other expenses.

"I for one would be happy if I never saw the child again." Lindy plopped the package just messengered from Now What? on Gayle's drawing board. "Ever."

"That's cold, Lindy." Gayle put down her pencil, opened the envelope, and pulled out the mocked-up catalog, version twelve. "Give her a chance."

"I never saw any benefit in the doubt." Lindy humphed and hovered, eyeing the catalog. She still hadn't gotten past the Tiffani bombshell, and since it was a misfire, Lindy was done, end of story. Even the letters Tiffani sent both Marcus and Pat on kitten stationery, apologizing for any problems her mistaken information had caused, left Lindy unmoved. She knew Pat and Gayle were her bosses, but that didn't stop her from treating them like her daughters—she'd raised five of her own—which meant they got liberal doses of her opinion.

Pat came and looked over Gayle's shoulder. "Drew says this one should be pretty much ready to go. We should call with any revisions when we're done. He also sent a couple of links to some Web designer's sites for us to look at." That was the e-mail he sent both of them. Then there was the one to Pat alone, telling her to break a leg with Tiffani.

—Lucky girl to be getting advice from you.

She wrote him back:

—Don't know if I have anything worthwhile to say.

His reply made her smile—they always did:

—I do.

Gayle had talked Pat into the tête-à-tête—reminded her how freaked she had been living in a dorm full of girls whose families wintered in Aspen or St. Bart's, and who had no clue what you do with Afro Sheen. "Time to put your mouth where your money is," she had said.

Lindy pointed to the star-filled sky on the catalog cover. "Either the sky should be darker or the stars should be brighter—if you ask me." Before she had a chance to add further comments, the buzzer sent her scurrying back to her battle station.

Pat had taken her deep breath, but let it out again when she heard Lindy's voice.

"Hey, Chicken."

"Hi, Mrs. Cheney."

Vanessa exploded into the office, peeling out of her blazer. "Gotta get out of this dork drag." Hair flying, she headed to the bathroom at the back of the office. Gayle shrugged at Pat. Mother and daughter had the uniform fight long ago. It was required and Vanessa had to wear it, at least from eight-fifteen to two. Gayle thought the Breton Collection—jackets, skirts, slacks, sweaters in gray, burgundy, and black worn with white shirts, or coordinating turtlenecks—looked classy, but Vanessa had other ideas. "She'd die if we saw one of her dance friends with her uniform on." With only a week of school left, three until Vanessa headed for the Catskills, Gayle hoped to keep the peace.

"Bless you my friend." *At least Tiffani is passing through.* Pat was just grateful Marcus hadn't brought up the B-word since she agreed to help Tiffani get into a better school. As long as he didn't bring up babies, she sure wasn't going to.

A few minutes later, Vanessa emerged, hair slicked back into a ponytail, wearing a CATS T-shirt and a wrinkled lilac chiffon skirt, the hem of which she had gathered in scallops using giant safety pins. "Ready?" She pulled a faded denim jacket and low-top, green Converses from her backpack and stuffed her school clothes inside.

"Almost." Gayle attached a sticky note with Lindy's suggestion on the catalog. "Go bother Lindy. She likes it."

"Whatever." Vanessa bounded off, dropped her stuff on

one of the chairs in the reception area, and sprawled opposite Lindy. "Hey, Mrs. Cheney, who's gonna win—Venus or Serena?" They debated which of the Williams sisters would prevail in the French Open until the buzzer interrupted them.

Lindy checked the new monitor on her desk, sucked her teeth, and pushed to unlock the recently installed wood-grain, steel-core door. She understood the security issues and was actually tickled that Terry Stuckey felt they had become important enough to be concerned about such things. But being cut off from the hallway drama, especially from the tattoo parlor upstairs, made Lindy miserable.

"I will let Ms. Reid know you are here." Lindy adopted her royally officious tone, and she didn't wait for a greeting before she disappeared into the back. She had an intercom, but Lindy wanted to mark her territory before she let the tiger cub loose.

"So you're her." Vanessa copped a look of recreational disinterest as she checked out this Tiffani she'd heard so much about. The hair arrangement—Vanessa would bet her tap shoes it was a weave. "I'm Vanessa." She dragged her backpack from the other chair, watched Tiffani smooth the skirt of her petal pink suit and sit down, and wondered if those were hand-me-downs or if she picked that stupid outfit herself. It looked like something Gayle would try to get her to wear.

"Wow. So you're the real Ell." Tiffani perched on the end of the chair, knees together, ankles crossed.

"There is no *real* Ell." Vanessa tried not to groan when she noticed the pink pumps, wondered if her panties were pink too. Vanessa crossed her leg, revealing her red, footless tights. "It's stupid."

Tiffani looked down at her hands, then back up at Vanessa. "I'd like it—it's like being the girl Barbie is named for and your mother owns Mattel or something."

"This ain't hardly Mattel." Vanessa gestured to the Ell book covers and posters that adorned the walls of the reception area.

"Could be." Tiffani sat back.

"Yeah. Right." Vanessa waggled a green-sneakered foot. "I don't even like little kids. I'm a dancer."

"You been in any videos?"

"Not that kind of dancing." Vanessa made it sound like an insult. "They have no technique. It's all gratuitous booty shaking and sweat." She picked up *Toy* magazine, flipped pages without looking at them. "I hear they're shipping you off to Aunt Pat's Stepford School."

"You mean like in that old movie?"

Vanessa nodded. "I go to one here. I hate it."

"This one didn't look so bad—especially compared to where I am now." Aunt Stephanie had taken Tiffani to tour the campus and scrutinized the offer for hidden strings that might further obligate her to a niece she hardly knew. After weighing the loss of her free babysitter against an extra mouth to feed, clothe, and shelter, she agreed to let Tiffani go—if she wanted to.

Tiffani had examined her options too, but really, the decision was a no-brainer. On one side was another year at the crumbling, crowded school where graduating was the exception not the rule, and that cot in a kitchen that smelled like old grease and diapers. On the other, the bucolic school grounds, state-of-the-art classrooms, and cozy residence houses. It beat getting caught up in the gang thang or playing Mary Poppins to the triple T's just for a roof over her head. And unlike her mother, she knew a good deal and how to play it.

"But at least yours is a boarding school. I'm going away for the summer, but I'd give anything to get away from my mother."

"Maybe not." Tiffani's voice was hollow, distant, and she folded and unfolded the hem of her skirt.

"Sorry." Embarrassed by her gaffe, Vanessa jumped up, gathered her belongings.

"I don't know—I'm gonna be gone all summer, but if you want to hang out or something when they parole you from school, call me or whatever." But Vanessa hoped she didn't.

"Yeah. OK." Tiffani planned to exercise that option only if necessary.

Pat and Gayle came out along with Lindy, who resumed her post. Gayle gave Tiffani a hug and congratulations, then tried to gauge Vanessa's reaction as they departed, leaving Pat face-to-face with her charge.

"Glad you could come, Tiffani." She extended her hand because she didn't know what else to do. In return she got Tiffani's girly-girl fingertip handshake. Pat definitely had something to say about that. "Let's back that up. A handshake should always be firm, like you mean it."

"But I thought—"

"Don't worry about being a lady. It's important people know you're confident. So look the person directly in the eye, grasp the whole hand."

Tiffani caught on quickly, and when they went out for a bite, Pat saw she had good table manners and wasn't shy about asking for what she wanted, including ice in her water and French dressing on the side.

"Were you afraid, being at school, all by yourself?"

"Sometimes." It was a good question. One Pat didn't want to dwell on since it cut a little close to home. "Lonely too."

"Guess you didn't make any friends."

"Sure I did—tennis friends and homework friends. Even some hanging-out friends. Not like Gayle. That's different." Pat hadn't thought about that in a while, how it was different. "Some of those people I talk to till this day—gotta keep your networking options open."

Tiffani looked to be soaking it all in.

"Don't let scared and lonely stop you from doing what you need to do. Mostly people don't know if you don't tell them." Pat looked at the face across the table, amazed that she could ever have looked so young. She always thought she looked mature, but she realized now how much of a front that was. "I lost my mother early too." She wasn't even sure why she said it, hadn't meant to make this personal. "It hurts, but you can make it."

They were on the street, hailing a cab, when Tiffani said, "Would it be OK if I call you sometimes—you know, to ask you stuff?"

"Absolutely."

A taxi stopped, but before she got in, Tiffani reached out her hand. Pat smiled, took it firmly, and they shook on it. Pat kept the smile on the way back to the office, not knowing exactly why. She gave Gayle a ring to let her know what happened, but she was still hip deep in leotards. Marcus was out of town. He'd surely be in the middle of some conversation, situation, negotiation, where he couldn't talk, so she didn't bother calling yet. Maybe later, although it seemed kind of strange to say she'd agreed to be his ex-girlfriend's daughter's mentor. At least she could check out those Web sites Drew had sent.

It was amazing how quickly their company was progressing. Catalogs, now a doll, and soon to be an Internet presence. It was a long way from where they started, from where she started, which was supposed to fill her up more than it did at the moment, in the office alone.

One of the Web designers seemed particularly good at mixing whimsy with a modern feel. She e-mailed Drew to say so, and that she'd confer with Gayle in the morning.

—U still at work 2.

Drew's reply came in thirty seconds.
Pat hit reply.

—Yep.
—How did it go?

It was odd, talking with Drew when he wasn't there. She could hear his voice, his inflection as she read the message, just like a conversation.

—Good. For both of us.

Somehow it was easier to type that than it would have been to say it. She waited to see what came next.

—Dinner?

Pat considered the offer, wouldn't have minded the company. And didn't exactly remember when Drew became a part of her day, like orange juice. Finally she wrote back:

—Just ate. Rain check?
—Deal.

•   •   •

"This shit is raw."

Marcus was not at all surprised when three weeks into his A-league season, DeJohn, fired up red-hot, called from a diner somewhere between Batavia, New York, and Lowell, Massachusetts. Six days on the road, three home, two away, two home, five away. He hated the bus, hated the crummy motels, the fast food, and his roommate—a shortstop from Missouri who recited Bible verses out loud every night until he fell asleep. "You take me out, show me around, tell me how great shit gon' be, and where am I? On a bus with twenty stinkin' dudes. I mean, they really stink. The damn uniform itches. I got mosquito bites on my scalp, man. I'm from Georgia and I never been bit on my head."

Marcus wasn't surprised—the guys they recruited right out of high school usually had the homesick breakdown somewhere in the first month. DeJohn was right on time. Marcus went into his pep-rally arsenal, spouting encouraging words about paying dues, the future—how it would all be worth it and one day they'd laugh about this. Knowing the answer would be no, Marcus said he'd come up to Lowell if DeJohn wanted him to. Fourteen minutes by the digital clock on his desk is what it took Marcus to talk DJ down from the ledge, but he was sure this wouldn't be the last time.

CHAPTER 10

This is not your little hobby anymore.

"In a sea of sameness and* shameless imitators, this holiday season, a charming newcomer stands head and shoulders above her vinyl competition. Ell Crawford, a new entry in an overcrowded, underimagined doll field slipped into the marketplace under the radar. Wow!" Each word was better than the next as Pat read the *Journal* article to Gayle and Drew. "No hype, TV commercials, or billboards heralded her arrival—and if you're not already on the mailing list of The

Ell & Me Company, which for the last four years has published storybooks featuring the eponymous, plucky, sturdily shod heroine, then you are probably too late to snag one in time for Christmas . . . at least this Christmas."

"That's pretty good." Her hands in fists, Gayle's whole body tensed as she listened.

"Are you kidding me? It couldn't have been better if I wrote it myself!" Drew stood up, put his coffee cup down. "And the timing is perfect. Early October starts the holiday push."

"Outstanding!" Pat tossed the paper in the air and threw her arms around Drew. The firmness of his muscles—arms, back, chest—startled her, made her aware she had actually thought about what he might feel like. Realizing what she had done, she quickly pulled Gayle into the hug before explanation, apology, or analysis made it awkward.

Pat thought last week's conversation with the *Journal* reporter had gone well, not overly solicitous but polite. Still, they had no idea what his take on Ell would be. Drew, who engineered the interview, had warned them the piece might not be an endorsement, and that despite calls from a fact-checker, it might not even run. Whether it did or not, one hundred thousand catalogs, featuring the very first Ell Crawford doll, as well as the new book, were already on their way to mailboxes across the country. But when they got word the story was a go, Pat, Gayle, and Drew decided to gather at Ell central to await the dawn arrival of the newspaper—just like a Broadway cast anticipating opening-night reviews.

Drew was the first to break from the three-way embrace. "This calls for a celebration—I'm aware it's seven a.m. so I suppose cocktails are out, but we could go for pancakes, or pizza—something festive. Because once this hits, you'll be too busy for breakfast with your old friends."

Pat felt giddy, intoxicated. "Hey, you get a share of the blame for this too."

"Glad to take it." Drew gathered up the newspaper pages. "We'll need lots of copies."

"She's right about the Drew factor." Gayle knew she needed to act as thrilled as they wanted her to be. "You've been a great accomplice." Being written up in the *Journal* was a big deal. It wasn't a touchy-feely puff piece. Their little company had three column inches in the business bible—Ell's photo included—which said to the industry and consumers alike, "Pay attention." But it was like Gayle was on a different wavelength. All she got was static and she couldn't find the off switch. "Isn't there still champagne from—I don't remember—somebody—in the fridge? And I know there's orange juice." Gayle hoped she sounded sparkly, not scared.

"A morning mimosa to mark the occasion?" Pat hoped she didn't sound surprised at Gayle's zeal.

"Works for me!" Drew went to retrieve the bottle, and when Lindy arrived a few minutes later, they toasted Ell and her many, many new friends.

The phones started ringing just after eight. By nine thirty the office buzzed, with everybody, including Drew, fielding calls nonstop. At noon Lindy switched the phones to voice mail. A message directed those who wanted to place an order or request a catalog to the 800 number for their fulfillment house and to the Web site. Media inquiries were directed to Now What? Vendors and suppliers were asked to mail or fax their requests for appointments. All others were asked to leave a message.

Pat wanted to slip in a call to Marcus to share the news right after she read the piece, but he was in L.A., three time zones away. It was midafternoon when she thought of calling again, but she stopped. He knew the story was running. By then he should have read it and called to congratulate her—the way she did when one of his players got good press. She had even left her cell phone on the desk so she wouldn't miss him. So she filed that slight away and kept moving. When he surfaced the next day, she was matter-of-fact. It was going well, no big thing because she just wouldn't let on he had hurt her feelings. He was supposed to know that.

By the weekend Gayle was fried. It was all happening so quickly—the company growing out, Vanessa growing up. And Gayle was the only one who wanted to put on the brakes, because the speed made her dizzy. She had only survived Vanessa's summer absence because there was so much work. Pat not only kept her on task, she kept Gayle going—out to lunch and dinner, a spa weekend in the Berkshires, to the beauty shop to have her hair trimmed and the premature gray washed away. "We're the same age, and you're making me look bad," Pat had teased.

They had visited Vanessa's camp twice. Each time she was sublimely happy, and Gayle cried all the way home. And all summer Pat kept prodding—sometimes gently, sometimes not—trying to get her friend to consider what she was going to do when Vanessa left to make her own life. "This will be her junior year. We couldn't wait to be out of high school. I'm sure she can't either. It's not that far off, you know. She could go away to college. And you were married and gone by what, twenty?"

Gayle couldn't hear it. "Biggest mistake I ever made." And there was no need for Vanessa to repeat it. In the hours Gayle had lain awake, alone, regretting the frozen cheesecake, the bucket of chicken, the cycle not broken, she convinced herself Vanessa didn't need to leave home. Home was comfortable, it was safe, and the city was an arts Mecca. She could dance if she wanted. Gayle would do whatever it took to keep her there, keep her happy.

By Monday morning it was official. Ell had sold out. Every doll had a new home waiting for her, and twice as many orders were pending. Book orders were coming in twice as fast as usual too, both for the new title and backlist selections.

Pat got on the horn first thing, reordered with their printer. Gayle hovered by the phone while Pat spoke with her contact at the toy plant. Gayle was relieved to hear they could handle another run immediately and get them dolls to ship before Thanksgiving.

"That's fantastic." Gayle couldn't believe she was saying that, but it looked as if her fears were for nothing.

"No need to rush." Fingers knit together, Pat swiveled her chair side to side, eyes sparkling. "I think we should make them wait."

For Gayle it was like going from sixty to zero by hitting a brick wall. "Are you nuts? That doesn't make any sense." Her voice was shrill, her arms tightly folded. "The orders are in our hands. Why wouldn't we try to fill them?" She was practically in Pat's face.

"Hear me out. We want Ell to be special." Pat got up

and perched on the edge of her desk to give herself leverage. She knew Gayle was overwhelmed, but this was no time for half-stepping.

"You can't buy her in a store. She already costs three times as much as other dolls. Isn't that special enough?" As far as Gayle was concerned, having people want more dolls meant they needed to make more dolls. They'd never discussed what would happen if they sold out, and frankly, she had never imagined it.

But Pat was adamant about keeping the first run limited. "A shortage creates buzz. Buzz means more interest, means if I don't have one, I gotta get it because this is *special*. Which means more sales." Pat glowed with excitement.

"It's Christmas. If it's not under the tree, they'll ask for a refund and buy something else. Then we are screwed." Frustration mounting, Gayle didn't get it. She had worried no one would be interested. Now that they were, why wouldn't they sell as many as they could?

"Ell is not some run-of-the-mill dolly. She can't be snatched up by the dozen from SuperCheap Mart at the Friday-after-Thanksgiving sale. More detail goes into—"

"But the Christmas season was the whole point! Everything was geared to that." Now Gayle just wanted to cry.

"They'll still want them after Christmas. You saw all those collectors at the expo. Some people won't rest until they have one. The laws of commerce, Gayle. Think about it. There will only be ten thousand first-edition Ell dolls. Ever—"

"Which has nothing to do with us!" Gayle voice had risen past office-decorum levels.

"It sets us apart. It sets our standard, but that's what we're about. We want to offer quality, give girls a doll with heart, soul, and as many stories as you and they can imagine—along with a wardrobe and a house and a bicycle and a covered wagon and—" Pat ticked off the items on her fingers.

"Enough!" Gayle didn't want to hear the litany of Pat's future plans. "It sounds greedy."

"It's business, Gayle. If you don't have the stomach for this, let me handle it. This is not your little hobby anymore."

The wounded look on Gayle's face told Pat her remark was blunter than she intended, but every time the company faced a new challenge, Gayle needed coddling. Walk one step, drag Gayle—another step, drag Gayle. Pat was tired of explaining, especially since it benefited her too. "I mean—"

Lindy buzzed, interrupting Pat's explanation. "It's Breton. About Vanessa."

The conversation was brief—and on the tense side. Pat could tell it wasn't good.

"I have to go." Voice shaking, Gayle grabbed her jacket and purse.

"What's up?"

"I don't exactly know." Pat walked with her downstairs as Gayle explained that for the past month, two or three times a week, Vanessa had been having afternoon doctor appointments, or so she told the school. They had become concerned and wanted to know if they needed to know anything about Vanessa's condition so they could ease her school day. "What is she doing three afternoons a week?"

Home was the only place she could think of to start. She nearly barreled into Mario before he could open the door. "Did you see Vanessa this afternoon?"

"No." He stepped to the side. "It's been spotty the past couple of weeks. Thought maybe her schedule changed— sometimes I'll see her go out—around three thirty or four— with some of her friends, so I assumed she got out early or something you know—before I came on duty."

Gayle headed upstairs, unable to remember the last time Mario had given her a weather report—which was obviously because he hadn't been seeing Vanessa. At the apartment Gayle paused, put her ear to the door—nothing. Feeling ridiculous, like a bad TV-detective imitation, and upset that her daughter had brought her to this, she entered.

Muffled music came from Vanessa's room, so Gayle knew she was home or had been. Before she tackled what was behind the closed door, she surveyed the rest of the apart- ment—nothing out of place. It took her a minute to notice the balcony, in great part because Gayle rarely thought of the four-by-five-foot shelf, with a view of air-conditioning ducts and fire escapes, as much of anything, except Vanessa's pout- ing room.

But she wasn't pouting now. Vanessa laughed and talked with friends whom Gayle didn't recognize from school. The blond waif took a final drag, flicked her cigarette butt over the railing, and stuffed her hands in her peacoat pocket. She and a boy with a flat brush of red hair watched a tall, skinny guy who appeared to be coaching Vanessa. He rested his hands at her waist, moved her hips side to side. She moved with him, as if his instruction and his hands were familiar. And Gayle was both detached from and enraged by these strangers in her house, including her daughter.

Finally the redhead noticed Gayle in the living room.

He elbowed the blonde, who was about to light up again. Then Vanessa swung around, looked straight at Gayle as if she were trespassing. Then there was a scrambled blur of doors, bags, mumbled words, and hasty exits. The tall boy was last to leave. As he passed, Gayle realized he wasn't so much skinny as lean, sinewy. Nor was he exactly a boy. His features were strong, prominent, manly. A wave of black hair flopped over one eye. He flipped it up with a toss of his head, gave Vanessa's arm a squeeze. Gayle noticed he had big, muscular hands. "Vanessa is an inspired dancer," he said, then slipped out.

"I hope you're satisfied." Vanessa trounced inside, leaned against the sliding-glass door, blocking the view. "You totally embarrassed me in front of my friends."

"No, I'm not satisfied." Gayle struggled to keep her voice even. "I won't be satisfied when you explain why you're here instead of in school. And you know what? I won't be satisfied when you tell me why those children were in my house in the middle of the day. Or even better, who they are?" She took a breath, moved toward Vanessa, who stood rooted to her spot. Gayle met her daughter's gaze, waited until she stepped aside. Then she saw what Vanessa was hiding—empty beer bottles. "The smoking was bad. You're drinking too? Have you lost your mind? How long has this been going on?"

"If you want me to answer all those questions, you have to repeat them." Vanessa flopped on the couch. "But I can answer the first one. I'm not in school because it's a waste of my time. Julian says so too."

"Who?!" The screech was right there, choking in the back of Gayle's throat.

"You just threw him out." Vanessa folded her legs under her and crossed her arms.

"Is he your boyfriend?"

"Julian is not my boyfriend." Vanessa rolled her eyes. "He was one of my instructors at camp, and for your information he's a brilliant choreographer."

"Dial back the sarcasm."

Vanessa, surprised by Gayle's unusually parental tone, folded herself tighter on the couch. "He's starting his own dance company, out of his loft in Williamsburg for now."

"How old is this Julian?"

"Twenty-two."

"Vanessa! You're still a teenager. You should be dating boys—"

"I told you we're not dating! Don't you ever listen?"

"He's a grown man. Or at least I'm sure he thinks he is. And I also know there's only one thing he's interested in." It was her voice, but it was her father's words Gayle heard coming out of her mouth. She remembered when he said them—on a Sunday morning, before she went to a champagne brunch with Ramsey.

Vanessa looked her mother in the eye, carefully examining her target. "We're not like that." Ready. "But, it would be just fine with me." Aim.

"What does that mean—it would be fine?!" Gayle felt as if her head would implode.

"Well, it's not like I'm a virgin or anything." Fire.

Gayle couldn't hold in the gasp. And Vanessa smiled, waiting to see where the shot landed and how much damage it did.

"Go to your room. I can't even look at you now."

They retreated to separate corners. Vanessa in her room, brooding. Gayle in hers, stewing. And whether a little girl in Phoenix who couldn't get an Ell doll for Christmas would still want one for Valentine's Day suddenly became inconsequential. Of course they had THE TALK years ago, but Vanessa was so focused on her dancing, on not being ordinary, on being angry, that there hadn't been room in her schedule for boys—at least not in a way that concerned Gayle. She'd gone to parties and the park—group things. There hadn't been a pick-you-up-at-your-house, burger-and-movie date. But there must have been something, and now Gayle had to figure out what to do.

Gayle called Pat because she had to, although she wasn't exactly in the mood to talk to her either. "Do what you want about the doll." She could only fight on one front at a time.

Gayle ranted about Vanessa, and Pat listened, said she'd hold down the fort for as long as needed. "I know you're mad, but talk to her about protecting herself—against disease, pregnancy, and idiots. We skated by the first one, but we both ran smack into two and three. Our choices were different. So were the outcomes. We survived, but we weren't smart. You can't protect her from getting hurt or making mistakes, but you gotta try."

Afternoon faded into evening and sank like a stone into night, and Gayle still wasn't ready to make nice. She drank endless cups of tea and scarfed down three boxes of cookies from the stash of comestibles she kept in the back of her closet for midnight emergencies—times when she couldn't quiet the panic and Vanessa was still up and about. She always gave in to Vanessa, allowed her to control the temperature in the room—just as she had done with Ramsey—and she was determined not to let her do it this time. She wasn't going to storm the barricade, read Vanessa the riot act, or get her fitted for a chastity belt. But for once, Gayle wasn't apologizing and she wasn't backing down.

There was no summons to supper, no soft knock on the door asking Vanessa if she was OK. And when she heard the safety chain slide into place and saw dark replace the sliver of light under her door, Vanessa was stunned, couldn't believe her mother would let her go to sleep hungry. But she did, and sometime after midnight, Vanessa dozed off, still pissed.

"I will call your school every day to make sure you are there." Gayle put her mug in the dishwasher. "I will call the doorman to make sure you're home—alone, by three o'clock. Then I will call you to make sure you are really here. You will go nowhere else without permission."

Vanessa stared, mouth open. "How long is my sentence, warden?" She snatched her backpack.

"Until I change my mind."

They rode the elevator in silence, parted in front of the building. Vanessa heading east, Gayle west. And so the staredown began. After four conversation-free mornings and evenings, and four sandwiches she'd made herself for dinner, Vanessa blinked. Around nine o'clock, she padded barefoot into her mother's room. The TV was on. Gayle was half watching, half sketching, sort of flipping through a magazine.

"I'm sorry." Vanessa's voice was barely audible.

"Good." Gayle put down her sketch pad. "Are you protecting yourself?"

Vanessa nodded.

"Are you smoking?"

"Nope."

"Anything—grass, meth, pills, crack—"

"Mom!" Vanessa wanted to say she wasn't stupid, but for once bit her tongue. "No." She smiled. "Am I released?"

"No." Gayle smiled back. "I'll let you know."

The Vanessa situation harnessed so much of Gayle's worry energy she had little left for Ell & Me. Pat was sorry for the reason, but glad to have Gayle off her back for a while. She, Drew, and their marketing plan marched full steam ahead. They brought in additional desks and a couple of temps to handle the calls, faxes, and e-mails that continued at a steady pace. Ell No. 1 and Ell No. 10,000 had not been offered for sale and were safely ensconced in the company archives.

February brought back-to-back Black History Month appearances for Ell and her mom and the debut of Ell Nos. 10,001–50,000. Minor changes identified the second-run doll—there were two stars next to the name Ell on the bottom of her right foot, and the dye lot of the velour for her shirt was slightly lighter, but orders remained robust over the next months.

Pat wondered when the novelty would wear off, but in the meantime she was grateful for the good fortune coming their way. She considered all options carefully, looked as far ahead as she could see before taking the next step, and held tight to Gayle's hand—not her drawing hand, because there were more adventures, outfits, and catalogs to create. And Drew was there—not always in person but on the phone or by e-mail. He helped Pat cut through the underbrush, climb over jagged barbs, somehow knowing when it was time to commiserate, cheer her on, or offer a thumbs-up—unlike Marcus, or even Gayle for that matter.

"Want to grab dinner?" Pat looked up from the folders on her desk and the spreadsheet on her monitor.

"You're ready to leave? It's only six o'clock." Gayle put down the fabric samples she was examining. "Are you feeling OK?"

"These numbers are starting to run together." For weeks, Pat had been comparing past and current budgets and sales—working on projections and charting their future. "Thought we could chill. We haven't been out in a long time."

Gayle couldn't tell Pat the real reason why.

It was becoming harder for her to eat out. And being on the road was a nightmare. By the end of the day, she had controlled the need to feed herself as long as she could, and she knew that once she started eating, it was nearly impossible to stop before she reached nirvana, the peaceful feeling that calmed her, enveloped her like a warm blanket. So she stayed close to home as much as she could—because it was easier.

"I don't know. Nessa's been pretty good, at least as far as I can tell, but spring is in the air and that could spell trouble." Starting right after Christmas, Vanessa's restrictions had gradually been eased, but she was still a good reason for Gayle to beg off. "I like her to know I'm home."

"Sooner or later you've got to stop hovering." Pat stretched, arms overhead.

"Don't remind me." Gayle dropped an envelope in her out bin. "But I also promised I'd let her explain why she should be allowed to go to that camp again. Apparently this

Julian won't be teaching, but I don't know if I'm convinced it's the right move. Of course if I don't let her go, I'll have to live with her bad attitude all summer."

"Doesn't seem like there's an upside."

"Why couldn't she be more like Tiffani? What a level head that kid has on her shoulders."

Pat had to admit the girl had proven them all wrong. Even Lindy, though not exactly singing Tiffani's praises, was less hostile toward her. She was doing well at Southridge, had adapted to her new environment pretty easily. Her grades were good—certainly better than Pat expected—and she wanted to pursue her interest in fashion retailing.

"Did I tell you she applied to FIT for the fall—fashion merchandising management?"

"About forty-two times." Sometimes Pat's horn-blowing was a little loud. Or maybe it was just that Gayle hadn't felt she had anything to toot about lately.

"Anyway, I told her to let me know when she gets her acceptance and I'll help her find scholarships. There are tons of corporate ones the Southridge counselors won't have on their radar. And I guess Marcus and I will continue to cover the rest, although somewhere along the line she became more my project than his."

"Maybe she kind of fills in for Darlene." Gayle knew Pat had been fond of the little girl from the shelter she used to mentor. Gayle was fond of her too. It's what had brought the two friends back together after so long.

"Maybe." Pat often wondered if Darlene was OK. They'd kept in touch after her family moved to Mississippi, but then there were other moves and Pat lost contact. "But nobody's filling the spot tonight. I'm up for some fun, but you have Vanessa waiting, Marcus is in Tokyo, Drew has a meeting—everybody's busy—guess I'll go home." Pat made a sad face.

"And sit in the corner eating worms? Please." Gayle gathered her things. "Unless they're served with a lovely Barolo."

Pat cleared the folders from her desk, stuck them back in the file cabinet, sat down at her computer, opened a new e-mail.

—U still there?

Pat typed her reply.

—Yep. What happened to your meeting?

Gayle turned out the lamp on her desk. "I thought you were ready to blow this joint."

"In a second."

By then Drew had answered.

—Meeting canceled :) U up for dinner? Or did U fill in your calendar with something more interesting? : (

"I knew you'd never leave this early."

"Huh?" Pat closed Drew's e-mail before Gayle could see it. "Just thought of one more thing I need to do."

—And what if I did?

She hit send quickly.

—Then I shall go home and have my usual boring evening alone.
—Ha! Nobody actually falls for that—do they?

Pat glanced up at Gayle. "Go ahead and leave. I won't be much longer."

—All the time. Just kidding.
—Sure U are.

"See you tomorrow." Suddenly Pat wanted Gayle to be gone. "Tell Vanessa I said to give you a break." She tried to appear casual as she glanced at the monitor.

—So can U squeeze me in?

"Don't hold your breath." Gayle was out the door.
Pat crossed her leg and typed.

—What's in it for me?

Pat wasn't sure what made her type it—or maybe she was. But there, all alone in the office, she felt tingly, alive. *It's just words.*

CHAPTER 11

There is no art in easy.

*R*amsey *had no dreams worth remembering,* and staying in bed past the sleep he needed to survive was a waste of time. So he was up and out with the garbage trucks groaning sluggishly down his narrow street. Like every day for the past year, the only living being who noticed him was the dusty gray stray with sad green eyes who waited by the gate in case he'd saved some of his dinner to share.

The Kingston subway stop was mostly deserted that time

of the morning. The token booth clerk never looked up from her *Daily News* when Ramsey pushed his money through the slot and she slid out a MetroCard. He didn't see the nurse in her flowered smock and white clogs who always rode the middle of the train. But the woman with a shopping cart brimful of whatever she owned covered in a brown-and-tan, crocheted afghan was in her usual spot—catching a few hours of shut-eye on the hard wooden bench on the platform.

Ramsey got on the train, walked to the front, stood at the window next to the motorman's cab because it gave him something to look at besides the other working stiffs trying to make it one step closer to payday. Watching the lights whiz by kept him from thinking about the way it used to be—the days when his hands were manicured, he wore a diamond horseshoe ring on his pinkie, and he ran the show.

Spring Street he got off, stopped at the corner for coffee and a buttered roll. Then he went in the garage, stocked the van for the day, and was on his way. His first stop on Thursdays was the consulate on East Seventy-ninth Street, but he was early. When he first started the job, he'd just wait in the van, but now, when time allowed, he headed up to the Eighties. He circled the block twice before he found a place to park near the building with the gleaming wall of windows. First he saw the wall of a man with the little orange dog at the end of a bright red lead. A noisy tangle of legs and leash, it was always impossible to tell which of the pair was leading the walk.

A little after eight, they came out together. Vanessa was taller than her mother and slim—all arms and legs in a navy blue blazer. When he first got back to the city, Ramsey had made a trip there on a hunch, just to see if Gayle still lived in Pat's building. He never saw Pat, so as time passed he assumed she'd moved. He'd read about their books—remembered Gayle drawing them. But Pat marrying Marcus—Youngblood? That was a real surprise.

They had all moved on, and he was sitting in a white van in a brown uniform waiting. One day it would be his turn. One day—but not yet.

• • •

"Who woulda thought this many people could draw?" Lindy stacked another portfolio on the back side of her new desk, a blond-wood and frosted-glass doughnut with her in the middle. "Or at least think they can. My grandchildren can do about as well as some of these."

"Looking at all these makes my stomach hurt." Gayle had been dreading this since they'd put out a call for illustrators to submit their work. "I'll start taking them back—"

"No such thing. I'll buzz Cassidy. That's why you have an assistant now. She gets to do the heavy lifting." Lindy readjusted her houndstooth jacket—she had acquired a new "executive" wardrobe as she called it, befitting the new digs. "Where do you want them?"

"The conference room." Gayle pushed up the sleeves of her taupe cardigan, folded her arms across her chest. She, on the other hand, had not purchased a new wardrobe. It was all she could do to keep her monthly hair appointment. But even she had finally accepted the gray had to go. "I'll be there in a second." She needed a preview of the work, before the artist was sitting across from her, so she could be calm enough to stay in control. These were people with degrees, trained illustrators. How could she be judging them?

It was less than a year from Ell's debut to new digs.

Gayle found it hard to believe that the doll and her accessories had propelled The Ell & Me Company into stratospheric growth. Pat had been right. Thus, the new office, three blocks east, but a world away. Gayle almost choked when she heard the rent. "A month?!" But they were squarely in the middle of toyland where other manufacturers had showrooms. Again, Pat held her hand, said they could do this. The building had security, which made Terry Stuckey happy. Some of the bigger companies had elaborate, 3-D showroom entrances, with forests, airplanes, playhouses, and a host of characters. But for the new kid on the block, theirs was pretty cute—a mural of Ell with her big smile and her big shoes surrounded the door, welcomed you inside. It was the first time anybody but Gayle had drawn Ell. She had sketched out the scene, specified colors, then couldn't look until it was done. Everyone, including Gayle, said it looked great, which only fed her insecurity.

Their office was one of the smaller suites, but it was more than double their previous square footage. In addition to a formal reception area, there was a conference room, a kitchenette, and a lunchroom. Pat and Gayle had separate offices now, each with space outside for her assistant's desk. Pat's was spare and elegant, as much as it could be with displays of dolls and picture books—ecru, with executive walnut and chrome accents, like the one she'd left as an advertising VP. Gayle's had white walls, cherry red bookcases, and a rainbow of fabrics and samples. She had cried when she walked in the first day and saw Pat's office-warming gift—the very first Ell book Gayle had drawn for Vanessa, in a bubble-gum-pink shadow box.

Then there was Ell's Room, with all of the books, the doll, and her accessories. The items in production were show-cased too, new outfits that went with previous stories as well as the two that were coming in the next quarter. Their first Ell produced in China, where they had switched manufactur-ing, was on display, and she was joined by the original doll of Bradley Curtis, Ell's cousin. She took him with her on an adventure, and now Bradley was going to star in his own book series. They weren't sure how a boy doll would fly, but Pat convinced Gayle that the books would do well and the Brad-ley doll would be a worthy experiment—which was why they needed to expand the Ell & Me creative department, as Pat called it. And there was still space in the suite for additional staff—room to grow in.

Gayle's office still had a window. It was eight feet tall, but it didn't let in as much sunlight because they were in a canyon of tall buildings. And since they were on the seventh floor, she couldn't sit at her board and watch the hustle-bustle pass her by. The best she could do for inspiration was pigeons on the ledge. They had gotten new, ergonomically designed office furniture, but Gayle insisted that her Brain Strain board make the trip intact. So she made Pat help her cover it in plastic and they walked it across Twenty-third Street, which turned into a comic journey, especially when a stiff breeze almost took them airborne.

Another thing Gayle missed was having a private bath-room in their suite. They had keys for the restrooms down the hall. Lindy fussed about nasty women and the kind of home they must live in and kept a canister of disinfectant in her desk drawer. Gayle didn't mention why the bathroom was such a big deal to her.

It was a half hour after her assistant set up the portfolios, a pad, an extrafine mechanical pencil, and a bottle of water before Gayle made herself go sit in front of the stack. She held the side of the table and rocked before she made herself unzip the first of twenty-seven eleven-by-fourteen folders.

Gayle pored over each a long time, even the ones she didn't like. She turned the pages slowly, first examining the whole composition, then zeroing in on the individual strokes, the colors, the energy in the lines, feeling the hand of the artist. She had narrowed the field to twelve when Pat pulled up a seat.

"Anything good?" Pat went for the first book, checked out page one, seven, and twelve, then dumped it and was on to the next.

"You didn't look at that."

"Didn't grab me. If I'm six years old, I'm not going for aesthetic nuance."

"You had more patience than that in kindergarten. I remember. I was there."

They had quibbled, laughed, and scraped through half the offerings when the phone rang. Pat picked it up, passed it to Gayle, hand over the receiver. "Vanessa's school."

And Gayle's face froze. "Yes, she left for school today. . . . We haven't spoken. . . . Five days? . . . I'll be in touch tomorrow."

Gayle's voice shook as she dialed her daughter's cell. "Vanessa's been absent for a whole week." She spoke at the beep. "Vanessa Josephine, where are you? Call me." Gayle dialed home, but only got the recorded reply, couldn't believe this was happening again. Gayle pushed away from the table. "Dammit, I know she's with that Julian. I should have known things were too mellow to stay that way. What am I supposed to do? Get her an ankle monitor?" Her voice crept higher, out of control.

"Want to call the police?" Pat was at a loss for where to begin. How do you manage a whole other person who is old enough to flex her will, but too young to know her own strength?

"And tell them what? My daughter cut class?"

"Let's go wait at your apartment."

"You stay here. On the slim chance she calls." Gayle tried to cover the bases, not dwell on the awful possibilities that scared her when she wasn't sleeping at night.

Gayle felt that she should be out looking, but where do you search for a teenager who has all of New York for a hiding place? She went through the motions, went home and called anyone Vanessa might consider a friend, but that only passed time. And she didn't have Julian's number, at least not the digits to his phone. Gayle thought of her parents, worrying about her when she ran off with Ramsey—for a whole week. Only being Vanessa's mother had given her an inkling of the horror that must have been. But her "lightbulb" moments were late and beside the point. She just wished there was somebody to tell her what to do now.

Gayle spoke to Pat every half hour. In between she ate half a loaf of bread with strawberry preserves, whacked off slivers of cheese until she'd gone through the package—didn't matter what she consumed, as long as she ate. Shortly after six the intercom buzz sent her heart pounding.

"She's on her way up."

Gayle took several deep breaths, steadied, waited in a living room chair for the door to open.

"How was school?" The question was as regular as Gayle could make it.

"Why are you in the dark?" Vanessa dropped her pack, turned up the lamp, headed for the kitchen.

"You didn't answer my question."

"Classes were OK."

The lie came so smoothly. Gayle wondered how many others she'd already swallowed. "How would you know?"

Vanessa turned.

"Breton called. Didn't you think I'd find out?"

"I said *class*, not *school*."

"Don't play word games."

Vanessa pulled off her blazer, let it drop to the floor. She drew up to a fully majestic posture. "If you want to know, I've decided to stop wasting my time."

"Do not say another word until you tell me where you've been and what you've been doing."

"Dancing. It's how I express myself to the world." Vanessa pulled several cards from the front zip compartment of her pack, handed them to her mother. "I take stretch and core-strengthening first thing. Then ballet to work my technique . . ."

The rest of her schedule was white noise as Gayle flipped through the ten-class cards, from a variety of studios based in different disciplines and techniques. The words melted on the page. Vanessa was still pontificating when Gayle snapped out of her trance. "You take dance classes after school."

"And waste the best part of my energy on meaningless trivia."

"Which is supposed to mean what?" Gayle felt sweaty and sick. She wanted to stand, but was afraid she'd faint.

"I'm done pretending I care about conventional school."

"You've only got one more year to *pretend*."

"That's three hundred and sixty-five days of my life I'll never get back. You can't lock me in the house. You can't make me pay attention." Then, switching voice from defiance to empathy: "You should understand. You're an artist too."

Definitely a new tact. Vanessa had never acknowledged artistic merit in Gayle's work. Now they were fellow artists? "I understand you're impatient, but you need to finish high school."

"Because society says I have to?"

The righteous indignation would have been funny if it weren't giving Gayle a pain in the head. "Because you need at least a high school diploma to get anywhere in life. College would be even better."

"You didn't go to college."

"Do you know how much easier it would have been—"

"Maybe it's not supposed to be easy. There is no art in easy."

Now Gayle just wanted to slap her. "Julian told you that, didn't he?"

"I can think for myself. Besides, you owe me."

"Excuse me?" Gayle couldn't believe what she was hearing.

"If it hadn't been for me, you would never have come up with Ell Crawford. She looks like me. She has shoes like I did. If it hadn't been for me, where would you be? This is what I need to do. The least you can do is support me."

A punch would have been less painful. Gayle felt the wind knocked out of her. "You cannot drop out of school, Vanessa." She said it with a mother's finality.

"I'm not asking permission." Vanessa answered with a daughter's rebellious ease.

"If you live in this house—"

"What are you gonna do, put me out?" Vanessa stared.

Yes was on her lips. She was the mother, she made the rules. But she knew her daughter was the better bluffer—must have gotten that from her poker-playing father. So this time Gayle blinked because Vanessa wasn't ready to be on her own, no matter what she thought. "We'll discuss this in the morning."

Gayle retired to her room, twisting her brain for some kind of answer, devouring a package of vanilla-crème-filled cookies, and a box of doughnut holes from her closet stash. She stared at the baby picture of Vanessa that still sat on her bedside table—the only place in the apartment her daughter could tolerate it. Resting a hand on each bronzed baby shoe, she looked at the smiling face, remembered how Vanessa used to love to hear that she was fourteen months old in the picture, and that those were the shoes she'd taken her first steps in. It was not supposed to come to this.

Before lights out, Gayle swallowed a handful of the pink laxatives hidden in her lingerie drawer. Since she'd spent as much on the dentist as she would have on a new car, she had tried to do better. She didn't want to make up a new explanation for the trouble with her teeth—or find another dentist.

Violent cramps got Gayle up twice, but then it was over and she felt lighter, calmer, and the next morning was almost normal. Vanessa had yogurt and grapes, Gayle had tea, and they left the house together, but this time the Breton blazer was nowhere in sight.

CHAPTER 12

Once complete, repeat.

"You're condoning it."

"What am I supposed to do, Pat? It's too late to spank her." Gayle spoke in sharp whispers. She was not planning to broadcast this debate to the rest of the staff, and despite Pat's closed door, she knew her assistant, Meg, was already at her desk. It was one of the things Gayle still wasn't used to. This wasn't two desks and a dream anymore—had it ever really been the same one? The Ell & Me Company was becoming an enterprise. That was progress—supposedly. "And I am not putting Vanessa out."

That was Lindy's solution. "Going to work was my job. Going to school was theirs. Everybody living under my roof had to be doing one or the other."

"I'd have to do something. Get a tutor. Send her to a military academy. She can not drop out of high school."

"Don't you think I'm looking for alternatives? Maybe in time for next semester, but right now she gets up and goes to some dance class every morning. It's how she spends her day. It's not like she's goofing off." Gayle wasn't planning to defend Vanessa, but she was fed up with cookie-cutter solutions for a problem neither Lindy or Pat had ever faced.

"Will they issue her a diploma?" Pat shook a packet of sweetener in her coffee.

"No, but—"

"Then it doesn't count."

"It's easy to be right when you have nobody at stake."

Pat opened her mouth, closed it again.

And Gayle left, headed for the sanctuary of her own office. Vanessa was never an academic all-star. Homework and tests had always been painful. Gayle understood that—it had been the same for her. Truth was, the last week or so had been almost peaceful at home. Vanessa was into her classes and what she was learning, and however much time she spent dancing, she craved more.

It reminded Gayle of when her drawing had been for pleasure, not for pay. Now she shouldered so much pressure—to meet deadlines, to make each book more clever than the last, to be creative on cue, and now to supervise another artist.

People's jobs and the company's growth depended on it. Gayle couldn't remember the last time she picked up a pencil or some markers and let her hand and her mind go with the flow.

Still, staying at home and doodling had left her at Ramsey's mercy. Gayle got respect and independence when she found an audience. And part of her wished Vanessa's classes had recitals, like when she was younger—a performance Gayle could see and point to and say to Pat and whomever else, "That's what she's striving for. It's not a waste of time."

Gayle even held her tongue when Vanessa joined Julian's newly formed dance company, Kinesthetica. She had to audition, along with many others, and she'd been so excited to make the cut this time. "Can you imagine being chosen as one of the first dancers by Martha Graham or Alvin Ailey." Gayle wasn't convinced Julian was a twenty-first-century dance master, but everyone started somewhere. If this was Vanessa's start, so be it. Pat had wanted to know if the dancers were paid. "Not yet. Money isn't everything." Gayle knew full well the thought of being without it gave her night terrors. But she could afford to spare Vanessa that for now.

It didn't help that FIT freshman Tiffani had started working in the office—a few hours a week right now, while she acclimated to college life. Tiffani had become Pat's poster child for how to successfully shape a young person's talent and character—the "do" to Vanessa's "don't." Gayle made sure not to hold that against Tiffani, although some days she had to tell Pat to stuff a sock in it.

Tiffani had made herself an all-purpose office assistant— their girl Tuesday and Thursday—so she breezed in right after her advertising-and-promotion class.

"Hi. Hi. How are you?" Her fizzy voice bubbled throughout the office. Pink-and-cream-plaid short trench, belted over cream trousers and turtleneck, she stood apart from the black and gray Manhattan environment like meringue on a mud pie. Unlike most college students, whose uniform involved denim and sweatshirts, all of it baggy, clean optional, Tiffani took the fashion part of the school's name seriously—the girl dressed.

"How's Vanessa?" she chirped as she passed Gayle in the hall. Nobody had exactly told her what was going on, but Tiffani knew there was some controversy and nobody was happy about it.

It caught Gayle off-balance, "Uh, she's OK. I'll tell her you asked."

Then Tiffani posed at Meg's desk, took a swallow from her can of passion-fruit-flavored caffeine punch. "Got anything for me?" The braids and fluff had been replaced by a flat-ironed drape that turned under just above her collar.

Meg was about to hand her a microcassette of dictated correspondence when Pat called out.

"Tiffani! I need to borrow you." Since the semester started, Pat had been getting a kick out of Tiffani's questions about advertising. She enjoyed sharing stories with someone who soaked up information as fast as the brand-named paper towel. And rather than needing constant supervision, Tiffani was a self-starter. After interviewing for staff, Pat knew how scarce a commodity that was.

"What can I do?" Tiffani bounced in, pushing hair out of her eyes and behind her ear with her manicured ring finger.

"I need you to run this over to Marcus at G and C. He's

got a flight out tonight, after the ball game, and I trust you with his passport." Pat handed her a manila envelope. "You know where the office is?"

"Sure. You'll let them know I'm coming?" It's where Tiffani had started this odyssey. She'd only wanted to get there for the last two years.

Pat nodded. "You can take off after that."

Time off for good behavior and a visit to the Marcus Carter prime-meat locker would make for an outstanding extracurricular activity. Tiffani charged outside, headed directly out to Twenty-third Street traffic, and walking backward waved for a cab like a native New Yorker. One stopped before it got to her and Tiffani trotted in that direction. A six-foot woman with a three-foot braid, hoop earrings the size of CDs, and carrying a giant fishing-tackle box got out, and a short guy wearing what Tiffani knew to be an expensive, multicolor Italian sweater was about to get in.

"Excuse me! Hello!" She went running up beside him. "That's my cab." She sounded sweet and distressed.

"Scusi?" One foot in, the man stopped, looked puzzled.

"My cab. I was there." She pointed, smiled. "You walked out right in front of me."

"Oh." He knit together bushy brows, thinking, then brightened. "You share?"

Tiffani knew most locals would have told her where to go and what to do when she got there, but tourists were easy. He let her get in first, was only going to Thirty-second and Madison, and left ten bucks toward the fare. *Ciao bella*.

That gave her plenty of time to explore the manila envelope. She got it out of her purse, ripped it open, examined

Marcus's passport photo. He was certified fine—maybe even more now than he had been the summer he spent with her mother. She flipped through the pages—Curacao, Yokohama, Johannesburg, Athens . . . How the hell had Simone let that walk out of her life and leave her in Losertown forever? That, Tiffani would never understand.

The tourist's ten covered the ride to G&C—the tip was lousy, but that was the driver's problem. Tiffani got a receipt to turn in for expenses. She knew Pat didn't expect change from the twenty she'd given her, so it was clean profit. A quick stop at an office supply store yielded a crisp manila envelope. She resealed the passport, good as new, and was ready to go.

Tiffani got a kick out of flashing her student ID at building security, and this time the call upstairs yielded a wave through the turnstile and directions to take the elevator bank on the left. On the ride up she checked her face in her compact, smoothed her hair, got ready for takeoff.

"Is Mr. Carter expecting you?"

"Yes. Ms. Reid called. I have a package for him." Tiffani had to admit the receptionist was pretty, in a Tammy-starlet kind of way—long hair, teeth done, amped-up assets. Tiffani figured it was a choice surveillance post. Tammy got first pick of every warm body who came through the door. If she had any smarts, she'd take advantage of it.

"You can leave it with me." Tammy reached out her hand.

"Ms. Reid asked that I deliver it personally." Tiffani wasn't too keen on the trusted-messenger MO, but she had not come all this way to be turned around before she crossed the threshold. So she perched on the circular sectional, ready to spring.

In moments an assistant came and walked her to the back. Photos lined the walls—men with bats, diving, leaping, barreling into each other, for what, a ball? Frankly, she didn't get the whole sports thing—running, sweating, spitting, and the uniforms were butt ugly, but there was a spot on the news for sports, not fashion, so she was definitely paying attention.

"You saved me." Marcus stood at his office door in shirtsleeves and ushered her in.

It was cushy—like she expected. "Glad to help." The most interesting appointment in the room was the tall, brown happy meal, checking out the model boat across the room. His dress was casual, but designer, current season. He wasn't shopping discounts or knockoffs, so this wasn't a flunky. And he didn't look up when Tiffani entered, which meant he was used to being the main attraction.

While Marcus tore open the envelope, Tiffani marched to the young man, hand outstretched. "Tiffani Alexander."

DeJohn was already quite used to women his age approaching him with squeals and giggles, all their goodies on display, hoping he'd notice. So the handshake from this sweet thing caught him off guard. She had nice, soft hands, pretty nails. "Hey. DeJohn Henderson." Her gaze surprised him too—straight in his eyes, her beauty mark dotted over the suggestion of a smile.

Tiffani could tell she got his attention—step one.

"We're headed to Shea." Marcus pulled on his suit jacket, stuffed the passport in his pocket. "Number fourteen here makes his major league debut tonight." After just two years DeJohn was getting his first shot. It was a quick rise, especially for a player coming straight from high school—less time than even Darryl Strawberry. But Marcus had struggled to keep him patient and playing to his potential.

DeJohn would fuss, "Why I gotta play with these lame-ass—"

"'Cause that's how you show you're better," Marcus would reply. "You think you're ready, but you need more time."

Between Marcus, Marvella, and DeWitt they'd managed to convince DeJohn to stay at home in the off-season, keep his money invested. He did splurge on a Corvette—megawatt yellow, "so they can see me coming." This last summer when he'd made it all the way up to the Tidewater Tides had been the hardest. He was playing AAA ball, the last step before the Show, and DeJohn could see the starting gate, knew players who had gone up and come back down again. He talked to Marcus almost daily, wanting to know when the call was coming. And in September it finally did.

"That's totally impressive." Tiffani's stint in prep school had been great for connections, eye-opening for what certain people were used to, what they took for granted. But it was lousy in the Saturday-night date department. And she'd only been there a short time, but college was shaping up the same way. At least DeJohn looked like a worthy practice partner.

"What I do tonight, now that's gonna be impressive." DeJohn's chest swelled and his feathers seemed to spread like a peacock's. "I can get you a ticket."

"That's so nice." She smiled. "But I've got plans." A date with her textiles textbook, but this looked like a guy who liked a challenge. Too available was yesterday's leftovers, but it was good to know he didn't have a companion for his big debut.

Marcus shepherded them out, under the GOOD LUCK #14 banner hanging above the entryway. He stood behind, feeling oddly like a chaperone, but they were two good kids.

The elevator ride brought more stats, such as DeJohn's sports car. "Don't have it here in New York. Yet." Tiffani told him she was in college, that Marcus's wife was her mentor.

"So you're into the dolls and everything." DeJohn thought she had a voice like a doll too, and he liked the pretty-in-pink outfit—very girlish.

"It's more learning about business I'm into." But Tiffani wasn't into getting specific. "A lot of athletes I knew were superstitious. So, what's your lucky charm?"

DeJohn's eyes were slits when he smiled. "Definitely seven and seven. Lucky fourteen, baby. And it's gonna be on my jersey."

"What's so special about fourteen?"

The doors opened in the lobby. DeJohn let her exit first. "I'll tell you one day."

A black sedan waited for DeJohn and Marcus at the curb. As soon as he saw them, the driver got out, opened the door. Time for Tiffani to make a memorable exit. She touched DeJohn's arm. "I've got to go. Hope you win."

Marcus got in the car to give them some privacy.

DeJohn seemed reluctant. "Can we like drop you off somewhere?"

She stood still, let DeJohn move in closer. "No. Thanks."

DeJohn rubbed his hands together, like it was chow time. "So, uh, can I get your number?"

Step two—interest—this was going well, but she didn't

want the digits to be the prize. "You've got a lot on your head today. Why don't you call me at Ell and Me, when you're ready. They'll give me the message if I'm not there." Tiffani leaned in, popped a kiss on his cheek. "Good luck." And then she walked away, hair flipping, no looking back.

Tiffani hopped the subway back to her dorm, feeling like she'd scored a home run. This had all gone better than she knew to imagine when she used to lie awake in her kitchen cot, watching headlights run across the wall, dreaming what if . . .

Tiffani had played what-if with Simone, when their heat was off and they huddled in bed together to keep warm. What if they were in a palazzo in Corfu? What if the cancer had not gone to her mother's liver? What if Simone had gotten pregnant by that baseball player instead of by a "for old times" lay with her lame ex-husband? Simone never told him. He could hardly take care of himself. The loser slithered back into the ooze he came from, and Simone chose to enjoy her baby girl instead of cursing the daddy. She told Tiffani when she was old enough to understand, but nobody knew except the two of them. And alone in that cot in Aunt Stephanie's kitchen, what-if seemed better than anything Tiffani had going, even if it just meant she met the man in the picture, but it became so much more. It changed her life.

Really it was perfect that his wife had gotten so involved. Pat's connections had panned out nicely. Tiffani found her a little hard to take sometimes. She had a story for every occasion and they always had some Aesop's fables corny moral. But Tiffani wasn't looking for mother love. She'd had that. This was affirmative action, Tiffani Alexander style.

So she spent the evening studying, made sure she turned on the eleven-o'clock news in time to catch sports. And there was DeJohn's blooper to the gap, which she figured was a good thing since it scored the winning run. There was a locker room interview. "I'm just happy to do what I can to help the team." She was sure somebody coached him to say that. They'd only spoken a few minutes, but DeJohn didn't strike her as the modest type.

Next morning the back-page headline read, "Could DeJohn Be De One?" She kept a copy, just in case, and wrote to congratulate him on the floral stationery she scented with rose potpourri. She still didn't include her phone number. When she had a break, she headed for Canal Street. She'd gone there originally because another student told her to check out the art supply stores, fabric outlets, and cheap, funky clothes, but she also found scads of jewelry stores that sold everything from wedding rings to medallions the size of manhole covers. Thus far she'd only gone window-shopping, but after careful hunting and deft bargaining she picked up a small 10k charm she had engraved with the number 14, for little more than the $20 she made in cab fares the day before. Tiffani mailed it in care of Marcus, considered it a speculative investment . . .

Which paid off a week later. DeJohn called early, while he waited for the team charter to taxi to the Jetway after a red-eye from the West Coast.

"I got a new chain for it."

Tiffani rolled over. "Hope it brings you luck."

DeJohn liked the sleepy in her voice. "Already has. I'm batting .302 since I came up. And we're three and one on this trip."

She could live without the stats, but the one number she played had paid off.

"I got a day off in two days. Wanna do something?"

"Sure." Tiffani had more ideas than just something. "I haven't seen much of the city. Have you?"

"Not really—my apartment and the stadium."

"I have this friend who says you have to see it by helicopter."

"For real?"

"Yeah. You can take sightseeing trips. Can you imagine— flying up close to the Statue of Liberty, all the skyscrapers?"

It had been in Tiffani's wish book since a classmate at Southridge told her how she always took a helicopter to the Hamptons for the weekends with her family. By the end of the conversation, she had DeJohn calling somebody at Marcus's office to arrange a sunset tour with dinner to follow, completing phase one of her marketing strategy. It was one of the first things she learned in her advertising class—A-I-D-A:

Attention leads to

Interest, which creates

Desire and leads to

Action

Once complete, repeat.

The next week Tiffani was in Pat's office, syncing her mentor's BlackBerry to the desktop, another of her trusted duties. She wondered if the dvoight@nowwhat.com who sent crisp e-mails about drop dates and appearance schedules was the same as the drewro1@whatever.com who wrote:

—Hey Stranger, I miss you.
—What do you propose we do about that?
—I'm sure you'll think of something.

Tiffani pressed print, folded the pages in her purse. When Pat returned, Tiffani decided to stir the pot and see what bubbled up. "Tell me if I go too far, but what was it like dating Mr. Carter? I mean, when he was still playing." Tiffani did give Pat credit for not using the baby trap. It was so overplayed. She liked it that Pat had options, with or without her husband, although she couldn't exactly figure out what Pat was waiting on now—time to start the dynasty. "I kind of have this date . . . with DeJohn Henderson."

"I know." Pat's eyes twinkled. "I was wondering if you were going to mention it." Marcus had come home with a proud-papa smirk. Pat thought it was pretty cute too. They had bragged about their "kids" and left it at that—no arguing, no snuggling.

"We weren't together during his playing days." That was an easy one to dodge.

"How do you keep it together now? I mean, you've been married kinda a long time and you're both so busy and everything."

"Well . . . we're friends first—have been since we were kids." That was safe. And Pat didn't much care for dwelling on how much they felt more parallel than together. More like roommates, but as soon as things slowed down . . . "Have a good time with DeJohn. You're both young, so keep it light. Don't let him make you lose your mind, like whoever this

Julian character is, who has Vanessa dropping out of school."

"Oh, sorry to hear that." Except Tiffani was glad to finally get the dirt. Vanessa was either a genius or an idiot, depended how she worked her show.

The day of her DeJohn date was perfect autumn in New York—like it said in the song, so inviting. Tiffani wore a flirty and femme baby-doll dress that revealed yards of leg, elongated by perilous pumps. When DeJohn picked her up in the semiconservative white sedan he had engaged for the day, he was suitably bug-eyed. Outerwear had been Tiffani's wardrobe dilemma—the coat that was warm enough didn't work with the dress, so sacrificing comfort for style, she tossed the lilac shawl casually over her shoulders, which left her shivering as the helicopter swooped and hovered over the canyons of steel. But the choice seemed inspired since it encouraged him to pull her close and put his big arm around her. It also prompted a stop at one of the exclusive stores DeJohn had been introduced to, where she modeled coats until they picked out the white cashmere number—très chic and way out of her student budget, even at a sample sale.

There was a quick stop at his apartment—a furnished one-bedroom in a la-di-da building kept for players in transition—so he could change into something more dapper for the evening. Tiffani felt tingly being greeted by the doorman. At one point DeJohn came out of the bathroom, wearing suit pants and a bare chest, allegedly to make a point, more likely to show off the physique—smooth skin with firm ripples in all the right places, definitely a yum.

Then DeJohn showed off his mastery of New York after dark with dinner at Lush. He had the routine down—handshake and "How you doin'?" from Jaleel at the door, who smoothly removed the velvet rope, ushered them in, and pocketed the tip. Rain was on the desk, had a smile and his reservation for Blue—he wasn't ready to venture into the other regions alone yet. But this time when he was shown to the bar, other patrons knew *his* name, pointed, talked to each other while looking in his direction. Tiffani saw it too, liked her first taste of the spotlight, even if this time it was shared.

She learned more than she cared to know about baseball over dinner, but Tiffani asked the right questions, hung on the answers. She was glad to hear he chewed bubble gum and not tobacco during games. "Maybe one day you'll have your own sneakers or clothing line or something. That's the kind of thing I'm going to school for. Merchandising."

"Oh, yeah? Guess I better keep you around."

And Bessie sent them dessert, the house special Blueberry cobbler with Blue-berry whipped cream. Then he stopped by the table to see if they enjoyed it. Bessie looked even bigger up close, but he made DeJohn feel like a champ. "You're shaking up the lineup, giving us something to watch down the stretch. Glad you came back to visit and brought such a lovely guest." Bessie kissed Tiffani's hand, wished them a good evening.

"That's the owner, you know."

DeJohn had an afternoon game so it was an early night. On the ride downtown he tested the waters, moved in for a kiss. His lips were so plush it startled her, like silky pillows.

Tiffani looked into his eyes, laid a hand on his chest. "I had an amazing day."

"We could stop off at my place. Ya know, kick it for a while."

She laid her head on DeJohn's shoulder. "I'd really like that . . . but I can't tonight." She rubbed a hand over his cheek; random whiskers spiked the smooth skin. "Next time?"

"Now see, you gon' have me thinking about next time when I'm supposed to be thinking about how I'm gonna hit the ball."

"Me too, not about hitting the ball, but I'll be thinking of you."

And DeJohn made sure next time took place during his next home stand. He got Tiffani box seats, where he could look up and see her from the dugout, which gave him a whole different feeling than seeing his family. One thing he had quickly learned about New York was that you can have anything delivered, any time of the day or night. So afterward, they went directly back to his place. It couldn't have been better. He started out sulky after the one-run loss, but Tiffani looked so pretty, and she smelled like a garden. On the drive back they ordered steak dinners from the brasserie around the corner, which arrived right after they got in, smothered in mushrooms, his new favorite delicacy. He'd never had steak like that at home.

And Tiffani wasn't like anything he'd had at home either. His high school girlfriends wore jeans, sneakers, and baseball caps to his games, but under that white coat, Tiffani had on a wrap dress. And once he unwrapped that . . . her round, soft flesh was veiled in sheer, fuchsia lingerie that made him want to touch her, squeeze her . . .

The overwhelmed excitement on DeJohn's face fired

Tiffani's jets—the way he couldn't take his eyes off her, had to feel her, kiss her, smell her, once, and again . . . and again. Until they rested in a slippery, panting heap. Smile on his face, DeJohn was just about to doze.

"I gotta go." Tiffani sat up, made some attempt to push her hair into place.

"In the morning. I'll get you a car." He pulled her close.

"I drag in tomorrow looking like this—won't be a secret what I did all night."

DeJohn lounged against a stack of pillows. They looked at each other, laughed. "Bet somebody will be jealous."

"Should be." Tiffani nestled in closer. "Mmmm. But your season's almost over." She traced lazy loops on his chest with her finger. "What will you do then?"

"Hadn't thought about it." He closed his eyes. "Guess I'll go back home—"

"Until when?" She kept the words purring, but her brain had snapped back into gear.

"Season starts in April."

"That's forever."

DeJohn squeezed an arm around her waist. "Guess I shouldn't leave you here by yourself that long, huh?"

"Uh-huh. I could get very lonely."

"And this city is pretty interesting."

"Every day."

They played getting to know you the rest of the fall. Through school Tiffani stayed connected to what was happening in town and brought DeJohn into the loop—clubs, concerts, even a museum or two. They met other athletes, rappers, radio DJs, actors, and a mogul or two. You never knew what a New York night might bring, and while he wasn't a luminary yet, DeJohn was on the "up-and-coming" list.

And when he missed his mama's cooking, Tiffani could handle that too—she'd been in the pots since she was young and she'd get dinner ready for herself and her mom. DeJohn liked the cozy arrangement, except she would never stay the whole night. "I need my own stuff in the morning," she told him.

Before the end of the year, management made it official. Based on the talent he showed in his stint with the team in September, they wanted DeJohn in training camp in the spring. "But you need to work on your upper-body strength, put on some muscle," Marcus advised him. It took more heft to blow one out of the park in the big leagues. "Eat some steak. Pump some iron over the winter." Still Marcus and Rich were able to negotiate a $500,000 first-year salary, a cut above the $300,000 rookie minimum . . .

. . . which Tiffani, DeJohn's newest adviser, thought was OK, but . . . "I don't know. Seems like it should be at least a million."

The Ell & Me Company gave Tiffani a nice bonus for the holidays. She wanted to show her appreciation on a budget, so Tiffani hunted down some beautiful remnants—a red tapestry for Pat and an aquamarine brocade for Gayle. She designed a tote bag, a simple square with coordinated lining and braided leather handles. The pockets for cell phones, keys, and other paraphernalia were near the bottom—the better to discourage pickpockets. She had one of the design students run up the bags in exchange for editing his term paper on how innovations in fabric composition influence design. And they were a big hit as presents.

Christmas break was the hardest. While DeJohn was home with his family, she got a reality wake-up. The dorms were closed and she was reduced to the Cinderella quarters in her aunt's kitchen again. It was not a merry Christmas, except for the charm bracelet DeJohn sent. There was a gold baseball with #14 on the back, but what she really loved was the T in pavé diamonds, her very first diamonds. She had it on at midnight, with a silk nightgown hidden under her flannel bathrobe. And as the ball lit up and her neighbors shot off firecrackers and pistol rounds to ring it in, Tiffani vowed it would be a happy new year.

There was snow on the ground in New York when spring-training camp started for DeJohn in Florida. During spring break Tiffani requested her first minivacation from her duties with Pat.

"He's flying you to Florida?" Pat knew she didn't date much in college, but nobody she remembered had dates involving plane tickets and hotel rooms.

"Just for the week. I'll have my own room. In a different hotel."

Pat smiled to herself, wanted to say, *I'm not that old.*

Marcus was more skeptical when Pat told him that night. "This is an important year for him. He doesn't need the distraction."

"I'm sure you had your distractions while you were playing." She curled up on her side of the bed.

"Not during camp." Marcus turned out the light.

And called DeJohn the next day to talk him out of it. DeJohn assured him he could handle it.

Port St. Lucie was hardly South Beach. To Tiffani it felt

like the capital of Baseball Nation. The place was crawling with sports reporters and devoted fans who wanted the pre-season scoop. But she caught a few rays in the afternoons, went to the malls, just to see what was out there, what people were buying. She'd save enough time to get cute in time for dinner. He liked picking her up in his yellow 'Vette, riding around. One day they went looking for houses he liked. "Someplace I can keep my boat." Because he knew Marcus had a boat.

And DeJohn was pretty whupped by night, so they kept it low-key. He liked lounging in her room. It was pretty average as hotels go, but Tiffani got candles to make it feel more exotic. DeJohn would fall asleep pretty early, but he woke up early too, liked having Tiffani there in the morning to talk to, about what was on the schedule for the day, about how much he hated calisthenics, hated the drills, the weights. "Just let me play. That's what I'm good at."

"So say it. There are reporters everywhere. You're not shy about telling me how big you're gonna be. Tell them."

The flap didn't reach the papers until she got back. Reports quoted DeJohn as saying he was what the team needed to shake them out of lame, lazy play. The teammate who'd preceded him in right field took exception, and the ink was flying. DeJohn would call Tiffani to have her read the columns to him. Marcus made the trip down to smooth ruffled egos. "Your name isn't even on your locker yet. Speak with your bat and your mitt." He got DeJohn to pull back, rephrase, and clarify until all shook hands and the situation blew over. But DeJohn liked his name in print, standing out, being quoted—liked hearing Tiffani egg him on. He liked the way people looked at her when they were out together. She had style, good ideas. And by opening day the Realtor G&C recommended had helped Tiffani find an apartment with DeJohn's name on the lease.

It was a studio in Chelsea, second floor—not far from campus. White tulips were already coming up in the window box. Tiffani loved the wood floors, the white marble mantel, the recessed alcove where her bed would go. The two closets were small, but she could make space for whatever DeJohn wanted to leave. And it was all hers. No more roommates with weird tastes in music. No more cots.

Tiffani's new bed was delivered the day she moved in. DeJohn was away for a three-day series in Baltimore. So she told him how she couldn't wait for him to see the apartment, dusty rose with silvery accents. But she was glad she'd have a few nights alone to savor her shiny new keys, her fresh white sheets with platinum pin-tucks at the hems, and the real beginning of the life she was writing for herself.

CHAPTER 13

*We all make our own beds, and you can't
keep changing her sheets.*

R*amsey climbed the stairs, pushed open* the door, and reentered the world. August, in all its glory, clung to the city like wet wool—heavy, hot, and oily. And the din of traffic, generators, air conditioners, and people was always a shock after he'd been in the cool, dry quiet of the church basement—whichever church it was. Some days he went back to Brooklyn after his shift, others he stayed in Manhattan, but finishing at two left plenty of idle time. He filled most of it at meetings and in the library—he really loved the Internet, you could find out almost anything, about almost anybody. But Tuesdays were good because his meeting was only a few blocks away from Twenty-third and Fifth.

Dodging hordes of cell-phoning pedestrians dashing down Broadway, Ramsey made his way to the coffee shop across from the Toy Building and found his favorite booth by the window empty. He checked his watch, ordered his usual—coffee and chocolate cake—and scanned the fifteen floors of windows wondering, as he did every time, which was theirs. He never went inside—never even checked out the lobby directory. He was still careful. Very careful. Even though he was hardly recognizable to anyone who had known him before.

Gayle wore a beige linen tank dress and carried a turquoise tote with flowers brimming from the top. Pat came out right behind her. It was a little after six. They both laughed at some shared story, then climbed in a livery car that was waiting in front of the building. And they were gone. Ramsey paid his tab and headed back out into the heat. The library was still open.

* * *

"This can't be it?" The driver had stopped in front of a dingy warehouse in the shadow of the Williamsburg Bridge. Gayle surveyed the block, lined with grimy factory buildings. Vanessa had said it was a performance space and Gayle was expecting a theater—which this was not.

"The number is right there." Pat pointed to the peel-and-stick hardware-store digits clinging to the frame above the battered gray steel door, propped open by a broken cinder block.

A New York sampler pack of alternative-arts types loitered around the entrance. Pat and Gayle had dressed down for the occasion, but they still stuck out like nuns at a biker bar. A young woman, with lapis blue streaks accenting jet-black hair, collected their ten dollars and handed them programs. "First right. You can sit anywhere."

It took a moment for Gayle's eyes to adjust from the summer twilight they left outside to the subterranean black of the theater—brick walls, ceiling, a scaffold fronting as a catwalk, were all painted matte black, like a Stealth plane. Pinpoints of light illuminated the floor, a patch of ebony-enameled cement with just enough scars and chips to legitimize its status as a stage. Right angles of tape marked the outermost corners of the ersatz proscenium.

"Look how many people," Gayle whispered, sounding surprised and relieved. "It's a nice crowd." The audience was a perfect slice of New York City pie, at least the artsy-subculture-flavored one—dance gypsies, young Wall Street bulls with power ties undone, old sixties radicals, theater junkies, SoHo fashionistas, and if they were lucky, a reviewer or two from some underground weekly whose write-up might tweak the curiosity of an angel investor.

"Up-and-coming artistes have quite a network—they spread the word, keep the seats filled. Events like this are happening in a dozen places tonight." Pat's roommate from Princeton was an actress, so Pat had been to more than her share of avant-garde productions in no-name black-box spaces like this one.

"Maybe it's a good thing Tiffani couldn't make it." At the last minute, Tiffani begged off. DeJohn was flying her to Denver to keep him company. "This isn't what I was expecting when I invited her." Gayle felt more than a little out of her element.

Pat knew that to Gayle, theater meant Broadway, Lincoln Center, or at the very least somewhere with a stage and a curtain. This concrete cavern had neither. "I bet she'd have gotten a kick out of it. Some classmate of hers might have done the costumes. Besides, she and DeJohn seem to be getting around all over town these days. Marcus and I ran into them at a Schomburg event last week. She gave one of her totes to a magazine editor I know."

"Going to school, coming to us twice a week, making her bags—you can't say she's afraid of work." They minced their way up makeshift risers, until they found two seats together. Gayle brushed off the folding chair with her program, making sure the spots weren't a recent deposit from the previous occupant. "They need to turn up the air-conditioning." Beads of sweat trickled down the middle of her back. "These will be wilted before I can give them to her." Gayle had a bouquet of summer wildflowers in her tote.

Pat laughed. "AC? Not. This is a rent-a-space. They barely make enough to keep the lights on." She took off her linen jacket and folded it on her lap. "Bet it's freezing in the winter." She fanned herself with the program. "Nervous?"

"For Vanessa? Of course." Gayle had seen her dance a hundred times—recitals, school shows—but this was her first professional gig, even though there was still no pay involved. Gayle was proud. Still not happy about the school situation, but maybe Vanessa was right. *What if this is her time?* A dancer's window only opens a crack. "She's dancing a piece Julian choreographed for her."

Pat stopped fanning, examined the program. "She's after intermission." She put the program down. "So, do you like him any better?"

"I don't know. I don't see him much. Her either for that matter. Between classes and practice, she's barely home. I will say she's been in a much better mood. But I'm also not sure I want to know if he's the reason. She hasn't said their relationship has changed."

"Would she?"

Gayle shook her head as the lights went out. In the pitch-darkness, the heat felt hotter, and the rustling, throat-clearing, seat-adjusting, breathing, and whispering sounded louder. All of which provided enough distraction for the girl with the blued-black hair to take center stage unnoticed.

When the spotlight came on, she introduced herself, welcomed guests, thanked them for supporting the nascent genius of Julian Drake's Kinesthetica. There was modest applause, then darkness. First, thundering djembe drums and a high-pitched whine—like a radio signal in search of the right frequency—then the plaintive wail of bagpipes joined the cacophony and seven dancers sprang into view. For the next hour they spun, slid, leapt, and catapulted in pairs, trios, quartets, and ensemble in what their announcer had called a one-world fusion of classic ballet, Afro-Asian-inspired modern dance, and mime.

"That was exhausting." The dancers, the rising heat in the airless space, and her own nerves made Gayle feel like a hot, wet mess when intermission arrived.

"It was certainly different." Pat stood, hoping to find a little air somewhere she was missing. She didn't. She tried to be inconspicuous as she jiggled her legs, hoping her pants would unstick from the backs of her thighs. They didn't.

Gayle dabbed at the perspiration on the back of her neck with a tissue. "I wonder what Nessa's piece is like."

They didn't have to wait long to find out. The music for her pas de deux, "Antediluvian Rumpus," was both mournful and pulsating. Vanessa, wearing a skin-toned leotard with a strategically placed, perfect triangle of fur, was dragged onto the stage by Julian—bare-chested, the crotch of his tights sporting a suspiciously conspicuous bulge. She had said something to Gayle about an homage to the Parisian Apache dancers from the twenties, but to Gayle it looked like assault. The piece was a mind-numbing cycle of raw aggression—followed seamlessly by raw sex. Vanessa and Julian pounded, kicked, flung, and wrestled each other, then unleashed an equally unrestrained sexual barrage. Gayle's fingers dug into Pat's arm. "What is she doing?" The hissed whisper scratched her throat. Julian mounted her from the front, from behind, slamming, humping, hands probing her body, seeking and finding her compliant. "How could he?" How could Vanessa let him? Gayle had no answers, no words. She found Pat's hand and held on. Trying to get through it, praying for the music to end.

When Vanessa reversed the dance, arching her back, thrusting herself onto Julian, tears burned Gayle's eyes, and a thick, sick feeling enveloped her. But she could still see—not whether Vanessa was graceful, skilled, accomplished. Only that her daughter was having virtual intercourse on a stage in front of a hundred strangers.

Pat wanted to go down there, kick Julian in that bulge, and snatch Vanessa offstage by her ponytail. Instead she squeezed Gayle's hand. She looked so devastated when the lights came up—wiped out, heartbroken.

"I don't know what to say." Gayle looked at her hands in her lap while Julian and company took their bows to measured applause.

"Let's go." Pat took the lead, weaved their way out.

"I have to say something."

"No, you don't. Not tonight." She walked Gayle to the waiting Town Car. "Go home. I'll talk to her."

"What are you going to say?" Gayle couldn't stop trembling.

"I don't know. But I'll call you."

"Give her these." Gayle handed Pat the flowers.

Pat wanted to scream, *Are you nuts?!* but she took the bouquet, closed the car door. As soon as Gayle drove off, Pat dumped the flowers in the trash can outside the theater door and went to find Vanessa. Pat spied her, now clad in a modest warm-up suit, towel tucked into the neck, emerging from backstage.

"Hi, Auntie Pat." She put her duffel bag down, straddled it. "Mom in the bathroom?" Vanessa smiled innocently.

"No. Your mother is on her way home." Pat took two steps closer and leveled her gaze at Vanessa. "You are eighteen years old, which means you have the right to make your own decisions about your life—even if they're stupid, like dropping out of school."

Vanessa opened her mouth as if she had something to say, but Pat's glare made it clear it was not her turn yet.

"And for reasons I don't get, your mother has decided to support you in those decisions. I don't agree, but that's not my business, so I let it go. But this is my business. Just so you get some context here—your mother is my best friend. We were watching out for each other long before there was a you. And I will not let you off the hook for what you did to her tonight."

"What are you—"

"Don't play dumb. You know what your mother was expecting, and you know what you showed her. And you knew it was an ambush. But what I want to know is, why?"

"It was creative expression—Julian's poem for me." Vanessa crossed her arms, looked off to the side.

"Look at me when I talk to you." Pat never raised her voice, waited for Vanessa to shift her eyes. "I'm not a prude and I recognize art when I see it. What I saw was soft-core porn. You knew it would hurt your mother, and you didn't have the decency to warn her."

"I don't have to listen to this." Vanessa turned away.

Pat gripped her arm. "You will not walk away, pout in a corner." Her voice, though still barely audible to those around them, now dropped to a low growl. "You are a mean, spiteful, ungrateful girl. I don't know what you perceive is the great wrong your mother did that requires you to pay her back like this. And frankly, I don't care. But I do care about her. I care about you—even though you don't seem to care about yourself. You are not the only kid whose childhood didn't work out the way she wanted it to. People leave. People die. People get sick. Things change. It's not your mother's fault. It's not about fault. It's about growing and going on."

"This isn't about her." Vanessa stared defiantly at Pat. "This is about me and what I want to do with my life."

Pat struggled to keep from laughing out loud. "Well, isn't it just always about you? But tonight—this is about her. You will go home. And even though I can't make you mean it, you will say you're sorry and it will sound like you mean it." Pat turned to go, turned back. "You can take this advice or leave it, but don't follow Julian blindly. Keep your eyes open or you might end up down the wrong road and you won't even know how you got there. I've done it. So has your mother. Believe me, it's not a good place."

Angry tears welled in Vanessa's eyes as she watched Pat go out the door.

"You OK?" Julian had watched the conversation, waited till it was over to emerge from the wings. He draped an arm around her shoulders.

"She has no right to talk to me like that."

He kissed Vanessa's temple. "Don't let her rattle your chain, love." Julian's accent—a curious mix of patrician Connecticut, cockney twang, a hint of the South with an overlay of City gritty—was as unidentifiable as his ethnicity. His jet-black hair was thick but the wavy texture unknowable. His skin wasn't distinctly black or white—he was some olive, golden, omni-ethnic mélange, but all he told Vanessa about his parents was that they never loved anyone but themselves and he hadn't seen them in five years.

"Auntie Pat my ass! She's not my family. I don't have any family."

"That makes two of us then. Orphans of the storm." He leaned close, his words touching her ear, drifting down her neck. "They don't understand us—what we do." Julian ran his hand down Vanessa's arm. "I told you this would happen. Didn't I? But for us, it's a calling. It is essential. We can't blame them because they can't see the art."

Vanessa let her head rest on his shoulder, closed her eyes.

"It is always the artists who struggle—against the puritanical, the plodding, the myopic, and powerful." He came round in front of her. "Then what happens?"

"After we're dead they say we were brilliant, ahead of our time." Vanessa smiled as she repeated the oft-heard lesson.

"Your mom is mad. Your auntie is mad. It's because they can't see you. Not like I do." Julian kissed her forehead, picked up Vanessa's bag. "Did I tell you my next piece will be based on *The Scarlet Letter*? It will be called 'Bloody A'—and you of course are my Hester Prynne."

Two days later, Vanessa showed up at Ell & Me midafternoon, breezed past Lindy with a quick hello, never slowed her pace at Cassidy's desk, and walked right into Gayle's office. "Sorry to interrupt your day."

"It's OK." Gayle put down the Bradley Curtis storyboards she had been going over. Things had been tense since the night of the performance, but they hadn't been arguing about it. Gayle hoped that performance was something she'd gotten out of her system, like rotten eggs, and the less said about it the better.

"I decided it would be simpler this way. But it probably won't." Vanessa shifted her weight from one foot to the other.

"Sit."

"I won't be that long." Vanessa took a deep breath. "I'm moving—out. Moved actually. This morning after you left."

"What?"

"Don't freak, OK? But we—I—wanted to skip the big hysterical scene, which is the same reason I came here instead of telling you at home."

Hands flat on her desk, Gayle needed to hold on to something solid. "You can't be serious."

"As a heart attack." Vanessa reached in her purse, dumped her keys in front of her mother. "So now, your *mean, ungrateful, spiteful* girl—I think I covered all the terms Auntie Pat used—is out of your hair. I can't make you crazy if I'm not there, can I?"

"What are you talking about?" All Gayle knew is that Pat had called right after she spoke to Vanessa and told her they'd talked. Vanessa came home later that night, said she was sorry. The apology felt halfhearted, but Gayle took it as a good sign.

"It really doesn't matter. Julian and I are together. It's what you've been expecting all along, isn't it? So you were right. Anyway, we're living in his place in Williamsburg." Vanessa handed her mother a sheet of notebook paper folded in quarters. "I'll be using my cell phone, but this is my new address. You can mail my allowance check here."

Dizzy, stunned into silence, Gayle played the frayed edges of the paper with her thumbnail. She did not open it. She couldn't breathe. She couldn't think. She felt her heart leap from her chest to her throat—the beat in her neck thudding, so hard, so fast. Couldn't Vanessa see it?—until it dropped into a rhythm half its own.

"So that's it? Nothing to say? This was easier than I expected." Vanessa kissed her mother on the cheek. "Bye." She pirouetted and was out the door.

For the next hour Gayle just sat there, the storyboards exactly where she'd put them when Vanessa showed up. The phone didn't ring. Lindy didn't pop in. Cassidy didn't buzz.

Pat didn't e-mail from next door. It was as though Vanessa came in, made her speech, and sucked all the air from the room when she walked out, leaving Gayle in a vacuum that could no longer support life. Gayle didn't realize she was, in fact, awake and alive. Not until a pigeon swooped in and landed on the window ledge. She finally unfolded the paper in her hand and knew she had not been dreaming. She dropped it on her desk, got up, opened her door, heard the chatter and buzz—voices, phones, faxes, copier—business as usual. She walked the ten feet to Pat's door, tapped, and poked her head in.

Pat waved her inside, held up a finger to let Gayle know she'd be off the phone in a minute. Gayle wasn't counting, but it was actually less. "Marcus. DeJohn shot his mouth off in front of some reporter again." Then Pat actually looked at Gayle. "You look like hell. Are you coming down with something?"

Gayle perched on the edge of the chair across from Pat's desk. "What did you say to Vanessa the other day?"

"After our night in Kinesthetica hell? I told her to stop making torturing you her hobby."

"Did you tell her she was spiteful and ungrateful?"

"And I think I said mean too. She's been bullying you for years. It was time for her to get pushed back."

"Oh, OK." Gayle stared at the poster behind Pat, from the first Ell book they had published together—Ell in her big shoes, helping the mama crocodile rescue her baby from the powerful Zambezi River currents.

"Gayle?" Pat waited a second.

Gayle got up. "OK." But it wasn't. When was the last

time her life had really been OK? If she was ready to be honest with herself, she would have to go back before Ramsey— to the time when her parents were still in charge of it. When her mistakes were small and didn't come with such a high price tag. If she was ready to be honest with herself, she would have to remember how much she loved those big price tags. The more it cost, the more it showed—what? Mostly how much she had paid, not what it was worth. But this price was so steep. If she was ready to be honest with herself, she could admit Vanessa wasn't hers forever. Gayle's departure from home had been just as abrupt, just as cruel. Gayle knew that through the natural evolution of things, Vanessa would find her own way, her own life. Just not like this. She had no skills, no education. And if she was ready to be honest with herself, deep down Gayle also knew Vanessa's dreams were greater than her talent.

But Gayle wasn't ready.

So for the next two weeks Gayle came and went as if nothing had changed. She got to the office at her usual time, gave no hint that her world had been radically altered. There were now more than one hundred Ell products, not including books, available by catalog and online. They were preparing to celebrate the Ell doll's third birthday, and there was so much to be done, it was easy for Gayle to let herself be consumed by it. Vanessa even called her at work a couple of times, so nothing seemed wrong to any who might have noticed.

Not until Gayle sat down to pay bills at the beginning of the month did she begin to unravel. She wrote out Vanessa's allowance check as usual. Gayle's hand shook as she addressed an envelope to the street and number on that piece of note-book paper she had folded and unfolded a thousand times.

But the simple act of dropping that envelope in the mail-box on the corner on her way to work—Gayle pulled the handle, and before she intended, the white rectangle slid from her fingers. It was gone. And she was inconsolable, holding the mailbox, sobbing as passersby averted their eyes or stared at the sidewalk freak show, relishing the good story they'd have to share over coffee when they got to the office.

"Are you quite all right?" The man's voice was deep, soothing, but the little dog yipped at his feet. "Well, no—it is quite apparent you are not." He pried Gayle's hands loose. "There, there. Let's get you home." With his tiny orange fur-ball leading the way, the big man with wiry, black hair gen-tled Gayle away from the box and guided her back to their building.

Since Gayle didn't appear injured, the doorman used her emergency contact numbers. When Pat showed up twenty minutes later, she found Gayle still sitting in the lobby. Dwarfed by a wingback chair, her face sad and tear-streaked, she looked like a little girl waiting to hear what her punish-ment would be for some childish infraction. Pat recognized the man who hovered nearby from when she'd lived in the building—third floor. He tapped his fingertips together and explained that he felt Gayle was too distraught to go upstairs by herself.

Pat thanked him for being so attentive and led Gayle to the elevator. "Is Vanessa OK?" But Gayle just kept saying she was sorry, over and over. Pat didn't know what for, so she didn't know what to expect. Had someone broken into the apartment? Had Gayle finally had enough sass and hit Vanessa in the mouth with her shoe? But when Pat opened the door, everything looked fine. She steered Gayle into the living room, sat next to her on the sofa. "You have to tell me what's wrong. Do you want me to call Vanessa? Maybe she should come home."

"No!"

"OK. Then tell me what happened." Pat stood up, noted that the apartment smelled a little funny, so she opened the patio door. "I'll make some tea and you can tell me what's going on." Pat headed to the kitchen before Gayle could protest.

What the . . . ? It looked as though they'd had a party—a big one. Dishes caked with dried bits of food, containers—pizza boxes, Chinese-food cartons, frozen-dinner trays, wrappers, bags and boxes from cookies, bread, crackers, chips—were piled in the sink, on the stove, counter, and stools. *Gayle, who cleans before the cleaning lady comes? Gayle, who can't go to bed with dishes in the sink?* Even if Rosie took her mop and feather duster and walked out, Gayle would never let it get like this.

Pat headed back to the living room. "OK, what is going on? You have to tell me." She knew it wasn't subtle, gentle, or coddling. But their best-friendship wasn't like that—never had been, no point going there now. Even the first time they were separated, when Pat was swept into the foster care system, the notes Gayle wrote to cheer her up had quarters and dimes taped to them—something Pat could use—not bunnies and butterflies. Their friendship had been to hell and back again and they loved each other like blood. They just weren't pink hearts and pinky swears BFFs.

Gayle looked up at Pat. Her face was unreadable.

"Did the cleaning woman quit? The kitchen looks like you've been feeding an army and no one was assigned KP. And it smells kinda funky in here too."

Gayle shook her head. "She's gone."

"She didn't quit but she's gone? What are you talking about?"

"Nessa." The story came in welled-up fits and agitated starts, ending with Vanessa's keys on the desk. "They're still in my purse."

"This happened two weeks ago? Why didn't you tell me?"

Gayle shrugged like a six-year-old caught in a lie. "At first—I was mad at you—because of the things you said to her."

"After that idiotic dance program?"

Gayle nodded. "But I really know it's my fault."

Pat sat next to Gayle again. "I'll tell you the same thing I told her—it's not about fault."

"But it is. Let's start when she was a child, and I was in my own la-di-da world, pretending the sky wasn't falling. Then I let Ramsey convince me it wasn't, even when it hit me in the head. I have been steadily making mistakes, and it looks like she watched me and learned."

"She could have picked up the good things too, like how hard you worked to turn your life around. And that all you ever wanted was for her to be happy and love you back. I'm sorry Gayle, but Vanessa's got a lot more learning to do. We all make our own beds, and you can't keep changing her sheets. She has to do that herself."

"But I'm supposed to be able to protect her." Gayle teared up again.

"Not after she has officially declared herself grown. And when you move out with a man, that's pretty much what you're saying. I know you're going to tell me I'm not a mother. And you're right. But it looks like our girl just went out and bought herself some sheets, and she's gonna have to sleep on them. With Mr. Julian."

"She said he told her she was his muse and they were going to be famous." Gayle accepted the tissue Pat handed her. "Even I know he's full of shit."

For her to swear, Pat knew Gayle had reached her outer limits. "Of course he is. She'll find out. Just like we did. The hard way."

"I don't want her to get hurt."

"You can't stop that. Nobody can. We all knew Ramsey was a snake, but you couldn't hear it. And you damn sure couldn't see it when it was right in front of you. You would have thought the same thing about PJ—if you'd ever met him. Because we can always see more clearly when it's somebody else's cobra dancing to the music.

Pat wanted to tell Gayle everything would be fine. Vanessa would weather this just as they had, even though Pat wasn't convinced it was true. But this didn't seem like the time. "So—you're going to call Miss Vanessa and make a lunch date, maybe one of those sprouts-and-weeds places she likes. You'll let her tell you how it's going. She'll lie, but at least you can watch her do it. She'll invite you over because she'll want to show off her grown-upedness. You'll take her a house-warming present—because what else can you do, except pray?

But the first thing we're going to do is clean up that kitchen."

Pat called the office to check in. Found there were no fires to put out and told Lindy she and Gayle would be out the rest of the day. Then, side by side, they worked together establishing an easy rhythm, filling the sink, loading the dishwasher, gathering trash, setting the mess to rights. At least the mess in the kitchen.

"I'll be back." Pat headed to the bathroom.

The door to Vanessa's room was ajar, and mostly it looked the same as it always did, including stars on the ceiling, tie-dyed mosquito netting over the bed, but Pat knew the closet and drawers were as empty as Gayle felt right now. When Pat reached the bathroom, the odor greeted her as soon as she opened the door. She didn't see anything, but the smell was distinct, unmistakable. Sick. Sour. Too-much-to-drink, worship-the-porcelain-goddess, college-bathroom sick. Pat did what she came to do and left quickly. On her way back to the kitchen, something made her stop outside Gayle's room—the room that had been hers when this apartment had been hers. The door was closed, and she paused, hand on the knob, debating whether she should invade her friend's privacy or mind her own business. It took a long moment to make up her mind.

"Are you sure you're all right?" Pat came back into the kitchen. "It's kinda ripe in the bathroom."

Startled, Gayle stopped unloading the dishwasher. *Does the smell stay in the air?* "Uh—I had kind of a stomach thing last night. I don't know if it was a bug, or something didn't agree with me." *Does it get in the towels or the shower curtain? How come I didn't notice? Did Vanessa smell it?* She always deodorized and sanitized when Vanessa was home, but it hadn't mattered since Gayle was alone. "I thought I'd cleaned that up." She hoped Pat couldn't hear the panic in her voice.

"I guess you did. I mean it's not all over the place or anything, but if your best friend doesn't tell you something stinks, who will?" Pat laughed.

"Nobody I guess."

"Listen, we've blown half the day, why don't we polish off the rest?"

"I'm sorry. I know we have so much to do at work and here I am falling apart because my kid is growing up."

"Forget work. We could go to the movies or to a museum—you know, the stuff we all say we'll do when we have time. Come on. It'll be fun. Get out of here and get your mind off your troubles for a little while."

"I feel like I've been in a fight—even if it was only with myself. I think I'll finish cleaning up, maybe take a nap. Then hopefully I'll have the energy to call Vanessa like you said. I'll be fine. And back in the office bright and early tomorrow."

"You sure? I can stick around."

"Don't be ridiculous—I'm in charge of that today. Go. I'll call you later." Gayle ushered Pat out of the kitchen. "Thanks. I needed that."

"No prob."

And they hugged, which they hadn't done in a long while. They saw each other almost daily, talked most of the days they didn't, but they rarely hugged, so they lingered a moment in each other's arms, feeling a kind of comfort that they could only get from each other.

Then Pat left with the nagging feeling there was something more to do, to worry about. She took out her cell when she got to the lobby. "Hey. It's me. Believe it or not, I'm out of the office. The sun is shining and I'm thinking about playing hooky for the rest of the day." Pat knew she was taking a chance. "Care to join me?" He was as busy as she was—with multiple clients and their needs to manage, maybe busier. But she needed to check out for a while, talk, think, be. She held her breath, hoped for a yes. "Great. The café at the Boat House. Half hour?"

It was a perfect September afternoon—neither too warm or too cool. Huge puffy clouds sailed high in a clear blue sky, and that early-autumn light cast long, crisp shadows on the sidewalks and buildings. It was the kind of day that made you glad New York was a walking city. So Pat headed west, then down Fifth Avenue along Central Park, replaying the morning, until she turned in at the Seventy-second Street entrance. Was it only Vanessa's sudden departure that had triggered Gayle's meltdown? What was with that kitchen? It seemed like way more food than anybody would have eaten in only two weeks—after all, Gayle wasn't even home during the day. And then there was the bathroom thing. None of it made sense. The lunch crowd had thinned and Pat was sitting at a table out on the deck when he arrived.

"Glad you could get away." Pat smiled, reached out, squeezed his hand—her right, his left, not a handshake but it was contact, a connection she needed.

"Me too." Drew pulled a chair next to hers. "But I know you. It takes more than the lure of a sunny afternoon for you to decide to ditch work—especially with Christmas only three months away." He folded his hands on the table, looked her right in the eye. "So what's up?"

"Let's walk." She led the way down toward to the water. "It's Gayle." Pat knew there was no point holding back—it's why she'd called him. Over the past three years, which sometimes seemed like forever, and other times like yesterday, Drew had become more than part of her day. He was her refuge. The person she went to when she was wrestling with a problem and couldn't talk to the people—Marcus, Gayle—in her life, mostly because the problem had something to do with them. Pat couldn't put her finger on exactly when Drew had assumed that role, but she did know how. He didn't need her to hold him up, to keep him together, to reinforce and reassure. There was no history to tread lightly around. No sensitive issues to gloss over. No tightrope of tension to try to cross. No egos to bolster or fears to assuage. She didn't have to do anything. He didn't think she worked too hard. He talked. He listened. He understood. He helped. And, he was always there when she needed him to be.

Pat knew she was dancing around the fringes of something that might prove perilous, but she couldn't stop herself. She liked Drew, a lot. But everything about this was wrong. They had a professional relationship. She was married. He was not. She was black. He was not. She was older—not by more than five years, but older. Still—when she couldn't see him, she thought about him, looked forward to their conversations and e-mails. And for reasons she had yet to discern, Drew was content—not only to dance with her, but to let her name the tune. Once she asked him why. He said sometimes you don't get to choose. "People happen in your life. They move in or pass through. You can't *make* it be either, but you have to enjoy whatever there is." So there was no promise—of anything—and they never went further than she led them. Which as far as Pat was concerned was close enough to the edge to be exhilarating, but not dangerous. Although she did stop at offering him a position, director of marketing, with Ell & Me. She thought about it long and hard—even discussed it with Gayle. In the end, she decided that while the temptation that would come with having him around every day might be greater, so would access, and she liked the feeling of anticipation that came with the way things were too much to give it up.

They left the water and wandered up the path toward Belvedere Castle. "Think she has an eating disorder?" Drew asked when Pat finished the story of her morning.

"That's for neurotic teenagers." Gayle was about the same size she had always been, not like one of those skeletal sixteen-year-olds obsessed about being skinny. "Gayle is almost forty." Pat wandered over to a bench.

"I'm not so sure the demographic is that narrow, Pat." Drew sat beside her, leaned forward, resting his arms on his knees. "There's a lot of new research."

"OK. But they're looking at . . . I'm sorry, they're looking at white women."

Drew looked at her. "Oh, come on, Pat. It's not about being white or black or even necessarily female. And it's not about eating either." He sat back, stretched his legs out, crossed them at the ankles, and clasped his hands behind his head. "It's not about food, it's about emotions. Are you going to sit there and tell me that black women are exempt because you're strong and can handle anything?"

Pat didn't know what to say. Although she and Drew talked about nearly everything, race—except as it applied to

marketing strategies for Ell—hadn't been one of their sub-
jects. Was it because race, religion, and politics were off the
current list of PC conversations in the workplace? Did they
have an unspoken acknowledgment of their racial difference
as irrelevant? Or had they chosen to avoid the entire topic?
*And what does he think he knows about black women and what
we can handle?* "I know it's emotional, Drew. But Gayle isn't
crazy. I know her better than anybody, and if something like
that was wrong with her—I'd know it." *Wouldn't I?*

"Would you?" Drew said it quietly. Gave Pat time to let
the question sink in.

She wondered, not for the first time, if he'd read her
thoughts.

"Aren't there things we can't even tell our best friends—
or our spouses?" He turned to face her, hung his arm over the
back of the bench.

"I don't know—"

"Not to mention the stuff we can't even admit to
ourselves?

"Maybe." *Like I've never told Marcus about the baby I didn't
have.* She raked her fingers through her hair, leaned forward,
put her head in her hands. "I don't know what I'm supposed
to do."

Drew pulled her up, kept his arm around her shoulders.
"You'll watch for signs. There's tons of information if you
need it. We'll keep an eye on her."

Pat thought about pulling away, but this time, this once,
she let herself relax, allowed her head to rest against his chest.

"It'll be OK." He held her a little tighter.

But Pat wasn't so sure.

. . . all she could do was watch the remake and root for a different ending.

*C*all Vanessa. What will she say? Suppose she hangs up? *Does she hate me?* Just in from a morning and afternoon of busywork, errands, and diversions, Gayle put on the kettle, shuffled through her apartment, repeating the chant, gathering the nerve to dial. She'd been picking up the phone, putting it down, since she got home from work on Friday—just like the Friday before. Ten p.m. was too late. Seven a.m. was too early. The longer she waited, the deeper the hole, the higher the climb. Gayle had been putting it off since Vanessa left, expected she would call after she got the first check. But she didn't. Eleven days ago Gayle had mailed the second, to the dismay of all those who considered themselves involved. "She has to learn to fend for herself." "Would you work if somebody paid your bills?" "How can you tell if she's serious?"

But Gayle could not let Vanessa be without money. Her own money. It gave her the chance to walk away—if she ever wanted. At this point, Gayle just wanted to know she was all right, maybe even happy, as slippery as that was. And she needed to extend some kind of olive branch to Julian, at least enough to keep him from becoming a wedge, because it was clear he was the boyfriend, the wizard, the guru, the one who took Vanessa's breath away. Gayle had been there, done that, paid the price, but all she could do was watch the remake and root for a different ending.

The kettle sang a mournful note, and Gayle brewed a cup of Moroccan mint tea. It was still so hard to be home alone, in control. There was no one to be strong for, or at least to pretend for. But when she let down her guard, Pat had come close to discovering Gayle's nasty little secret. Too close. It was too humiliating to admit, even to someone she had known her whole life. Even to someone who loved her.

Shortly after the day of the mailbox meltdown, Pat had come into her office, fidgeted about nothing in particular, looked out the window, then asked, sort of sideways, "Are you in trouble? I mean about eating. I mean—is there something you need to tell me?"

"No." It was the first thing, the only thing, Gayle could say. "What are you talking about?"

"Nothing. I don't know. I was worried."

Gayle was a grown woman. She had to act like one. She didn't want Pat to worry, didn't want to disappoint. And Gayle was trying so hard not to give in. But there had been slips, because nothing made her feel more calm, more in charge. And she still hadn't talked to her daughter.

Pick up the phone. Gayle needed to get on with it. Every week Pat would ask, "Did you call yet? Do you want me to do it? What are you waiting for?" Besides, turkey and stuffing were in the stores and she and Vanessa had never spent Thanksgiving apart.

Eleven digits, and every one of them burned as she pressed the button. Gayle waited for the connection, barely breathing. Vanessa's first phone had the opening of *The Sleeping Beauty* as a ringtone. It changed depending on her favorite dance theme of the moment, and it made Gayle's eyes well, realizing she didn't know what music it was now. She just hoped Vanessa would—

"Hello, Mother."

Gayle couldn't place the inflection—warmer than "Why are you bothering me?" but not quite "I'm happy to hear from you." There was water running in the background. Gayle wondered what Vanessa was doing, what it looked like in the room where she stood.

"It's good to hear your voice." Sappy beginning, but true. "Did you get the check—"

"Yep. It got here fine."

There was an awkward silence on the end of that instead of a thank-you, so Gayle moved on. "How's Julian?"

"He's OK. I'm a little busy right now. We're having people over."

Gayle hadn't seen her daughter's place yet, but others would be there, eating, drinking, laughing. *Don't give in.* "I won't keep you. I'd like to see you. See your place. Whenever is good for you."

The water stopped, another long pause. "I work three nights a week, hostessing at this place down the block. They make really authentic brick-oven pizza."

Vanessa had never had a job. *Maybe it's a step.* "I could come in the afternoon—if that's better." Gayle was not allowing for the possibility of no.

"Um, what about Tuesday, around three. I should be in from—"

"Perfect."

There were only two days to wait, and this time Gayle was past the shock of the neighborhood. She wanted to bring a present, something for their home, their space, whatever they called it. Gayle didn't know what Julian did or liked yet, but she and Vanessa often drank tea. So she shopped for a teapot, something modern, edgy. She found a cast-iron one, with elegant, Japanese lines, the color and texture of a cantaloupe, with four matching tea bowls.

Gayle stayed home Tuesday morning, didn't want office chatter, or Pat's well-intentioned pep talks. She considered taking the train. "The L is just a few blocks away," Vanessa said so proudly. But Gayle opted for a car, so she could be alone with whatever mishmash of feelings came up. She called Miles Ahead in plenty of time. The dispatcher's voice seemed so familiar.

"Your pick up at two fifteen is confirmed. Car 387. And how have you been, Ms. Saunders? This is Miles. The limo from Newark Airport, three or four years ago . . ."

"I remember." *Amber skin, easygoing, dinner invitation . . . has it been that long?* She couldn't imagine where the time had gone. "You sure get around. Do you fix the cars too?"

"No, I draw the line there."

"I hope you're well."

"I'm excellent. Business is good and I'm a newlywed—two months."

Gayle could hear the smile in his voice. "Congratulations." She hoped she sounded happy. He seemed like such a good guy, he deserved to be happy. She just couldn't shake the hollow sensation inside, like she was missing what she never had.

The car was downstairs when she walked outside, carrying the gift bag. Vanessa's keys were in Gayle's purse, just in case she wanted them. In no time at all they pulled up outside the yellow clapboard house wedged between a muddy, unpaved truck-storage lot on one side and a nearly complete gray concrete monolith with a MODERN URBAN LIVING condos for-sale sign on the other. As soon as she rang the bell, she heard footsteps galloping on the stairs, and the door swung open.

Vanessa was always adopting some new getup; still, Gayle wasn't prepared for the transformation. The long, smooth curtain of hair had been chopped to a short, spiky orb that reminded Gayle of a porcupine or an asteroid. It was just hair, but somehow it made Gayle want to cry. Dark eye shadow and pale lips gave Vanessa a haunted look. Gayle wanted to snatch her and wash her face. An unfamiliar baggy, striped turtleneck, probably his, topped leggings and scuffy, platformed Mary Janes.

"Hi. Come on up." Vanessa sounded perky, acted as though nothing had changed.

So Gayle followed upstairs, past the pasta masterpiece— shells, wheels, penne, rigatoni, glued to the wall in a representation of the solar system.

The white walls in Vanessa and Julian's apartment had been attacked with slashes of red and black, as had the furniture, a hodgepodge of thrift-store finds as far as Gayle could tell. It reminded her of the first place they had lived in, after they lost the house. That was a nightmare she never expected either of them to revisit, let alone call home by choice. Despite the weirdness it was neat, more than she expected considering the usual condition of Vanessa's room and her aversion to chores.

"This is for you . . . and Julian." Gayle handed her the shopping bag. She could find those words, make them seem normal.

"Thanks. Um. Have a seat."

The gray corduroy couch was almost on the floor, so Gayle perched on the tooled-leather stool, watched Vanessa dig the teapot out of the froth of tissue paper. "This is so neat."

But Gayle noticed the smile came only from her lips, not her eyes, which seemed flat, not even defiant, or mischievous, but vacant. *It's the makeup.* "There are cups, and the tea you always liked."

"I'll make some."

In the kitchen, a slim galley with metal cabinets, circa 1952, that had been painted so often they barely closed, Vanessa put water on to boil in a blackened copper kettle and talked about the neighborhood—how stimulating it was. "It's real, you know. You get *wiejska* and pierogi from the Polish markets, where they still speak Polish."

Gayle knew you could get kielbasa and all kinds of other regional specialties in Yorkville, a Manhattan neighborhood within walking distance of their apartment, but Vanessa had never shown any interest. She barely ate meat.

Vanessa shook loose tea in the strainer, washed the cups. "Around here they make real espresso, served in glasses with sugar around the rim, not some frappé, latte, artificial rip-offs in throwaway containers. And there are all these cafés and bars and bookstores where people discuss real ideas, not mundane drivel."

Gayle was up for something real. "Tell me about your job."

Vanessa shrugged. "You know, the people are nice. They grow their own herbs. I'm learning Italian."

All of which was impersonal crap—not what Gayle needed to hear. "So, what made you cut your hair?" She figured she'd waited long enough to keep the question from being a flashpoint.

"Hair is a bourgeois emblem of femininity." Vanessa patted the pointy tips. "Hair is dead. I need to feel alive."

Gayle wanted to shake her, or laugh, but she clasped her hands in front of her. *It's only hair.* Then she went for what was really on her mind. "So . . . tell me about Julian."

Vanessa got the yogurt container where she kept sugar packets she pocketed from her restaurant. "What do you want me to say? He has insight into human beings—into our basic, kinetic connections."

Right. Gayle had no idea what that meant. "OK, but does he love kittens? Does he have ugly feet? Does he make you laugh? Does he have a good heart?" *Does he tell you who you are? Does he screw you till you don't know your name, or what you believe or how to say no?* Those were the real questions, but she didn't know how to ask them.

Before Vanessa answered, boiling water sputtered from the kettle spout. She bunched a dish towel around the handle, poured water in the teapot to steep the leaves. "I can't explain it. He knows things. Teaches me things. My dancing is freer since I've been with him." Cups on the counter, Vanessa poured one for her mother, then one for herself, stirred in sugar.

"Are you still taking class every day?"

"I don't need it as much. I train with the company." Vanessa lifted the cup to her lips, but it slipped through her fingers, spilled hot, sweet liquid down the front of her sweater, then crashed to the floor.

Vanessa yelled.

"Oh my God—" Gayle sprang to yank Vanessa's sweater and camisole over her head to keep the searing water and fabric away from her skin. Gayle grabbed a dish towel, soaked it in cool water, and bathed her stomach where the water had landed. "Is that better?" Gayle wrapped an arm around her waist.

"I'm OK." Vanessa's voice cracked. "I'm so stupid."

"It was just a mistake." Gayle stifled a smirk when she saw the bloom of a hickey on Vanessa's neck, but then she noticed the circlet of black-and-blue fingertips around Vanessa's upper arms. "What is this?"

"What?" Vanessa crossed her arms over her chest, hands covering the five bruised spots on each arm.

But Gayle moved Vanessa's hands away. "This."

"Must be from dancing. We were working on lifts—"

"Does he hurt you?" Gayle had thought about lots of ways Julian wasn't good for Vanessa, but not that he hit her.

"Don't be so dramatic."

"You don't have to put up with that."

"I'm getting another shirt." Vanessa left the room.

And Gayle picked up the broken pieces from the floor, her mind racing for what to do now, what to say. It was true. Vanessa had been banged up, scraped, and strained before, but there was something purposeful, mean, about those fingerprints.

Soon Vanessa reappeared in a turtleneck and enormous plaid shirt.

"Vanessa, I have your keys, to home . . . to my house . . . just in case . . ."

"I don't need them. You still think I'm a baby, but I'm not."

Yes, you are. But there was no way to say it without making her back up even more. "No, it's not that. Well, I thought maybe we could go out, get a bite. You pick the place."

"I'm not really hungry." Vanessa got a mug from the cupboard, poured another cup of tea.

"We can wait until later, till Julian gets home. I'll take the two of you out."

"He's teaching. He won't be home until late. And I've got to work."

The rest of the visit was hurried wrap-up chatter, all of it seeming to move Gayle closer to the door. So soon she called for a car to take her home. Only the pressure of having it waiting downstairs forced the rest of what she wanted to say. "You know, Thanksgiving is coming and I wanted to invite you two to come for dinner."

"We already have plans, Mom."

She left off the *And they don't include you*, but Gayle heard it. "OK, well, maybe sometime that weekend, for turkey sandwiches and cranberry sauce." Her smile felt brittle, as if it would crack. So Gayle gathered her things, was ready to walk out. "If you need anything . . ."

"I, uh, I could use some extra money. Um, the apartment and stuff . . . I can pay you back. I'm looking for another job." Vanessa's words came in a flustered rush.

Gayle emptied what was in her wallet. "I can send you a check."

"Um. OK. Whenever." Somehow the money talk seemed to make Vanessa withdraw even more.

Good-bye was awkward. Gayle wanted to say, *Just come with me. We'll get you new stuff*. Or, *Don't be stupid*. Instead she looked at her daughter, said, "I love you," and headed downstairs.

Midway down the first landing, Gayle was startled as the outside door opened. Julian rushed in, as if blown by the wind, a muted Guatemalan scarf wrapped at the neck of his short leather jacket.

"What a surprise." In a second he had bounded up the stairs, stood in Gayle's path.

"Yes, well, I came by for a visit." Standing so close, he smelled of cinnamon and sweat. Julian wasn't as tall as he seemed from a distance, but Gayle was glad she had the leverage of the step above him.

"So sorry I have almost missed you. Perhaps another time."

"I look forward to that." Gayle found something about him theatrical, like a performance in search of a stage, almost laughable, but it didn't feel like a comedy.

"Until then." He gave a curt bow of his head.

Gayle pressed against the macaroni, let him pass. She waited on the stairs a moment, recovering her balance. That's when she heard them.

"What was she doing here?"

"She just dropped by."

"I hope at least you asked for more money. She owes you that."

Gayle had the driver stop at the first bodega they passed and picked up a sleeve of coconut cookies. "Just to tide me over. I lost track of the time," she told him, like he cared as long as he got a tip. She crunched all the way back to her apartment, in spurts—mad at Julian, Vanessa, herself. Nothing had changed after she got home and attacked a bag of chips.

A few times during the evening Gayle called Vanessa, hung up on her voice mail.

"If he's hitting her, we have to stop him. We have to go over there. I'll talk to Marcus."

"She swears he's not. And I don't know."

I don't know. I don't know. I don't know. It repeated in her head, mocking her.

So Gayle did what she usually did, then lay in bed praying: for an answer, for Vanessa's safety, for some way to get hold of the pieces of her life she felt slipping through her fingers. She fell asleep in a heap, awoke in a hot panic, heart beating in quick ripples, short of breath, in the dark, then it passed—that had become usual too.

Vanessa did call the next day, thanked her for the teapot and the money. "Julian says we have to get together."

Gayle knew better than to hold her breath.

● ● ●

"This is the part of the meal where I wish I'd used paper plates. You know, the pretty ones with the matching napkins." Roberta scraped turkey bones and cranberry scraps into the trash and handed the plate to Gayle.

"But the table looked so pretty with the crystal, and napkins, and candles." Gayle rinsed the plate and loaded it in the dishwasher. Pat had insisted Gayle spend Thanksgiving at her house, along with Marcus and Booker. And Roberta, who accompanied Booker to New York for the first time. Gayle wasn't quite sure if it fell under the heading of "that's what friends are for" or "misery loves company." Probably somewhere in between.

"I guess candles aren't a good idea with the paper plates." Pat dug in a cabinet, looking for the lid that went to the container where she'd crammed the leftover mac and cheese. "Personally, I'd be happy to make reservations."

"Not for Thanksgiving." Gayle was glad Pat had insisted.

Home alone would have been unbearable. And whether they were together or apart, they always touched each other somehow on Thanksgiving because it was the anniversary of the day that fate and faith brought their friendship full circle.

Roberta was an easy edition to the holiday mix—for everyone but Marcus. Down-to-earth and good with a story, she didn't stand on ceremony. Roberta was a roll-up-your-sleeves-and-do-it kind of person. For dessert, she baked a German chocolate cake, from scratch, that made your mouth happy with every bite. And she had made Booker into a new person. He had been downtrodden from the time they were all in grade school. That had multiplied to the nth degree after Freddy died and Ethel fell apart. But he had already planned what he and Bert were going to do on Friday—check out the animated store windows along Fifth Avenue, have lunch, watch the skaters in Rockefeller Center, and take in the show at Radio City. He'd ordered tickets before they came. "Never went while I lived here. Now's the time."

Pat made the mistake of asking Marcus if they'd be staying in the guest room, like Booker always did. "He can not lay up in here with that woman," Marcus said. And Pat left it alone since she hadn't spent any real time with Roberta. She had made herself scarce during Marcus and Pat's stops in Wilmington, which had become pretty sporadic in the last few years.

"Which one of you girls is a Tar Heel?" Roberta looked as if she'd been living all her days not inside or under a parasol, but out in the open, under the sun, in the wind, not afraid of a little rain. Scores of age moles dotted her cheeks and neck, and her belly stuck out farther than her bust, but it was clear none of it had stopped her from having a good time.

"Did you hear that, Pat? She called us *girls*." It had been a while since either of them had hung out with anybody they were tempted to call ma'am. Lindy didn't count.

"We used to be." Pat cut one more teeny slice of cake, before she sealed the rest in cling wrap.

"Tell you a little secret." Roberta rested a hand up on each of their shoulders. "There's a piece of you that's always a girl, no matter what the calendar says."

Pat wasn't sure she knew where to find that piece, but she went along. "In that case, I'm the Carolina girl, but I think my citizenship has been revoked."

"Can't happen. That red Carolina clay is in your blood." Roberta folded the dishcloth and draped it over the faucet. "Still got people there?"

Pat started to say no, but something about Roberta made her stay closer to the truth. "Kinda. But we're not close."

"How long has it been?"

Pat hadn't thought about Verna in years—she was part of another life.

"That long? Well, sometimes it's good to close the door and throw away the key. Then again, I have been known to find just what I'm looking for on the other side of that door if I let myself open it again. Next time you're down, we'll have to take a homecoming tour. Just us girls." Roberta rolled down her sleeves. "It's mighty quiet in there. I bet one of those two is asleep. And I know which one."

Roberta headed for the living room with Pat and Gayle right behind her.

They found Marcus and his father, lips sealed, staring at the football game like statues. Roberta stood behind Booker. "Who's ahead?"

"Doesn't even matter. Neither one deserves to win." Booker stood, stretched his legs. "And I think our time would be better spent getting back to the hotel. Lots to do tomorrow."

Marcus voiced no objection. "I've got an early-morning flight."

"You won't even be here for leftovers? That's the best part." Booker stepped past Marcus and stood by Roberta.

"Got things to take care of, Dad."

"Watch out they don't take care of you first."

Gayle left with Book and Bert. Pat settled in on the couch. "She's really a nice lady."

"And my mother is by herself in a nursing home."

"You think she knows that?"

"That's not the point."

"Think they still love each other—your parents?" Pat wasn't sure where the question came from, but now it was out there.

"In their way." Marcus handed her the remote and got up. "I need to finish packing. Dinner was great."

"Compliments to the caterer." Pat reached out, grabbed his hand, rubbed it against her cheek.

He kissed her forehead. "Come, help me pick out ties."

"So you don't pack the ugly ones? In a minute."

In their way. Pat knew Marcus was heading into a busy time of year—free-agent negotiations, salary-arbitration deadlines, blahdy, blahdy, blah. Tomorrow, before heading to Tucson to check out some college players, he was making a quick stop in Miami to visit DeJohn at the Miami Beach condo he'd bought for the off-season. Marcus said he was planning to read him the riot act about building his conditioning before spring training—DeJohn's rookie season had a strong start and a limp finish.

Pat had lots on her plate too. The Ell & Me Company was involved in a ton of children's charity events this time of year, not to mention keeping everybody focused on their deadlines for the next quarter, including Gayle. As much as Gayle hated it, Pat was glad they had other artists to rely on now. Oh, and besides work, she and Marcus had a fair share of command-performance parties, some separate, others joint appearances—attendance was not really optional. December was so hectic, they'd stopped buying presents for each other—it had became one more chore dumped on the pile. They were grown-ups with their own charge cards and checking accounts. If they wanted something, they could buy it.

They were good partners—compatible, entertaining. *What's our way to love each other?*

• • •

"The season is one hundred sixty-two games long. Longer than your high school season, longer than your minor league season. And you need to be in prime shape for every one of them." Marcus plopped a wedge of fried egg on his steak and ate it. "They're not paying you for half-steppin'."

DeJohn had picked this Ocean Drive restaurant. It was open twenty-four hours, so he was acquainted with it all times of the night, mostly feeding a club-crawling food jones. This meeting was earlier in the day than his current schedule called for. They sat outside, a light breeze rustling the green umbrella above them. "I hear ya, man." Hiding behind Armani shades, DeJohn was about ready to fall in his fried-ham-and-egg sandwich on toasted French bread. He took a swig of Coke, followed the intro and outro of a golden beach goddess in a slight, white bikini as she rollerbladed past, flinging much hair in her wake. "Da-yum."

"There will be twenty more lollipops rolling by before I get the check." Marcus yanked DeJohn's glasses off, dropped them in the bread basket. "You need to remember how you can afford to live here if you intend to stay." Marcus had been miserable watching DeJohn's midseason meltdown. He knew from experience how hard it was to stay focused, stay strong, especially that first year. By July you are sore, jet-lagged, sun-dried, and sick of balls, strikes, the smell of pine tar, and honking wads of tobacco spit in the dugout. And there are still at least two months to go. "I can hook you up with a trainer."

"I can handle it." DeJohn retrieved his glasses, blew off the crumbs, and put them back on.

"How's Tiffani?" DeJohn's renting her a love nest was a nightmare in search of a pillow—too much, too close, too soon. But it was a done deal by the time Marcus heard about it. He had asked Pat why she didn't stop it. "Talk to your boy. She didn't exactly ask my permission," Pat had snapped back.

"Bitch is gettin' on my nerves." DeJohn dropped his head in his hand.

"She's got a name and that's not it."

"Sorry, man. But I was out last week and I met this honey. Umph, umph, umph . . ."

"There's always gonna be a honey. And they're gonna like your money." Marcus dropped his napkin over his plate. "You couldn't be too mad at Tiffani. I heard about the earrings you bought her."

DeJohn snickered into his hand. "That was off the chain. We went pre-Christmas shopping with this jeweler one of the guys hooked me up with. They brought out trays of stones, like they was peanuts or somethin'. I got three carats for me."

Marcus had noted the new edition to DeJohn's left earlobe, but hadn't commented on it.

"Then I got four carats for her—two in each ear. I'm sayin', that was stompin'."

"Look, bottom line, you gotta trim the nightlife and concentrate. It ain't fun finding your ass back on the bus, telling stories about what it was like when you went to the show."

"Aw-ite. I'ma handle it."

On the ride back to Miami International, Marcus wanted to get on another plane, to fly and talk to some more people about baseball, like he wanted to live on Mars. He wanted to go get on his boat and chart a course for someplace where nobody had questions for him to answer or dreams for him to fulfill. He could barely remember the last time he and Pat had done that. At first they did it every year on their anniversary. Then she got him the model of the boat as a present and they hadn't been on the real one since.

Think they still love each other? What kind of question was that? He twirled his wedding band on his finger. It was tighter than it used to be. You take care of the people you love, make sure they're safe, well provided for. That's why he was going to get on the plane. But it was so hard to figure out how to take care of Pat—always had been. And part of him ached for a son or daughter to take care of. He was sure he'd know how to do that. And he didn't know how much longer he could wait.

• CHAPTER 15 •

. . . a way to finally say "the end."

D*ecember 26 was a monumental relief* for Gayle. All the last-minute rushing, shipping, promoting, and worrying about units sold and the bottom line were done, at least until the beginning of the New Year. With Christmas on a Thursday, she and Pat had given the staff Friday off. But Gayle had a key. It would be quiet at the office, and she needed to be away from home, where she didn't put up a tree or get out the angel pillows or the crèche or festoon the doorways with Christmas cards. It didn't smell like pine or ham with cloves cooking in the oven. Gayle had not been up for the mandatory merriment of the occasion, so she told Pat she was spending the day with Danitha, Danitha she was spending it with Pat, and she never left the building.

Gayle only got out of her nightgown because Vanessa called, said she and Julian were dropping by. They brought her a mulberry soy candle and stayed a hot few minutes—long enough to collect a Christmas check and the indigo cashmere hoodie she got Vanessa, because she had to buy her something. Vanessa seemed so deferential to Julian, watching for his reaction to what she said—waiting for pearls of wisdom to drop from his tongue. She gushed about Kinesthetica's invitation to videotape two pieces as part of an online alternative-arts festival. Gayle hoped "Antediluvian Rumpus" was not on the bill.

She got Vanessa alone in the kitchen long enough to ask if she was alright. Her eyes still seemed opaque, unsatisfying. The only skin Vanessa had visible was her face and her hands. Gayle couldn't tell anything from that, and all she read in her eyes was a kind of steadfast bewilderment. Gayle had seen that look before—a long time ago in the mirror. What troubled her more was when she raised her hand to cup Vanessa's cheek and she flinched. "You startled me," Vanessa had said. And Gayle wanted to know why.

So Gayle needed to leave the turmoil of her home for a while, before the walls folded in. Outside, the whole city seemed drowsy, hungover from the fun. When she got to the office, it was odd unlocking the door, finding the light switches, without even the baseline buzz of people talking, typing, breathing. It reminded her of the old days, in the walk-up with the picture window. Back then she was often the first one in, so she and Ell would be together in the early-morning half-light.

These days Ell felt more like a commodity than the happy sprite through whose inquisitive eyes Gayle got to look at the world, at least some of the time. That was a vision she was finding harder to conjure. She didn't remember the last time she added a new leaf or picture or whatnot to her Brain Strain board. Ideas for new adventures used to swim in Gayle's head. Now she had to dredge for them.

And in the cushy silence she realized she was exhausted—tired had become her new normal. Some days more, some less, but she was always dragging. *Gotta get some vitamins.* And stop releasing food before it had a chance to sustain her. Gayle taped a piece of paper to her board and stared. She fingered the pencils she kept in a tin cup, kneaded a gum eraser. She had started to leave the "office closed" message on the phones, but she was actually grateful for the distraction of the occasional call. She answered some e-mail—some fans had already written to say how happy they were with their new dolls and books. She still found it odd getting e-mail from seven- and eight-year-olds. She missed their earnest, if wobbly, printing, but even children preferred cyberspace these days.

Gayle nuked a can of soup and got some crackers from the pantry for lunch, stared at her blank paper awhile longer. Then she put her head down on her arm, closed her eyes to let images float across the black screen of her mind . . .

. . . and she jangled awake when the phone rang, she had no

idea how much later. "The Ell and Me Company." She did her best Lindy impression, trying not to sound like she'd been sleeping. Silence. "Hello." She was about to do the Lindy slam.

"*Uh . . . hello.*"

The man sounded unsure. She expected him to apologize for dialing the wrong number.

"*Gayle, uh, Saunders, please.*"

A prickly shiver ran down her arms, up the back of her neck. The voice sounded gravelly, but oddly familiar. *You're overreacting.* "Who may I say is calling?"

A three-Mississippi pause. "*The name's Hilliard.*" It was as if he wanted to add something else, but didn't know what.

And there he was, out of the ether and the millions of moments since he'd disappeared down that dark street. That's when Gayle realized she had always known she'd hear from him again.

Before she could answer, he added, "If she's not in, I'll call—"

"Ramsey?" Gayle could hardly find air to support her voice. It came out in a fluttery whisper.

"Gayle?"

They hung on the line, connected, but not speaking until Ramsey finally said, "Figured you'd be off today. I called to see if I could make myself say your name. I haven't been up to it till now."

He would never have said that before. "What do you want, Ramsey?" She had to be strong. The last time she saw him he sold her a lie, wrapped in velvet promises.

"I want to talk to you, in person if you let me. I want to make amends."

"You said that the last time."

"I was lying."

A simple statement, but it echoed to the depths of whatever they had meant to each other. Gayle let it sink in. "Why should I believe you?"

"I can't tell you what you should do. I can admit I was powerless over my gambling. It took me down, and I took you and Vanessa down with me."

Powerless was never how she thought of Ramsey. And he said it so humbly, so matter-of-fact. "Where are you?" She had sworn she would never see him, speak to him.

"In New York. Been here the last few years—working myself up to this."

"Oh, you're here?" Gayle figured he was somewhere else, stricken with holiday loneliness and remorse.

"Will you meet with me? I won't keep you long. Anyplace you want, anytime—even now."

"Now?"

"I worked today. I'm off now."

Now. To go from zero to Ramsey with no speed bumps, no caution light? But it would save her the anticipation, the worry about what-ifs and why. "Alright."

He suggested a coffee shop, but sitting across a table, that was too intimate, too confined.

"Grand Central." Even on a semiholiday there would be lots of people. "The information booth." The room was cavernous, big enough to have its own sky and for her to be with Ramsey.

"I'll be there."

Gayle did no primping. What she looked like didn't matter. It wasn't that kind of reunion. She closed up the office, walked the twenty blocks to take up the time, breathe in cold, sober air, revive herself, numb herself.

Holiday music bounced off the marble walls and swirled around the station when she arrived, competing with the final-boarding call for the 4:01 departing on track 12. There were always tourists peering up at the constellations on the vaulted Main Concourse ceiling, but even some of the locals had paused long enough to take in the laser light show, watching blue snowmen and green snowflakes, trains and candy canes, swirl over the bull, the crab, and the stars. Commuters and travelers hustled to make connections, toting day-after presents, and after-Christmas-sale shopping bags.

Gayle made her way to the booth. It hadn't occurred to her to ask Ramsey what he looked like. She still had that image burned in her head from the first day she looked up at him, standing next to her car, long and lean in a silvery suit.

"Hello, Gayle."

So the chunky man in the brown nylon parka and work pants, with the mushroom of hair, stippled with gray, was a shock. He had the scraggly beard that last day she saw him, in the cemetery, when he scared her half to death, but even then he had looked more like himself. "Ramsey."

He saw it in her eyes, had tried to prepare for that first moment, but although he had seen her from a distance for a long time, he still wasn't prepared to stand beside Gayle, for her to see him. A hug, a handshake, even a slap, felt like too much contact. So they stood there a moment, alone in the crowd.

"Your hair. It's so . . . big."

That smile made his heart swell and he wanted so bad to call her Nightingale, his Nightingale, but he'd forfeited that right with all the other rights and privileges he'd pissed away. The three-fingered hand he kept in his pocket reminded him of that. "You know, I'm still good at growing things. Plants. Hair." Wasn't any reason for her to know he kept it long to hide the ear they'd sliced off with a machete that night in the van. That was after the two fingers. They called it a box set to take back to Bessie, laughed about what else they were going to put in the box. Hair was good camouflage. The beard covered the chunk of cheek he lost to a gun butt. And if he didn't smile too wide, which hadn't been difficult, he could hide the teeth that had been broken in the pistol-whipping too.

Gayle needed to move, started to stroll toward the perimeter of the concourse, and Ramsey followed, oblivious to those racing past them. "Where have you been?"

"I lived a lot of places, mostly between here and Kentucky. I been trying to get control of my life."

"You escaped from Stuckey that night?" Gayle had been so mad at him, at the money he had hidden from her and Vanessa, right under her nose. And to have the nerve to try to trick her to get it back. She had wanted him locked up, but it looked as if he had been in his own prison and found his own penance.

"I escaped." Barely. Stuckey had gotten her payoff and split. Moe, Larry, and Moses drove him around in a van for a while, Ramsey couldn't tell where. Not long after they stopped and collected souvenirs for Bessie, Moses, the albino bullfrog in the Kangol, got dropped off, took the offerings, and left Moe and Larry to finish the deed.

They continued the road trip, drinking Private Stock and arguing about where to take Ramsey. He passed in and out of consciousness, but awakened with the dipping and rolling of the van as it went off road. That's when they opened the doors, dragged Ramsey out, and untaped him. Moe, a biscuit-eating slob in a black tracksuit with crooked, fuzzy cornrows, had the gun, kept pushing it in Ramsey's back, saying, "You 'bout to die now." Larry, who was scrawny, with jeans hanging halfway down his butt and plaid boxers, carried a shovel. And clearly they had both watched one gangster movie too many because when they got into the woods, Larry handed Ramsey the shovel, and Moe said, "You gon' dig your own grave, nigga." Larry snickered. After a few shovelfuls, Ramsey knew he'd rather just be shot than continue the drama, so he summoned his strength and desperation, swung as hard as he could, and hit Moe in the head with the shovel. The gun went flying in the dark and Ramsey ran, harder than ever in his life, for his life.

A motorist saw Ramsey by the side of the road, called 911. At the hospital he swore he did it himself, the ear, the fingers. The last thing Ramsey wanted was to press charges, and at that moment it wasn't hard for him to act crazy. He spent some observation time in a psych bin after that, but it gave him time to think, and for his wounds to heal. He figured nobody bothered telling Bessie about the screwup, so when they let Ramsey out, he took the first thing on wheels heading west out of New York State—forever, or so he thought.

"Detective Stuckey has retired. She does security for our company now."

Ramsey made a mental note, but said nothing. "Could

we find someplace quiet?" Ramsey had things he needed to say. He had been practicing a long time.

Quiet was in short order in the terminal. The waiting room in Vanderbilt Hall had morphed into a winter bazaar, filled with stalls of crafts and gift items. So they headed to the relative peace of the bricked Roman arches in the cavernlike lower level. It felt like a shrine. That's where Ramsey made his confession.

He wanted to hold Gayle's hand. Instead he kept his clasped behind him. "You are a loving, beautiful person, Gayle. And almost from the first time I met you, I dishonored you because gambling had already taken hold of my life. You made me feel special, and I repaid you by lying, by trying to cut you down so I felt bigger. I took all I could and was mad when there wasn't more."

A tear spilled from the corner of Gayle's eye. She brushed it away, but it was replaced by another. And she looked at him straight on, maybe for the first time ever. Not listening for what she wanted to hear. Not manufacturing what wasn't there.

"I stole from your family. I took you away from your friends. I took things I can never replace or repay. For that I am deeply sorry."

Ramsey's eyes seemed ancient, but Gayle didn't see deceit in them. She would never forget what his actions had cost. And she didn't want to run into Ramsey's arms and be with him again. "I forgive you." She had thought the words, but they were new on her tongue—a way to finally say "the end."

Ramsey closed his eyes, dug his nails into the palm of his hand to focus. He was not going to cry. "I thank God every day you're doing well. I know I told you those stories weren't nothing. I was jealous because I didn't know what to do to make Vanessa as happy as she was with you."

Gayle remembered how happy Vanessa had been then. A group of tourists, speaking some language that sounded Scandinavian, chattered as they passed Gayle and Ramsey on their way to the food court. Their voices echoed brightly until the last word was gone. "Vanessa's a dancer now."

"I remember those little pink tights."

Gayle could see Ramsey trying to reconcile the past he remembered with all that had gone on without him. "She moved out last fall—with her boyfriend."

He shook his head in disbelief. "You like him?"

Gayle looked for the answer. "No. But I'm trying."

"I'd like to see Vanessa too. To make amends. If that's alright."

Gayle wasn't sure how to handle that. First she had to let Vanessa know her father wasn't dead. "I'll talk to her about it."

"I've taken enough of your time. I want you to know I will help you in any way I can. Just call me."

Gayle found a pad and a pen in her purse, handed it to him.

"My cell. I'll stay put for a while, but I'm planning to head back to Kentucky, or who knows where. New York is a tough place to live without any roots." But that wasn't her problem.

• • • •

At 8:18 on Saturday morning, traffic and weather played on the radio and Ramsey was still in bed. He'd been awake most of the night, half-listening to the same stories loop every half hour on the all-news station. He didn't know what he expected to feel after talking with Gayle. Not exactly proud—relieved maybe, that he had done something right by her, at least told the truth, but relief was elusive too. He had gone to a meeting last evening, needing some support for the sense of guilt and regret that accompanied him out of Grand Central. But they continued to gnaw at him through the night, along with a big piece of the past that had unexpectedly jumped into his lap—Detective Teresa Stuckey.

It had been hard for him to maintain his composure when Gayle said that name. Not because of any anger he felt toward Stuckey—a dirty cop was part of the trouble he'd brought on himself. But now Stuckey was involved with Gayle—doing security no less. And although he was no longer a betting man, Ramsey was sure the odds were better than even that Bessie was somewhere close by. And what did that mean for Gayle?

Ramsey made himself get up, shower before the old man down the hall funked up the bathroom. He moved the pieces around in his head, trying to figure out what to do. Thanks to the Internet, Ramsey knew about Lush, knew Bessie had, as always, found a new way to satisfy people's appetites for a price. But was Bessie keeping an eye on Gayle? Would he follow the money, look to collect Ramsey's old debts from a fresh money stream? He couldn't let that happen. Would Gayle have mentioned Ramsey to Stuckey as innocently as she'd brought up Stuckey to him? When he was working the steps of his program, they stressed that you only make amends if it doesn't put the other person in jeopardy. Had he done that without meaning to because it made him feel better? He didn't want to tell Gayle about Stuckey—that she'd been on the take, had delivered him to Bessie's thugs on a platter—because he didn't want Gayle to feel in any way responsible for that. The possibilities bubbled and multiplied like the fuzzy scum in jars of old food in the back of the refrigerator. And Ramsey did something he hadn't in years—he got back in the bed, with the radio on, racking his brain for the answers, trying to think it through.

By afternoon he was at the library, queued up for a computer. It took longer to get one on the weekends with schoolkids doing homework, working people trying to turn their lackluster jobs into résumé gold, the way it said in the how-to books. Finally he sat down at a terminal, got out his notebook, a little one, like those he used to use to keep track of his wins and losses. He got to the search engine, put in her name. Ramsey wrote slower and more deliberately now, but he still pressed hard, leaving ruts on the pages underneath.

Sunday morning he was out with the church folks going to Sunday school. He took the train uptown. If it was like the old days, it was a good time to catch Bessie, sitting at the bar, drinking coffee and looking over paperwork before brunch. Ramsey didn't care about his own safety. Whatever happened, happened. He just needed to keep Gayle out of this equation.

Nightspots always looked forlorn in the straight-up daylight, with no shadows to promise intrigue and no glitter to hide the wear and tear. Ramsey knocked at the flamingo doors, kept knocking until a vexed-looking man with a polishing cloth in his hand opened one a crack.

"Read the sign. Closed till noon."

"I'm here to see Bessie Austin." Ramsey spoke loud so his voice would carry.

"Look, we're not hiring and I got—"

"Tell him it's Ramsey Hilliard."

"Ain't tellin' him shit. I told you—"

"Let him in."

The porter stepped aside, waggled his rag in the direction of the Blue bar, and walked away. A bag of trash sat open on the glass oval desk, with extra bags draped over the arm of one of the bronze nudes. A vacuum hummed on an upstairs floor.

There was no time to back down or second-guess. Hands at his sides, Ramsey strode through the archway. Bessie's handlebar mustache was gone, and his head was shaved clean, but Ramsey would have recognized the big man. Seeing him gave Ramsey a bilious, wobbly feeling, took him back to the awful high of walking up the stairs to that back room at Bessie's old place and playing poker days and nights on end in a crazed trance, not eating, not sleeping, just the cards, the chips, the wins, and the losses.

Bessie had swiveled around on his stool, gave Ramsey the up and down, searched his face with a skeptical eye.

Ramsey held up his hand in a three-fingered salute. "It's me."

Bessie's face went deadpan.

"Need to see this too?" Ramsey lifted the flap of hair that hid the hole at the side of his head, outlined by a ragged semicircle of cartilage. Ramsey walked closer, stood face-to-face at the bar. In a quiet voice he said, "I'm not here to stir up nothin'. I know I owed you."

"Don't know what you're talking about." Bessie's voice was calm, like he was discussing the weather or a day at the park.

"Just leave my family out of it. They didn't know. Whatever you want from me—"

"You don't owe me a thing." Bessie waved his hand. "And we don't ever have to speak about this again."

Ramsey nodded, held out his hand, and they shook on it.

Monday, Ramsey took off work, went to Millennium Security. And Terry Stuckey looked as if she'd seen a zombie.

"I've been to see Bessie."

"You saw Bessie?" Red blotches broke out on Terry's throat, traveled up to her cheeks.

"I'll say the same thing to you I said to him. Just leave my family out of it. I know you work for Gayle."

"You could have come to me first. I would have—"

"It was you who turned me over the first time. Sorry if I don't trust you."

Ramsey left her sitting behind her desk, rocking.

•   •   •

"Are you crazy? You went to see him alone? Nobody knew where you were, Gayle." Pat was beside herself on Monday when Gayle told her about meeting Ramsey.

"I'm not afraid of him. He's changed."

"That's what you thought the last time."

"He seems, I don't know, peaceful. Ramsey was never peaceful. And bottom line, I'm not in love with him, anymore."

"And you thought you were?"

"I don't know. Maybe." Or still wanting to be excused from trying again.

"You should give Terry Stuckey his number."

"Why? That's over and done. *But what will I tell Vanessa?*"

CHAPTER 16

. . . a tempest in a snow globe.

"I f *you're not scared senseless—you're not* trying hard enough!" Pat roused the audience. "Don't be afraid," she called.

"Do it scared!" they responded, and broke into applause. She had flown into Albany and taken a car to Saratoga Springs to be the keynote speaker for the Your Business–Your Way conference.

"And if you haven't heard enough from me, I'll be happy

to take questions." It was always odd doing the speech without the other half of the team. Pat pointed to a man in the third row, then zigzagged her way through the ballroom, fielding inquiries that ranged from the mundane—patents, corporate structure, and business plans—to the personal—managing your time and family obligations—and ultimately to the inane—where did she get her shoes?

Pat handled the final question—"Would you ever take The Ell & Me Company public?"—by saying, "I never say never." Then she was surprised to spot Drew, slight smile, almost imperceptible head nod, leaning against the back wall. She would know that hair anywhere. She thanked the enterprising entrepreneurs, and he waited by the door as she made her way though the crowd, still shaking hands and answering questions. She graciously accepted kudos—"You made me believe I can start over." "It was great to know you really can start with only an idea and make it work." "You've inspired me!"—until she reached the exit.

"Got me thinking about starting up my own shop—almost." Drew added his applause.

"How long have you been here?" Pat didn't want to admit how happy it made her to see him on this unscheduled drop-in. Glad she wouldn't be dining alone.

"Long enough."

A man approached Pat, business card in hand. "Edmund Douglas. Excellent presentation. I'm sorry your other half wasn't here too. I came especially to see you."

Pat was surprised. Looking at him in his tweed jacket, with elbow patches, she wouldn't have taken him for an Ell & Me fan. "Thank you. I'm sure she wishes she was here too."

"I have a proposition which might be of interest to you. I'll give you a call next week." His smile was polite, reserved, and orthodontically flawless. Then he went on his way.

Pat shrugged at Drew, slipped the card in her pocket along with the three-by-five cards with speech notes she always carried, but never used.

"Don't you want to know who he is?" Drew asked.

"Nope. Another inventor from Podunk whose idea will set the world on fire if only we'll help him find financing for his widget or become his partner and finance the widget. Lindy will handle it. She loves telling them we're not in the widget business."

"Where's your accomplice?"

"The flu—I did Chicago solo too." She saw his skeptical look. Pat had been monitoring Gayle's actions as well as she could. "She's really sick—achy, chills, fever. I made a chicken-soup delivery before I left. Didn't stay long though. Both of us couldn't be sick. Chicago was too important." Pat had gone to Chi-town for meetings about setting up a Midwestern distribution center. "And I didn't want to blow this conference. But she looked fine—not fine—she looks like hell, but you know what I mean."

"No more from her ex?"

"Not a peep. She let him say his piece—which is more than I would have done. Hopefully that's the last chapter. But the real question is, what are you doing here? It's Saturday afternoon. Aren't you supposed to be on the slopes in Vermont?"

"I've been gone a week, or haven't you missed me?" Drew ran a hand through his hair. "In any case, I've had enough speed to keep me stoked, and I remembered you guys were here today. Saratoga is only a ninety-minute ride—and on the way home—sort of. So I thought I'd check you out, then head home. The weather, however, has thrown a shovel in my plans."

"What's it doing out there?" The hotel ballroom and meeting spaces were windowless pods. Pat hadn't seen outside since she left her room at ten thirty. She looked at her watch—three forty-five.

"I heard in the car it's a nor'easter."

"Why didn't you keep going?"

"Wasn't it you who asked me why men can't resist a damsel in distress?"

"You remember that?"

"I remember lots of things. But it wasn't snowing that hard when I left Killington." Drew shoved his hands in his jeans pockets. "I know you're scheduled to drive home tomorrow. I'll be happy to give you a lift back tonight. What's another stop on the road to Hoboken?"

"Sounds like a song from a bad musical." Pat led the way through the maze of hallways. "Let's see if I can get my rental early and get out of here." She stopped at the auto desk in the lobby.

"We have your car, but it's not gonna matter." The perky girl in the yellow blazer looked at her monitor, then at Pat. "The road from here to the Thruway is closed. The airport stopped flights an hour ago. Have you looked out there?"

Pat joined Drew at the front entrance. What had been a landscaped circular drive with a picturesque dusting of snow on the evergreens now looked like a tempest in a snow globe.

"Bellman says the nor'easter met an Alberta clipper. It was love at first sight and they've formed a union that would make George and Martha look like Jack and Jill." Drew knew Pat would get it. They had joked about the Taylor-Burton *Who's Afraid of Virginia Woolf?* last week when they saw a genteel-looking old couple cussing each other out on the corner of Broadway and Twentieth.

"Damn." Pat tapped her foot.

"Slow down. It's just weather. Storm should blow over by morning. The roads will get cleared and life will go on."

"But if it keeps coming like this—"

"They're used to this here. It's called winter. Not like in the city. Fewer people, fewer cars, more plows per capita. It's a winning combination."

"And how did you come by all this upstate knowledge?"

"I spent lots of time here."

And Pat wondered why. She was struck by how little she really knew about Andrew Voight—other than facts that might appear on a résumé. "You can't get back on the road. Have you checked for a room?"

"On my way in. Nothing here. They found me a place a few miles away. I can make it that far. I've got a macho four-wheel drive."

"And I've got a two-bedroom suite and a missing accomplice. There's a blizzard out there."

"Seriously. This is situation irregular. You sure you're OK with that?"

"Absolutely." Which was a lie. Pat wasn't sure at all. She also wasn't sure what OK meant. "There's two bedrooms, two baths, with a sitting room in between. No dividing some tiny space with a flimsy blanket, à la *It Happened One Night*." Pat recalled the romantic comedy where the dashing, but amusingly inept, leading man and the daffy, but beautiful, heroine get stranded and are forced to share close quarters. Zany high jinks ensue, resulting in a long-anticipated romantic interlude. This, however, was not the movies. "Better get your stuff while you can still find your car."

In a few minutes Drew returned with a small satchel. "That it?" Pat asked.

"Got what I need—I'll spare you the particulars."

The lobby was packed with perturbed guests—the arriving who had made it through the storm, and those whose failure to depart had created a room shortage. Pat and Drew chatted as they waited in the front-desk line to get an additional room key. She watched the desk clerk sneak glances at her, then at Drew. *Wonder what he thinks? Do I care?* She and Drew had certainly gotten their share of stares—in restaurants, airports, even on the streets of New York—from people who had opinions about who they were to each other and what that meant, but Drew seemed oblivious. Pat satisfied herself with the fact they worked together—he worked for her actually—and people could think whatever they chose. But there was something salacious about getting the key. Handing it to him made Pat tingly.

The conference center sat on several acres, constructed on the site of a quaint old hotel. Upon arrival, guests could only see the sprawling, state-of-the-art addition—brick, glass, atriums, adjacent golf course, stables, tennis court. But tucked away in an inner courtyard was what made The Brecker special—the original hotel. The ground floor housed meeting rooms, but the five upper floors had been converted to distinctive luxury suites reserved for special guests—conference speakers, visiting politicians, luminaries, even a movie star or two.

So when they reached Pat's suite, Drew found more than he expected. "This is bigger than my apartment."

"Swank digs, huh?" Pat waved her arm around the huge room, which was decorated in understated, traditional style—substantial, upholstered sofa and chairs, mahogany tables and bookshelves, silk-shaded lamps, formal drapes with tasseled tiebacks and sheers beneath. The colors were quiet and dense—greens, golds, and burgundies. And all of it might have felt too heavy in August, but this was January, and like Baby Bear's bed, it was just right.

"There's even another fireplace in the master bedroom—which I have already claimed." Pat pointed. "Yours is there. Dump your stuff and we'll—"

"Make a plan? Play checkers? Find some food?"

"All of the above. I'm starved." Pat went to the big bay windows. It was only four o'clock, but it was that winter stormy almost dark. She watched snow plummet sideways from the sky, then headed to her room, this once not fighting how happy she was for Drew's company. For one night she was spared from conference people who wanted to hear about Ell & Me ad nauseam. From worrying if there was really something wrong with Gayle. And from Marcus, who was full of frustration from work and frustration with her and had taken them both with him to San Diego. Drew was simple. Easy. Pat quickly changed into jeans and a cashmere sweater, ran a comb through her hair.

"You look relaxed. Nice." Drew smiled, tugged down his own sweater. "I don't see this Pat too often. Shall we?" He held out his arm, she hooked hers through his.

Pat and Drew peeked into the bistro off the lobby—every table was filled and the disgruntled and thirsty were six deep at the bar. They tried the two other restaurants, found both mobbed, with waits of more than an hour.

"Plan B—the conference sent one of those gargantuan welcome baskets. We can see if that will tide us over until the crowd thins."

"The motion carries."

When they got back to the room, Pat found the remote, turned on the TV. "Guess we should see what's going on out there." She channel surfed.

"Looks like one of those easy-start deals for the fire-challenged." Drew stood in front of the fireplace, which was already laid, logs picture-perfect, ready for the photo shoot. "Shall I?"

It seemed so—romantic? "Why not?"

By the time Drew got the wood crackling, Pat had found weather reports. Every news broadcast had reporters in arctic wear with microphones and yardsticks, prognosticating whether this was the storm of the year, decade, or century. The only thing they all agreed on was that snow would continue at the current rate throughout the night.

"We're officially stranded." Pat clicked off the set.

Drew closed the fireplace screen. "It's starting to feel like one of those movie clichés. 'It was a dark and stormy night—'"

And right on time, there was a knock at the door.

"You should write those things." Pat went to see who it was.

"Hospitality."

"Aha!" Drew squinted. "But who is it really? The mad scientist's assistant? The kindly innkeeper who's been secretly doing dastardly deeds?"

Pat rolled her eyes. "Not scared." She opened the door.

"Checking to see you have whatever you need and to assure you the hotel is fully staffed and prepared to handle this unfortunate weather situation." He handed Pat a small shopping bag from the batch he carried. "We have a backup generator, but just in case, this is a flashlight, candles, and matches."

"Thank you"—Pat read his name tag—"David. We're fine."

"If there's anything else, please call."

Drew came up behind Pat. "Is it possible to order a bottle of wine or should we call room service directly?"

"I can get whatever you like, sir, but the suite has a fully stocked bar and wine cabinet. May I?" He headed across the room. "This only looks like a bookcase. Right here." He pressed a wood-grain button on the side. "It's a Prohibition bar." The front, books and all, sprang open to display the bar's contents. "This is original to the hotel." He did the same on the opposite bookshelf and revealed a temperature-controlled wine cellar. "This, however, was added." He left the doors open. "Is there anything else I can do for you and your wife, sir?"

"Uh—no. Thank you." Drew tipped him as he left, then headed to the bar. "Brandy? Seems like a snowed-in kind of drink." Pat nodded and he grabbed the calvados, two snifters. "It's been a long time since I've heard that." He poured, handed a glass to Pat, perched on the arm of the sofa, and put the bottle on the table.

"Heard what?" Pat sat on the opposite end of the couch.

He swirled the amber liquid in his glass, inhaled the fragrant oaky apple.

"Someone referred to as my wife." He took a sip and breathed deeply, letting the brandy fill his head, trickle slowly down his throat. "I was married once—a long time ago. We were young. It was over before we had much of a chance."

Pat knew Drew dated—not details, those she sidestepped. Now a wife had landed in the middle of Pat's fantasy of Drew's life. She played with the fringe on a throw pillow. "We all do stupid things in the name of love when we're young."

"It wasn't a stupid thing." Drew's answer was instant, and pointed.

Pat felt the sharp edge. "Sorry. I didn't mean anything." She took a bigger swallow than she intended; the brandy burned her throat.

"It's OK." Drew stared into the fire. "How would you know?"

"Do you want to tell me?" The question seemed polite, but Pat wasn't sure it was the box she wanted to open.

"I don't know, Pat." He slid from the arm onto the couch, turned toward her. "Do you really want to hear this?" The fire caught gold flecks in his green eyes.

Pat looked down into her glass, at the silk fringe in her fingers, at her wedding ring. She had made Drew privy to the details of her life and those of the people closest to her. So far the door had just swung one way. But if she let him in, made it personal, then what were they doing really?

But safely cocooned in the foothills of the Adirondacks and away from all things familiar, she allowed herself to want more. First, she took in his hands—long, strong fingers with squared even nails holding his brandy snifter, stainless steel Chronolog peeking from the sleeve of his bulky orange sweater. He crossed his leg over one knee, revealing scuffed leather boots with a lot of mileage on them. Finally she let her eyes travel back to his face—slightly windburned and tanned after his week outdoors. There was the hint of fuzz—had she ever seen that before? Then there were his eyes, waiting for an answer, and for the first time Pat admitted to herself she saw Drew as a man—one in whom she had more than collegial interest.

Suddenly she had a million questions—all the things she'd never asked, but the answers would have to come at their own pace. Pat curled into the corner of the couch, hugging the pillow to her stomach. "Tell me."

Drew rested his head on the sofa, looked up at the ceiling. "Her name was Sabine." They met third year at Emerson, and an easy friendship quickly grew deeper. The wedding—just family and close friends—took place right after graduation. Career-launching, write-your-own-future kind of jobs—his with WGBH, hers with the *Globe*—kept them in Boston. And seven blissful weeks after they said "I do," Sabine was killed in a hit-and-run on her way home from work. The driver was never found.

"That's devastating." Not the story Pat expected.

"I grieved for a year—could barely get out of bed. Spent

another three mad as hell before I found peace—or it found me, you know?"

Pat nodded, although she really didn't know. Being strong, overcoming adversity, yes, but what did she know about peace?

"I started looking at the whole thing the way I thought she would. Sabine was all about being alive." Drew paused, savored another sip of his drink. "It didn't matter if it was an ass-kicking final thesis, her birthday, or a broken water pipe. She was all in, hands-on with each and every thing that happened to her, around her. In time I came to accept that enjoying her—I mean just knowing her, for whatever amount of time, that was a gift. Then I was grateful."

Drew didn't seem sad or even wistful as he related the story, and there was no longing in his telling. In fact, he seemed almost joyful. So much so that Pat didn't quite know what to say, but she leaned in closer.

"You don't have to say anything." He got up, put another log on the fire. "I just want you to know."

There he went again, reading her mind. But hard as she tried, Pat couldn't find anything to add, wasn't sure what she wanted to take away because this wasn't as simple as typing words to each other on a blank screen.

"Let's see what your basket has to offer. I don't know about you, but I need to feed this brandy a little something." He went over to the towering cellophane-wrapped wicker hamper on the dining table, giving her a detour, an exit if she wanted it.

But despite the convenient escape route offered by Drew's dead wife, and the warning signal alarming in Pat's own head, she couldn't bail yet—didn't want to. But she was also unsure of what to do or say next. "I haven't been a very good friend, Drew. And I haven't been fair either." *That was pretty lame.*

Drew turned to face her. "Oh, come on, Pat. I didn't tell you this because I wanted you to feel sorry for me or be my fishing buddy."

"But it's true. I've been totally selfish." Pat joined him at the table. "You've listened to me complain, helped me celebrate . . ."

"You haven't made me do anything I didn't want to." Drew reached for her hand, rubbed his thumb over the back. "And you know as well as I do that I'd be lying if I said I wasn't attracted to you."

So would I. Although Pat felt herself easing closer and closer to the edge, she hung on, if only by a thread. "But why me? It doesn't make sense."

"Sense to who?" Drew let go of her hand. "Why not you?"

"I don't know." Pat tried to undo the raffia bow. The cellophane rattled, but her fingers weren't working. "It's just that none of this is what I was expecting when I brushed my teeth this morning."

"I know you weren't." He stilled her hand with his. "Me either."

I'm married. She loved Marcus—and he loved her, in his way. *What the hell does that mean?* She screamed at herself in her head. What did she feel for Drew? Curiosity? A change of flavor? Something more serious? More dangerous? She had so many questions and some of them needed quick answers, which was usually her specialty, but not tonight. Pat was at war with herself. She had gone into battle with that worthy opponent many times. She could weigh strategies, strengths, weaknesses and move forward with clarity and precision. Yes or no. Most of her major life decisions had been made that way—up to and including marrying Marcus. He asked, she deliberated, said yes, and within days the deed was done. For Pat, choices were pretty much black-and-white, but this one, despite the obvious parallel, was not.

"Soup's on."

She was so involved in her bout, she didn't realize Drew had undone the wrapping. Cheese, bread sticks, pâté, caviar, nuts, fruit, chocolate, were all spread out on the table.

"Pat?" Drew rested his hand on her back, at her waist. Allowing the casual gesture a new familiarity.

She felt his nearness, his heat. The slow build, the simmer—he said that a long time ago, about his hobby, but she had let his words play mischief in her head, wondered what that simmer would feel like. It had taken years to admit, but every part of her wanted to find out, wanted him.

And right then, his hand on her back, it was so easy. All she had to do was turn into his arm. Open that door. And she did.

He pulled her close, held her tight, strong, warm. She closed her eyes, let herself sink into him, breathe him, for once not thinking. And whatever energy fueled their connection coursed through them both. Finally she lifted her head, lips parted, heart racing. They looked at each other, saw each other a long moment. And then they kissed. His lips were softer than she expected. His tongue gentle, reaching deep for her, and she opened, welcomed, reached back. The sharp prickle from his stubble on her cheek, the smoky tang of brandy that filled her as she inhaled their kisses, swallowed them, were the only reminders this was real.

Then Drew slowed, eased himself away from her—only inches, but he pulled back. "We have to talk about this," he whispered, hoarse and low against her ear.

Pat didn't want to stop, didn't want to talk. She wanted more of him, of them. She shook her head.

"Yes," Drew insisted, widening the space between them. "I want this. You know I do. But this can't be something you'll regret. Not tomorrow, not next month. I don't ever want you to regret . . . us."

"But I do want this . . . you. Drew."

"I know, sweetie." He kissed the tip of her nose. "But we're on a cloud here—in our very own snow bubble. Real life is still out there, and we're going to have to face it." Drew held her face. "This isn't a game. It's not let's pretend. And it's not let's fuck."

"Damn it." Pat's head sank in his hands. "Who died and made you wise King Solomon?" She slipped out of his grip, the ache for him still burning, unlike the fire, which was down to the last few embers. But like her, with a little prodding, another log, it would blaze again.

He chuckled. "Hardly. But I'm a big boy. A patient man. I've waited this long. But I'm unencumbered, Pat. Free—I have no serious attachments or obligations. You do. And I have to respect that—I've tried to. And I don't know if you'll get this or not, but—as far as I'm concerned, whether we take the next step or not, what we have won't go away. Don't get me wrong, I want you in my life in so many ways, but having you in my life at all may have to be enough, and I can accept that. And somehow today, knowing that we've given it a place, made it real—makes me happy."

"What planet did you fall from?" Pat struggled to find her footing, as if the floor had shifted under her feet, the lights too bright, the focus too sharp, too real.

"After Sabine, I read—poets, philosophers, spiritualists, saints, prophets, you name it. Nobody seemed to have all of the answers, so I took pieces that worked for me from each, things that made sense." He winked at her. "And created my own Tenets for the Life of Andrew Voight—the first one: Love Is." Drew twirled her around, caught her in a hug. "Let's eat."

It was hard to believe it was still early evening. So much had been packed in so short a time. They transferred the feast to the coffee table, but at first Pat had trouble eating, speaking, so he let her set the pace. Eventually, between bites, snatches of weather, sips of wine, keeping the fire going, Pat asked some of the questions she had never before broached.

Drew had been a corporate brat—from birth to seventeen—five states, three countries, and nine cities—two in Texas. Family—Dad worked himself to death, Mom remarried, living in Palm Springs, sister married, living in London, no brothers, but a suitable number of aunts, uncles, and cousins. He spent most childhood summers and a few winter vacations with grandparents in Lake George, until a bitter divorce, after forty-five years of marriage, resulted in a sale of the property—his upstate experience. He had his tonsils out at eight, broke his right arm when he was eleven, his left ankle at fifteen. He played basketball and soccer in high school and was the yearbook editor. He had painful, embarrassing acne and his first girlfriend at sixteen. She had acne too. Images, their inherent messages about identity, had always fascinated him, and RISD and Emerson had been his only college choices. Accepted to both, he tossed a coin. Sabine was his only wife. She died in 1994. Yes, there had been other women since. All just passing through, none moved in.

They fell asleep on the couch, Pat curled in the corner, her hand on his chest, Drew's head in her lap, arms around her waist—neither willing to separate, each wanting to hold on to as much of the day and each other as they could.

Morning dawned with that poststorm quiet. Crisp, clear, sparkling, it brought with it news that the main roads would be passable by ten. And just like that the spell was broken. They disentangled, slipped back into their usual easy, teasing banter, and prepared to face the real world. Two bedrooms, two baths, made it easy to shower, dress, pack, and meet back on neutral ground. But she finally got to see how his hair achieved its tousled state. He towel-dried it and however it finished was it. No blowing, no brushing, no fuss.

Drew went out, hunted down pastry and coffee. Pat reconfirmed her rental car. He offered a ride he knew she wouldn't accept. A three-hour trip back to the city with Drew would not allow her time to think of anything but them. He had made it clear this decision was hers alone, and she needed some distance, perspective.

Outside, the sun—bright, brittle, blinding—glinted off the snowscape. Pat's car idled, ready for takeoff. He stowed her suitcase, she waited, leaning against the driver's door. The thud of the trunk lid sounded so final, made her eyes fill, but she blinked back the tears. Drew put his bag on the roof, his hands against the car on either side of her. He looked at her long enough for the heat of her embarrassment to flush up her legs, back, neck, as if it might melt the snow right where she stood. Their kiss was long, sweet, and light—last night's urgency a declaration neither needed to reconfirm. He traced her jaw with his index finger, cupped her chin, smiled, and left.

Pat watched him walk down the drive toward the parking lot before she pulled off. What had happened? How could she? How couldn't she? Then she'd be in a moment and a moan would slip through her lips and she'd shake herself loose, concentrate on the road, the cars, the immediate priorities. Every mile along the I-87 snow canyon brought more questions. What was cheating? Had she? Was she wrong? Her father-in-law obviously loved two women—did the fact that Ethel wasn't in her right mind make it OK? Or was he wrong too? Was Marcus right to be upset with his father?

She was twenty-five miles south of Albany when Marcus called from California. He'd heard about the storm. She tried to sound nonchalant. "It was pretty bad yesterday, but it's fine now. . . . The speech was good. . . . Chicago too. . . . Lucky you. No, it's not seventy-five—but I'm plenty warm. . . . OK. See you Wednesday." She removed her earphone and the questions in her head picked up where they'd left off, but she still had no answers when she got home.

A quick check on Gayle—better but still not up to speed— a lame attempt at the Sunday *Times*, and Pat fell asleep on the couch, her BlackBerry nearby for the telltale red blinking light. She awoke a while later, but she wasn't quite ready to go to bed—their bed. She spent another night on a couch.

Pat was at the office by seven the next morning. Messages, mail, and e-mail—none of it from Drew—kept her busy till Lindy and Meg got there and the office came to life. She worked—attempting to square away the clog in the inventory pipeline, follow up on her Chicago meetings. And she tried not to check her e-mail in-box every five minutes. The day was full. As was the next. Drew's e-mails were friendly and funny as ever, but there was none of the intimate sparring she had grown used to, and no mention of the weekend. By noon Wednesday she couldn't stand it anymore. Marcus was coming home. She wasn't sure what she had done, or what she was going to do. Pat left her BlackBerry on her desk, grabbed her coat. "I'm going out for a while."

"I don't have a lunch on your schedule, Pat." Meg checked the computer. "Last-minute meeting?"

"No. I'm going for a walk."

"A what?" Lindy looked at Pat over her glasses. "In all the years I've known you, you have never left the office to take a walk—not without a destination. Is everything OK?"

"I'm fine. I just need some air." Pat wrapped her pashmina around her neck and headed for the elevator. The city had gotten only a dusting of the white stuff that had paralyzed upstate, so the street had its usual midday madness. Strollers, dawdlers, joggers, shoppers, messengers, and folks on a mission—finding food on the run, making the sale at Loehmann's and back at their desk in an hour, getting to the make-or-break meeting at Cafeteria just late enough to be the most important—they all converged on a few square blocks for the noontime Chelsea carnival.

Pat joined the strollers. She wasn't in a hurry. She didn't

have a destination—she just needed to be out, clear her head so she could focus on what she got out of the Chicago meetings and not on Drew, or Marcus. South on Fifth for a couple of blocks, then west and north again until she found herself where this had all started—Twenty-third and Eighth. She stood across the street staring in their old windows. It was a nail salon now.

She could still see Gayle sitting in the window at her drawing board, remember the day they hired Lindy—their first employee, the instant she saw the little brown girl clutching a doll while she waited at the bus stop with her mother and the idea for the Ell doll popped into her head. But today, what she remembered most was Drew barreling into Ell & Me, ten minutes early for his pitch appointment, full of ideas, his energy and enthusiasm nearly overwhelming their little office. "Lord, Lord, Lord! What's that white boy on?" Lindy had joked. "'Cause whatever it is, I want me some."

Did I feel it even then? And ignored it because it was crazy? Just like it is now? Several people on Twenty-third Street slowed, looked up at the windows, trying to see whatever Pat saw. But of course they couldn't. They looked back at her, shook their heads, and went about their business.

The first time Pat felt this kind of disturbance deep in her core was way back when Marcus kissed her in Gayle's basement. They were kids, he was Gayle's boyfriend then, and it felt both right and wrong. The next time it happened was with PJ—it was heady, lusty, and loving—or so she thought, right up until he married someone else. It had felt so right, but been so wrong. *Was it? Could he really have loved me? And Edwina? Both of us? And he married her because he had said he would and didn't know how not to?* Until now the very idea had been unthinkable, incomprehensible. And now there was Drew. What they had was close, real, powerful, true. It felt exactly right and totally wrong.

"What are you doing here?" Gayle was talking to Lindy when Pat got back.

"I still work here, don't I?" Gayle, still a bit green around the gills, sounded better than she looked.

"Yep. But you've been slacking off lately." Pat took off her coat. "So did you take the miracle cure? We thought you'd be out all week."

"I'm feeling better and I didn't want you to give away my desk. Besides, the doctor says I'm not contagious. So I thought I'd come in for a couple of hours, give myself a test run."

"OK. You wanna talk about Chicago?" Because Pat certainly wasn't going to talk about Saratoga.

"Let me look at Alicia's sketches for *Ell's Hospital Adventure*. It won't take long. I just need to see if she's going in the right direction."

"Swell. You know where I'll be."

Lindy waved a stack of message slips. "The one on top says it's important. Of course they all think that. But he said he ran into you in Saratoga last week and that you were expecting to hear from him. He's from TaDToY."

"You mean A TaDToY Is FoREveR, TaDToYs?" Gayle asked.

Their slogan was their brand, and they were right up there with Mattel and Hasbro.

"Why don't I remember this?" Pat was pretty sure she

would recall talking to someone from one of the largest toy companies in the world. Then she remembered Edmund Douglas, right before she left the ballroom with Drew. His card was probably still in her suit pocket. *He was from TaD-ToY? Why didn't he say that?* "But I'll give him a call and maybe he'll refresh my memory."

Pat was just getting off the phone when Gayle came in thirty minutes later.

"Alicia's stuff looks good. So tell me about Chicago." Gayle sat down.

Pat had a glazed look on her face. "They want to acquire us. They'd like a meeting." Pat got up.

"Huh?" Gayle got up.

"TaDToY." Pat sat down. "They want to buy our company."

. . . the destination might not be as good as the journey.

"I still can't believe any of this is happening." Gayle swiveled the white leather seat to face Pat. "You and me? In a private jet?" Even though she was dragging, she kept rerunning the tape of the day's events. Remnants of the flu still lingered a week and a half later. It was hard to find enough energy to get through a regular day. And this one had not been regular.

"Nothing has happened yet." Pat was tired too. She hadn't caught the flu but there was so much going on. She and Marcus were still running in place, getting nowhere. Drew was still—there, either a solution or a problem. It was barely February, and out of all the things that could possibly have come along to add to the hyperhectic new year, a potential buyout offer from TaDToY would not have made her top ten thousand list.

"And we have no clue if anything will happen." The idea that The Ell & Me Company, and probably she and Gayle, had been monitored, for who knows how long, and been the subject of corporate conversations they knew nothing about was unnerving to Pat. And TaDToY's sleuthing had stayed under the radar—there was no buzz, no gossip, no phone calls from nosy reporters or envious competitors trying to size up the rumors as fact, fiction, or mere speculation. Just a man who handed her a business card in the middle of a blizzard. Pat was wary—she'd been ambushed in the workplace before. It was a long time ago, but some things you don't forget.

A barrage of phone calls and e-mails followed Pat's initial conversation with the toothful Edmund Douglas—whose job it was to search out delectable, easily digested morsels to feed the ever-increasing appetite of his sovereign, King TaDToY. He was the official royal taster, and Ell & Me, at least initially, looked like a nice little bite—enticing enough to warrant a trip to HQ, as "call me Ed" referred to their center of worldwide operations. So this morning at seven they had taken off aboard the TaDToY jet, for Tadton, Missouri. Apparently Toy and Doll of America, the name they started out with, had named an entire town after themselves, built from the ground up. More than half of Tadton's residents were employed by the company—the rest provided services to those who were.

"Don't be such a killjoy. Am I talking to the same Patricia Reid who has been so focused on 'growing' this company? You even have me saying stuff like 'grow a company' and 'market share.' I thought this was the league you wanted to play in."

"I know." *Be careful what you ask for.* Pat glanced around the cabin of the ultraluxe plane. White leather walls, seats, dueling divans, a conference area complete with gleaming mahogany table, credenza, cabinets, plasma TV, telephones, fax machines, computers—it was snazzier and more state-of-the-art than most offices, including theirs. But she had spent the day smiling, nodding, and saying, "Thank you!" "Amazing!" "No, we didn't know you had offices in Mexico and Australia," "The Dongguan operation is very impressive," with a level of forced enthusiasm that was exhausting. "All we've done is spend the day in Missouri seeing how the other one ten-thousandth percent lives." *It was all so perfect, so polite, so clean and shiny.*

"Well, it sure beats a ride to Twenty-third Street on the IRT." *And everything so nice, so clean, so quiet.* Gayle reclined her seat—no looking behind to make sure she wasn't disturbing another passenger because, other than the flight crew, they had this nice jet all to themselves. Besides, the nearest seat was a yard and a half away. "I could get used to this. It kinda makes first class look like Greyhound."

"Don't be so sure they really want to share the wealth, or the Gulfstream." The day had been pretty heady, and it wouldn't take much to get drunk on this stuff, Pat would give Gayle that. The TaDToY driver had delivered them to the plane at the private airport in Morristown, New Jersey. No tickets, no shoes to take off, no check-in—it was limo to a plane where each seat was both an aisle and a window, then coffee, pastry, omelets, or whatever they wanted, available from a leatherbound menu, worthy of any fine restaurant. All meticulously managed by a well-spoken, attractive, forty-something brunette "in-flight *assistant*."

Back in her grunt days at the ad agency, Pat had flown private a couple of times—on clients' planes. But she would spend the whole plane ride doing the same thing she did during the three days in Miami or Tahoe or wherever the ad shoot was—trying to keep flak at bay, models and actors coddled and/or sober, and her bosses happy. She had been the in-flight flunky, never on the receiving end of the white-glove experience. Pat traced the grain of the sleek mahogany shelf beneath the window, looked out into the night sky, and had to admit, it felt really swell. *But who are these people and why us?*

Tadton was located in an inconvenient patch of Missouri, between Joplin and Branson, but it became miraculously convenient when you built your own airport—even if it only served one client, with five planes. They had been met by their new friend, Ed, and whisked to HQ, laid-back Midwest style, in a tank-size, black SUV.

"Why would they go through all this if they weren't serious?"

"Talk is cheap."

"Well, I think they are serious and I thought they were nice."

"Three Horsemen of the Apocalypse? Nice?" Pat snorted.

"First off, there were Four Horsemen, and these guys weren't that bad."

"I know there are four. They're saving one for later, in case the other three can't get the job done."

"Pat! What an awful thing to say."

"We asked if we should bring our 'team' and they said no need. This was just an informal chat so they didn't overwhelm us with the whole herd. Trust me, today was TaDToY light."

Danitha had been chomping at the bit to come with them, and she had lined up three attorney friends to ride shotgun. Not that they could match TaDToY's legal force, but Danitha didn't want them to think Ell & Me was underrepresented. She would make sure the offer, if extended, and whether they decided to take it or not, was respectable. Drew also volunteered to come along and bring his assistant—to plump up their presence. Even Rich, Marcus's partner, was ready to join the posse. He knew Danitha's work, that she could handle the deal, should it come to pass, but he just loved the smell of burning negotiations and was happy to help them look as lawyered-up as possible.

Marcus was another story. He wished them well, but Pat could feel restraint. As if every step she took diminished him—not deliberately, but by comparison. Gallagher & Carter now had more cred with recruits since DeJohn. But Marcus still seemed distant, as if he were receding and neither knew how to reach for the other. And Pat wanted to reach for Drew, but that wasn't as simple as it used to be.

So Pat had said no thank you to all of her deputies and took Ed at his word. "You'll have a look-see at our operation, meet a few folks, have some lunch. We'll chat a bit and have you back to New York before the ten-o'clock news." Pat didn't remind him that news was on at eleven in their part of the universe.

"So they told the rider on the pale horse to lay low, and our friend Ed and a couple of his buddies showed us the TaDToY they know and love—and, oh, yeah, the one that pays them quite handsomely for finding fodder—that would be us."

"What do you think the offer will be? How much?" Gayle looked like a kid dreaming about her Halloween candy haul.

"Who knows?" Pat shrugged. She wasn't ready to hazard a guess.

There were mentions of Gayle continuing as "Ell's mom" and CCO—chief creative officer—Ed chuckled when he said that. He said Pat would head up the Ell & Me division—no specific title was floated, but Pat was assured it would be commensurate with their highest executive levels. No numbers were even uttered. Conversation had been light and nonspecific while they toured the campus in a candy-colored, heated golf cart—one of their fleet of one hundred—which ran on electricity they produced themselves at their wind farm a few miles away. "TaDToY is mindful of our planet's depleting resources. We do our part however we can," one of Mr. Ed's equestrian chums had volunteered. Pat wanted to ask about their jets, limos, SUVs, and the planet, but it didn't seem the time. It also made her aware that while A TaDToY Is FoR-EVeR was the slogan, most of the actual playthings seemed flimsy, designed to last half as long as a child would like them and then be tossed away—sending parents out for replacements. It was good for the bottom line, but that's not how Ell & Me was designed.

Pat definitely kept her antennae up as their hosts dropped tidbits about taking Ell global. All meant to sound unstudied, off-the-cuff, but, Pat was sure, carefully chosen and sprinkled in a timely way throughout their day in playland.

"Could it be millions and millions?"

"Let's not put the cart before the horse, even if it is environmentally conscious." Pat wasn't going to let the razzmatazz get the best of her good sense. "We'll see what the next conversation is like. That should tell us a lot—whatever we choose to do." Pat was content to take the ride—nice, leisurely, happily enjoying the scenery from the window of a private jet at forty thousand feet because the destination might not be as good as the journey. "Anyway, we shouldn't talk about this now. You never know who's listening." Pat, only half-kidding, darted her eyes around the cabin. "Or watching."

"You're crazy." But it didn't matter, Gayle was still moving the decimal point farther to the right.

"Never underestimate or oversimplify the enormity of how deep a corporation will dig to resource and effectively actuate their goals."

"I have no idea what you're talking about."

"Exactly. That's the kind of opaque, obtuse subterfuge we're going to have to wade through before we're done here." Pat wanted to slow Gayle down.

Gayle's mind raced ahead at warp speed. With enough money maybe she wouldn't worry it would all turn to ash like it did before.

Pat could see Gayle's "on" light, and she knew her friend had drunk the TaDToY Kool-Aid. Pat wanted a martini, but asked the flight attendant for water instead. At their next dinner meeting—and she knew there would be one—she didn't want to find her cocktail waiting. *We took the liberty . . .* TaDToY wasn't exactly Big Brother, but she knew how the game was played.

"On another subject—did you decide what to tell Vanessa about Ramsey?" Pat waved away the offer of a glass and sipped her sparkling water from the bottle. "You know I'm no fan of daddies-come-lately—hers or mine—but she needs to be the one to choose what to do about it."

Vanessa. Her greatest joy and her greatest sadness. Gayle's stomach lurched—the same pitch that happened when a plane hit unexpected turbulence. Her belly flux was now reflex, triggered by tension and anxiety. Whether she had eaten a lot, a little, or nothing at all, now her body had been trained and knew what it was expected to do. It was a horrible feeling to have about her own child. Money wouldn't make that any better. It might make it worse, and she just hadn't figured out how to incorporate Ramsey into the mix.

"I know. I'm not trying to decide for her—which would blow up in my face. But you have to admit, it's been a crazy few weeks—I'll call her tomorrow. Plan something."

Pat let it go. She wasn't exactly in a position to press the issue—she had her own issues to keep her busy. She wanted to call Drew. She should call Marcus. She didn't do either, instead pondering how they would handle the staff tomorrow.

From the moment Pat had returned that call from TaD-ToY, the atmosphere in the office changed. Everyone who worked for them, everyone who worked in toys or had a child, knew "A TaDToY Is FoREveR," so Pat and Gayle didn't try to keep the potential offer secret.

The full-time in-house staff was small—sixteen including administrative and creative. Their gal Tiffani had such success at street markets with her TiffiBags that she had given notice and left them, which made Pat extremely proud. Ell & Me had half a dozen freelancers—copy editors, illustrators, and writers they used regularly. Then their were the vendors—manufacturing plant, distribution, transportation, printing, advertising and marketing, accounting, legal—whose services they either contracted or kept on retainer, which, when they added it up, came to about two hundred people who would be directly affected by a TaDToY deal—more if they counted those affected indirectly. They knew they had come a long way from an idea, two desks, and a telephone, but it wasn't until the possibility of being acquired dropped out of the sky that they realized how far.

After Pat and Gayle's Missouri meeting was set, the office vibrated at a different frequency. Chatter went from awkwardly loud one minute to hushed the next, and conversation interruptus was the order of the day. People showed extra interest when the fax machine chugged to life or the overnight guy showed up. If Pat came out of her office, or Gayle went down the hall to Ell's Room, the office held its breath. Will TaDToY make an offer? Will Pat and Gayle sell? And the biggest question of all—will I have a job? Pat knew what they were going through. She had been on the employees' end of a takeover target before.

So the day after they got back from Tadton, they held a staff meeting—including the freelancers—a rare occurrence in their informal shop. But this time it was necessary.

Pat and Gayle sat in the middle of the big table in the

conference room—no head-of-the-table positioning for them, and Pat laid it out. There was interest from TaDToY, but no offer yet. No decisions had been made. She promised to keep them in the loop. They could expect regular e-mail updates. She praised them for their contributions, told them they were valuable members of the Ell family, and that as far as she and Gayle were concerned it was still business as usual. They clapped, cheered, and went back to work, a little more enlightened, but just as unsure.

A thanks-for-coming-out-to-Tadton call came later that day.

Pat still wasn't as excited as Gayle, but she was curious about the process. She wanted to see firsthand how a deal like this came down.

And it came down fast. Ed called the day after that with the offer—told Pat and Gayle the letter of intent would arrive the next morning. It was just that simple, no fanfare or ceremony. The copresidents of The Ell & Me Company said they'd get back to TaDToY within a week. They had taken the call in their separate offices, so when they ran to meet each other in the middle, the staff knew something was up. They announced the offer was official—but the decision was yet to be made.

. . .

"What do you mean you're not sure you want to take it?" It was as if Pat were speaking another language and Gayle didn't have an interpreter.

They had just spent five and a half hours with Danitha, going over TaDToY's letter of intent, which sketched out the deal in general terms. They asked questions, tweaked points, noted where they wanted more clarification—exactly what does *administrate, advise, adjust* mean? But no real red flags, nothing came up that was a deal breaker. Danitha had left them with the letter to sign, agreeing to entertain the offer. Then due diligence could begin. Now Pat was saying she had reservations?

"Just that. I'm not sure." Pat got up from the conference table.

"It's late, but if you need to ask more questions, we can call Danitha tomorrow."

"It's not that . . . Gayle. We've invested a lot in Ell. We've grown her up and I don't know if I want to put her up for adoption." Pat didn't think there was anything inherently wrong with the deal. The money was good, a little more than she expected, and the rest of the terms were generous. Which made her wonder if Ell & Me was worth holding on to. Wonder if she and Gayle could take the company the same places TADTOY outlined, without TADTOY—even if it took them ten or twenty years instead of five. "I know it's decent money, Gayle, but money isn't everything. It's money we can make ourselves—over time."

"It's too hard, Pat. The pressure, the deadlines. I hardly make up stories anymore—or draw. I don't see the Ell readers anymore. I'm too busy seeing vendors and going to trade conventions. What's the point?"

Pat threw up her hands. "Whenever I try to get you more help, you say I'm undermining your creative process. You can't have it both ways."

Gayle tried to keep her hands from trembling. "I want my money and I want out. At least out of the way it is now."

"And you're willing to toss what we've accomplished—give it away?"

"We're not giving it away. We're getting one hundred and ten million dollars! Which is about a hundred and ten times more than most people earn in a lifetime."

But Pat wasn't convinced Ell would enjoy being related to all those TaDToY suckups and sycophants. If Tadton, Missouri, had been any indication, they didn't seem like her kind of people.

• • •

Pat found Marcus on the sofa, head thrown back, open bottle of Macallan on the coffee table, glass in his hand. Marcus rarely drank anything more than a beer or two, so she knew something was up, and whatever it was wasn't good.

"That bad, huh? Who died?" Even though she didn't feel like it, Pat thought she'd try to lighten the mood.

"Terry."

"Terry who?" Marcus was always talking about some old-time Hall of Famer or Negro League player she'd never heard of. "Who'd he play for?"

"Terry Stuckey." Marcus took a gulp, stared at the ceiling.

Pat felt hot, cold, and out of breath. "What?" She dropped her coat on a chair and sat next to him. "How?"

"Don't know much." He sat forward, turned to her. "They found her this morning, in her car, in a parking lot by the Staten Island ferry. Gunshot wound to the head." He drained his glass and poured another.

"Was it a robbery? Was she working?"

"They said it looked self-inflicted, but they don't know anything definite yet."

Pat had left her a message about the buyout offer earlier in the day—just keeping her in the loop along with the rest of the Ell & Me family. Terry hadn't called back, but Pat hadn't said it was urgent, and so much else was going on she didn't think about her again—until now. "Terry Stuckey didn't seem like the suicide type to me."

"Me either—which doesn't change the bullet in her head."

They sat side by side lost in separate meditations. Death was never a welcome caller, especially when it arrived with no warning. Freddy had been dead more than twenty years and Marcus sat there still trying to "if only" it into a different outcome. Pat couldn't help but think how suddenly Drew had lost Sabine. From time to time Terry had mentioned family—nieces, sister—just in passing. Pat wondered if Terry had a someone who would forever be changed by the time they had spent together.

So for this one night, Pat held her misgivings about the buyout and her clash with Gayle. Marcus didn't brag about signing a player who had decided to leave UMG. And when they finally went to bed, for the first time in months they fell asleep in each other's arms, clinging to what they had—each other.

News of Teresa Stuckey had hit the office by the time Pat got in the next morning, and she and Gayle declared a de facto truce—at least temporarily. The death of a friend was a more than reasonable excuse to delay their response to TaD-ToY, so Danitha made that call. And between Terry and the buyout speculation, not much got done for the next few days. And aside from snarking, "That woman didn't no more shoot herself than I did," even Lindy was quiet.

But the coroner disagreed, ruled Terry's death a suicide. And on a rainy February morning, a week after her body was found, she was buried in Westchester, not far from Gayle's old house. Rich, Marcus, Pat, and Gayle went together. None of them knew her well, but they felt as if they did—at least well enough to attend her funeral. Stuckey's family was small, but her former police department was well represented. Gayle saw the ex–chief of police, who was Vanessa's old friend's father, but he didn't recognize her and she didn't try to make him. Others who were obviously Millennium clients were in attendance. Marcus and Rich shook hands with a manager from Lush who was present. Bessie was not.

The next day Pat walked into Gayle's office with the term sheet. Without saying a word, she put it down on the desk, signed it, handed Gayle the pen, and left. Gayle was relieved. She understood they were still a long way from a two-comma check, but it was the beginning.

Pat decided the letter of intent was just that. It wasn't a binding contract, so what the hell? TaDToY's exploration of Ell & Me would be like the company getting a complete physical—the kind the president has—with scores of doctors, nurses, and technicians utilizing every diagnostic tool available. Except for them it would be attorneys, accountants, auditors, product analysts—maybe even a private investigator. The final pronouncement of tip-top shape, or the discovery of a minor problem or something more serious, would determine their worth. And that valuation, not just TaDToY's interest, could and ultimately would shape Ell & Me's future.

• CHAPTER 14 •

He'll rot in hell first.

T he *fight with Pat, Terry's suicide,* and how to tell Vanessa about Ramsey added to Gayle's misery mix, and something had to give or she would explode. So she tackled the one thing she knew she could do something about and called her daughter.

"Well—OK." Vanessa sounded so much farther away than Brooklyn. "But I'll come to the city—so you don't have to schlep to Brooklyn."

"Fine." Gayle was surprised to find Vanessa so accommodating, but it was alright with her. "I can work around your schedule. I know you have your job and classes."

"Um . . . I'm off this week." Vanessa paused. Gayle heard her swallow, and the rest of her words came in a rush, without a breath in between. "And classes are in the morning, and I have a workshop I'm rehearsing for after that, but four or four thirty tomorrow is good if that's good for you. I mean, I know you have to work and stuff."

And there was lots of stuff. The office had become an alien nation, invaded by emissaries from TaDToY, questioning everything from what kind of graphics programs the artists used to how frequently they had water delivered or ordered paper clips. Pat and Gayle asked the staff to be cooperative and truthful, said the inquisitors should have full access—and promised that no one was going to lose his or her job whether the deal closed or not.

The tension between Gayle and Pat had eased only enough to get them through the days without snapping—at each other or anyone else—but the issue wasn't resolved. Danitha, negotiator extraordinaire, tried her best to engineer détente—at least to start peace talks—but right now, they were still in opposing camps.

The morning of her conversation with Vanessa, Gayle kept the monster at bay until noon—but then it was out of her hands. She had two lunches. A frozen diet entrée she popped in the microwave, chowed down in the kitchenette with Lindy and Cassidy. Door closed in her office, she inhaled the turkey and Swiss on a hard roll and the three snack bags of chips she grabbed from the deli on her way in—they were less noticeable than one big bag. Two chocolate bars and half a box of pecan Sandies later, she was headed for the loo.

Relieved to have found it empty, Gayle picked her favorite stall, closed the door, and flushed several times—the rush of water a noisy enough cover. Finished and tranquilized, she washed her hands and face, rinsed her mouth, and popped a breath mint. But she did feel better—ready to see Vanessa. Well, not exactly ready, but it was time to get off the pot.

Gayle examined her face in the mirror—not a regular activity these days, but she knew how beat she looked. She didn't want to startle Vanessa. She dabbed concealer under her eyes, tinted gloss on her lips, rubbed some on her cheeks. Gayle told Lindy and Cassidy she'd be gone the rest of the day, skipped the announcement to Pat, and was out the door early, worried she'd have trouble finding Avenue C because she'd never been there before. Gayle arrived at the coffeehouse fifteen minutes early. Beanzz, with its crisp green-and-white awning, was sardined between a rent-a-potty company and a bicycle shop.

Gayle opened the door tentatively—looked around, but didn't see Vanessa. A young woman with blond dreadlocks told her she could sit anywhere—which seemed to be the only kinds of places Vanessa went to. *Maybe she thinks it's less bourgeois—but she works in a restaurant where her job is showing people to tables.* Gayle decided not to look for a reason, just find a table and wait.

The place was mostly empty and surprisingly retro—Goodwill meets grandma's—for the newly chic Lower East Side. Doilies were draped over worn spots on horsehair-stuffed sofas and chairs, covered in shiny velvet, faded tapestry, and shabby cabbage roses. A potbellied stove warmed one corner. All manner of occasional tables, accented by bric-a-brac and dried flowers, made conversation groupings. Gayle couldn't smell wood, but it looked authentic enough—not at all what she was expecting.

She decided on the red velvet settee near the window—the better to watch for Vanessa. She took off her coat, folded it over the arm, and told the server, a young man with a seventies-style Afro globe, she was waiting for her daughter—which Gayle could tell was of no interest to him. He nodded absently, put his order pad back in his pocket, and returned to his post, leaning against a large sideboard.

Gayle checked her purse to make sure the paper with Ramsey's number was still there. It was. She looked out the window, at the waiter, the door, her watch, and waited. The days were longer, but it was getting dark, and Gayle wasn't at all sure this was a neighborhood she wanted to be in, or wanted Vanessa to be in, at night.

It was four twenty-five when Gayle saw Vanessa. She stopped, looked around before she opened the door. Gayle was glad to see her being careful.

"Sorry I'm late." She sounded out of breath. "I ran from the subway 'cause I know how you are about the time thing." Vanessa sat opposite Gayle in a threadbare Victorian chair.

Gayle couldn't see her well in the dimly lit room, but at least the pale lipstick had been replaced by bright red—her hair, a little less angry-looking than last time, was still short. Her coat, which she hadn't taken off yet, was tweed and looked like a man's topcoat circa 1956—which it may have been. Gayle could see she had on black pants of some variety and the same scuffed brown shoes.

"Take off your coat, stay a minute." Gayle tried to sound informal, nonjudgmental.

"Soon as I get warm." Vanessa shoved her hands into her pockets. "Can we order something?"

"Of course." Gayle waved to the waiter. She hadn't figured out whether to get right to Ramsey or build up to him. Nor had she decided what to tell Vanessa about TaDToY. Would she see it as the recognition and accomplishment it was? Or would she only be interested in how it would get her a permanent seat on the Easy Street Express? So Gayle treaded water. "How did you get the week off? Have you worked there long enough for a vacation?"

"No. They're doing work on the restaurant—remodeling or something—so they're closed for a few days."

"When do you go back?"

"Probably Saturday. Saturday's our busiest night. Great tips."

"I see." Gayle ordered regular coffee and a plate of cookies, Vanessa, one of those frappé, grande, latte, mocha concoctions she had been so disparaging of and excused herself to the restroom.

When she came back, at least her coat was unbuttoned. "Isn't this place cool?" Vanessa slouched in her chair, letting it and her coat swallow her.

"Yes. And such a surprise in this neighborhood." Gayle thought she'd try to let Vanessa lead the conversation until she found an opening. She only wished she could see her a little better. See if her eyes still had that unreadable dullness.

"It's owned by this black woman—about your age I guess, maybe a little younger. She's in here sometimes. Anyway she opened her first one in New Jersey, a few years ago, and now she has a whole bunch of them. They're not like a chain or anything so corporate. Each one is totally different. Except they all always have white roses." Vanessa was on fast-forward, no pause button in sight. "There's a really beautiful one in Harlem called Jewellzz. And one by the Museum of Natural History. The owner is hooked up with this hip-hop record guy and he's got like a gazillion dollars. Everybody says they're married, but nobody seems to know for sure. Isn't that great? No stupid celebrity wedding on some dumb island nobody ever heard of. This way they can't have a stupid celebrity divorce and fight over their stupid houses and who gets the stupid celebrity kids for Christmas." She finally took a breath, picked up her coffee, and gingerly blew on the foam.

"Good for them." Gayle bit a cookie, melted it with a sip of coffee. "Vanessa, I need to tell you—I need to tell you something about your father." Gayle put her cup down, thought about what it had taken for Ramsey to come to her, to admit what he had done, not to blame anyone, not to ask for forgiveness. And hoped she could do the same. She scooched forward to the edge of the settee.

"I didn't tell you the whole truth." It was a start. "For a long time I didn't know whether he was dead or alive, but I let you believe he was dead. Now I know he isn't." Gayle tried to see some hint of reaction, but the shadowy light made that a challenge. Vanessa didn't react or say word, so Gayle continued, telling Vanessa everything—the gambling, the disappearance, how he faked his death, the hidden money that had been there all along, the whole of it. Gayle tried to keep her tone even, didn't want to sound angry or critical. And she didn't want Vanessa to hate her father any more than she claimed she already did. She wanted her to understand that he had an illness. And he was recovering.

"Your gram told me that not telling you the truth about things was protecting myself—not you. She was right. I'm not asking you to forgive me for lying. And I can't ask you to forgive your father either. That decision is yours. But I'm so sorry, Vanessa. I should have explained, helped you understand, and I didn't. I really didn't completely understand myself until I saw him. Let him talk."

"You what?!" Vanessa growled. "When?"

"Right after Christmas. He called and said he wanted to make amends."

"And you fell for that after what he did to us?" Vanessa folded her arms. "How much money did he hit you up for?"

"That's not what he wanted."

"No. Of course not. He just wanted to make nice and say he was sorry."

"As a matter of fact, yes."

"Well, I couldn't care less. He is sorry. A sorry excuse for a father. A sorry excuse for a man." Vanessa crossed her legs, waggled her foot.

Gayle opened her purse. "He wants to apologize to you too—he asked me to give you this." Gayle reached across, offered the paper to Vanessa. "It's his cell number."

Vanessa reached back, snatched the paper, tore it to shreds, and let it fall to the floor. And stared defiantly at Gayle. "He'll rot in hell first."

And Gayle saw Vanessa in the light for the first time. Gayle leaned across the table, cupped Vanessa's face. "What happened to you?!" The left side of Vanessa's jaw, the side she'd kept in the shadows, was bruised—she'd tried to cover it with makeup. Her bottom lip bore a cut she used the red lipstick to camouflage.

"Nothing." Vanessa shoved her mother's hand away.

"Is this why you're off from work?!"

Vanessa retreated back into the half-light. "I fell. You saw those stupid stairs at our house." And even further into the lie. "I told you they're closed."

Gayle felt the panic rise again, sure Vanessa was lying. "I asked you before if Julian was hitting you. Is he?"

"Julian has nothing to do with this. How many times do I have to say it? I fell. Period. I'm not the kind of girl who'd let some guy push her around."

Vanessa's bravado rang false, especially to a mother's ear. "None of us were." Gayle didn't believe a word Vanessa was saying. And she didn't know what to do about it.

"I have to go." Vanessa stood, brushed the remaining flakes of Daddy confetti from her lap.

"Wait. I'll leave with you." Gayle wanted to snatch Vanessa, grab hold and not let her go. Not back to Julian. Not back to Brooklyn. Just hold her close until—until Mommy kissed it and made it OK? Until Vanessa was thirty? Until she cared enough to stand up for herself? "Just let me pay—"

Vanessa gave Gayle the same get-a-life-and-leave-me-alone look she used to when Gayle wanted to take her to school or a party. "I'm out of here, Mother."

Gayle watched her storm out, door slamming in her wake. But again, she looked furtively to her right and left before she stepped out onto the sidewalk. And Gayle knew why. She had once felt the same way. Ramsey never laid a hand on her but in the end, she was still afraid. Afraid he was lurking in the shadows, around the corner, in the house. She used to freeze when the doorbell rang—terrified he was on the other side. And she forced herself to stop reacting that way only when she watched her own panic reflected in Vanessa's reaction to hearing a doorbell.

Gayle knew about shelters and programs for battered women—interventions, rescues, escapes—but she never expected those things to apply to her again, or to her daughter. Two weeks ago, she would have called Terry, explained the situation, and known that at the very least Terry would lay out Vanessa's options in a clear and concise way. And Gayle knew that whatever hairs they were currently splitting, Pat would help if she could—so would Marcus. But what would they do? Kidnap Vanessa? Hire a hit man? Find one of those deprogramming people?

Gayle snatched her coat, left a twenty, and found herself back on Avenue C, looking for a taxi and a way to save her child.

When she got home, she headed for the kitchen, yanked open the refrigerator door—in search of a solution, security, sedation. But all she could see was Vanessa's face, the bad makeup job covering her bruises, probably as bad as her own attempt to hide her woes had been—was.

Like mother, like daughter. Gayle rubbed her eyes until she was sure the concealer was gone and sank to the floor with a jar of mayonnaise and a spoon. The gelatinous cream slid down her throat, cool, quiet, satisfying. It was so smooth, so easy, and the jar was empty. Then, without warning, or coaxing, all by itself, it turned on her. Her throat and mouth refilled with the oily, oozing slime, and the jar was replenished.

Heart thudding in her ears, Gayle ached for Vanessa, searched for an answer with every beat. She got up, went to the sink. She knew Vanessa wouldn't listen to her, if only out of stubborn pride. She splashed her face—the cold water cooling her hot tears down to a bearable temperature. *What am I going to do?* Gayle had no idea how long she stood at the sink or how many times the question ricocheted in her head—but she didn't move until she had the answer. She went to find her purse, removed the notepad, took it to her drawing board. She tried a couple of charcoal sticks before she found exactly the right one. Vanessa had torn up the page, thrown it away, but his handwriting was as familiar to Gayle as her own. It only took a few soft strokes for the numbers to appear. She knew they would.

Gayle stared at the paper until nearly midnight. Could she call? Would he help? If you had asked her, she would have told you she was done, through. No need to see or speak to him again. But in spite of disappointment, betrayal, lies, rejection, death—the longer she looked at his number, the clearer the choice became. They were still connected, their lives forever attached—because they had a child. And she didn't care what time it was.

• • •

People in the house next door were kicking butt, cussing each other out—a semiregular occurrence—so Ramsey was awake when his phone buzzed on the table next to his bed. Even so, he was still startled. Except for the occasional call from work about filling in for someone, or a check-in call from his sponsor, his phone never rang—mainly because there was no one else to call. He answered on the fourth ring. And in less than ten minutes he was dressed, out the door, flagging down a livery cab. Ramsey didn't know exactly what he was going to say, or do—except whatever he had to, whatever it took.

He had promised himself that once he spoke to Gayle,

he would stop watching—keeping an eye on her. And since December 26 he hadn't been to the coffee shop or looked for an early-in-the-morning temporary parking spot on her block. Staying away hadn't been easy—the only part of his day, his week, he had really looked forward to was gone. But he kept his word, if only to himself.

Ramsey climbed in the back of the battered black car, gave the driver the address. Which is what Gayle could give him—that and a name. It would be enough.

When he'd read about the discovery of the body of "Teresa Stuckey, former Westchester police detective and current president of Millennium Security," in the paper, he knew that whatever the medical examiner's report said, he would never be sure whether her death was suicide by choice or suicide by Bessie—since both added up to the same thing. But Ramsey was sure that Bessie was the kind of man who could forgive a debt much more easily than he could betrayal or disloyalty.

And after Stuckey, Ramsey had wanted to check on Gayle—see if she was alright. But he talked himself out of it. He was tempted to take a bus to Westchester the day of the funeral, just to make sure she was really dead, but he went to work instead—finally feeling certain that he and Bessie were finished. For good.

And although he hoped, Ramsey never really expected to hear from Vanessa. Why would she want to talk to him? He was ashamed, maybe even more ashamed of the way he had treated her than what he had done to Gayle. From the beginning—the moment Gayle told him she was pregnant—his child had been another chip, something to wager on. And there was nothing he had done that was more shameful than deciding he would marry her mother if he won a poker game. If not—too bad. His daughter—he didn't even know how to think of her that way. Their history was circumstantial, their relationship had been biological. He didn't know her. Never tried. Gayle and Vanessa were accoutrements he needed for the life he thought he should have, like props for his movie set. And he never loved them the way he should, never loved them more than a bet, never loved them enough—until they were gone.

This was his chance—not to make up for anything—he couldn't undo what he had done. And it wasn't a chance to say I'm sorry—an apology was too little a plug for the hole he'd blown in Vanessa's life. This was a chance to do the right thing, for the right reason, and hope it would make a difference.

Somehow the yellow house wasn't what Ramsey had been expecting. He paid the driver and never thought about what he would do if he couldn't get in. But he needn't have been concerned. Two guys, one white, one black, both bald, hands in each other's hip pockets, were leaving as he came to the door, and they obligingly held it open for him. Being polite to the old guy—which was fine with Ramsey.

He took the stairs two at a time until he got to the second landing and saw her sitting on the top step, arms wrapped around her knees.

"I'll call the cops," she cautioned him. "Get out of here. My boyfriend is right inside."

Ramsey could hear the fear through her threat. Of him—who he might be and what he might intend to do. And of Julian, who was on the other side of the door.

"What happened to your hair?" It was out of his mouth before he realized he'd said it, realized it would only frighten her more. She didn't know he had watched her—go to school, come home again, her hair long, wild, free—the way her mother's had been.

"Who the fuck are you?!" Vanessa's eyes widened, she scrambled to her feet, pounded on the door.

"Vanessa—it's Daddy."

Her mouth opened, but nothing came out. This raggedy, old man in work clothes? Her father was handsome. Young. A sharp dresser. Dead. Not dead. She shook her head in disbelief.

He could see blood on her mouth, a fresh bruise blossomed on her cheek. And he came the rest of the way up the stairs. "Is he in there?"

But before she could answer, Julian spoke through the door. "I told you to stop knocking on *my* door. I'll let you back in when I'm damn good and ready. You'll think about it before you see her again and come back empty-handed."

And the door was ripped from its hinges with one solid shoulder thrust. Julian stood there in his boxers and a T-shirt. "It's OK, man, take whatever you want. I don't have much. No cash, but whatever is here, it's yours. Just take it and get the—"

Before the sentence was finished, Ramsey had his eight fingers around Julian's throat, lifted him off his feet. He let him dangle for a few seconds before he backed him up against the wall, never letting go of his neck.

"I'm only going to say this once. So you better pay attention." Ramsey's face was only inches from Julian's. "That is my daughter." He nodded toward Vanessa, who stood frozen in the doorway, her eyes darting between her father and Julian. "Do you understand?" Ramsey squeezed a little tighter. Pressed his knee against Julian's legs so he couldn't kick.

Julian, whose head was immobilized, tried to nod.

"Good. That's a real good start." Ramsey moved in a little closer. "You probably don't know any more about me than I know about you. But you're about to find out. If you ever—and I mean for all eternity ever—come near my daughter, call her, or in any other way make your presence on the planet known to her—I will kill you. Now I want to be real clear. Make sure you understand me. So I mean—if you see her on the street, you find another street. If you see her in a theater, you'll want to see another movie. I don't care if you have to jump off a moving train—you will not ever bother her with your skinny, spineless, simple-ass self again."

Ramsey relaxed his grip long enough for Julian to sputter, gasp for air. Julian looked at Vanessa, his eyes pleading for her to make Ramsey stop. But she glanced away. And Ramsey squeezed Julian's throat again.

"You had her mother worried. And me? I'm just mad. And the one thing you ought to know about me, youngblood, is that I'm already a ghost. Been dead and gone, there and back, so I'm not worried about dying—like I would be if I was you, 'cause I'm not worried about killing you." Ramsey let him go. Julian started to slip down the wall, but Ramsey pulled him up again. "Are you sure you got all that?"

Julian stared blankly at Ramsey.

"Because I really want to make sure you don't forget one single word I said." And Ramsey reared his fist back and punched Julian in the face. Julian dropped to his knees; the blood gushing from his nose down his white shirt matched the red paint splashes on the walls.

"You stay right there, son. We're going to gather up Vanessa's things now and we'll be gone before you know it."

Ramsey turned to Vanessa. "Come on, grab what you need and let's get you out of here."

Tears streamed down her face. "I—I—don't want anything."

"You got a coat?"

Vanessa nodded, took it from the hook by where the door used to be. Her father helped her into it. Julian was still moaning on the floor. "How did you know?"

"Your mother's expecting you." They started down the stairs.

"Wait! There is something I want." Vanessa ran back up, Ramsey behind her. She ducked into the kitchen, grabbed the cantaloupe-colored teapot, and wrapped the cups in a dish towel. "OK. I'm ready."

In the taxi, Vanessa sat in disbelief. She had no sense of time, wasn't sure what she thought happened really had. So she grabbed snatches of her day, her week, her life, and kept turning the pieces around in her head, trying to recognize their shapes, make them fit together so she could see what was in the picture. It was easier than talking to the mysterious rescuer sitting next to her, who had swooped in and scooped her out of the way of the oncoming train. A familiar stranger, this tired-looking man with big hair, frightening yet somehow also comforting—she couldn't explain any of it, so she didn't.

Ramsey didn't try to talk to her, touch her. He left her alone with whatever was going through her head. But when they got close to home, he cleared his throat. This was his chance to say what was on his heart, and he expected nothing from her in return. "I let my sickness cause so much harm—to you, your mother, your grandmother—to everyone who loved you better than I did. I haven't gambled for many years, and I am grateful for every day I can make myself remember why I don't. I can't make up for what I did to you and your mother. I was pretty bad at being a dad. But I am your father—I always will be. Don't worry—I don't expect you to love me. I don't expect to be a part of your life—your mother's either. That's on me and I've made peace with it." He paused, breathed. "I'm going back to Louisville. It's quieter there—more room. Been here long enough. But I want you to know, if you ever need me—for anything—I'll be there." He chuckled. "I don't have much these days, but I'm gonna try and start a business again one day, and if I got it, it's yours."

"I—I—" Vanessa searched for something to say, a way to say whatever it might be.

The taxi stopped. "Shush. You don't need to say anything." Ramsey came around, opened Vanessa's door, helped her and her teapot out of the taxi. "Go on up to your mother. She's waiting for you."

Vanessa clutched her coat close, tucked the teapot under her arm. She wiped a tear away with the heel of her hand, leaned over, kissed her father on the cheek. "Thank you."

That night and the next three, Vanessa fell asleep in her mother's arms. Gayle would watch her breath slow and deepen until she drifted off, watch her eyes twitch, flutter, and become still again in the wax and wane of a dream. She watched the bruises on her jaw and cheek change color, the cut on her lip heal closed. Sometimes Vanessa cried, sometimes Gayle, sometimes both. Vanessa didn't talk much and Gayle didn't press or probe for details of what happened, not with Julian, not with Ramsey. She was just glad Vanessa was safe, home. There would be time for answers, for reasons, but it wasn't now.

CHAPTER 19

Let's have it out, or let it go.

"This is fabulous." *Tiffani's eyes widened* like beach balls when she stepped into DeJohn's South Beach condo. When he said his mother helped him decorate, she was expecting plastic-covered sofas with crocheted afghans, but Mom did alright. At least she didn't blow the flow. Tiffani could see the ocean from the door, and in one panorama you caught the living room, kitchen, and dining room. The wide-open space was Miami hot.

"Let me show you my favorite spot." DeJohn swept her off her feet, leaving her platformed thongs in the hall. He carried her to the sliding door, which she opened, and walked her onto the deck.

"It's like a room." With a terrazzo tile floor and the Atlantic as a welcome mat.

"This here's the place." He took her around to the opposite end where an open cabana shaded what looked like the pasha's lounge from a harem. He dropped to a seat, landing both of them in a heap in the ample red pillows.

"Welcome to the tropics, baby." Twelve stories up and with no neighbors across the way, they mixed their own welcome cocktail. And it had been a long time.

So long that Tiffani was surprised by the new bulk to DeJohn's biceps, the definition to his pecs. She smoothed a hand over his chest. "Somebody's been working it."

It wasn't because Tiffani didn't *want* to make the trip. More than school, TiffiBags had become nearly her full-time job. Business at the market on Prince hadn't gone terrifically well for Tiffani's boothmate, whose deconstructed-reconstructed jackets looked a lot like something the dog had at. But Tiffani's side of the booth stayed busy. New Yorkers, who don't have car trunks to carry their daily supplies, can't live without bags to haul their stuff. A bag with style gets a big plus. Make it affordable, and you've got a winner. Tiffani had stayed on top of the season's color trends and shopped for great remnants all over town. She had the bags made in brunch, workday, and shopping sizes, and on a lark she did evening totes that folded into clutches.

The big leap came when a writer for an online city guide

saw her stuff and listed it as one of its Essential Ten. That week Tiffani had sold out her two-day supply by 2 p.m. on Saturday.

That's when she talked to Pat, about how to set up a Web presence. Pat hooked her up with the designer Ell & Me used. They put together a basic site, and Tiffani became an online retailer. Pat was also happy to introduce her to a fulfillment house, and an entrepreneur was on her way.

Tiffani was a working girl, so romp time in paradise had been hard to come by, and DeJohn had been in the wind once the season ended, so they hadn't had much face time. Tiffani called and e-mailed constantly since he never answered his text messages, got PO'd when DeJohn didn't share her cyber enthusiasm. But he kept paying the rent on her Chelsea crib, even while he had a good time exploring his new city—and its female residents.

As much as he complained to Marcus, Tiffani might have been on DeJohn's nerves, but he wasn't ready to cut her loose yet. Yin and yang, push and pull, some days he was ready to kick her to the curb, and the next he couldn't get enough, would fly into the city for a pick-me-up, which, as he told her, was a sacrifice—"I hate me some cold weather." He had planned to fly her down in February for the first anniversary of their spring-training fantasy camp week together, but she had lobbied hard for a week in January in Miami instead. Tiffani needed the sizzle, not the pop fly.

Tiffani loved being in his place. It lived up to her fantasy of the good life. At least the starter edition. For the first few days they were dancing to the same music. DeJohn, who was trying to keep his word to Marcus, got up, if not early, at least while it was still a.m. and did the sweating he needed to do with his buddy from the minors, who had been brought up by a rival team. Tiffani made the rounds of trendy boutiques showing samples of her TiffiBags.

And the nights were for socializing, which in South Beach was an art form. They'd hit the clubs on Ocean and Collins, one night went for a cruise on a real estate developer's yacht, the next attended an intimate house party for one hundred on Star Island. It was all good and plenty. Until the morning Tiffani stayed in to relax while DeJohn left to hit the weights. After coffee and a shower, a mani and a pedi, she had time on her hands. Instead of sunbathing on the patio, she took herself for a little ramble among his personal items. She found statements from his accountant with lists of checks he had written for DeJohn. The mortgage on the condo was a nice chunk of change—made her rent, which was also on the list, look like spare change. The 'Vette was a lease, so was the new minivan he'd got for his parents. But it was the credit card bills that sent her into a slow burn.

DeJohn had flown her to some of his away games during the season. "I get lonely on the road," he had said. Well, apparently he had a whole booster squad. Tiffani found round-trips purchased from Miami, D.C., Augusta, L.A., even from New York for trips she knew she hadn't taken. And there was some jewelry she was sure was not for his mother, his grandma, or his cousin Betty Lou. Then there were the phone numbers—on ticket stubs, matchbooks from clubs, grocery-store receipts. He kept those in his sock drawer.

By the time he returned, she was done with her exploration, dolled up, bubbly, and ready to rock. But Tiffani was not a happy camper. It wasn't so much that she loved him. It was the principle of the thing. He had gone behind her back. Who knew what kind of bimbos he was hittin' it with—not cool in her book.

In February she surprised DeJohn, made the sacrifice and came to training camp. "I know how hard you work." DeJohn was loving it up—calisthenics and drills in the daytime and pampering at night.

DeJohn got massages from the trainers as a routine part of his conditioning. But he sure liked his Tiffani massages a whole lot better—sometimes better than sex. Tiffani's gentle hands, rubbing him from feet to head with sweet oils and a special cream she ordered just for him. "I'm gonna have the softest skin in the National League," DeJohn had said, while he rolled over for some more. He hated to see her go. Got her a watch with a diamond bezel as a going-away present.

And training camp was going great. Coaches were quick to notice his improved upper-body strength. It showed in the way he put a hurting on the ball. Reporters and bloggers noticed too—were hopeful the promise he had shown early the previous year would be fulfilled in his sophomore season. DeJohn was loving it, playing like it was truly a game and he was having fun.

Marcus was having fun too. He came down to check on DeJohn. "See what happens when you listen to me?"

The team had a fast start to the season, and DeJohn played like a pro, like he belonged. So the headline struck him like an express bus: "Girlfriend Alleges DeJohn Is DeJuiced."

Rich called Marcus at home screaming, "Did you see this shit!"

Marcus shot out of bed so fast, Pat thought something had happened to one of his parents. It might as well have been family—he took it that hard.

DeJohn was in town for a home stand. He called not long after, yelling like a madman, "I didn't do it. Swear to God. Test me, I'm clean. Bitch is lying!"

Pat was jangled too—couldn't believe Tiffani would lie about something so damaging. Pat tried her cell. It went straight to her cheery voice mail—"Hi, hi, hi! This is Tiffani of TiffiBags. Leave a message and we'll talk."

Since they couldn't reach her by phone, Marcus called Millennium, now run by Terry Stuckey's second-in-command. Marcus had them send someone to Tiffani's apartment, just in case DeJohn got it in his head to do something crazy. Her upstairs neighbor said she'd moved out over the weekend. Aunt Stephanie didn't know where she was either.

The rest of the day was circling the wagons and damage control. Marvella and DeWitt were beyond upset. DeJohn's little brother, Calvin, wouldn't go to school. Marcus was torn up for DeJohn and thrown back in time to his own personal media hell. He knew how a well-placed story, even a false one, could end a promising career. It did for him.

By the afternoon there were dueling interviews. DeJohn had a press conference at G&C's office. Holding back tears, he declared his innocence. The team issued supportively noncommittal statements. And from the office of her newly acquired PR firm, hair freshly flat-ironed, wearing a stylish pink jacket, with a TiffiBag placed prominently nearby, Tiffani Alexander made her multimedia debut, said on several occasions she had witnessed DeJohn rubbing testosterone cream on his buttocks and thighs. "He said it was harmless—that it would make him more manly."

That night Marcus looked as downtrodden as Pat had ever seen him. It was the first time she really noticed how much he resembled his father. He sat on the side of the bed, head in his hands. "I know she's lying. I can feel it, but I can't prove a damn thing. And I brought that girl into our lives." Pat had a mind to add a hearty *Hell, yeah,* but instead of piling on she sat beside him. "You had no way to know. Maybe there's some explanation."

By the next day the on-air, online, and press speculation derby had started. Much mention was made of DeJohn's changed physique—before and after pictures included. People took sides, her word against his—stupid, cheating jock versus lying gold digger. But it all left DeJohn dangling in the wind.

The Tiffani controversy was the last thing Pat needed while the office was still in the throes of TaDToY due diligence. The air in the office was still thick. She and Gayle were semifriendly, but still at arm's length, which was pretty obvious to the staff. Pat kept trying to reach Tiffani—still couldn't believe she could be telling such a bold-faced lie.

"Then why doesn't she call you back?" Gayle asked.

Pat could hear the dig—knew that a little part of Gayle enjoyed watching Tiffani's golden-girl status get tarnished. Lindy, however, felt vindicated. "Didn't trust that girl from the day she sashayed in here. She knew then Marcus wasn't her daddy."

And DeJohn's team authorized a "random" drug test—which DeJohn positively failed. He was baffled and devastated, and he faced a ten-game suspension. But more than that, he became a suspect, with his own personal cloud and a sour note that would always be attached to his name.

Pat continued to reach out to Tiffani—through her school, through her PR flak, but there was no reaching back. She walked into work one morning, stopped at Lindy's desk. "Did you ever call Tiffani from your cell phone?"

"I'd sooner call Satan."

"Give it to me."

Pat went in her office, dialed.

"Hi, hi . . ."

"Hello, Tiffani." Pat felt the frost on the line. "Marcus and I would like to come talk to you. No cameras, no—"

"I don't know if I—"

"You owe us at least that."

Tiffani wouldn't give up her home address, but grudgingly agreed to meet them at her PR agent's office.

Pat had still hoped Tiffani had an explanation for her behavior, that somehow this would make sense once they could see it from her perspective. But while flipping through the morning papers on the way to the meeting, she noticed a well-placed item about a certain übertrendy Meatpacking District boutique that had just placed a TiffiBag order, and Pat didn't get a good feeling.

When they got to the office, it was hard to remember the earnest, fresh-faced cutie, "Tiffani with an i," as she'd introduced herself, not all that long ago. She had blossomed into a character made for lights and camera—a little too coarse, a little too garish, for real life.

Tiffani stood up when Pat and Marcus walked in the

room. She extended her hand to Pat, grasped firmly, shook twice, looked directly in her eyes, and said, "Good to see you," as if they were just meeting on a receiving line. And Pat felt the sting of the first lesson she'd ever given Tiffani bite her back.

Pat noticed Tiffani still had on the diamond studs. She'd never seen the watch, but somehow felt DeJohn had a hand in it. The baseball with #14 was gone from the bracelet he'd given her. Only the pavé T remained.

Marcus just wanted to cut through the crap. "Where'd all this come from, Tiffani?"

"Ask DeJohn. He tested positive."

Pat could feel the force field radiating from Marcus. Jaw clenched tight, he was trying to stay cool, trying to maintain.

"When did you see him using this . . . this cream."

"Nobody asks you what you see and do in your intimate moments. Let's just say I was around him when we both had our guard down, so to speak."

Marcus sucked in a breath to keep himself in the seat, used his hands to shape the question. "Is there anyplace else you think this substance might have come from? Accidentally maybe."

"You heard my statement."

"But as you said, you had the intimate access."

"Which doesn't mean I know everything." If you were paying attention, you could see Tiffani coil, her aspartame-sweetened venom rise. "I assume you and your wife have intimate access, but I'm sure there are things you don't know about her. Like who does she swap e-mails with and they say stuff like 'Hope you're free for dinner. I miss you, sweetie'?"

Pat felt Tiffani's fangs puncture her skin. And it happened so fast she almost didn't feel a thing. The little garter
snake had turned into a full-grown viper.

Tiffini tilted her head, lips curled in an insipid little smirk
"I have copies if you—"

"We're done here." Marcus stormed out.

There was nothing more to say. Pat wanted to spit in
her eye, but instead she collected her purse, leveled one
final, blistering stare . . . until Tiffani looked away. Then Pat
walked out—

—to see where the other shoe had dropped and what
it would take to pick it up. But Marcus didn't mention the
e-mails. She found him in the hall, and he said he was going
back to the office. Rich was working on an appeal of DeJohn's
mandatory ten-day suspension. Marcus looked in her direction, but not really at her. Their lips met, but it wasn't really
a kiss when they parted.

At that moment Pat wanted to get in an air balloon and fly
off to Oz. She'd even deal with the tornado and the flying mon-
keys if she could just escape this moment and all it implied.
In less than five minutes she had been both betrayed and the
betrayer, and there was no way to tell which was more painful.
The office would be no refuge, but it's where she had to go.

"And?" Lindy's raised eyebrows met her as she walked
through the office.

Pat shook her head and kept walking. At least her office
had a door. Gayle buzzed from down the hall, asked how it
went. "From bad to worse," she said, assuming Gayle hadn't
called just to gloat.

Marcus was already home by the time she arrived. Flat out on the floor by the stereo, eyes closed, jeans and a T-shirt, headphones on. He stayed that way a long time. She had changed into sweats, washed off her makeup, and was bent over, scoping the fridge for dinner options.

"I know—"

Pat almost leapt out of her slippers. "Sorry. You startled me." Marcus watched her set sealed bowls of leftovers on the counter. "Do you want . . ." She looked at him and it was clear it wasn't about the food.

"I know Tiffani is a liar. I can't prove it so it helps DeJohn, but I'm sure."

Pat put down the dish of orzo with spinach and Parmesan to listen.

"This thing about the e-mails . . ."

Marcus was dressed the way he had been that afternoon when they were kids and the two of them ended up in Gayle's basement. He was soaked to the bone that day, and they argued about his playing baseball or going to college. And for the first time they kissed and acknowledged a connection they had already shared for years.

". . . is it true?"

Pat had spent the rest of the afternoon in her office with the door closed, trying to prepare for this moment. You're supposed to feel better when the truth is out, but she had been quite content with her secret and had prepared to lie to keep it. *No* was short and sweet and he would believe her and that would be the end of it. Except she would always have that slim film between them. But they wouldn't argue.

Yes felt like a hurricane, a monstrous, unpredictable wind that would level whatever they had built and saved and cherished. And how would they rebuild? *Yes* was complicated. He would assume it meant something it didn't, but even if she explained, would it be better?

"Yes." She spat it out before she could change her mind.

His eyes closed. His head dropped.

And what was the next sentence? *"But I didn't love him?"* *"But we didn't do it—not capital It?"* *"But it was just once?"*

Pat hadn't picked one before he left the kitchen. She found him sprawled on the sofa. She stood in front of him, waiting for words. "I don't—"

"I can't talk to you right now."

"But we have to—"

"No!" It was a bellow, then he dropped back. "You don't get to decide."

It was as if he had overheard her conversations with Drew. "And you don't get to shut this down, Marcus." They didn't used to be such obedient, quiet helpmates. Feisty was part of the fun, part of what kept them connected.

"I don't want to argue with you."

"And I don't want you to package this some kinda way that keeps it buried and quiet. Let's have it out, or let it go." That bubbled up from someplace Pat usually had a lid on.

Marcus sat up, but looked straight ahead, not at her. "I'm not the one with a sweetie."

Drew's term of endearment sounded like a curse coming from Marcus's mouth. "No. You're not." Pat hated to be on the wrong side, but she had to admit that. "And I'm not the one with a cape who has time to save every damn body but himself."

"Tiffani was a mistake. Alright, I admit that. Maybe if I worked with you, you'd have time for me. I assume *sweetie* is one of your band of devoted followers."

"It doesn't matter. I needed someone, something. I don't know. But I didn't come to you."

"You never need anything. Especially me."

"Do you want me to need you? Is that the problem?"

"You had somebody to scratch your itch. I'm not the one with the rash." Marcus got up and walked toward the door.

"Doesn't it count when you have glitter on your pants, or am I not supposed to know what goes on at Lush Pink?"

"It doesn't mean anything," Marcus answered quickly, as if he wanted the question to go away.

"And that makes it better?" Marcus headed for the door. "Don't walk out."

"Why? Because you said so?"

"Because I don't want us to be married fifty years just because we said so."

Marcus paused. "What's that supposed to mean?"

"It means I'm drowning here." Pat sank to the couch. "What are we doing?"

"I don't know." Marcus yanked a jacket out of the closet and walked out.

And Pat needed them to know or feel or something more than obey. She banged dishes back in the refrigerator, angry she was the one caught and there still were no answers. She thought about Drew, about how simple it was with him, but they had never been tested. She had wanted to call this afternoon, tell him they had been exposed, but what would she say: "He knows"—like some tawdry melodrama? Then the music swells and she swoons on the fainting couch?

That night Pat moved out of their bedroom. It seemed only fitting since she was the one who'd strayed. The pillows were hard, her sleep was spotty, and morning just meant this wasn't a dream and she had to face this situation head-on, out in the open, not shrouded by a convenient lie.

Pat and Marcus met at the coffeepot the next morning. She poured his, then her own, passed the sugar.

"Are you and sweetie over?" Marcus poured milk in his cup.

Pat stirred, took a breath and a leap of faith. "Yes."

Marcus fixed a bowl of oat flakes, half a banana, and some 1 percent. He leaned against the counter, eating. "Do you think I'd be a terrible father? Is that why you . . ."

"Is that the only reason you need a wife?" Pat put down her coffee so she wouldn't spill it.

"If that was the case, I'd have a new one by now."

Pat had to catch her breath before she could speak. "It's not like I've been sitting around picking lint out of my navel."

"And nobody asked you to give up your shoes and stay pregnant and happy. You'd probably set some kind of record for best competitive mothering."

"Clearly my skills are lacking. I didn't do such a hot job with Tiffani, so maybe I'm not cut out for it."

"Or maybe that's what you'd like to believe so you can keep blaming your mother—for what she did or couldn't do. You'll never know unless you try."

And Marcus didn't know she did once—believe she could

be someone's mommy, until daddy bailed and she didn't want to treat the child like some painful reminder of her poor judgment of character. But since she was letting it all hang out, she decided to float this while she could make a timely exit.

"I was pregnant once—before you."

Marcus looked startled.

It was hard for Pat to go there, to tell him that whole story, to its unhappy ending.

Marcus rinsed his bowl, put it in the dishwasher. "I'm sorry he left you out on a limb. I'm sorry you felt that was your only choice. But you have to know that's not me. I'm not like this boyfriend. I'm not like your father. I'm not leaving."

"You don't know that. And I don't want you to stick around just because it's your sworn duty." Pat gave him a snappy salute. "I don't want to be some kind of joyless obligation."

"Do you think my mother made herself crazy on purpose?" Marcus flung his cup into the sink. It made a dull thud before it shattered in thick pieces.

"What?" Pat wasn't sure what she'd hit, but it hurt and she didn't mean it to.

"Do you think that's what she wanted?" Marcus grabbed the side of the sink, shook it as if he wanted to tear it free. "I remember when Moms and my pops used to get dressed up on Saturday night—once a month—and go up on Linden to some joint. I used to hate it 'cause they'd leave Freddy in charge, but Mom would put on lipstick and some perfume, and Pops had this brim he'd bring out to go with his shiny gray suit. They didn't even stay out that late, but they looked happy. And all that stopped after my brother . . ."

"Marcus, you can't ever replace Freddy, you know." Pat

couldn't walk in his shoes, but she knew where the muddy soles came from.

"That's not what I'm doing."

"Yes, it is. DeJohn, Randall, all your boys. You'd go to the end of the world for them. You can't make your mother better. You can't make Roberta go away."

"I'm tryin' the best I know how."

"And if that's what you want, you're doomed to frustration."

"I gotta get to the office." Marcus left the kitchen.

And Pat had to get to work too. But her hardest assignment for the day had nothing to do with Gayle or Ell or even TaDToY.

Pat knew Drew's number by heart, but making herself dial it was torture. They agreed to meet for a drink after work. Then she dreaded going all day.

It was their usual watering hole, between her office and his. Not a trendy spot, dark and quiet, they met at a table near the back of the bar, ordered a bottle of cabernet. After small talk, Pat swallowed what was left in her glass.

"You know what you said about me being the decider? Well, I've come to a decision." Pat expected a quip, but there wasn't one. She reached her hands across the table. He rested his on top. She fought to find her voice. "I've decided that you'll always be my friend." She saw the slightest shift in his expression, the twitch of a muscle that changed his look from hopefulness to resignation. "And that I'll never, ever regret anything about us."

The corners of Drew's mouth turned up, an effort to smile, but not a real one. He kissed her fingertips, patted her hands, then let them go. "Forgive me for drinking and running." He got up, squeezed her shoulders. "I need to go." And he was gone.

Pat was glad she could sleep alone that night. She ached and she mourned for what she imagined could have been.

But by morning she was ready to fight for what she and Marcus had let slip by the wayside.

• CHAPTER 20 •

Let it go.

For two months now, *Ell & Me* hadn't been itself. The normal rhythm that revved up or slowed down in direct correlation to the next quarter's catalog or marketing schedule, or to who got engaged or left a mess in the kitchen or whose turn it was to bring the bagels on Tuesday, was long gone. Pat's and Gayle's unraveling personal lives, their professional dissension, the presence of a steady stream of TaDToY snoops, made for pretty strained working conditions. Lindy cussed out one of TaDToY's lawyers. Meg quit twice. Gayle came in late and left early. Pat never seemed to go home. Spring wasn't in the air or in anybody's step. Nothing was the way it used to be, and it didn't feel as if it would ever be that way again.

So even when the final report decreed Ell & Me in fine shape and TaDToY ready to proceed with closing, it didn't make anyone actually feel better.

Pat sent Gayle an e-mail.

To: GS
Since your hours in the office are so flexible these days, we should schedule a time to meet. Time is of the essence—according to everyone's lawyers.

To: PR
tomorrow? after hours?—considering what happened last time?

To: GS
6:30. Ell's Room.

This room was their memory. Not Gayle's, not Pat's, but theirs. And while it was neither of their offices, it was the least neutral space for the meeting.

Gayle got there first, sat at the round oak table in front of the case that displayed first editions of every Ell and Bradley Curtis title. She didn't think Pat had played fair by picking Ell's Room—then again, they weren't playing. But Gayle didn't complain. *And I haven't changed my mind.*

"So—how's Vanessa?" Pat came in with a stack of folders

and manila envelopes. She knew Ramsey had rescued Vanessa from the bad boyfriend, but Gayle hadn't shared much more. From twin beds to twin desks to twin offices—the gap between them grew greater every day.

"Better. She's improving. We'll see." Gayle wanted to continue, to talk the way they used to, fill Pat in on the progress Vanessa was making with the therapist—tell her about the family counselor they were seeing together. The sessions had just started, but already Gayle had begun to realize that Vanessa carried as much guilt as she did about things that had gone wrong years ago—especially her grandmother's death. But it didn't feel right to make this personal—at least no more than it already was.

"That's good. I know it isn't easy."

"Not much is these days. How's Marcus?"

Gayle was aware the damage Typhoon Tiffani had done to Marcus's professional life, but she had no idea Pat had also been a casualty. Pat hadn't shared her marriage woes. And Gayle didn't know that Drew's decision to move to London had little to do with his sister or a tantalizing job offer—or how much Pat missed him being around. She and Gayle weren't exactly having heart-to-hearts these days.

"Hanging in there. Let's get to it then." Pat folded her hands. "I don't want to go through with this. I've thought about it all these weeks and I still think it's not right for us."

"Are you insane?!" Gayle pushed back from the table, took a few breaths, tried to stop her heart from racing. "By June we could be relaxing in a villa in the south of France before we start our new positions."

The deal gave Ell & Me space in TaDToY's New York

executive offices—just four floors up from where they were. Gayle, as chief creative officer, would lead her team, generate ideas, and TaDToY elves around the globe would "advise and implement" them. As Ell's mom, Gayle would make a limited number of appearances—book and doll signings, travel on a TaDToY plane, and get the same fringes and juicy salary as other execs on her level. Pat's package—making her a TaD-ToY VP and director of the Ell & Me Division—was comparable and loaded with the same perks, so Gayle couldn't figure out what was wrong with Pat.

"It's not just the money, Gayle." Pat got up, perched on the edge of the windowsill, her backdrop a checkerboard of light from a neighboring office building where the workday didn't end at five either.

"What is it about then? Because you're the one with a rich husband and a stock portfolio."

"Marcus is not rich—he was smart with his ball money, didn't burn through it like some of his buddies. Like I didn't spend every cent I got my hands on." Pat folded her arms across her chest.

"You mean like I did. And if I had been as smart as you, I wouldn't have ended up like I did after Ramsey?" Gayle slammed her binder closed.

"You really should stop. Do you have any idea how stupid that sounds?" Pat walked over to the chalkboard on the far side of the room—the one from *Ell's Strange School Adventure*. "And, for your information, not that it's any of your business, Marcus and Rich lose as much as they make."

"Right." Gayle smirked. "I'm not the IRS, Pat."

"And I'm not kidding. It looks good, but that's part of the

show. Every cent that comes into Gallagher and Carter Pro Sports, goes out." Pat snatched a piece of red chalk, wrote + 100 − 100 = 0 on the board, and turned back around.

"Then why on earth wouldn't you want to sell?! They promise to keep Ell's dignity. We'll both have jobs or titles or whatever—bottom line, you can still be somebody's boss. We get stock in TaDToY, seats on the board of directors, *and* a hundred and ten million dollars!" Gayle gripped the edge of the table to keep her hands from trembling, and from grabbing Pat by the shoulders and shaking her until she made some sense.

"What they promise, and what they'll deliver, can be entirely different, Gayle. Yeah you'll be CCO, but they'll be able to *'adjust, administrate, and align all Ell products with TaD- ToY brand philosophy and direction.'* Don't you get it? That really means, 'We'll listen, but in the end we'll do what we want.' Ell and Me is ours. It's not some valve or sprocket or circuit board. This is us." Pat held out her arms wide—Ell in all her sturdy-shoed, spunky, let's-make-it-better glory was all around them. "Especially after the valuation we got. The sky's the limit for us. Do we want to let them turn her into a hula-skirted ninja hoochie from outer space—or something equally ridiculous?"

"They wouldn't do that." Gayle took a breath. "Besides, without my ideas, my drawings—my daughter, for that matter—none of this would exist." She stood, pulled herself up as tall as she could. "So if you want to be accurate, Ell and Me is *me*. Not *us*." She put her hands on her hips. "All you had was money. And this is my chance to get some and you don't want me to have it? Is this still some of that shoe-on-the-other-foot stuff left over from when we were kids?" She shoved a chair aside and moved as far away from Pat as she could go.

"I won't even dignify that, Gayle. We make good money." Pat was trying to lead them back to safe ground, away from the muddy past.

"And you get to decide how much is good?" But Gayle didn't want to go back.

"No. *I* don't. We both decided what our salaries would be and they've always been exactly the same. Even when you didn't do much besides sit around whining and complaining about—what? Let's see . . ." Pat didn't even know how she slipped and joined Gayle in the muck of held tongues, buried hurts, and unspoken resentments, but she was there now. She tilted her head, put her finger to her chin. "'We're moving too fast.' 'We shouldn't do a doll.' 'Why can't we make more dolls?' 'What am I going to do about Vanessa?' Pat shook her head, shrugged her shoulders, covered her mouth with each example. "'I have to go to Vanessa's school?' 'Vanessa's sick.' 'I'm sick.' The list goes on, but I don't have the energy." Pat finished her performance and sat down.

"And so now you want to punish me because I was cautious—and trying to be a good mother?" Gayle stayed at the far end of the room.

"Maybe I should've encouraged you to try a little harder—considering. So what will you do if we sell, Gayle? Give Vanessa more money for doing nothing? See if she can ruin her life faster and more expensively than she has already?" Pat knew it was mean, but she was tired of coddling Gayle, dragging her forward, dealing with her fear of everything including her own success.

I already know I could have been a better mother. Gayle couldn't believe Pat had brought Vanessa into this. "Well, at least I try—which is more than I can say for you. You don't want anything to do with your own mother. You don't want to be one. Why bother building something when you won't have anyone to leave your share to?"

"What's the difference? You've got someone who could give a fat rat's ass about Ell and Me, as long as it pays her bills. The generations are different, but maybe that saying about the apple and the tree is true—for both of us." Pat headed for the door. "But I thought you might need to be reminded that we are not just the copresidents of this company, we're co-owners. And you can't do a damn thing if I don't agree." Pat slid the folders she'd brought in with her toward Gayle. "Some bedtime reading for you. I'm going home."

Gayle was vibrating, but prepared. "That's true—about the business. But Ell is an intellectual property and I own her outright." She shoved the folders back at Pat. "And I don't have to read anything to know that."

"We'll just have to see who's right about that, won't we?"

"You can't always be right.

"Maybe not, but—"

"And you can't just walk out—I'm not through—uh, *we* aren't through."

"Maybe we are." Pat yanked the door open so hard, it banged into a display case. Ell in her covered wagon toppled off the shelf and cracked the glass case right down the middle . . .

. . . which was exactly the way Gayle felt watching Pat walk away. She sat at the table until she settled down, and her heart stopped racing, at least enough for her to get home. She gripped the armrest in the taxi and rode all the way uptown on waves of sadness, her equilibrium shifting, her breath refusing to fill her lungs. In the door, forget the mail, in the elevator, push the button, find the key. If she kept the steps small, one at a time, she could do it.

Gayle dropped her things on the chair, heard the shower running, but it sounded far away. She didn't call out her usual "I'm home" to Vanessa. She didn't go to the kitchen—didn't want to eat because she felt so full. It was as if she had swallowed too much already during that meeting and it was still lodged in her throat, her chest. And then it started again, her heart quickening—little fingers strumming it faster and faster. *If I lie down, it will stop.* It always did. She edged her way down the hall, feeling the walls close in, then let her go. Every few wobbly steps, she touched the wall for support, couldn't catch her breath—*it always stopped by now.*

Pat had been in her life since kindergarten—thirty-five years, minus a decade for bad behavior. How did they get to this place again? How much was a company worth? How much a friendship?

She didn't make it past the foot of the bed, didn't make it out of her clothes. She just curled up in a ball in the dark, tried to breathe, to rest, to let the galloping stop.

"Mom?" Vanessa stood in the doorway, wrapped in a towel. She came closer when Gayle didn't answer. Touched her mother's face—she was damp, clammy. "Mom—what's wrong?"

Gayle shook her head and tried to say "Nothing," but she couldn't get enough air to push the word out of her mouth.

Vanessa flipped the light, took one look at her mother's vacant eyes, the gray-green pallor to her skin. "I'm calling 911."

Once the EMTs arrived, time sped up, keeping pace with her heart. They got her onto the stretcher, into the ambulance, screaming through the streets. Gayle wanted it all to slow down, drop back into control, be normal again.

As soon as they rolled her through the big double doors, she was surrounded by doctors, nurses, technicians. Gayle looked up into the faces looming above her—they were all talking—at her, at each other, a jumble of words, and there was no air.

"What's your name?"

"Gayle." It was hardly a whisper.

Hands pulling off her shirt, attaching leads to her chest.

"Are you on any medication?"

"Any allergies, Gayle?"

"Her heart rate is over two fifty."

Gayle closed her eyes, to make it slow down, to make it all stop.

"Are you with us, Gayle?"

"Gayle?"

       . . .

"Where is she?" Pat found Vanessa in the emergency waiting room. "Have they told you anything?" Pat tried to keep her mind from drifting back to that hospital corridor where she sat with Gayle and her mother, drinking bad coffee, waiting for news about Gayle's father—praying it was good, that Uncle Joe would be all right.

"Something with her heart—Auntie Pat." Vanessa's voice quavered.

"Her heart?" Pat put her arm around Vanessa. "She's too young . . ."

"They said it was beating too fast." The panic Vanessa had shoved down started to rise. "I found her curled up on the bed. She looked so . . ."

"She'll be alright." *She has to be alright.* Jagged bits of their argument pierced Pat's thoughts. *I shouldn't have pushed her.* "Uncle Marcus is on his way."

"This is my fault."

"Stop it. Mothers are built tough enough to endure their kids. God planned it that way."

Pat knew hospital waiting rooms, like funerals, somehow force people to reach into the places where they've tucked things away—either on purpose or by accident—things they had not been ready, or able, to deal with. So she held Vanessa's hand and let her talk—about her grandmother and how much she still missed her, about her father and how she wished she missed him. The more Vanessa talked, the more Pat could see how much she had been holding in—how afraid she was and had been all along. Finally, they called for Vanessa.

"Curtain five, down there." The man in blue scrubs pointed down the warren of pale yellow curtains.

"Mom?" Hand on the rail of the gurney, Vanessa's eyes brimmed, but didn't flow. Gayle was hooked up to so many monitors—blipping, beeping, flashing LED readouts.

"Honey. I'm OK." Gayle's voice was as watery as Vanessa's eyes. Gayle remembered how shocked she had been seeing her father in a hospital bed, attached to machines. "I know it's a lot of stuff. But it's not a heart attack. OK?" She stretched out her hand—the one without the IV, oximeter, and blood-pressure cuff—and played her fingers along the back of Vanessa's hand.

"I'm sorry. I messed up. I know this is my fault. Auntie Pat said it wasn't but—"

"She's here?"

Vanessa nodded.

"Ms. Saunders?" A resident badly in need of a shave

popped his head in the curtain. "We've got some initial results. I can go over them—"

"Nessa? Would you get Pat? She can help me understand what the doctor says—she's good at that stuff. Then you can come back. OK?" Gayle knew the doctors knew.

Gayle had become oddly serene while they worked to stabilize her. There were shots, consultations, commands swirling around her. Then they thought they had a solution. It felt like they had shot warm gelatin into her veins, like her blood slowed, time slowed, but not her heart. She had opened her eyes, saw the quietly panicked looks, closed them again. More hushed chatter, then they tried one more time. It was so sudden, like a switch finally flipped, and her regular, steady beat returned. The immediate crisis was over.

After that she heard them talking, just outside the curtain. "Are you sure?" "She doesn't fit the profile." "Symptoms are classic though." But she didn't want Vanessa to hear it from them—Gayle didn't want to hear it alone. And since the hateful things they'd said to each other earlier hadn't kept her away, Gayle had to believe Pat would help her hear this.

Pat peeked her head through the curtain. Gayle looked like hell, but if Pat thought about it, not so different from the way she had looked at the office. Drawn, depleted—frail almost. The dark circles under her eyes, her skin tight, waxy. *How long has she looked that way? How long have I not really seen her?* "OK. You win. So you're not having a heart attack, but you sure went to a lot of trouble." Pat had to joke. "Sold. Check is in the mail." Try to make the situation seem lighter than it looked. "I'll call 'em now if you want me to."

."Funny." Gayle managed a weak smile. "Listen, Pat—the doctor's coming back to talk to me, and he's going to say some stuff. I—I've been . . ." She didn't know how to begin. She had never said it, but she knew the word.

"OK." The doctor was back. There were lots of terms—electrolytes, potassium imbalance, tachycardia. He sidled up to the last one. "Ah, Ms. Saunders, do you . . . have you been purging regularly? I mean . . ."

"Yes."

It was out. Pat reached for Gayle's hand, squeezed gently—enough to make her raise her eyes. They shared a look, knowing—and the world didn't end.

"How long would you say you've been bulimic?"

"A lot of years."

They held hands while the doctor explained the condition of her esophagus, her teeth, probably her colon from laxatives, her muscles from dehydration. "The heart is a strong muscle, but over time it can be affected by the sustained purging. Bulimia is rough on your whole system." He broke it down, said they would admit her, keep her long enough to get her current imbalances in shape, and to have a psych evaluation. "You'll get moved soon as we have a bed."

Tears seeped down Gayle's cheeks. She stared straight ahead. "I'm so ashamed of myself. I kept trying to stop—doing this."

"I'm ashamed. I didn't know—or I didn't want to. I asked you a while ago. You said no and I left it alone. I shouldn't have. There was something wrong. I could feel it, but I was so hell-bent on the company and having things my way—I think I stopped looking at your way, at you. But we're going to get through this."

"I don't know how to tell Vanessa."

"You just have to tell her. We've all spent too much time not being straight. Me, you, Vanessa, Marcus too. She's not a child anymore, Gayle. Yes, she'll always be your child, but you've got to start making her feel like a grown-up if you want her to act like one. She loves you, Gayle. She really does. Just like you loved your mother, even when you acted—" Pat grinned. "You know how you acted!"

"Don't remind me."

"We'll take Vanessa home with us tonight—she shouldn't be by herself."

"Thanks."

If they looked at each other much longer, they were both going to dissolve.

"I'm going to let you get some rest. I'll send Vanessa in." When Pat came out, Marcus was waiting. They stayed until Gayle was taken to a room, got settled in.

When they got home, Marcus made midnight scrambled eggs. Vanessa kept him company and Pat slipped into her guest-room outpost—stripped the sheets, gathered evidence of her exile—made it ready for company.

She and Marcus had been taking small steps toward each other—talking in snatches about more than business, and their schedules. They hadn't returned to the same bed yet, but she wasn't going to put Vanessa on the couch. And maybe it was time to cross that bridge again.

The three of them sat at the table together, like family, eating, talking, easing each other's worry. Afterward, Vanessa went straight off to sleep. Pat fiddled in the kitchen, washing pans, loading the dishwasher.

Marcus came up beside her, held out his hand. "Come on. Let's go to bed."

As soon as she closed the door, Pat started to cry, deep, wrenching sobs that had been collecting for so long. Pat didn't cry—always felt she was too strong for that. She held in, she held on, she got mad, she got even, she got her way—but she didn't cry. Ever.

Not since Marcus had known her. He wrapped her in his arms, cushioned the torrent until she was spent. And Pat felt calm in a way she hadn't expected, relieved to be back in their room. Home.

They didn't fall asleep when they turned out the lights. They let their bodies find a fit, their arms a place to rest, and they talked—about the day, about signs that had been overlooked, about arguing over the sale, and about being scared. So much had gone on, gone wrong.

"I missed you, Pat."

"I missed us." She could still see his eyes, shining in the darkness. Pat looked directly into them, didn't know how to begin. "Marcus, I'm sorry. For risking what we have, for looking someplace else for what I can find here, with you."

Marcus squeezed her. "Don't." He kissed her softly. "I messed up too. We just have to pay attention so it doesn't happen again."

Vanessa left early the next morning, to pick up things her mother would need and head back to the hospital. Pat and Marcus would go for evening visiting hours, but Pat called to check on Gayle. And for the first time in longer than either could recall, Marcus and Pat skipped work and stayed home together—e-mail off, voice mail on, with no schedule or demands that couldn't or wouldn't wait. They put on favorite music neither had played in a long time, let the day direct itself—and they talked.

"I'm going down to Wilmington to see Dad—and Roberta." Marcus didn't miss Pat's raised eyebrow. "If she makes him happy, then I'm happy."

"Good."

"I'm also thinking about taking the boat out. Don't have a destination yet—but I could sure use a first mate."

"Ay captain. If you still got a berth for me." Pat smiled, thinking about that first time they sailed together. How it felt so free and they were easy with each other. *After I stopped pushing.* It was past time for an encore.

●　●　●

"If I close my eyes, it feels like we're at the beach." The midafternoon sun was strong in the hospital solarium. Gayle sat on the sofa next to Pat. She already looked healthier, less like she would break.

"I hate to bring this up while you're catching rays, but lawyers await." It was the last subject Pat wanted to revisit right now, but TaDToY was ready to close. "And I'm ready to sign." She had almost lost Gayle twice in the same day, which was unthinkable. They had created something unique, they had done it together. And together was more important than whatever they had been fighting about. Now Pat could see that whatever happened, they were in a winning position. "You were right. You created Ell Crawford, and your vote breaks a tie. I'm so sorry for the things I said the other day."

"I started it. And I'm sorry too. But I don't want to sign."

"What?"

"It's hard to sleep around here so I've had time to think—

about lots of stuff. It bothered me when you wanted to bring in other artists because I was afraid of what they would do with my little Ell. And I know that whatever they pay me, I'm not ready to lose her. Not to them. The jet was nice—more than nice—but I don't want to be a TaDToY soldier. You were right. I'm not hurting for money. We're not hundred-and-ten millionaires, but we've done alright."

"None of that matters if it's making you sick."

"I'm going to work on that—I have to. I've already spoken with a counselor here. I can't keep hurting myself. This . . . this scared me."

"So we can go ahead and do the deal, Gayle—relieve the pressure."

"That won't keep me from inventing new worries—does TaDToY really like my work? Am I worth what they're paying me? No deal will cure that." Gayle curled a philodendron leaf around her finger. "I can't push as hard as you do. I never could."

"And I need to pull back. Get a life." They were quiet a moment. "Are you sure about this?"

"Yep. I'm tired of doing or not doing things because I've cooked up a reason why it will all go wrong. I'm sick of being afraid."

"Me too."

"Of what?"

"That someone might see that fat, nappy-headed little girl from North Carolina who didn't have a mother or a friend. That I'm not as strong as I pretend to be. That Marcus could have done better."

"That's quite a list." Gayle searched her friend's face—

past the flawless makeup, the impeccable coif, beyond the steady, defiant, confident gaze that was her daily mask; and there, right in front of her, was the same Pat who arrived in that St. Alban's kindergarten class all those years ago.

"Tell me about it." Pat clasped her perfectly manicured hands tightly in her lap. "And I'm afraid I won't be a good mother."

Gayle raised an eyebrow—would've jumped straight up if she could have. "Is there something you're trying to tell me?"

Pat laughed. "Not yet. But I promise, you'll be the second to know."

"Worry doesn't help that one anyway—it's strictly on-the-job training, learn as you go—trust me, I've been at it for twenty years and I still feel like I don't know anything." Gayle watched a nurse wheel a teenage girl into the solarium and park her by the window. "But I do know that I don't want to sell anymore. Besides, it's not every day you get to turn down that much money. It's kind of exhilarating."

"Have they checked your meds?"

"Every four hours."

"So—I guess we're not through yet?" They had come so close—too close.

"No way."

The day Gayle was discharged, Pat took her home. And the first thing they did was go through Gayle's hiding places. She cried as they cleared out the cookies in the closet, the bin under the bed—all of her secret food stashes.

"I'm so embarrassed." Gayle dropped the last of the laxatives she had concealed in coat pockets and purses into the trash bag.

"This is brave. I'm proud of you," Pat said. "Hiding is easy. Letting it all hang out takes guts."

That evening they sat on the floor around the coffee table with Vanessa, who had voluntarily made dinner—burgers and salad. Vanessa showed them a magazine photo of Tiffani at a party in Saint-Tropez, hanging off the arm of a giant-size rapper named Big Dippa.

"I'm sure we haven't heard the last of her." Gayle shook her head.

Pat tossed the magazine aside. "Yeah. Rats thrive in a variety of climates."

Vanessa laughed. "I want you to know I'm not giving up on dance—but I did enroll in a GED program, because it's the smart thing to do." She paused, took a breath, let her announcement sink in before she continued, "And since I'm pretty sure my job at the pizza place is long gone, I was wondering if—if there was anything part-time at Ell and Me."

"Lindy will probably make you fill out an application." Pat reached for Gayle's empty plate, winked at her, then passed both their plates to Vanessa. "But you can tell her you have an in with the owners."

* * *

Pat took on the task of managing the TaDToY fallout. They weren't happy with the last-minute about-face, but they would live to devour another company, another day.

Gayle had plenty to keep her busy—follow-up doctor appointments, a first session with a new therapist. And learning to get through her day using food as fuel, not a tranquilizer, took monumental effort. Some days were easy, others not so. She had a lot of work to do, and sometimes thinking about

Ramsey, working his steps, one at a time, helped her truly believe she could change too.

And she and Pat talked more than they had in years—about the things that mattered in their lives. Pat even came clean, told Gayle about Drew, and what she and Marcus had been through. But they also left room to recapture some of the joy they had lost.

● ● ●

Pat waltzed into Gayle's office. Gayle could tell by her look that something was up. "We leave Thursday—I called Verna."

"You what?"

"Marcus found her a few years ago, but I couldn't deal." Pat waited for the words to settle on Gayle. "I'm going to see her when we're in Wilmington. She's only an hour away. I gotta get past that. Let it go. And that won't happen until I talk to her. Whatever she says, I need to hear it, make peace—because two weeks on a boat is a long time without these." She tossed Gayle her birth control pills.

"I'm honored." Gayle spun her desk chair around and ceremoniously dropped the pills in the trash.

"You have to promise to help me, if we have—"

"When you have—"

"But I'm forty." Pat knew the stats.

"Forty smorty." Gayle ignored her. "And if it's a girl, she could be Ell's little sister, and a boy could be Bradley's brother, and then—"

"You're out of your mind." But Pat smiled, sure that whatever happened they would be there together.

DEAR READERS,

Gotta Keep on Tryin' is not only a title, it was our mantra as we wrote this book. When *Tryin' to Sleep in the Bed You Made* was published in 1997, thoughts of a sequel *never* entered our minds. Our writing philosophy is not to wrap up a story in a tidy "And they lived happily ever after" bow. Life doesn't work like that—at least nobody's we know. When we manage to resolve one set of circumstances in our lives—good or bad—others are always poking us for attention. So in our books, we choose to leave our characters at a new beginning, rather than at an end.

But we never anticipated how much readers would identify with Pat, Gayle, and Marcus—their friendship, their struggles, their weaknesses and strengths. It seems their journey struck a chord with lots of us who have made choices and had to deal with the consequences. So much so that for ten years readers have asked, "What happened next?" For that, we thank you—it's an honor when you invite our characters into your life. And as we wrote *Far From the Tree* and *Better Than I Know Myself*, we debated whether to check back in on Pat, Gayle, and Marcus. Finally we decided to knock on that door and go for a visit.

A lot can happen in ten years. Some situations you can see coming a mile away. Others drop in out of nowhere—life's pop quizzes that test our relationships, our nerves, our faith, and some days it feels like even our sanity. We've had those tests, and we've given them to Pat, Gayle, and Marcus too. Some days we pass, others we need a do-over, but the one thing we've gotta do is keep on tryin'!

Most of all we wanted to be true to the characters we created as we brought their lives forward. For *Tryin'* fans, we aimed to give you more of the lives of your friends—not to compete with or take away from their earlier story. For new readers, we hope to engage you with their story and spark a little curiosity about their past.

Writing *Gotta Keep on Tryin'* was an incredible journey for us, one that was both exciting and scary enough to make us weak in the knees, but one that we are ultimately happy we embarked on.

Thank you for letting us share our stories, for supporting our work, and for taking the time to write and let us know how you feel. We enjoy the dialogue!

Keep tryin',

VIRGINIA & DONNA

www.deberryandgrant.com
virginiaanddonna@aol.com
DeBerry & Grant
P.O. Box 5224
Kendall Park, NJ 08824

P.S. Please check our Web site for our travel schedule—we enjoy meeting with you. And we'll keep you posted on *Tryin' to Sleep in the Bed You Made*—the movie!

Gotta Keep on Tryin'

Summary

In this sequel to *Tryin' to Sleep in the Bed You Made*, Gayle Saunders and Patricia Reid are working their way up the corporate ladder—but as joint owners of the Ell & Me Company; the corporation is their own, and that makes the ladder that much more difficult to navigate. Business partners and childhood friends, Gayle and Pat find themselves on the verge of explosive growth. The pressure takes its toll on Gayle, who has trouble shaking doubts that her creation can really be a grand success. Pat is confident in their product, but suffers from the intense devotion she must show their burgeoning business. This devotion causes her to feel more and more distant from her husband, Marcus. And, despite her success, she still lacks confidence in her potential to be a good mother, which is a problem since Marcus wants desperately to have a child.

To make matters more complicated, a teenager named Tiffani Alexander appears claiming to be Marcus's daughter, heightening the tension between Pat and Marcus over their empty nest. Gayle also has family drama: despite dating new men, she has never really gotten over her husband, Ramsey, the gambler who left her and her daughter Vanessa in financial and personal ruin. And Vanessa, Gayle's reason for being, is growing up too fast as she pushes to start her own, separate life. While Marcus and Pat figure out how Tiffani does or doesn't fit into their lives, Gayle and Vanessa face an unknown danger. The years go by, but things only seem to get worse. Will Ell & Me, and the families the company revolves around, thrive or be destroyed in the face of so many challenges?

Discussion Points

1. When you read the opening prologue, did you think Pat was talking about her friend or her husband? What about her friendship with Gayle is like a romantic relationship? Do you think these elements ultimately help or hurt their dynamic?

2. Pat and Gayle are two women working hard to create success on their own terms. What else makes them similar? What makes them different? How do they complement each other as friends and business partners?

3. What is it that drives Tiffani to go to Marcus? Did you agree with Marcus's sympathetic view of her? At what point did you lose sympathy for her, or didn't you? Why?

4. How does Vanessa's "can't-do" attitude reflect Gayle's? What other traits of Gayle's does Vanessa pick up on? Do you think children unconsciously absorb their parents' attitudes and behaviors, or do you think it takes a more active role to instill both negative and positive characteristics in children?

5. Gayle knows that Pat is uncomfortable not being in control. Yet, on some level, Gayle's binging and purging arises out of a similar discomfort. How does a need for control affect the characters in this novel? What consequences do they suffer because of it?

6. Pat claims that she's afraid of not being a good mother, yet she has no problem telling Gayle what she should do with her own child. What is really at the root of Pat's reluctance to have a baby?

7. Despite Marcus' warnings about gold-diggers, DeJohn takes up with Tiffani. And, against Gayle's wishes, Vanessa moves

in and stays with Julian. How do you feel about what happens to DeJohn and Vanessa, both of whom suffer from their mistakes? Do you think they deserve what they get? Why or why not?

8. When you first learned that Ramsey was alive and well, and that he'd been spying on Gayle and Vanessa, what did you suspect he was up to? How much responsibility for Gayle's and Vanessa's emotional problems can be laid at Ramsey's feet? Given the lasting repercussions of his actions, do you think he has paid sufficiently for his crimes?

9. Pat loves Marcus. But she can't stay away from Drew, who takes on a more important role in her life as her loneliness grows. Do you think she's pursuing a relationship that isn't good for her?

10. On page 274, Pat struggles with the concept of loving two people at once. She is mystified—it's an idea that has never really occurred to her, and now she finds herself in a difficult situation. Compare her relationship with Drew to Booker's relationship with Roberta. Do you think Pat has "cheated?" Do you agree with Marcus that his father and Roberta are having a morally wrong affair?

11. There are many different types of relationships examined in this novel. Identify and discuss the rewards and challenges of each. Which relationships seem healthy to you? Which seem unhealthy, and why? If you were any of these characters, what would you do differently?

12. What did you think Terry Stuckey was up to by remaining close to Gayle in the years since Ramsey's disappearance? Did you think her interest in Ell & Me was suspicious, or do you think she was genuinely concerned about Gayle's safety? Why

might she have killed herself, and for what reason might she have been murdered?

13. As the title states, you gotta keep on tryin'. Describe some of the ways that the characters in this novel are "tryin'." Why or why aren't they successful?

14. If you've read *Tryin' to Sleep in the Bed You Made*, how does it compare to *Gotta Keep on Tryin'*? Did the characters from the first novel end up the way you expected? Why or why not?

15. What would you like to see happen in future novels about these characters? Do you think the authors leave room for another sequel as they tie up loose ends?

Enhance Your Book Club Experience

1. Tiffani, DeJohn, Ramsey, and other characters in the novel are blinded by the glitter of the "high life," which leaves them doing almost anything to achieve the lifestyle they think they deserve. Get a taste of temptation by taking your club on the road to the swankiest restaurant or night club in town. Try searching on www.citysearch.com or www.zagats.com for the right place, make a reservation, don your hottest outfit, and go wild.

2. The Ell & Me books and dolls are a fictional part of a very real American tradition—the expansive world of doll collecting and enjoyment. Get a glimpse of Pat and Gayle's intricate business by attending a local convention for toy makers or visiting a collector's shop. You can start by checking out your local business listings or visit http://en.wikipedia.org/wiki/Doll to learn more about the history of dolls.

3. Take some time to visit and browse the authors' Web site at www.deberryandgrant.com and their blog at www.twominds full.blogspot.com. Come to your next Book Club meeting prepared to share how reading the authors' thoughts on life has given you an insight into *Gotta Keep On Tryin'*.

Q&A with Virginia DeBerry & Donna Grant

Pat and Gayle are best friends and business partners. You two are also women who've made their friendship into a successful working partnership. How has your experience working together influenced this story?

After so many years of writing together we have seen both the high points and the pitfalls of combining work and friendship. So far we have navigated smoothly, but we wanted to take a look at what could happen if a business situation puts the friends on different sides of a solution. Getting along when you agree is easy. Maintaining the friendship when you disagree takes work.

You've written five novels together now. Have either of you written anything independent of the other? How does the process of collaborating differ from writing alone?

We have not written for publication separately, although we both have ideas tucked in the files to pursue independently. A lot of why our partnership works is because we respect each other's writing skills and have managed to adapt our individual methods of getting the words on the page so they work together. When we are each writing alone we use more of our individual methods—Virginia lets the words flow on the page then edits. Donna gets the words organized in her head, then once she likes them puts them on the page.

What prompted the decision to write a sequel to Tryin' to Sleep in the Bed You Made?

From the moment *Tryin'* was published, readers wanted more. They told us how much they cared about the characters and wanted to know what happened next in their lives. People connected with Pat, Gayle, and Marcus—their challenges, triumphs, and their friendship. Such strong identification with a character and their situation is the highest compliment you can give an author, but it's terrifying when it comes to writing a continuation of their story! Having ten years pass meant there was time for new situations to develop, and children to have grown into young adults. It gave us lots of new material to explore, so we decided to dive in.

You are both former models. How have your experiences in an industry of image, controversial for its influence on female body issues, changed how you write your female characters? How do you relate your former occupations to your characters' participation in the doll industry, which is also sometimes accused as having a negative impact on young girls' self-esteem?

Our whole participation in the fashion business was aimed at exploding size-ist tyranny. We were both plus size models, back when the industry first began. At the time it was a radical idea to photograph women who accurately represent the size of those who will buy and wear the clothes. Manufacturers thought women wanted a size 8 fantasy, even if they wore a size 18. Even some photographers didn't understand why they were taking pictures of large women. Our philosophy was and is, forget numbers, wear the size that *fits* you, make yourself look good the way you are and go on with the rest of your life. Not to suggest that some of us don't have weight-related health issues we need to address, but so do thin women. We have found it's hard to make positive change when you feel negative about yourself.

And yes, dolls can promote an idealized version of what we're supposed to look like. It's the reason Ell Crawford has her big, clodhoppers. As little girls we both had to wear unattractive oxfords— Virginia really did throw hers down the laundry chute to hide them. But it's also the reason we gave the shoes the power to transport her. The thing that makes her different is the thing that gives her strength—makes her truly outstanding.

You tackle a number of serious real-life issues in this novel, such as infidelity, domestic violence, illegitimacy, criminal corruption, forgiveness, eating disorders . . . the list goes on. Where do you find inspiration for your stories? How do you choose what issues to throw at your characters?

Inspiration is all around us. Sometimes we choose issues because we hear them discussed regularly—like what constitutes cheating in a relationship. Other times we choose topics we haven't heard anyone mention—like eating disorders in adult women. We try not to be preachy. We just want to show how someone can be affected by a particular problem, and hopefully find ways to overcome it.

The characters in Gotta Keep on Tryin' *seem to contradict the notion that fame and fortune bring happiness. Are you trying to send a message to your readers?*

There's no question that life is hard—harder for some than for others, and having enough is critical to our wellbeing, but stuff doesn't bring you happiness—not real joy. Oh, we all find momentary pleasure in things, but the real feeling of joy comes from within—from realizing the good things we do have like—family, friends, health, or simply another day!

Race doesn't play a major role in this story, though it does come up, such as in the generally unspoken racial difference between Drew and Pat. How much of a role does race play in the creation of your characters' fictional lives? Do you see the novel strictly as "African American fiction?" Why or why not?

We have readers of every race—and pretty much every age. So, no we don't think our stories are strictly African American. We write about the lives of women and the situations that affect them. Our characters happen to be black but the things that happen to them are universal—which is what we hear in letters and e-mails that start

"I'm not African-American but I completely identified with . . ." We think our stories about women, family, and friends are just as universal as those of Amy Tan or Anne Tyler.

Gotta Keep on Tryin' *takes readers inside high style clubs and the sometimes treacherous lifestyles of moneymakers on the rise. What research did you do to create the authentic feel of the novel?*

We worked in New York, in the fashion business in the 80's—which might have been the greatest preparation of all! It was the time when club life and ladder climbing became twin art forms. So we relied heavily on our memories of what we used to do, our collective imagination, and researched the rest.

Gayle seems to be a very weak character, while Pat is stronger—almost too strong, too independent. They both suffer tremendously in ways that seem natural given their flaws. What was your intention behind drawing these characters in this way?

When we originally drew these two, Pat and Gayle, we saw them as flip sides of coin, halves of a whole. If you were to put them together, you'd have a great character—complicated, complex, challenging, flawed, but ultimately compelling.

Many first-time authors write semi-autobiographical novels. With several books under your collective belt, how much of your own lives still end up in your novels?

Readers would be surprised how little of our stories are actually autobiographical. We are always asked which of us is which character—Pat and Gayle especially, and our answer is "neither and both." Of course, we write from our collective and individual experiences, but we strive to stay away from directly taking from our lives—because that always involves other people too, and we don't think the lives of our family and friends are fair game. So we use things like locations—cities, houses, apartments, some job experiences.

What was it like writing your first sequel? Do you find that you prefer creating characters for a first novel in a series, or taking the time to explore them in sequels?

It was terrifying. Mostly because we know how attached readers were to the *Tryin'* characters—Pat, Gayle, Marcus—even Ramsey took on a significance we never expected, so deciding to re-visit them was something we thought about long and hard. When we wrote *Tryin'* readers undertook a journey with the characters—one we had mapped out. They had no expectations about where they were going or what they would do when they arrived. But we knew, from all the mail we received, that readers had very definite ideas about what they wanted/expected to happen next in the lives of Pat, Gayle, and Marcus. We hoped that picking them up several years later, instead of immediately after *Tryin'* might make the transition a bit easier—and give us more leeway to once again map the continuation of their journey.

Do you see yourselves writing more novels about the characters in
Gotta Keep on Tryin'*? Why or why not?*

When we wrote *Tryin' to Sleep in the Bed You Made*, we never once thought of a sequel. When we got to "the end" that's really what we believed. But then the letters, e-mails, book club meetings started to ask for a sequel. And as you see, it took us ten years to do it—so the answer is. . . . We don't know. Let's see how readers feel about this installment—and we'll let you know!

What meaning does the title phrase, **Gotta Keep on Tryin'***, hold for you?*

Life is fraught with difficulties, some greater, some smaller, but we all have struggles, obstacles we need to overcome in order to make it to the next place. It's a long story and the past four or five years were quite a challenge for us—but despite problems we faced we knew we had to keep on tryin', that we couldn't allow the hard times to keep us from believing there was something better around the corner. There's a Stevie Wonder lyric that also echoed in our heads and kept us going—"Gonna keep on tryin' 'til I reach my highest ground."